CONTENTS

LEXXIE COUPER

the
De Luca Sisters
collection

ALONG CAME AN AUSSIE

THE DE LUCA SISTERS BOOK 1

DEDICATION

*For all the people out there who've had plans change on them at the
last minute
And for Vicky, one of my best friends, who fought chondrosarcoma
and won. Love you, Vic. xo*

CHAPTER ONE

Maybe this is a bad idea?

Owen Blackthorne scanned the rooftop courtyard filled with sexy vampires, sexy witches, sexy superheroes, and sexy just about everything else one could buy at a costume shop. Lot of sexy characters at this party, that was for certain.

Biting back a chuckle, he adjusted his grip on the cold beer someone had thrust into his hand a few minutes ago.

"Sorry it's not Fosters," the sexy zombie NASCAR driver had said as he lurched away before Owen could tell him real Aussies didn't drink Fosters.

Having said that, the non-Fosters *had* helped Owen any time someone cast a judgmental eye on him, or rather, a judgmental eye on the costume he'd chosen to wear to the party. After every critical look, he'd taken a sip from the can. Which meant he'd taken a hell of a lot of fucking sips from the can by this stage.

Yeah, definitely a bad idea.

He plucked at the large, soft-toy stingray he'd pinned to his khaki shirt an hour ago, its tail "embedded" in his chest via some very dodgy stitching on his behalf, and wondered where his sister was. He'd flown all the way to San Diego from

Australia to see her, and on his second night in the country, she'd dragged him to a Halloween party on the rooftop of her apartment complex. Of course, Tilly being Tilly, she had offered to help him with his costume. In fact, she'd had a few possible options already selected on her phone from somewhere called *Costumes-R-Us* when she'd collected him at the airport. As far as Tilly was concerned, her big brother was coming to the party as either Thor or a US Postal worker.

However, while she was at work today, he'd gotten his clever on and created his own costume: that of the expired Steve Irwin. Owen was a high-school mathematics teacher back in Sydney, after all. He was good at getting his clever on. Who knew people wouldn't appreciate his sense of humor over here?

A sexy fairy sashayed past, eyeing him up. She smiled, biting her lip and playing with a glittering strand of purple hair, before her gaze fell on the stingray partially hidden by the non-Fosters can in his hand, and disgust filled her face.

"Yeah, very much a bad idea, Blackthorne," he muttered to himself as she hurried away.

Maybe if he told everyone here he was the second cousin to one of the world's biggest rock stars, they'd give him a break about his costume choices? Then again, cashing in on the Blackthorne fame had never been his thing. He'd traveled down that path once as a teenager, and it had only ended in... Well, self-contempt.

Taking another pull from his beer, he accepted he had no idea where Tilly was and decided maybe it was time to head back down to her apartment without her. She'd come to the party dressed as a sexy scientist. It was a little disturbing to see his little sister showing off way more flesh than a scientist normally would. Tilly's IQ was off the scale, and the garb she normally wore to work at the Salk Institute for Biological Studies had way more fabric.

Seriously, mate, stop being a prude. She's just turned twenty-six. You need to freaking relax.

True. He did.

He also needed to head back to her apartment and get some sleep. His body was still operating on Aussie time, and Tilly had five years of sightseeing planned for tomorrow.

He'd try for some shut-eye, and maybe his thirty-two-year-old body wouldn't feel like it was 100 tomorrow.

Sculling the rest of his non-Fosters, he placed the empty can on the chest-high concrete bar table he stood next to, nodded at the sexy wizard—or was that a BDSM wizard?—looking at him and his stingray. He turned to go and bumped straight into a vision in fluffy brown and black.

"Steve Irwin!" the vision said before he could apologize, sweeping ice blue eyes over him, her lips stretching into a wide smile. "You're a dead Steve Irwin, am I right?"

"I am." He dipped his head in a quick nod. "Wait, I mean, crikey, mate. That's fair dinkum." She laughed. He grinned. "Thank you. You're the first person here to approve of it."

The vision laughed again, and a shot of liquid lust sank straight into Owen's balls. Holy smokes, he liked the sound of that laugh: throaty and uninhibited.

She brushed at a strand of copper-red hair hanging over her eyes. "My sense of humor always tends to err on the weird side."

"Weird is good," he approved.

"I agree."

Trying not to be obvious, he took her in. An hour into the party, and he still wasn't sure of the Halloween-costume protocol. Was it okay to openly check out a person's costume? Or was that considered unacceptable?

As if sensing his uncertainty, the vision held her arms wide and did a slow 360 in front of him, showing off the baggy, brown onesie with its long tail and black splotches, the brown dog-ears headband, and the blue dog collar around her neck. "Scooby-Doo," she said. Damn it, even her American accent with its slight European lilt pushed his buttons. "From, well, *Scooby-Doo.*"

"Is there a Shaggy?" he asked and then internally winced. Shit, what kind of question was that? Now she'd be thinking he was hitting on her?

Aren't you?

"God, I hope not," she said, a devilish light glinting in her eyes. "And if there was, I'd knee him in the nuts."

Owen blinked. And retreated a fraction of a step.

She grinned. "Sorry. If there *was* a Shaggy to go with my Scooby-Doo, that hypothetical Shaggy is a dick who can't keep *his* dick in his pants."

Something in her eyes suggested the hypothetical Shaggy may not be as hypothetical as she let on. Damn it.

"Dicks who can't control their dicks deserve to be kneed. In the dick," he said. And winced again. Fuck a duck, he sounded like an idiot.

Talk about smooth, Owen.

The vision studied him, chewing on her bottom lip as she swirled the straw of her drink and then frowned. "So what's the deal? I wasn't aware of any Aussies in the *Lumia* apartment community. Mind you, there *are* twenty floors, and I haven't met everyone, but still..." She narrowed her eyes, a smile playing with her lips. "Did you crash the party?"

"No." He pressed his palm to his stingray. "Promise. My sister lives here. On the fifth floor. I'm visiting her for her birthday. She dragged me along."

The vision studied him, and he tried not to shift his feet under the obvious inspection.

"Okay then," she suddenly proclaimed, grabbing his hand and pulling him through all the sexy beings. "Let's go."

"Where?" He laughed, letting her.

She threw a look over her fuzzy brown shoulder. "To fuck."

He spluttered and stumbled to a halt. "What?"

"Kidding." She laughed, lips twitching. "To meet my girls."

"Okay," Owen said, holding up a finger. "I should point out Tilly calls her boobs her 'girls', so I'm still not sure of our destination."

"My *sisters*," the vision clarified, that devilish light back in her eyes. "Let's go meet my *sisters*, not my boobs. I'm one of three. We're triplets. I'm the eldest and the odd one out because Elisa and Zeta are identical, so don't freak out when you meet them." She flicked a look over him before meeting his gaze again. "As for meeting my boobs... Maybe later."

Before he could respond, she grabbed his hand once more and resumed dragging him through the crowd.

He willingly let her. Clearly going to back Tilly's apartment right now was not an option. Screw being tired tomorrow for sightseeing.

Whatever was about to happen next was bound to be more fun.

"I found Steve Irwin," Bria De Luca declared loudly over the crowd as she dragged the insanely hot Australian tourist to where Zeta and Elisa stood at the bar table they'd commandeered upon arriving at the party.

Zeta and Elisa turned in unison, checking out the tall man now standing directly beside Bria radiating all sorts of calm, male sexiness.

"Owen Blackthorne," he said, smiling at them both.

"I like the stingray," Zeta declared.

"It's what drew me to him," Bria said. It was a lie, of course. His six-foot-three-plus muscular form, shaggy dark hair, stubble-covered square jaw, and killer hawkish nose had drawn her to him. His obviously quirky sense of humor had merely been the icing on the cake.

Elisa offered Owen a very typical Elisa greeting—a shy duck of her head, tiny wave, and almost-whispered, "Hello".

Of the three of them, she was definitely the shyest. Their mom always said Bria made up for it. Neither minded.

"What do you do for a living, Owen?" Zeta asked, straightforward as always, before taking a sip of her margarita.

"Maths teacher," Owen supplied, a faint hint of pride in his voice. "High school. We say maths in Australia, not math." He smiled. "Just in case you wondered about the *s*."

"Math*sss*." Zeta shook her head with a smile. "Nope. Sounds wrong. Sorry."

He laughed.

Bria arched a look up at him. "So you're a numbers freak?"

He met her gaze. "I'm very good with figures."

A delicious little sensation fluttered in the pit of her belly. She bit her lip, totally a-okay with the extended eye contact. Hell, maybe a Halloween hookup with a hot Aussie was exactly what she needed? It had been six months since her accident, after all. And the doc had told her everything was okay a month ago. The only thing holding her back from returning to a normal life was her.

As normal a life as one could live being a professional skydiving instructor six months after shattering her hip in a bad landing.

It had also been a while since she'd had any kind of "action" apart from her vibrator. Of course, finding her boyfriend well and truly making out with her physiotherapist—her physiotherapist, of all people—five months ago had contributed to that situation. Although, to be fair, she'd come to realize she'd loved Simon's butt more than his brain.

Owen Blackthorne had both—butt *and* brain.

But was he also a cheater?

You're not planning on falling in love with him, stupido.

Narrowing her eyes at him again, she took another sip of her cocktail. He slowly cocked an eyebrow. The flutter in her belly intensified.

Damn it, why hadn't she and Elisa and Zeta tee'd up a

secret code for "I'm going to be banging my brains out tonight so be prepared if you come home early?"

Sliding her attention to her sisters, she opened her mouth to tell them she was going to show Owen around, wink wink, nudge nudge, when Zeta's face darkened into a scowl. "Umm…Bri," Zeta muttered, her stare drilling into the space over Bria's right shoulder.

Elisa gasped softly, shaking her head. "Is he really coming over?"

"What? Who?" Bria turned, the dog-ears headband on her head taking a second to catch up, and locked eyes with Simon Galston.

Her stomach clenched. He looked good, even wearing a ridiculous He-Man costume. But then he always did like to show off his body, the duplicitous bastard. He unfortunately had an ego to match the size of his cock, which led him to foolishly believe he could do whatever he damn well wanted.

Like coming up to her at a party five months after being caught out.

Prick.

"Umm…" Owen said, even as he seemed to draw a little closer to her side.

Simon flicked Owen a look, somehow puffing up his chest even more like a goddamn peacock, and then slid his attention to Bria. He raked a look over her, raising his eyebrows. "Hey, Bri Bri. We didn't think you'd come."

Bria grit her teeth at the "we". God, why did her ex-physiotherapist have to live in the same apartment building as she did?

That's why *you* picked *her in the first place, stupido. Proximity.*

Unfortunately, that proximity had turned out to be far more convenient for Simon than her.

"Fuck off, Si Si," Zeta snarled.

Simon shot her a sneer. "I haven't missed you at all, Zeta."

Simon had always hated how vocal Elisa and Zeta were about their opinion of him. "Nice costume, Elisa," he said, smirking at Elisa's Very Hungry Caterpillar costume. "Going for your intellectual level, I see."

Elisa flashed a wide, cold smile at him. "Stupido coglione imbroglione."

He frowned. "What?"

Bria grit her teeth. For all her joking earlier about kneeing him in the balls if she saw him tonight, she *was* trying to behave herself somewhat. Putting Simon and his wandering dick behind her had been a part of her recovery therapy after the accident, no thanks to her physiotherapist.

Besides, today *was* only her sixth day not walking on crutches, and her ball-kneeing leg was the one attached to her recently healed shattered hip, and she'd never been the type for clichés.

Still…

"Who's the dude?" Simon threw a contemptuous thumb at Owen, his attention returning to Bria. "If you're trying to get my attention, Bri Bri, you could have just sent me a text. You didn't need to drag some poor guy along just to make me jeal—"

"Ah, screw this," she muttered. She clamped her gloved fingers around his shoulders and yanked him down hard toward her rapidly upward-striking knee. "Stop calling me Bri Bri."

The collision was perfection.

He *oof*ed.

Beside Bria, Owen let out a soft hiss, no doubt feeling the pain for his fellow male. For a second, she accepted she'd probably lost any chance of getting to know him better after putting on such a display, but the humiliated grunt from her ex made it worth it.

Simon crumpled forward just as she released her grip on

his shoulders and stepped back. "Fuck," he groaned. "You bitc—"

"Hey," Owen said, a steel to his voice that made Bria's pulse quicken. "You don't talk to a woman like that."

She looked up at Owen, the disgust in his face as he watched Simon sink to his knees tightening her chest.

God, she liked him.

Simon groaned louder from the floor.

"Oh wow, Bria." Elisa gasped. "I've been wanting you to do that for so long."

"Me too." Zeta laughed, flicking Simon a look. "But I didn't think you'd do it quite so hard."

"What can I say? My physiotherapist was very good at her job." She shrugged and looked at Simon, who was currently cupping his groin, his face decidedly pale. "Or should that be ex-physiotherapist?"

Simon grunted, still doubled over, refusing to look at them.

Zeta chuckled. "I love the irony."

Elisa laughed, grinning at Bria. "And I love the fluid leg movement. The hip really is doing well, sis."

Bria laughed. "It is."

Zeta hooked Elisa's elbow with her own and grinned at Bria. "Well enough to dance, I say. What do you think? Coming?"

Without waiting for a response, she dragged Elisa into the throng of partygoers.

Bria watched them go, chest tightening again. She needed a few minutes to get her head around what had just happened, and maybe thrashing about on the rooftop's makeshift dance floor would help her decide where exactly she wanted the rest of the night to go.

As long as Owen comes along, the rest of the night can go anywhere…

"Coming?" she asked, turning to him.

He raised his eyebrows. "Where? To dance?"

She grinned. "Why not?"

He laughed. "I'm a maths teacher. I can't dance."

"Ahh, sure you can." She grabbed his hand. "And if you can't, who cares. It's just moving your body so it feels good, right?"

He held her gaze, a whole world of promise in his hazel-green eyes. "So it feels good. Right."

Bria shivered. The promise in his voice was as suggestive as the promise in his eyes. Given her current situation, had she bitten off more than she could chew?

Or maybe you're freaking out because it's been a looong time? Maybe you're worried you won't live up to his *expectations? Or your own?*

"C'mon," she said, ignoring the creeping doubt. Sex was like a riding a bike. Once you knew how to do it…

"Okay then," he said back with a grin.

Her girlie parts grew warm and tight, and she sucked in a breath. "Okay then," she echoed under her breath, pulling him through the crowd toward the dance area.

She spied Zeta and Elisa a few feet away, weaving through the partygoers. Zeta caught her eye across the throng, flicked Owen a glance, and then gave her a little wave. *Have fun,* she mouthed.

Coming to a halt, Bria's heart quickened. Oh boy, was she ready for this?

For what? How far are you planning to go tonight?

"Okay then," she muttered again, chewing on her lip as she watched Zeta and Elisa hurry away from the crowded dance floor.

Hmmm.

Owen stopped beside her, his very nearness making her pulse quicken. "So we're really dancing?"

She gave him an askew look. "Are you that scared?"

"Maybe," he said with a laugh.

"Sorry, buddy." She snagged his hand again, threading her

fingers through his. "It's now my *mission* to see you dance. It's imperative."

He opened his mouth, but she didn't let him talk. Instead, she dragged him to where most of the people bumping and grinding to the music were grouped together. Making her way through the crowd, she found the spot that felt right and pivoted on her heel, lifting a challenging eyebrow at him. "Ready?"

Sucking in a deep breath, he rolled his shoulders, his neck, and stretched his triceps and quads. Even with the stingray pinned to the front of his shirt and the relatively baggy khaki shorts he wore, Bria couldn't help but notice his subtle muscles flexing and coiling with the playful routine.

She wanted to touch them so much.

He looked at her, doing a small toe-to-toe shuffle. "Ready."

A laugh bubbled from her. "Why do I feel like you're conning me right now?"

Around them, their fellow partygoers continued to dance, the current song loud and frenetic.

"Just moving your body so it feels good, right?" he said, starting to widen his subtle toe-to-toe shuffle. "Like this?" His hips and arms moved with it, not even close to being in time with the music. He closed his eyes, affecting an over-the-top enrapt expression and began clicking. Also not in time to the beat.

Bria couldn't help but laugh again. "I hope you teach math better than you dance."

He opened his eyes, fixed her with those hazel-green eyes of his and smiled. "I do."

"Good." She began to move to the music herself, holding his gaze.

"Can I ask a question?" he shouted over the noise.

She nodded.

"Was that Shaggy?"

A thick lump filled her throat. "That was Shaggy."

He considered the answer for a heartbeat. "And he hurt you at some point?"

"He did."

"Fair enough." He continued to dance. "Remind me never to hurt you."

She smiled. God, he was easy to like. "Okay."

The music thumped out its wild, thrashing beat.

Any second now, it's gonna change to a slow dance, and everyone will partner up, and we'll be forced to press out bodies together, like in all those corny prom scenes in movies.

Bria prepared herself. If she *had* to press her body to Owen's, she could handle that. The soft-toy stingray would keep her libido tempered somewhat, surely?

The music didn't change.

But, holy crap, Owen did.

Before her eyes, his self-conscious, self-mocking, awkward shuffling slowly morphed into insanely sexy moves that told her there and then that he'd totally been conning her.

And that he'd be fucking incredible in bed.

"You *can* dance," she accused, whacking the back of her hand to the stingray.

Mischief and a certain level of triumph glinted in his eyes at her realization, and he snagged her wrist with gentle pressure, drawing her to his body. Her heartbeat tripled, and she looked up at him as he brought his lips down to her ear. "If I tell you I paid my way through my degree working as a stripper, would you believe me? Or be offended?"

Oh baby.

He pulled away a little, loosening his fingers on her wrist, a question in eyes.

For an answer, she snaked her arms around his neck and kissed him.

It was, in all practicality, the only answer she could give.

CHAPTER TWO

Well, this was a tad inconvenient.

He hadn't planned on showing off his dance moves at the party his sister had insisted he go to. He also hadn't planned on getting a boner while wearing shorts, in all honesty, a size too small. And he *sure* as hell hadn't planned on being kissed by anyone tonight. But here he was, sporting a boner and being kissed by the sexy-as-sin woman whose name he still didn't actually know.

Being kissed by her and thoroughly kissing her back.

Head swimming with a base male lust he hadn't experienced for quite a while, he met her tongue with his own as he grabbed fistfuls of the fuzzy costume she wore and pulled her hips closer to his.

Inconvenient boner or not, he wanted her against his body. Now.

She moaned into his mouth and tangled her hands in his hair, her lips moving over his with a hungry intensity as she rolled her hips, grinding the curve of her sex—padded by the voluminous onesie—to his erection.

Fuck. A. Duck.

With every ounce of self-will in his ridiculously horny body, he pulled his mouth from hers.

She whimpered and pouted up at him, sliding her hands down from his hair to fist his shirtfront. "Why'd you stop?"

"I feel like I should actually know your name before we—"

"Bria," she answered, her voice shaky. "De Luca. My name's Bria De Luca."

"Hi, Bria." He smiled, his body thrumming, impatient to get back to the making out. "I'm Owen."

She laughed, eyes twinkling with delight. "I know that, doofus. You told me already."

He winced. "Sorry. I wasn't planning—"

"On hooking up with anyone tonight?" She bit her bottom lip, and he was almost undone with the urge to replace her teeth with his own on the plump pinkness.

"It's been a while," he confessed.

She narrowed her eyes, studying him. Around them, the partygoers continued to thrash to the wild music. Oblivious to them, or just indifferent?

"What's your backstory, Owen?" she asked suddenly. "Because I really want to fuck you, but I'm not in the market for any kind of drama or baggage."

Hell, he loved how upfront and direct she was. It was as addictive as the devilish mischief in her eyes.

"No drama. No baggage. Promise. I'm a simple maths teacher. Planning to be head of the maths department next year if things go well. I own a dog, a Great Dane called Reg. He's being cared for by my younger brother while I'm here. I also have a second-hand Range Rover and a mortgage. Although, to be brutally honest, the mortgage probably owns me."

He stopped. Wow. Why the hell had he blurted all that out?

Because you really want to fuck her. And getting all the shit out of the road will make that happen quicker.

True. There was something to be said for upfront and direct.

Of course, you didn't mention…

"And that's about it," he said, cutting the unwanted thought short. Hooking up with Bria tonight had no bearing on his impending diagnosis. He either had chondrosarcoma in his brain—a rare place for it to be—or he didn't. Having incredible sex with a beautiful woman while he was in the US wasn't going to change that.

"And that's about it?" she repeated, tilting her head slightly to the side. "Promise?"

"Scout's honor."

"Were you a scout?"

"No."

She laughed, pressing her body to his again, fingers once more tangling in his hair. "In that case…" She took possession of his lips with hers.

Groaning, he surrendered to the wild kiss, grabbing at her arse through her costume and hauling her hips to his again.

His erection sprang to attention once more. He'd have to do something about it soon. But not yet. Right now, he was happy to lose himself kissing Bria.

Fuck, she knew how to kiss. Wild wasn't the word. Fierce. Fearless. Hungry. Sensual. Hell, *all* of those were the word.

Her tongue tangled with his, and he groaned, pulling away.

She stared up at him, her breaths shallow. "What's wrong?"

"I think we need to take this somewhere—"

Someone hit him. Whacked him on the arm. Hard. Really hard. "You fucking prick bastard!" a female voice shouted over the music.

He yanked his hands from Bria, spun around to face the assailant, and let out a sharp breath. "Seriously, Tilly? What the *hell?*"

His sister glared back. "You've got some explaining to do."

Owen shot Bria a look, ready to apologize for Tilly's inter-ruption and to make the introductions, when his heart sank.

She was gone.

"Crap," he muttered.

Tilly whacked him on the arm again. "Why didn't you *tell* me?"

He swung back to her, just in time to narrowly miss being struck by her phone as she shoved it way too close to his face.

"What the hell, Tilly?" he repeated, plucking her phone from her hand. He'd left his reading glasses in her apartment, but he didn't need to have them on to see how angry she was.

"Chondrosarcoma?" she shot back. "In your brain?"

A low groan tore at the back of his throat, and he sighed. "Who texted you? Mum or Mick?" He squinted at the blurred text on her phone. Nope. No idea.

Only two people apart from his doctor knew about the biopsy results he was waiting for: his mum and his younger brother, Mick. His mum had promised not to say a word to anyone, and he'd honestly thought Mick would stuck to the whole patient-doctor-confidentiality rule, even if Mick wasn't his doctor *per se*. Although did the worried-twin-sibling rule override it? Tilly and Mick almost had the same brain sometimes.

The fact Mick had been the doctor-in-charge of the emer-gency department the day Owen had first collapsed at school with a killer headache and had been subsequently rushed to hospital had been…bad timing.

He'd rather *no* one knew what the hell was going on with his brain until he knew himself, but what was he going to do? He came from a small town in Australia where almost everyone knew everyone else. And there were very few secrets in his family. Hell, Mick had told them all over dinner the night he'd lost his virginity, and Tilly had filled their mum in on how to administer a blowjob after their mum—a widow of fifteen years—professed to not having a clue.

He squinted at Tilly's phone again. Bloody family.

"Mum told me," Tilly said, snatching it back. She glared harder at him as she shoved it into one of the pockets of her super-sexy scientist's coat. "She said you've ignored her texts for twenty-four hours, and so she's worried. I asked why."

Owen groaned. Because his phone went flat, their mum blabbed. *Great.* "And she told you?"

Tilly rolled her eyes. "Of course she did. She said I wasn't to tell you she told, but you're waiting to find out if you have chondrosarcoma in your brain."

He laughed. He couldn't help himself.

"Hey!" Tilly slapped his shoulder. Hard. "She's worried. And now I am. Who gets chondrosarcoma in their brain? Only you would do something so odd."

"Thank you."

"What the hell are you doing here at a party?"

"*You* dragged me here."

"And *you* clearly have been enjoying yourself. Making out with Scooby-Doo."

"Which *you* interrupted."

"You're welcome. Do you even know her?"

"Not really. I'd like to, but you scared her off."

She scowled. "Too bad. I have to look after you. Now get your arse back to my apartment and make yourself some chicken soup."

"Chicken soup? It's brain cancer, not a cold."

Tilly's eyes widened, and her face bleached white. "So you *do* have brain cancer?" Tears filled her eyes, and she shook her head. "No, you're not allowed to have brain cancer. I won't let—"

"No, no." Shit. He grabbed her arms and gave her a warm smile. "I mean, I *might* have brain cancer. I don't know yet."

His sister stared at him. Around them, the partygoers continued to dance to the music. "You're not lying to me?"

"I'm not." He pulled her into his body and gave her a hug,

rubbing his chin on the top of her head. "I promise. I didn't mean to scare you. I misspoke. But, Ro—" he pulled away, holding her arms gently as he looked into her eyes, "—it's going to be okay. And until I get the results, I'm going to live every moment to its fullest. Do you know what I mean?"

She bit her lip, a tear spilling over her lashes to trickle down her cheek. "I do. But aren't you scared?"

"Would Dad have wanted us to live life in fear?"

She shook her head.

He tapped her nose. "So I'm not."

"And does living every moment to its fullest involve Scooby-Doo?"

"It might." His chest tightened at the thought of Bria. Why had she taken off? And would he be able to find her again? The party was packed, spread over the entire apartment complex's rooftop. If nothing else, he'd like to find her so he could maybe go somewhere quiet and…

What? Chat? Isn't it merely lust you're feeling for her?

Lust. Interest. Carnal attraction. Mental attraction. All of the above. Did it really matter?

Tilly narrowed her eyes. "Hmmm. Okay. But I'm giving you a curfew. And if she hurts you, I won't be responsible for what I do. I'm a microbiologist, remember. I'm pretty certain I can infect her with bacteria that'll devour her from the inside out."

He chuckled. "You have no idea how scary you can be, Tilly."

She beamed. "Yes, I do. Now go. Be home by eleven."

"Eleven?"

"Eleven. And don't worry. I'll text Mum now and tell her you're in my kitchen eating Vegemite on toast. How's that sound?"

He laughed.

She plucked at the stingray on his chest. "And maybe ditch the stingray. Unless it worked for her."

"It did."

Tilly snorted. "Someone else who has your weird sense of humor? Maybe she's a keeper?"

He grinned. "She's definitely a *kisser*."

"And I'm out." Tilly turned away. "Remember, eleven p.m. A minute later, and I'm calling Mum *and* Mick."

Owen laughed. "Bye, sis. See you tomorrow."

She threw a look at him over her shoulder and walked back into the throng of dancers.

He let out a sigh. There was something to be said for being in a family who didn't do dramatics. Of course, Tilly would be a mess if he did get bad news—

"Nope. Not thinking of that," he muttered, scanning the crowd. "Now, where the hell did Bria go?"

Bria sipped the gin and tonic she'd grabbed from one of the party's many bars after absconding from her...tete-a-tete with Owen. Thank God for the shadows crowding around her and the noisy partygoers doing some weird TikTok dance nearby. If she couldn't hear her own thumping heart in her ears, maybe she could convince herself she wasn't rattled by what had just happened. A dry snort tore at the back of her throat, and she took another sip.

Who was she kidding? She *was* rattled, damn it.

This was not meant to happen. When she'd approached the hot guy dressed with the stingray attached to his shirt, she hadn't expected to be assaulted by memories of Simon's betrayal a few minutes later.

Hell, she'd thought her ex's betrayal had slid right off her until now. She hadn't been that emotionally invested in him, and she'd accepted he was more goodtime beefcake than anything else. She didn't even cry when she busted him and her physiotherapist doing their own type of stretching, bending, and moving together.

She'd told Elisa and Zeta that evening, and she'd been fine every day for a good week after. Totally fine. Whenever they'd asked how she was feeling, and if she was okay, she'd laughed and said she'd actually dodged a bullet.

But whoa, when the woman dressed like some kind of sex-kitten scientist interrupted her and Owen, clearly furious and emotionally hurt, it had all rushed back to her—the second she'd busted Simon with her physiotherapist—and...well, she'd basically bolted.

Not her finest hour. But she'd never been good with impulse control. She jumped out of airplanes for a living, after all, *and* she'd kneed Simon in the nuts right in front of the hot Aussie she was trying to impress.

Impulse control was not her strongest personal trait.

Of course, she normally wasn't a chicken either. And taking off without any word to Owen was very much a cowardly thing to do. Another sip of gin and tonic slid down her throat, doing little to calm her nerves.

Okay, she needed to get her shit together. A Halloween party on the rooftop of her apartment building was *not* the place to have an emotional meltdown or an existential crisis, or whatever the hell she was having.

"You know what you're having," she muttered against the rim of her gin and tonic. "You know what this is. This is you liking Owen more than you should and freaking the fuck out about it."

She scowled, downed the rest of her drink in one mouthful, and then pulled out her phone from the tiny pocket she'd stitched into the Scooby-Doo costume. She'd touch base with Elisa and Zeta, see how they were.

Okay, De Lucas. Safety check time. You know what to do. She included a crazy-face emoji to the text for good measure.

The term "safety check" required a specific response, a specific emoji. A secret code answer so when they were out with someone new, if one of them *wasn't* okay, the other two would know straight away, locate them via their phone's GPS, and go kick butt.

Zeta replied within a minute with her appropriate emoji: the frog face.

A few seconds after that, Elisa replied with hers: the artist pallette.

Bria smiled. They were both good. Probably having a great time.

And you're not?

Hey! Zeta text back. **Where's yours?**

"Shit," she muttered. She'd forgotten her own emoji.

She tapped in the umbrella emoji, hit send, and slipped her phone back into her pocket. Her sisters were safe and well, which meant she couldn't use them as an excuse for hiding in the shadows avoiding people.

That made zero sense. Since when did she avoid people?

Bria De Luca didn't avoid people. Bria De Luca was the extrovert of the siblings, the Manic Pixie Dream Girl. The freaking skydiving instructor.

Is Bria De Luca now also the wounded girl with trust issues?

"Fuck that for a joke." She threw herself out of the shadows. "Watch out, Owen, here I come."

CHAPTER THREE

Hmmm, okay. Where had the sexy sonofabitch got to?

Stopping beside the rooftop pool, its underwater light casting everything around it in a crystal-blue sheen, she chewed on her bottom lip.

She'd weaved her way through the party twice and hadn't caught a glimpse of him. She had, however, dodged a slurred invitation from an inebriated Captain America—with an extremely un-Captain America paunch—to fill her mouth with *his* 'Scooby snack', which was both lame and *eww*. She'd spotted Elisa and Zeta checking out a sexy vampire standing near them, and she'd spotted the sex-kitten scientist who'd smacked Owen.

Bria actually stalked her through the party for a few minutes, on the troubling chance of finding Owen that way, but whoever the scientist was, she hadn't gone anywhere near Owen again, and Owen hadn't gone anywhere near her. At least, not while Bria followed her.

Now, nursing a sedate glass of ice water, Bria scanned the mass of people mingling around the pool's edge.

No sign of Owen here, either.

Fuck, what if he'd gone home?

To Australia? Or to where his sister—

"Oh, you fucking idiot," she groaned, dropping her face into her fuzzy-brown gloved hand. His *sister*. What if the woman who'd approached him was his sister? He'd said his sister lived in the building.

Of course, that made more sense.

But you don't know how long he's been here in the US. He could've been breaking hearts from one coast to the other, for all you know.

She grit her teeth, getting seriously pissed off with her internal monologue's Negative-Nelly attitude. When had she become a pessimist?

Since she'd almost died in a failed landing. Or since she'd caught Simon fucking the woman who was meant to help her get back into physical?

"Fuck." Maybe everything that had happened to her in the last six months had screwed her up more than she'd thought.

So what did she do about it? Therapy? Or would wild monkey sex with Owen fix it? Or at least start the ball roll—

"Hey, Bria," a familiar male voice uttered behind her.

She swung her head around a heartbeat before Simon pressed his palms to her back and shoved.

The world tilted. Blurred.

And she hit the water.

She went under, the voluminous Scooby-Doo onesie sucking up the pool with greedy haste, weighing her down.

Shock fought with rage. Rage won.

Fucking jerk.

She planted her feet on the pool's bottom, let her knees bend a little, and launched herself upward with a powerful downward swipe of her arms. Her hip protested, and a tight, drilling pain stabbed into her pubis bone, but she ignored it.

Coughing, spluttering, she breached the surface, water

streaming over her face, blurring her vision. "Prick!" she shouted, wiping at her eyes with sodden gloves.

She heard him laugh. And then she heard him shout, shocked and indignant, and suddenly the water next to her displaced, splashing all over her.

She stumbled sideways. *What the—*

Rubbing at her eyes again, she looked at the lurching, stumbling, swearing cheater beside her, and then up at the side of the pool.

"G'day." Owen extended his hand towards her, a lopsided grin playing with his lips. "Want some help?"

"Did you do that?" she asked, slapping her drenched palm to his.

He closed his fingers around hers, nodded, and hauled her from the pool as if she were a feather, albeit a very big, wet one.

Whoa, hot, *and* strong.

She steadied herself, ignoring the gawking people around them, and the laughing people filming the situation on their phones. Ignoring Simon cursing and swearing and promising to break Owen's ass when he got out of the water.

Ignoring everything except Owen.

"I'm not sure if what I just did is grounds for being deported," he said, "but I hate seeing a wanker go unpunished. Goes against my—"

She threw herself at him, wrapped her soggy arms around his neck, and crushed his mouth with hers.

He thoroughly joined in with the kiss, grabbing her sodden ass with strong, firm hands and hauling her hips closer to his.

Her mind registered a rather impressive, rather hard bulge, and liquid appreciation flooded her core.

Oh yeah, baby!

"Bitch!" Simon's whiney shout sank into her pleasure, and she broke away from Owen, breath ragged. Ignoring Simon— and everyone else around them—she looked up into Owen's gorgeous hazel-green eyes. "I need to get out of these wet clothes."

Something dirty flickered in his gaze. "You do."

"Wanna help?"

His nostrils flared. "Bloody oath."

"What?"

His smile turned as dirty as his eyes. "Means hell yeah."

"Hell yeah," she echoed, slipping out of his arms. She lifted her right hand to her mouth, pulled off her dripping fuzzy brown Scooby-Doo glove with her teeth and tossed it over her shoulder.

In the pool, Simon continued to rant and insult her.

Owen flicked him a glare, but she stopped him with a gentle palm on the side of his face. "Forget about him," she ordered. "He's a snake. Not worth your time or mine."

"Fuck you, bitch," Simon snarled, splashing water at her from the pool.

Owen's eyes narrowed, and he looked back at her. "Okay."

God, she loved how easygoing he was.

She snagged one of his hands with her bare one, threaded their fingers together, and pulled him closer to her again. His head dipped down to hers, his lips hovering barely an inch from her own. "Ready?" she murmured.

"Lead the way," he murmured back.

She turned and led him through the crowd, headed for the apartment she shared with Elisa and Zeta. Her feet squelched with each step, the thick, brown fluffy socks she'd worn as part of the Scooby-Doo costume now more like thick, brown sponges wrapped around her feet.

"Screw this," she muttered, stopping abruptly.

Owen stopped beside her, his curious smile turning to a grin as she used him as a balancing wall while she yanked off her left sock.

"Consider this foreplay," she instructed with a smirk, switching feet.

He laughed and caught her with a quick hand as a shard of cold pain sank into her left hip, making her yelp and crumple toward the ground.

Concern filled his eyes as he watched her straighten, his hands on her upper arm and elbow gentle but still firm. "You okay?"

Letting out a huff, she gave her hip a rub and scowled. "Yeah."

"Old football injury?"

She looked up at him, frowning. What? Football? What on earth was he on about?

"Sorry," he said, giving his head a little shake. "Bad joke."

"Ahh." She chuckled. "I get it. No, old skydiving injury."

His eyebrows rose. "Skydiving? You're braver than me."

"You've never done it?"

"I'm scared of heights."

She laughed. Couldn't help herself.

He grinned. "Your subtle compassion at my flaw is noted."

"If it helps, I'm scared of…" She petered off. What *was* she scared of? Maybe the ground? Landing on it incorrectly? Having her heart broken again? God, that was so lame.

And yet so true.

"Finishing sentences?" Owen offered.

She snorted, shutting out the unsettling thought as she rubbed at her hip again.

Her hand slid over something hard, and her stomach dropped. "Ah shit," she muttered, pulling her phone from the costume's pocket.

She held it up, sighing as water dribbled from it.

"That doesn't look good."

Giving her phone a little shake, she grimaced at Owen. "Nope. Hopefully, it really *is* as waterproof as the marketing says it is." She swiped her thumb over the screen, and her phone woke up. "Hey, look at that. It survived."

He laughed.

"Give me a sec?" she asked, opening up her text thread with Elisa and Zeta.

"Go for it."

She studied him for a moment, chewing on her bottom lip. *Go for it.* What an apt instruction for tonight. Once she got him back to the apartment, she definitely planned on *going for it,* dodgy hip or not.

Hey, she tapped out a message with her thumbs. **Simon pushed me into the pool. And then Owen pushed Simon into the pool. It's been fun. I'm wet. In more ways than one. Going back to our place to strip off. Taking Owen with me. I cannot be held responsible for what you might walk in on if you come back within the hour. You have been warned. Love you both. Stay safe. Have fun. B. xo**

She added the umbrella emoji and hit send.

"Done," she said, shoving her phone back into her damp pocket. "Ready?"

Before he could answer, she snagged his hand and started walking again.

"So, really a skydiving accident?" he asked, falling in beside her.

"Yeah." She nodded, liking more than she probably should the way he casually linked their fingers together. "I landed badly."

"Do you skydive often?"

"I'm an instructor."

A low chuckle rumbled from him. "That explains it."

She shot him a quick frown. "Explains what?"

"The absolute fearlessness I sense in you."

Warmth bloomed inside her at the compliment.

"Some people don't like it. They find it intimidating." Her chest tightened. Simon had been one of those people, and he'd found himself someone less...fearless.

Owen's eyes held hers for a second. "I think it's fucking sexy."

Liquid heat pooled in the junction of Bria's thighs, and she tugged him closer to her. "I'm going to fuck your brains out, Owen Blackthorne."

He lowered his head to hers. "I have no problem with that at all."

"G—"

He silenced her *good* with a brief kiss so hot and hungry and downright horny that she almost came on the spot.

Pulling away, she gazed up at him, breath ragged and shallow.

Jesus, what was it going to be like when they were behind closed doors and didn't have to stop for public-decency reasons?

"C'mon." She spun on her heel and hurried through the party. She didn't want to wait any longer to find out.

It was fucking time.

Both metaphorically *and* literally.

Thank bloody God they were almost at Bria's apartment.

It was tricky walking with a hard-on, especially in shorts a size too small for him. Owen tried to discreetly adjust himself again as he powered along beside Bria. One of the wings of the massive stingray pinned to his shirt kept getting in the way, and he'd mistakenly palmed *it* more than once instead of his cock, trying to get his imprisoned erection into a more comfortable position.

He was in mid-stride/adjust, Bria weaving them in and out of the crowd, when he caught sight of Tilly a few feet away laughing with a group of people all dressed like sexy scientists save for one, who no doubt was meant to be a sexy Frankenstein's monster.

As if alerted to his attention via some kind of sibling psychic connection, she locked eyes with him across the distance, raised her left hand up a little, and tapped her index finger to the watch on her wrist. He was pretty certain she was reminding him of the curfew she'd given him, and not merely acknowledging the fact he'd given her the watch for her eighteenth birthday.

He pointed to his own watch-less wrist, pulled an *oops* face, and kept following Bria.

Even with the slight limp, Bria had the sexiest stride of any woman he'd ever known. Fierce, determined, deliberate.

His cock throbbed in eager anticipation.

She was unlike any woman—any *person*—he'd met, and it was doing his head in. In the few moments he'd been with her, he'd felt more alive, less on the edge of possible expiration, than he had for months. Since his first headache that had turned into a seizure back in July, and even more so since his biopsy a week ago, he'd been existing in a holding pattern. Coming to visit Tilly was meant to shake him out of it. It hadn't, not really. Not until he'd met Bria. Whether she knew it or not, Bria had taken that holding pattern and kissed it into oblivion.

What would it be like to spend every remaining day of his short life with her? Not just tonight?

Whoa, mate. Pump the breaks there. For one, you don't have an assigned used-by-date yet. And for another, this is only a hookup.

Was it though? He'd had more than one hookup in his time, although to be fair, you could count the number on one hand. This felt…more than that.

He swallowed, swiped at his mouth, and took a deep breath.

"Everything okay?" Bria asked at his side.

He flicked her a quick glance, and it suddenly dawned on him the dog-ears headband she'd worn when he'd first met her was nowhere to be seen. Back in the pool perhaps? Her unconstrained hair now streamed over her shoulders in long, damp waves of deep-copper red he wanted to run his fingers through.

Everything about her appealed to him; her personality, her fearlessness, her humor, her feistiness, and her body.

Yeah, everything.

His cock pulsed again, even as his chest tightened. She was the kind of woman a man *could* spend the rest of his life getting to know better.

The rest of his life. How long *was* that for him?

"Owen?"

"Everything's okay," he answered.

"No second thoughts?"

"Not even close."

"Good." She studied him, her strides slowing a little. "I…I should explain why I took off earlier."

He shook his head. "It's okay."

"No, no. It isn't." She stopped, turning to look at him. "When that other woman came up to you, clearly very upset and angry with you—"

"My sister," he said with a gentle smile. "Tilly."

A shaky laugh fell from Bria. "Sister. Yeah, once I stopped freaking out, I thought that's who she might have been. But—"

"You thought I was a lying, cheating bastard?" he said. "Like Shaggy? Simon, I mean?"

Biting at her bottom lip, her eyes impossible to read, she nodded. "Like Simon. And seriously, I didn't think I was that wounded by what he did to me until that moment, but…" She raised her shoulders in a shrug. "Apparently, I am. Who knew I was so fragile?"

Taking a small step closer to her, he cupped her face in his palms. "I'm not a bastard, Bria. I promise. I hate lying, and I'm of the opinion cheaters need their dicks cut off. And if you want, I am more than happy to be your rebound guy."

She snorted out a laugh.

He brushed her bottom lip with his thumb, watching her process what he'd said, waiting for her to make the next move. She'd been hurt. She was allowed to take as long as she needed.

"I didn't tell you what I'm scared of earlier, did I?" she said.

"You didn't."

"Not spending the night with you," she confessed. "That's what I'm scared of. Right now, at this moment, I'm scared something will happen before we get to my apartment, and I won't get to spend the night with you."

He sucked in a slow breath, his head rushing, and took her fingers in his. "Bria, if anyone tries to stop this…" He trailed off. Not because he'd lost his words—although in all honesty, he had no fucking clue *how* to vocalize how much he wanted her at this point—but because walking towards them, fury contorting his face, was Simon.

Great.

"The wanker's coming towards us," he muttered, straightening a little as the guy locked eyes on him. "Simon."

She swung around. "Shit."

Simon's jaw bunched as he quickened his pace.

Bria's hand squeezed Owen's, and she grinned over her shoulder at him. "How fast can you run?"

"Fa—"

She burst into a sudden sprint, dragging him along, her laughter filling his ears and pulling out his own.

They dodged and weaved through the other partiers, laughing, fingers threaded until she drew to a halt near the entrance of the elevator lobby.

Letting out a wobbly chuckle, Owen dragged a hand through his hair. "Thank God I wasn't wearing thongs."

Bria leant her back to the wall beside one of the rooftop's massive potted palms and raked a gaze over him. "I had you pegged more for a boxer-briefs kinda guy."

He frowned.

She raised her eyebrows, as if expecting him to say something, and then laughed. "Oh, you meant *flip-flops*, didn't you?"

"Ah, I see." He grinned. "Yeah, flip-flops." Balls growing heavy, he closed the small distance between them, planted his hands on the wall either side of her head, and pressed his hips to her. "And for what it's worth—" he lowered his head until their foreheads touched, "—I'm a commando kinda guy."

She let out a soft groan, snaked her arms around his neck, and rolled her hips into his, pressing the soft curve of her sex to his hard-on. "Even better," she whispered, before capturing his lips with hers.

Her tongue lashed against his, and he groaned, grabbing her arse, squeezing it through the still-wet onesie.

She buried her hands in his hair and deepened the kiss, driving him wild with her tongue before nipping his bottom lip with her teeth.

Hot shards of liquid lust stabbed into his body, sinking into his groin. He snared her wrists and pinned them to the wall above her head, holding them there as he took control of the kiss, losing himself in her uninhibited response.

Fuck, she's amazing.

She rolled her hips again, grinding against his engorged cock, detonating fresh hunger in his body even as the front of his shorts grew damp from her costume.

Tearing his lips from hers, he gazed down into her eyes, his breath choppy. "I need to get you out of these damp clothes."

She arched an eyebrow, her breath as shallow and shaky as his. "You do. But that won't stop me being wet."

He chuckled, the sound part needful groan, and kissed her again, hungry for everything she was.

She moaned with approval, her lips and tongue as impatient and demanding as his. When he dragged his mouth from hers, charting a path along her jawline and up to her ear, she let out a ragged whimper. When he caught her earlobe with his teeth, she pushed her hips forward once more. "Fuck yes," she ground out, rolling her head to the side.

He left her earlobe and explored the side of her neck, nipping gently.

"Oh yeah," she repeated, the words a husky groan.

He journeyed back to her mouth, capturing it, exploring it.

She matched his urgency, and his head swam, a wave of giddy pressure rolling over him. His heart thumped faster, up into his throat, his ears. He broke the kiss again, studying her upturned face, reveling in the pleasure on it.

"Let's get the fuck inside," she whispered.

Releasing her wrists, he sucked in a slow breath. Getting inside was a good idea.

"Unless you want to fuck out here?" she said, sliding her fingertips down over the stingray to settle on the button of his fly. "Because I don't think I can wait much longer to feel you moving inside me."

His head swam again. His breath quickened.

Entirely the same sensation before he'd blacked out at school, and yet entirely different. God, was it possible to be so turned on you could pass out?

"Lead the way," he murmured.

Gaze holding his, she took his right hand, turned, and walked into the lobby.

They lasted five seconds in the elevator before he slammed her to the wall and kissed her, hands roaming her throat, her butt, tangling in her hair.

She'd barely yanked open his fly's button when the elevator came to a halt, the door opening with a soft chime.

"Oh my goodness," a surprised female voice uttered.

He tore his lips from Bria's, finding a woman possibly in her sixties, maybe her seventies, dressed as Dorothy from Oz gaping at them from the eighteenth floor's landing.

Laughing, Bria grabbed his hand and dragged him from elevator. "Sorry, Mrs. Benchley."

"G'day," he mumbled, with a tip of his head as he passed the now-smiling Dorothy. "Happy Halloween."

Bria laughed again and lengthened her stride. She pulled him along the corridor behind her and stopped at a door with a fake spiderweb draped over its frame. She pulled a set of keys from the same pocket as her phone and slid one into the lock. "Ready?"

CHAPTER FOUR

He kissed her to show her how ready he was. Pressed her to the door and fucked her mouth with his tongue. She kissed him back, bit his bottom lip, shoved him away, and held his stare. His nostrils flared, his chest heaving as she turned the key in the lock and pushed the door open.

He took one step toward her.

Oh God. Oh God. Oh God.

Her heart hammered into her throat. This was it. No interruptions, no snakes or sisters or anyone else to stop what was about to happen.

She took a step backward into the apartment she shared with Elisa and Zeta, flicked the light switch beside the doorframe, and hooked a finger at Owen.

He crossed the threshold in two strides, cupped her face in his hands, and crushed her mouth with his. She groaned into the kiss, fisting her hands in his hair as he propelled her backward. Her ass bumped into the back of the sofa in the living area, and she laughed, the sound captured by his hungry lips before he lifted his head.

"Unzip me," she ordered, pivoting on her heel to present him her back.

Without a word, he did, slowly lowering the onesie's zipper down to the small of her back before gently sliding his fingers beneath the parted material. A shiver rippled through her at his warm skin on her cool, damp back. Her nipples pinched tight. Her pussy clenched. Contracted. Squeezing a cock that wasn't there yet.

"Oh yeah…" she murmured, bending forward a little at the hip to press her ass against his groin.

"We're alone?" he asked on a breath at the back of her neck, his lips feathering her skin.

"We're alone," she confirmed. Elisa and Zeta were no doubt having their own adventures elsewhere. "I live here with my sisters, and I told them to stay away for at least an hour."

"Good," he whispered before sliding his palms up over the backs of her shoulders, coaxing the Scooby-Doo onesie off them. The damp costume slipped down her torso and passed her hips, revealing her naughty secret.

"Holy fuck," he ground out, his voice almost strangled.

She looked at him over her shoulder and wriggled her bare ass. "Disappointed?"

"Hell no. I'm a fan of commando," he said, raking his gaze over her naked ass before meeting her gaze again. "Also a fan of eagles."

She flicked a glance at the small soaring-eagle tattoo on the curve above her right butt cheek. She'd had it done to celebrate getting her skydiving instructor's license. "You like?"

His nostrils flared, and he drew in a slow, deep breath, lifting his gaze to hers. "You have no fucking clue."

"Hmm." She gave the impressive bulge straining against his fly a smile. "I think I do."

A low growl rumbled in his chest.

Meeting his stare again over her shoulder, she lifted one leg and then the other, freeing them completely of the damp onesie and kicking it away with a backward flick of her right foot.

Owen's nostrils flared again, his stare once more on her ass. Did he notice the faint purple scar running over the curve of her left hip? Did he care?

Let's find out.

Slowly, watching his eyes, she turned until the scar was fully visible.

For the first time since her bad landing and ensuing operation, she offered herself completely revealed to someone.

Completely exposed.

Completely horny.

And completely…nervous. What if Owen—

"Is it wrong I find your scar sexy?" he asked.

She puffed out a breath, her pulse quickening at the way he looked at her. "You do?"

"Fearless," he said, lifting his gaze to hers. "You are fearless. And you wear it so fucking well."

Holy crap, if she wasn't careful, she'd fall in love with him.

Holding her breath, she finished turning until she faced him directly. "Ta-dah," she said, holding her arms out a little at her side.

He let out a shaky chuckle, the sound turning into a groan as she moved her hand to her breast and feathered her fingertips over her right nipple. His nostrils flared, and his chest heaved. "If I'm already dead," he mumbled under his breath, swiping at his mouth, "I don't care."

She frowned at the weird choice of words—already dead? But then he buried his hands in her hair and kissed away any ability to think. Whimpering into the incredible assault on her mouth, she moved her hands to his shirt, tugging at the buttons on it. She ripped them open until the damn stingray got in the way.

She pulled her lips from his, scowling at the offending soft toy. "Make it be gone," she demanded, flicking at its tail.

"Done," he rasped, reaching up behind his head. With a

quick yank on the back of his collar, he pulled the shirt off, stingray and all.

"Oh baby," she whispered, taking in what he'd revealed—a body that liked sport and food in equal measure. A body that was fit but not to the extreme. A body lived in well, with a latent strength that made her pulse quicken. "You have the sexiest dad bod."

Another one of those low chuckles rumbled from him, and he ducked his head, rubbing at the back of his neck. God, could he be any more adorable? "I'm no Chris Hemsworth," he said, looking at her from behind the shaggy hair hanging over his eyebrows. "But can he name the Pythagorean triples, or solve polynomials by radicals?"

"Chris who?" she murmured, stepping up to him and smoothing her palms over his chest. "Polywhat?"

He sucked in a slow breath, and his eyes fluttered closed for a second before she made him open them with a gentle brush of her thumbs over his nipples. She held his gaze as she slid her fingers over his chest, down over his solar plexus and the plane of his abs to the soft snail's trail disappearing into the waistband of his shorts.

He pulled in another breath, this one shaky, and let it out just as slowly as she snagged the toggle of his zipper and lowered his fly.

The firm, warm hardness of his erection nudged her fingers through the opening, and she wrapped them around it without hesitation.

"Fuck," he ground out, eyes closing again for a heartbeat. "This is really..." His Adam's apple jerked up and down his throat and then, with a growl, he cupped the back of her head and captured her mouth with his. He kissed her as she squeezed and pumped his cock. Plundered her mouth with his tongue as she massaged his heavy balls and gently pressed her index finger to his perineum.

"This is really happening," he groaned, breaking the kiss.

"Hell yeah," she murmured, skimming her fingers over his hips to coax the shorts down.

They pooled at his feet in a puddle of khaki, which he immediately stepped out of and pushed aside with one foot.

Trailing her fingertips up the length of his cock, she arched an eyebrow at him. "You realize you're now wearing nothing but a pair of hiking boots, right?"

His lips curled a little. "It'll give me better grip on the floor."

She burst out laughing. He grinned. She took his cock in her hand again, giving it a firm squeeze and a slow pump.

Sucking in a deep breath, he closed his eyes. "I don't think you have any idea how good that feels."

"I think I do," she whispered, leaning forward to brush her nipples against his bare chest as she nipped his bottom lip.

He laughed out a groan, the sound turning raw when ran her hands up and over his stomach to his chest again. She teased his nipples once again with a featherlight caress, loving the way his chest heaved and a low moan tore from him. It seemed no matter where she touched him, he responded.

She liked that. A lot.

"You know what else I think?" she asked, rising up on tiptoe to drag the curve of her pussy up the length of his erection.

"F... I...ffff..." he groaned, grabbing at her waist with firm hands, pushing his hips forward, grinding his cock harder to her. "N-no."

Chuckling at the raw arousal in his response, she nipped his bottom lip again. "I think I want you to go down on me."

He let out a low growl, smoothing his palms over the curve of her waist and down her hips. "I think you're right." His right fingers traced the line of her scar, making her catch her breath. He slowly sank to his knees in front of her, looking up at her as his hands moved to her inner thighs.

"Yeah yeah," she encouraged, her breath growing shallow.

Still holding her stare, he gently parted her folds with his thumbs and ran his tongue up over her clit in a slow, deliberate stroke.

"Fuck," she whispered, rolling her hip to push her pussy closer to his mouth.

He stroked her clit with his tongue again, a little bit faster this time, his palms on her inner thighs, his thumbs keeping her folds parted.

An exquisite shudder wracked her body, and she moaned her approval and delight. "That's an impressive tongue you have there, sir."

He chuckled, blew a fine stream of air on her wet clit, and then painted it again with a slower swipe, this time teasing the sensitive nub with a swirl and flick.

"Oh fuck, yes," she moaned.

He lifted his head, pressed a soft kiss on the top of the scar on her hip, and returned his mouth to her pussy again. She closed her eyes and fisted one hand in his hair, gripping the back of the sofa with her other. She needed an anchor. Who knew being so simply licked would make her knees tremble so much? It was as if she were being swept away in a tsunami of pleasure.

He licked her seam over and over, concentrating on her clit for delirious seconds each time, driving her to an edge she hadn't balanced on for six months.

"You taste fucking incredible," he murmured against her inner thigh, his thumb rolling over her clit in lazy circles that made her want to whimper. His teeth nipped her flesh, his tongue laved the tiny bruise, and then he was licking her pussy again, harder this time. Faster.

Deeper.

His hands moved to her ass, cupping and kneading with an almost frenzied hunger that made her sex constrict.

Hell, she was so close to coming, and he'd only just started.

She tightened her hand in his hair and tugged his mouth

free of her sex, looking down at him through a pleasure-fogged haze. "Not yet," she rasped with a slight shake of her head.

His nostrils flared, and he vibrated his thumb over her clit, watching her.

She tried not to close her eyes, tried not to melt against the sofa, but it was too damn good.

"Okay," he murmured, a heartbeat before his breath fanned her folds and his tongue claimed her clit once again.

He worshipped her pussy. She had no other way of processing what he was doing down there with his tongue and teeth. Worshipped her clit, her seam, her sex. He nipped at her flesh, sucked it, licked it, probed it, all with a building rhythm that tore groan after groan after keening, pleading groan from her.

She clawed at his scalp, his shoulders, the back of his neck, gritting her teeth as a wave of concentrated pleasure rolled through her.

Hell, she was going to come. There was no stopping it. She could feel it tingling in her core, the soles of her feet, her brain…

Grabbing a fistful of his hair again, she rammed her butt to the back of the sofa and planted her feet on his shoulders, spreading her thighs as wide as her hips would allow.

A tiny shard of pain stabbed at her left one, protesting the unfamiliar position, and then her orgasm erupted, and there was nothing but intense, amazing, pulsing pleasure and Owen's tongue and hands.

"Holy fuck," she cried, bucking into his mouth as she held his head exactly where she wanted it.

Her release throbbed through her, from her.

He lapped at it, teased it from her, didn't slow or break his rhythm, and she cried out as another orgasm rocked through her.

"Holy fuck," she ground out again, vision fogging, her whole body thrumming.

She clung to his hair, toes actually curling, breath little more than shallow, hitching pants, until—with one last slow lick of her clit—he drew back from between her thighs and looked up at her.

"Whoa," she breathed, letting her fingers fall from his hair as she returned her feet to the floor.

He smiled, and leant forward and kissed a slow path along the curve of her sex, to her navel—acknowledging her belly-button piercing with a playful flick of his tongue—and over her rib cage.

She moaned, knowing exactly what his destination was. Her breasts grew heavy in anticipation. Her nipples puckered.

He followed the curve of her waist with his palms, a barely there contact that made her shiver as much as his lips made her already spent sex constrict again. He spent a few languid moments brushing his lips over the underswell of her left breast and then her right.

Her nipples ached with need, harder than they'd ever been. An exquisite hardness waiting for his oh-so-talented mouth.

"Oh yeah, oh yeah…" she moaned when he closed his lips around her left nipple and sucked, cupping her right breast in his hand. "That's it. That's…"

Words deserted her as he lashed her nipple with his tongue, sliding his hand back down to her sex to penetrate her with a confident finger.

"Oh fuck…" she groaned, rolling her hips to take it deeper, holding his head to her breast with a far-from-gentle hand at the back of his head.

He feasted on her nipple and fucked her with his finger, in utter control of her pleasure. In utter control of her body's response.

She rode his hand, wrapping her legs around his hips as he moved his mouth to her other breast, propelling her to the edge of a precipice she hadn't anticipated.

Her third orgasm took her by surprise; a short, tight, and fierce climax that tore a strangled cry from her throat.

"Holy crap," she gasped, squeezing her eyes shut, her pussy clamping around his thrusting finger. "Holy—"

He captured her mouth with his.

Her own juices slicked his tongue and lips. She didn't care. In fact, it was time *she* tasted him…

Pulling away from the kiss, she pressed her palms to his chest and met his gaze. "My turn," she said and dropped her legs from around his hips, shoving him back a step.

A shaky laugh fell from him. "If you in—"

She didn't give him a chance to finish the word. Wrapping one hand around his balls, she dropped to her knees and slid her mouth down his engorged cock.

"Fuck me," Owen groaned, hips bucking forward.

Sucking up his length entirely, she pulled off him with a pop and grinned up at him. "Later. For now, I'm having fun."

He breathed out a laugh, his eyes on hers. "Go for it. I'm not going to stop you."

Flashing another grin, she cupped his sac and gave it a little tug. "Better not."

He laughed again, and once again, the sound melted into a raw groan as she closed her mouth over his length.

His fingers combed through her hair, gently holding on to a fistful, not so much guiding her motion but engaging with it. Something about the subtle connection sent a hot lick of happiness through her, and she increased her speed and suction, taking him deeper still, cupping and squeezing his balls.

His breathing quickened, turning erratic and hitching. His hand in her hair grew tighter. She flattened her tongue to the rigid length of his erection and drew her lips up, stopping when she reached the rim of his cockhead and flicking at the tiny slit at its crown before plunging down again.

"F...fuck, I'm going to bl- come in your mouth if you don't stop," he warned.

A part of her wanted exactly that. A part of her wanted to bring him to the most intense orgasm of his life with only her mouth the way he had done with her.

Another part though, a selfish part, wanted to see his face when he came. Wanted to see the pleasure she'd given him there. Hearing it in his ragged breaths and groans was one thing, seeing it...

His fist tightened in her hair, and almost grounding out a low laugh, he jerked his length from her mouth and staggered back a step.

She sat back on her ankles, licking at her bottom lip as she looked up at him. Once again, her hip reminded her this kind of movement was all very new and unexpected, but she didn't care. She was having way too much fun.

Eyes fluttering closed for a second, Owen wrapped his hand around his dick and squeezed, shaking his head. "Fuck, I didn't realize I had such willpower."

"I'm both impressed and shattered," she said, her body aching for him already. It felt wrong not having a part of him inside her in some way.

His ragged chuckle fell from him, and he met her gaze. "You have no idea how much I wanted to fucking explode in your mouth."

"So why didn't you?"

An uncertain frown twisted his eyebrows, and he ducked his head. "I didn't want to be presumptuous."

Bria laughed, shook her head and laughed again. "Oh my God, Owen, I—"

She stopped herself just before she said she could fall in love with him. No man wanted to hear the L word during a wild hookup. No woman only recently out of a semi-serious relationship and in her right mind should utter it either. But damn, he was so freaking incredible and sexy and funny and sweet and…

Stop it. Ride him like a fucking pole, Bria, and then say good night. Goodbye. The guy lives in Australia for Pete's sake. Remember that.

He watched her.

Heart racing, she slowly straightened to her feet—biting back a wince as her hip complained a little—and closed the small space between them. "Do you have a condom?" she asked, feathering her fingers up the underside of his jutting cock.

His chest swelled as he sucked in a slow breath. "I have a condom," he confirmed, voice low and husky, stare holding hers.

She closed her fingers around his thick dick and brushed her nipples to his chest. "Get it."

CHAPTER FIVE

He got it.

It took him a few fumbling seconds to locate his wallet in the pocket of his discarded shorts. A few more fumbling seconds to withdraw the damn thing *from* his wallet. He dropped it once he'd done that, but he eventually he got it.

"Hope ribbed and studded is okay?" he asked, holding up the square packet for Bria to see.

Mischief danced in her eyes. "Hmm, let me think…"

Before he could reply, she plucked it from his fingers and tore the packet open.

Cock throbbing in anticipation, he chuckled. "I take it you approve?"

Holding his gaze, she gently slid the condom free. "May I?"

His cock jerked, answering for him.

"This is a very impressive specimen you have here, sir," she commented, trailing her fingertips up the straining length of his erection.

"Thank you," he croaked. "I'm glad you—"

Like it dissolved into a drawn-out groan as she placed the condom on the crown of his dick and slowly—her fingers a firm ring around his girth—sheathed him to the balls.

"Very impressive," she murmured, sliding her palm down to cup the heavy globes.

He let out a steadying breath, watching her admire her handy work. When she lifted her gaze to his, he cupped the back of her head and brushed his lips over hers. A shiver rippled through her, and she sighed into his featherlight kiss, skimming her palms up over his stomach to his chest. She stroked his nipples with her thumbs as he nibbled a path along her jaw up to her earlobe, giving it a gentle bite.

"I like that," she whispered, pressing the curve of her sex to his latex-covered cock. "Do it again."

He did, sucking on the fleshy pad for a split second before moving his lips up to her temple. "We've got two options here," he stated on a shaky breath, smoothing his hands down over her back and cupping her delectable arse. "Hard and fast to start with, followed by slow, languid fucking after."

She *hmmmed* as she dragged her nails along the back of his shoulders. "I like that idea. What's the second option?"

He kissed a path back to her lips, explored her mouth with his for a dizzying second, and lifted his head. "Pretty much the same thing," he confessed.

She chuckled, rolling her hips to grind harder to his aching hard-on. "I see."

Giving her a lopsided smile, he squeezed her arse. "I want to be inside you so fucking much, there's no way the first time is going to be anything less than fast. Sorry."

A throaty laugh fell from her, and she shook her head. "You've already made me come three times, so no apologies allowed." She dipped her head and flicked her tongue over his right nipple, sending a shard of liquid pleasure into his groin. Smiling up at him, she closed her fingers around his cock. "Ready when you—"

He crushed her mouth with his. She kissed him back with equal ferocity and hunger. His head swam, a carnal, base need to claim her rushing through him. Hell, he'd never wanted anyone as much as he wanted her. She pumped his cock with a tight grip between their bodies, pushing him closer to an edge he didn't want to fall over yet.

Not until he was inside her.

Tearing his mouth from hers, he swept his stare around the room. "Which way to your room?"

"You don't want to fuck me here on the sofa?" She gave his cock a playful squeeze. "The kitchen counter?"

"I want to fuck you everywhere," he confessed. "Here. The floor. The sofa, the counter, the shower, the balcony, the bed. I don't care. I just want to fuck you."

Her eyes closed at his rasped declaration, and she let out a soft laugh. "Tempting…" She opened her eyes, grinning up at him. "But if either Elisa or Zeta walk in and see your sexy naked ass, I'll have to fight them off."

"Ahh." He grinned. "In that case…"

"This way," she said, suddenly snagging his left hand and pulling him toward the hallway leading off the living area.

This is happening. This is actually happening.

The surreal, euphoric thought whispered through his swirling head a second before she hurried through the second door on the left.

"Welcome to my room," she said, turning to him.

He had a brief second to take it in—a large bed covered in an aqua-green duvet and a truckload of pillows and cushions of various colors, a massive black dreamcatcher on one wall, a framed photograph of her skydiving, both thumbs up, grin wide and fearless, on the other wall—and then all that existed was Bria as she wrapped her arms around his neck and kissed him.

He kissed her back. Drove his throbbing cock harder to the firm plane of her stomach, grabbed her arse again, and kissed her back. A distant part of his mind reminded him he was waiting to learn if he was dying or not, that perhaps losing himself to the addictive pleasure of Bria wasn't wise, but the rest of his mind told that part to fuck off.

If he was dying, he couldn't think of anything better than amazing sex with an amazing woman. He could spend the rest of his life with her, and it wouldn't be enough.

With a growl, he hauled her up off her feet without breaking their kiss. She locked her ankles at the base of his spine, growling back at him as he carried her in the direction of her bed. His shins bumped into its end, and he pulled his lips from hers. "Can I throw you on the bed? I've never thrown anyone onto a bed before."

"Throw away," she said, grinning.

He did.

She hit the mattress just as he lost his balance and toppled onto it, halting his awkward fall a second before he could face-plant into her stomach. She burst out laughing.

"Well, that didn't go the way I wanted it to," he grumbled, meeting her gaze.

"That was fucking sexy as all hell," she declared, wriggling into a reclining position between his splayed arms. "I give you ten out of ten for enthusiasm and commitment."

"And for style and execution?"

Devilish delight danced in her eyes. "Oh, definitely a four."

He snorted and then shoved her thighs wide and swiped his tongue up the wet seam of her sex.

"Now that gets ten out of ten for execution," she murmured, dragging her heels up his back.

He allowed himself a long second to drown in her juices, teasing her clit with his tongue, before rising up between her spread legs.

His cock—still as hard as it had been when she'd sheathed it in the condom—jutted upright, aching with anticipation.

"Hard and fast, remember," she said, thrusting her hips upward, her breasts heaving.

Hard and fast.

He studied her. If he sank into her now, he'd be done for.

"I'm thinking," he placed one knee on the bed beside her thigh, "I might do *this* first."

Her breath caught. "What?"

He crawled up over her body until his lips drew level with her breasts. "This," he whispered, holding her stare as he lowered his head and took her right nipple in his mouth.

He sucked.

She whimpered.

He sucked deeper, smoothing his palm up over her ribcage to her breast, rolling his tongue against the puckered form of her nipple.

"Oh God, that's good," she moaned, raking her nails over his back.

He surrendered to the carnal need her response awoke in him. Fell into it. Gave himself completely to the moment. To her.

She moaned again, her nails far from gentle on his back, her hips bucking. Moving his mouth to her other breast, he closed his lips around her nipple, sucking on it as he sought out her clit with his index finger.

"Fuck yeah," she approved, ramming her hips upward. He slid his finger inside her, still feasting on her breast as he stroked the sweet spot within her warm, tight, wet walls.

A shudder claimed her, and she let out a keening cry, clawing at his scalp. "Fuck, Owen, Fuck, I'm come... I'm coming *again*."

Her inner muscles contracted. Her release wet his hand. He increased the speed of his finger inside her, wanting more.

She cried out again, pulling at his hair, and then she slumped back onto the bed, limp and panting, her hands slipping from his head and back.

Body thrumming with urgent lust and need, he withdrew his finger from her sex and lifted his head from her breast.

"Okay," he said, rising up onto his knees between her thighs. "Now, we're ready."

She let out a shaky, breathy laugh. "This is the best fucking fuck I've ever had."

"Remember what I said earlier," he commented, taking his rigid cock into his hand. "I'm not going to last long."

"Don't fucking care." She shook her head, grinning up at him, eyes now fully closed. "It's still the best."

A rush of happiness swept through him at her declaration. *And with that...* Pulling in a deep, slow breath, preparing himself for the sensations to come, he aligned the tip of his cock to her glistening pussy lips and stroked it over the tiny, swollen button of her pink clit.

"Oh God, yeah..." She moaned.

Here we go.

He pressed his free hand on the mattress beside her waist, locked his stare on her face, and slowly, slowly rolled his hips forward.

Penetrating her.

She moaned again, wrapping her legs around his hips as he fully embedded himself in her slick heat. "That's it. That's it," she rasped, nails once again clawing over his back.

He looked down the lengths of their bodies, his head swimming at the sight of his cock disappearing into her sex.

"Jesus, you're tight," he murmured, withdrawing in a slow stroke until her folds hugged the rim of his cock, and thrust back into her again.

"Kegels," she rasped back, arching into his stroke.

"What?" He lifted his attention to her face even as he continued to roll his hips. So fucking good. It felt so fucking good.

A soft chuckle fell from her, and her inner muscles constricted around his dick. "Kegal exercises."

"I don't know what you're saying," he murmured, his

rhythm growing faster. Yep, he was getting close. Damn close. "But I don't care. This is too fucking good."

She laughed again, unlocked her ankles from behind his back, and drew her left knee up to her side. "Hell yeah."

He followed her unspoken lead, hooking his elbow under her bent knee and drawing it higher, pumping into her deeper and deeper with each thrust.

"Don't stop," she ordered, her muscles squeezing him again. Whatever kegels were, he loved them.

"Not even thinking about stopping," he ground out, burying his face into the side of her neck, slamming into her over and over and over again.

She bucked into each thrust, her nails dragging over his shoulders. "Oh God, Owen... Oh God..."

The soles of his feet began to tingle. A searing tension shot up his spine, all the way from his balls to his brain. Rhythm deserted him. "F...fuck..." He panted, shaking his head as a shudder wracked through him. "I'm...I'm..."

He erupted, filling the condom with spurt after spurt, just as Bria slammed her hips upward and cried out.

Energy deserted him. His whole body burned—the best burn he'd ever experienced. Heart pounding, he relaxed his arm, letting her leg fall back to the bed. He stopped himself slumping on top of her with a trembling elbow, even as her sex continued to pulse and constricted around his spent cock. Lifting his head from the side of her neck, he looked down at her flushed face. "Fair dinkum, you're beautiful," he murmured.

She gazed up at him, her eyes seemingly searching his as she gave her head a little shake. "I can't believe you're real, Owen Blackthorne. You're too incredible. Too amazing."

"Wait until you hear me fart on the loo."

She burst out laughing, the action vibrating through her body and into his cock. "Such a charmer."

"Yep." He brushed a strand of her hair from her eyes and

dropped a soft kiss onto her lips. "Aren't you glad I didn't skip the party like I planned?"

A scowl crossed her face. "Life wouldn't be that unfair. I was meant to meet you tonight. I can feel it in my bones."

"Speaking of bones—" he took more of his weight on his elbow and knees, shooting a quick look down their bodies, "— how's your hip?"

With a gentle laugh, she stretched her leg out beside his thigh. "All good. Little twingey at the halfway point, but I gritted through."

"Thank you for that." He grinned. "But how about I get my sizeable arse off you and—"

A sharp pain sank into his head, just above the top of his spine.

He winced, squeezing his eyes shut for a split second before the pain vanished.

"You okay?" Bria frowned up at him.

Throat thick, pulse pounding, he nodded, letting out a wobbly chuckle. "Jet-lag headache, I think." He arched an eyebrow at her. "Or maybe you just blew my mind?"

"You better believe it, bud." She gave his cock a little squeeze with her inner muscles and arched her own eyebrow. "Wanna take a shower with me?"

"Hell yeah."

Making certain the condom came with him, he rolled off her. He bit back another wince as a dull pain pressed at the back of his head again and straightened to his feet beside the bed.

Thirty minutes—and a blowjob that really *did* almost blow his mind—later, Bria strutted out of the bathroom wrapped only in a towel. "I'm getting us some ice cream," she threw over her shoulder as Owen shut off the water.

He scanned the room, looking for a towel. Two big fluffy ones hung from the racks—presumably her sisters—and four more folded ones were piled on a shelf opposite the shower. He shook himself off as best he could, crossed the floor, and snagged the top one. He had no idea if Bria was getting them ice cream from the freezer or going out somewhere. Could be either, with what he'd discerned about her so far. A chuckle bubbled up in his chest as he toweled off. Guess he'd find out when he finished in here.

Giving his damp hair a quick comb-slash-tussle with his fingers, he studied his reflection in the small mirror above the basin. No dark circles under his eyes, no residue hint of the pain that had shot through his head earlier.

Good.

He didn't want to think about what that pain was right now. Right now, all he wanted to do was surrender to the absolute pleasure of Bria's company. With one last, long stare into his own eyes, he let out a breath. "You've got this, mate."

Wrapping the borrowed towel around his hips, he exited the bathroom and made his way down the short hallway, clearing his throat loudly as he approached the living room, just in case. "Bria?"

"Chocolate, vanilla, peanut-butter fudge, rocky road or peppermint chocolate-chip?" her voice wafted back to him.

She stood in the kitchen, studying the contents of the freezer, wearing the skimpiest pair of black undies he'd ever seen and a little black singlet that stopped a centimeter or two below her last rib.

His cock pulsed beneath his towel, and he drew in a slow breath. He wanted to stride into the kitchen, lose the towel along the way, bend her over the counter, and bury himself into her tight heat, but he suspected she might be feeling a tad tender after their rather vigorous interactions. Plus, he'd only had one condom in his wallet, and…well, it was now well and truly disposed of.

"Peppermint choc-chip," he said, scooping up his shorts from the floor. Where the hell was his shirt? And his stingray?

"A man after my own heart." She closed the freezer door

and turned to face him, a brown and green tub in her hand, a grin in her eyes. "You okay with eating it straight outta the tub, or would you like a bowl?"

He arched an eyebrow. "Who eats ice cream out of a bowl?"

She laughed.

He pulled his shorts on, flung the towel aside with dramatic flair, flicked a look at where it landed on the floor, and then hurried over to it. "Sorry," he said with a wry chuckle. "If I don't hang this up somewhere, it'll bug me for the rest of the night."

Bria's lips curled in a smile. "There's a laundry hamper in the bathroom."

He nodded, took the towel to the hamper, and came back, throat thick. Every minute with her was wonderful, and he was beginning to panic. This was only meant to be a one-night hookup. This wasn't how he'd expected to feel. There was weight to this, significance. How was he meant to walk away from this when it was over?

Returning to the living area, he found Bria sitting crossed-legged on the kitchen counter, open tub of ice cream in one hand, ice cream-laden spoon in another. Her eyes connected with his as she parted her lips and slipped the spoon into her mouth.

Yeah, he was not gonna walk away from this unscarred, that was for certain. He crossed to where she sat, pressing his palms to the counter's edge on either side of her knees.

Removing the spoon from her mouth, she lifted an eyebrow at him. "So...what's your favorite color?"

He laughed. "We've reached that part of the relationship, have we?"

"We have." She dug some ice cream from the tub and offered it to him. "I'm partial to blue, myself."

"I'm a green man," he said before opening his mouth.

With a laugh, she fed him the ice cream and dug out some more. "Favorite movie?"

"*Aliens.*"

"Seriously?" She snorted. "Too much gore for me. I love *The Proposal.*"

"Sandra Bullock fan?"

"Ryan Reynolds, thank you very much." She flashed a mischievous grin. "If there'd been anyone dressed as Deadpool or the Green Lantern at the party, you wouldn't have stood a chance, just so you know."

He snagged the spoon from her and dug into the ice cream, holding her gaze, his pulse thumping fast at the notion of never getting this moment with her. "In that case," he said, bringing the loaded spoon up to his mouth, "thank bloody God there wasn't."

She grabbed his wrist, redirected the spoon into her mouth, and then preened after pulling it out. "You like me," she said. "Go on, you can admit it."

He pulled a contemplative face and laughed. Playing it cool had never been one of his strengths. "Yeah. You're all right."

"All right?" She gasped in mock indignation.

Laughing again, he scooped out more ice cream and shoved it into his mouth.

She narrowed her eyes and studied him, running her index finger around the inside rim of the tub. "Favorite book?"

"Stephen Hawking's *A Brief History of Time.*"

"Really?"

He shook his head. "No. I wanted to sound impressive. It's actually *The Hobbit.* Nerd, remember?"

"Oh my fucking God, are you kidding me?" Eyes wide, she gave his chest a gentle shove. "I love Tolkien. Have you been to Hobbiton in New Zealand?"

"I'm ashamed to say I haven't."

"We *have* to go! You will love it. And then we can go bungee jumping in Queenstown—that was the first place I ever bungee-jumped, and it's freaking amazing—and then after that we can go on the Shotover Jet."

Heart pounding faster, he looked at her. Did she realize she'd just sent them both on an international trip together? Of course, it was also possible she was speaking rhetorically, but damn, now she'd put the idea into his head…

"What about you?" he asked. Fuck, he desperately needed to get a grip on himself. "What's *your* favorite book?"

"Well, given my Italian heritage, my first favorite is *Arturo's Island* by Elsa Morante, but my favorite book originally in English is Douglas Adams's *The Hitchhiker's Guide to the Galaxy*."

Yep, even *that* answer made him like her more. He'd read the irreverent sci-fi comedy back when he was in high school and close to every year after that. In fact, he'd almost gotten a quote from the book tattooed on his calf during a drunken party back in his university days.

Almost.

Tilly had stopped him.

Just.

"Don't panic," he said with a smile, reciting the quote.

Her eyes grew wide, and her smile grew wider. "Yes! Oh my God, Owen? Did I *dream* you? Not a single guy I've dated has even known about *Hitchhiker's*, and here you are. When I tried to get Simon to read it…" She trailed off, her teeth catching her bottom lip.

He swallowed, a little knot of irrational jealousy twisting in his gut.

"He didn't know where his towel was?" he asked instead, making an obscure reference to a joke from the book.

Her soft, somehow-wounded smile tugged at his heart. "He didn't," she whispered, her eyes holding his.

"I do though," he murmured.

"You do," she whispered.

He leant forward and kissed her. Her lips and mouth tasted

of peppermint and chocolate. She *hmmmed* into the kiss, swiping her tongue against his before pulling back. "Favorite animal?"

"Stingray. Naturally."

She burst out laughing. Fuck a duck, he liked the sound of her laugh.

Smiling, he took the ice cream tub from her hands, stabbed the spoon into its center, and deposited the tub on the counter beside her. Cupping her jaw in his hands, her brushed his thumb along her bottom lip. "Can I make love to you again?"

"I thought you'd never fucking ask," she murmured and captured his lips with hers in a fierce, brief kiss.

CHAPTER SIX

S he pulled away, her heart pounding in her ears. "Have you got another condom?"

He shook his head. "Sorry."

"Fuck," she muttered. "Let me go check Elisa and Zeta's drawers…"

She scrambled off the counter and ran to Zeta's bedroom. A slight finger of guilt traced up her spine as she yanked open her sister's bedside drawers. Like most triplets, they were close, but this still felt like an invasion of privacy. Of course, when they were kids and teenagers, they'd shared everything, including bras.

Of course, when they were kids and teenagers, none of them had the dire need for a condom so she could have sex again—no, not just sex. Incredible, amazing, mind-blowing sex with the incredible, amazing Aussie waiting for her in the kitchen.

Damn it, the three of them had always joked about having a bowl full of condoms sitting on the coffee table. Why hadn't they done that?

Because it'd only ever been intended as a joke to freak Mom and Dad out.

She shoved the drawer closed and clawed at her hair. Whoever decided not to do that joke deserved a damn good talking to.

"I'm coming," she yelled as she bolted into Elisa's room.

"I hope not without me," Owen called back, a chuckle in his voice.

She snorted. God, he was adorable. Searching Elisa's room provided no condom. She did, however, find a big purple vibrator that made her pause for a second.

"Merda santa, sis," she muttered, staring at in in shock. "It's always the shy ones."

She returned Elisa's vibrator to its hiding place in the drawer, promising herself never to think of it again, and let out a sigh.

Okay. No condoms. "Damn it."

Body thrumming with need and frustration, she hurried back to Owen.

He now sat on one of the sofas in the living area, bare-chested and gorgeous, holding the stingray that had once been fixed to his shirt. His attention lifted from it to her as she stopped a few feet away, a wry laugh escaping him. "Do we need to go shopping?"

Clearly frustration and the failure to find a condom was evident on her face.

"We need to go shopping," she said. "There's a convenience store on the corner. We can go buy what we need and be back in twenty-minutes. That okay?"

He straightened to his feet and tossed the stingray aside. "That's more than okay. I'm a fan of delayed gratification."

She laughed, running her gaze over him. "I'm a fan of *you*, Owen. I think you are the best thing that's ever entered my life." The earnest statement slipped out before she could reel it back in, and she bit her bottom lip. True, their natural chemistry seemed off the charts, and their hookup so far was far from conventional, but no guy she knew of wanted such an open declaration after only an hour or so. "I mean—" she swallowed and gave a nervous laugh, "—after peppermint chocolate-chip ice cream."

His Adam's apple jerked up and down. "Bria—"

"Let's go get that condom," she cut him off, snagging his wrist and dragging him toward the apartment's door. Whatever he was going to say, she wasn't prepared to hear it.

Chicken.

He cleared his throat behind her. "You reckon we should get dressed first?"

Stopping her powerwalk to the door, she dropped his wrist and looked back at him. "Well, if you want to be boring…"

He laughed. "Hey, I'm game if you are."

She grinned. "Tempting."

He laughed again. God, she liked him so much. If she asked him to stay here in the US with her for a while longer, would he?

With a roll of her eyes at her own rash fantasy, she shook her head. "I want to spend the rest of the night fucking you, Owen," she said. "Not in a cell separated from you because we've been arrested for public indecency, so I guess we should probably get dressed."

His nostrils flared a little. "I'm completely okay with the idea of spending the night fucking you as well. Clothes it is."

Leaving him to find his shirt, she hurried into her bedroom and yanked on the first things she put her hands on: a pair of jeans, her old Padres bomber jacket, and her trusty white sneakers.

"Ready," she declared, almost running back into the living room.

He stood at the door, hand on the knob, grin wide. "Ready."

Grabbing her keys and phone, she shoved them into her back pocket and then destroyed the space between them. She wrapped her arms around his neck, rose up on tiptoe, and brushed her lips to his. "So I see," she murmured.

His hands found their way beneath her jacket and he smoothed them up her back. A shiver of delight and anticipation shot through her, and she smiled. "Let's buy two boxes, okay?"

He arched an eyebrow. "Only two?"

"Okay, four."

He nodded, drawing her closer. "Done."

She laughed, yanked open the door, and pulled him through it by his hand. They'd just reached the elevator when her phone buzzed with an incoming text message.

"Give me a sec," she muttered, pulling it from her pocket.

There was a text from Zeta. **Hey, sis, I know you're probably having insane amounts of fun right now, but if you see this message, is there any chance you could come back up to the party for a few minutes? I think Elisa might be heading into an anxiety attack.**

"Oh no," she whispered, re-reading the text.

"Everything okay?" Owen asked at her side.

She looked up at him. "We're just going whip back up to the party for a few minutes, okay? I need to check on one of my sisters."

"Sure."

She studied him for a heartbeat. No questions, no sign of a frown, no reluctance or irritation, despite the change to their plans.

"In fact," he said with a gentle smile, "I'll find *my* sister and tell her I'm breaking curfew."

"Curfew?"

"It's a…" He rubbed at the back of his neck, his eyes sliding from hers for a second. "It's a long story."

A long story. Why did that sound…ominous?

"Can you hit the rooftop button, please?" she asked,

tapping out a reply to Zeta: **On my way. Tell her to take a deep breath and count backwards from 10 in Italian.**

Elisa's anxiety rarely raised its head these days, not since she'd removed herself from a toxic relationship that had almost destroyed her self-confidence, but perhaps the sheer number of people at the party was triggering it?

The elevator door chimed open, and she shoved her phone back into her pocket. "Sorry," she said to Owen, hurrying into the carriage.

"No worries at all." He followed, hit the close-door button and leant his back against the wall. "Is everything okay?"

She leant against the opposite wall, taking a slow breath. "Hope so."

"If I can help in any way, let me know."

Smiling, she shook her head. "I'm going to say something I might regret later, and I hope it doesn't scare you off, but I have to say it anyway."

His gaze held hers. "Okay."

"I know this was only meant to be a party-hookup kinda thing," she said, her chest growing tight, "but I really *really* like you, which sounds ridiculous given we've only known each other for a few seconds, but I really really do. You're uncomplicated, insanely easy to be with, sexy as all hell, intelligent and funny, and I'm wondering if you'd be interested in maybe exploring the possibility of this, you and me, being something *more* than a one-night—"

He crossed the floor in one step, cupped her face in his hands, and kissed her. Deeply. Thoroughly.

He didn't break the kiss until the elevator gently jolted to a stop and the door chimed open again.

"So that's a yes?" she asked, looking up at him as he rested his forehead to hers. Somehow, the thumping of her heart seemed to drown out the sounds of the party still raging on the rooftop.

"That's an I'm in San Diego for the next week and want to

spend every one of those seven days with you," he said, straightening. "It's also a have you ever thought about moving to Australia?"

She laughed. "So a yes, then."

"Definitely a—"

The elevator door started to close.

"Shit." He threw his body in the way, grinning back at her.

She threaded her fingers through his and headed for the party. "Let's go find Elisa and Zeta."

It took her five minutes. Zeta was standing on a stool next to one of the bars set up for the party, scanning the crowd with squinted eyes, no doubt looking for her. When she saw Bria, she waved her hands frantically. The massive silk and wire monarch-butterfly wings she wore as part of her costume flapped about just as frantically behind her.

"There she is," Bria said, tightening her grip on Owen's hand as she made a beeline for her sister.

The crowd—a tad more inebriated than it had been the last time she'd passed through it—surged and pressed into them both. She shoved at people's backs and sides, growing agitated. No wonder Elisa's social anxiety was flaring up.

"Move your arses out of the way," Owen suddenly growled, stepping past her, forging a clear path through the partygoers.

She smiled at him and then at Zeta as they arrived at the bar.

"Thank God." Zeta leapt down to the ground, crashed-tackled her in a fierce hug, and let her go with equal ferocity. "*I* was beginning to freak out." She flicked Owen a glance. "Sorry for interrupting."

"No worries," he said. "Family comes first."

Bria's chest tightened. He meant that. She could see it in his face and hear it in his voice.

"Where's Lis?" she asked, taking Zeta's hand.

"This way." Zeta pivoted on her ballet-flats heel and slipped behind the grove of potted palms creating a green screen a few feet away.

Bria started to follow and then turned back to Owen. "You okay to wait a bit? Elisa struggles with anxiety, and I think the party has probably maxed her out, social wise."

He nodded. "My brother's battled anxiety and depression almost his whole life. I understand completely. Do what you need to do. I'm not going anywhere."

She stepped back to him, went up on tiptoe, and kissed him quickly. "You are incredible, and I think I love you," she whispered and then hightailed it after Zeta behind the palms.

Elisa looked up at her from where she sat on the floor, knees hugged to her chest, eyes wide and haunted. Her padded Very-Hungry-Caterpillar costume seemed to devour her. "I'm sorry, Bri," she said, her words almost lost in the party's din. "I'm sorry."

"Hey hey hey." Bria dropped to her knees in front of Elisa and smoothed her hands up Elisa's shins. "Don't you dare apologize. I dragged you here. *I* should be apologizing."

Elisa shook her head, giving Bria a wobbly smile. "This was your comeback, sis. After what Simon did to you, and then finally getting off your crutches... This was your time to cut loose, and I messed it up." She scrunched up her face and let out a sob as wobbly as her smile. "And I probably interrupted you and your hot Aussie from...you know..."

Bria flashed her a grin. "Nah. We got it happening more than once before Zet sent me the SOS text. In your room in fact."

Elisa's eyes widened and her mouth fell open. "Eww. Are you kidding?"

"Do I ever kid?"

"All the freaking time!"

Bria laughed. The sight of the smile on Elisa's face made her heart sing. Worry still shone in her sister's eyes, but nowhere near the same haunted grief as before.

"Was he good?" Zeta asked, crouching down beside Elisa to rest an elbow on her shoulder.

Elisa snorted out a shocked laughed. "Zet! You can't ask that."

"Just did." Zeta preened, giving Elisa's shoulder a little nudge with her arm.

Bria bit back a grin. One of the best ways to help Elisa through an anxiety attack was to make her laugh. Distracting her with humor helped her mind release all the feel-good neurotransmitters—dopamine, endorphins, and serotonin. Making Elisa smile and laugh had become an art form for Bria and Zeta when she was at her worst a year ago. Bria's sex life was always Zeta's go-to to make Elisa laugh. For Bria, it was their parents' ludicrous hairstyles when they were teenagers. She kept a whole slew of images of their mom and dad from the 80s on her phone especially to make Elisa laugh. That and really bad cartoon Aquaman gifs.

It had been a long while since the gifs and photos had been required, but it hadn't taken Zeta long to go straight to her weapon of choice.

Bria didn't mind. If kissing and telling was needed to help Elisa, then kissing and telling it was.

"He was fucking incredible," she said, rolling her eyes to emphasis just how incredible Owen had been. "At everything. He made me freaking come three times with just his—"

"Dio," Elisa slapped her hands to her ears, laughing. "Stop. Stop."

"He's funny, smart, very good with his hands *and* his tongue," Bria went on, her heart thumping a little faster at the memory of all the minutes she'd spent with him. "Uncomplicated. Grounded. Unpretentious. Did I say funny? *And* he picked up a towel from the floor. Couldn't leave it there. He has fantastic taste in films and books, and oh, he loves *The Hitchhiker's Guide to the Galaxy*. Can you believe it? I've finally found a guy who not only knows of *Hitchhikers*, but actually *loves* it. He freaking quoted it to me. I think I'm in—"

She stopped, a prickling heat crawling up over her scalp. Biting her lip, she frowned, slumping a little, her heart hammering in her throat.

"Huh," she muttered, lifting her stare to Zeta and Elisa.

Was it possible? *Had* she actually gone and fallen in love with Owen? Had she?

"Huh what?" Elisa asked, studying her.

Zeta's eyes narrowed. "Are you thinking what I think you're thinking, Bri?"

Bria swallowed at the desert suddenly making itself at home in her mouth. "Do you think love at first sight is a real thing?"

Elisa's eyes widened. "Seriously?"

Zeta burst out laughing. "If it was going to happen to anyone, it'd be you."

Bria blinked.

Elisa chuckled, nodding as she smiled at first Zeta and then Bria. "It's true, sis. You're the one who always lives life without a safety net. Of course you'd be the one who'd fall in love with a total stranger straight away."

Bria stared at them. It wasn't love. She knew that. Not yet. But holy shit, it could be. Really quickly.

"By the way—" Elisa reached forward and gently squeezed Bria's hand, "—if this is part of your plan to help me tonight, it's worked. Spectacularly."

Zeta snorted. "*You* might be feeling better, Lis, but I think our big sister is now shell-shocked."

"Never seen her shell-shocked before." Elisa flashed a mischievous smirk. "It suits her."

"It does *not*." Bria threw up her hands. "I'm not shell-shocked. I'm…"

"In lurve?" Zeta drawled with a grin.

"Oh, shut up." Bria glared, straightened to her feet and

pointed back and forth between her sisters. "This moment, this right now, this is about Lis, not me. We're fixing Lis up."

"Oh, I'm well and truly fixed up." Elisa's grin mirrored Zeta's. "I haven't felt this good in a long time."

Zeta burst out laughing. Elisa beamed.

Bria sighed and then chuckled. "Well, at least you're not freaking out any more." She shot a look over shoulder. Was Owen still out there on the other side of the palm-tree screen? Waiting for her?

God, she hoped he was. She really did like him a lot. More than she ever had Simon. She'd never even considered the L word with Simon, and here she was pondering if it could be a part of her vocabulary with Owen already...

"Go get him, Bri." Zeta gave her a little shove on the shoulder.

Elisa got to her feet, brushed off her Very-Hungry-Caterpillar costume and squeezed Bria's fingers. "And tell him we expect to see him at the breakfast table at eight so we can get to know him better."

"Eight?" Zeta rolled her eyes at Elisa. "I'm not getting up at eight."

"Eight-thirty?"

"Eighty-thirty, I can do." Zeta nodded and then smirked at Bria. "Tell Steve Irwin we'll interrogate him at eight-thirty tomorrow morning during breakfast."

Bria raised her eyebrows, shook her head with a huffed sigh, and squeezed Elisa's fingers back. "Are you *sure* you're okay?"

Elisa smiled. "I'm very much okay. Go have fun with the possible love of your life. Zet and I will go buy some earplugs before we come back to the apartment."

"Speak for yourself." Zeta snorted. "I'm planning to listen to all of it. Glass to the door and everything."

"And I'm outta here." Bria laughed. "We'll set the ground rules for the interrogation at eight-fifteen. Don't be late."

She leant forward, kissed Elisa on the cheek, followed up with one for Zeta, and then weaved her way back out from behind the palm trees.

His heart kicked its way up into second gear at the sight of Bria walking towards him again. He leant back against the bar, propping his elbows on the cool surface, and lifted the can of beer in his right hand as she stopped in front of him.

"People keep giving me these," he said. "I open my mouth and say something, and suddenly they give me a Fosters. I don't have the heart to tell them real Aussies don't drink it."

Without a word, she took the can from him, placed it on the bar next to his elbow, pressed her body to his, and kissed him.

Without hesitation, he smoothed his hands around her waist and up and back, returning her kiss. Hell, he loved kissing her. Loved seeing her. Loved listening to her.

Everything about her was amazing, and he hadn't planned to find amazing on the other side of the world as he waited to find out if he had many days left.

What did he do now?

Surrender to every second you have with her. And make every second count.

He pulled her closer, kissed her deeper, and refused to think of anything else.

Letting out a soft moan, she pulled away a little and met his gaze. "If I were to ask you to stay the night with me—"

"I'd say yes."

She laughed, pulling back a fraction more. "There's a condition, a qualifier. Well, two, actually."

Lips twitching, he cocked an eyebrow, resting his hands on the curve of her hips. "And they are?"

"One, my sisters are going to interrogate the hell out of you in the morning during breakfast."

"I can handle that." He pursed his lips with a melodramatic frown. "I think. And two?"

She grew still against his body, her stare holding his. "Even though this might scare you off, I'm all about being honest and upfront, so I need to tell you there is a very distinct possibility I might already be falling for you. Quite substantially."

Owen's throat grew tight. Upfront and honest.

You should tell her. Be as upfront as she is. Tell her what you're waiting to find out. You like her, and she likes you, and this could go…somewhere. Now's the perfect time to tell her you've got your own qualifier before things get too serious.

Pulse pounding, he opened his mouth. "While I've been waiting for you, I've been wondering how similar the US education system is to the Australian one."

That wasn't what he'd planned to say. He *had* been wondering that while waiting for her to come back out from behind the palms, but the two countries' education systems had nothing to do with being upfront about his possible diagnosis.

She bit her bottom lip, a smile in her eyes. "Why?"

"In case there's a need for me to move here."

If he was still alive, that was.

Oh for fuck's sake, shut up.

A grin split her lips, and she rolled her hips to his, dancing her fingers up his chest and into his hair. "Let's go buy every box of condoms we can find."

He chuckled. "Okay."

Better to think of a night of incredible sex with Bria than his upcoming results.

She wriggled her eyebrows and ground the curve of her sex to his stiffening cock. "And use them all before eight-thirty."

"Before your sisters interrogate me, you mean?"

"Yep."

He chuckled again. "I may be too exhausted to answer."

Mischief danced in her eyes. "Which will be the most honest answer, yes?"

Hell, he liked her so fucking much.

"Speaking of sisters—" he traced his fingertips up the line of her spine, "—how is… Elisa, was it? How is Elisa going? She okay?"

Bria let out a soft breath. "Ah, man, you are amazing. You remembered." She gave him a quick kiss. "She's okay. Sometimes she just needs something to make her laugh. Tonight, it was my—" She paused, twisting her lips as she clearly reconsidered what she was going to say. "Tonight, it was me."

"Sometimes, the most important role of a sibling is to make the other laugh. Been there, done that." What had she been going to say?

An irritating little voice insisted she'd been about to say "my taste in men". She was stunning and funny, and he was, well, he did have a dad bod, and he was a maths teacher, and Australian, and possibly a few years older than her.

Plus, you might be dying.

Oh for fuck's sake, the sooner he got the phone call with the results, the better. One way or the other, he'd be out of this holding pattern and not wondering if every decision he was making was a wasted one or the right—

"Owen?"

He blinked at Bria's soft voice, shaking himself out of the bleak funk trying to drag him under.

"Sorry." He rubbed at the back of his neck, giving her a smile. How could he be bleak and down when he was with her? Talk about wasted minutes. "Jet lag."

It was the second time he'd dipped into that well for an excuse. The second time he'd fudged the truth. He didn't like it.

"Let's go fuck that jet lag right out of your system," she said, taking his hand in hers.

He chuckled, even as his chest tightened with the realization that however many days/hours/months he had left, he wanted to spend them with her.

Fuck a duck, this trip wasn't meant to get this complicated.

Without a word, he pulled her to him, cupped the back of her head, and kissed her.

Pulling away, she flashed him a grin. "I'm taking that as a yes."

"Bloody oath," he drawled.

She shivered. "Have I mentioned how much I love your accent?"

Before he could respond, she dragged him away from the bar, heading back in the direction of the elevator lobby.

You should find Tilly. Tell her you won't make curfew. Tell her you're going to spend the night with—

"Hey, Kangaroo Jack," a familiar male voice snarled on his right a split second before something hard smashed into his jaw.

CHAPTER SEVEN

The night exploded. His *head* exploded. Black stars detonated in his vision as pain shattered everything.

He lurched sideways, looking for what had hit him, *who* had hit him. His blurring vision locked on a familiar shape—Simon?—and then Bria shouted, and Owen's knees crumpled beneath him.

He hit the floor, head a throbbing mass of pain.

"What the fuck is wrong with you?" Bria shouted.

I've just been hit, he thought, propping himself up with one hand, rubbing at his jaw with the other. His fuzzy vision jumped around the place, focused on nothing. *Shit, did Simon punched me?*

"You fucking jerk," Bria went on above him. "How could you—"

"That's what you get, Bri Bri," the familiar male voice cut her off.

Yep. Definitely Simon. Owen lifted his head, squinting through a black cloud of agony up at the Simon-shaped blur. Great, so the ex had decided to pick a fight. Awesome.

Get up. Punch the bastard back.

A shard of fresh pain sank into the back of his head, and he squeezed his eyes shut for a second. Punching anyone at this point in time was a no-go. Hell, it was a wonder his brain was still in his skull.

"I'm okay," he croaked, trying to push himself to his feet.

No, you're not.

"You don't just fucking sucker punch someone, you prick," Bria growled, shoving at Simon's chest.

"What the hell did you do to my brother?" a new voice shouted from behind Owen, and his gut dropped.

Tilly was here. Had she seen Simon hit him? If she had, Simon was in for a whole world of shit.

"Til," he said, wincing as the pain in his head dialed up to a hundred. He squinted through it up at her. "It's okay. I'm—"

"Who the hell are you?" Simon yelped, staggering backward as Tilly launched herself at him, sexy-scientist lab coat flapping behind her as she rammed her hands into his chest.

"What kind of idiot wanker punches someone with brain cancer?" she shouted, slamming her palms into Simon's chest again.

"I don't know if it's—" Owen mumbled, trying to make his knees work. Shit, he needed to stand up. He needed to stop all this before it got out of hand.

"Brain cancer?" Bria echoed Tilly's words.

The world wobbled. Owen wobbled with it. Or maybe it was his brain wobbling. Holy crap, his head felt like it was about to explode.

"I'm okay," he said again, blinking, trying to clear his vision. "I'm—"

"Brain cancer?" Bria repeated, confusion in her voice.

He closed his eyes. Fuck, his head hurt. What had Simon hit him with? A cricket bat? No, it'd be a baseball bat in this country. He looked up at Bria, his vision clearing a little as he straightened to his feet.

She stared at him, expression unreadable. "You have brain cancer?"

"I…" He swallowed, his chest tightening. "I don't know."

His brain—cancer-riddled or not—told him Tilly was making Simon's life hell. He'd intervene in a second, rescue the bastard from his sister's wrath, but right now, he needed to make it right with Bria. She was all about being upfront and open, and he hadn't been that with her. From the second he'd realized there was something special between them, he should have—

"You didn't think you should tell me?" Bria asked.

"Not to start with."

She stared at him, a stiffness to her he hadn't seen before, not even when Simon had first given her grief at the party, and a pity in her eyes that tore at his heart.

"It's not exactly a conversation opener, is it?" he went on. "G'day, I'm Owen. I might have brain cancer. And this—me and you—wasn't meant to be anything more than… Well, a hookup, right? But then it started to feel like it could be more. It started to feel perfect, and I didn't know how I could bring it up. How I could tell you without scaring—"

"Hey, dude?" Simon tapped Owen's forearm, cutting him off. "Owen."

For a brief second, barely a heartbeat, Owen held Bria's unreadable gaze, and then he turned to face Simon, his head still aching, the side of his face a throbbing sting. "Mate, if you want to continue the fight, you're going to be sorely disappointed."

"No, no." Simon shook his head. "I want to say sorry. I didn't know. I didn't mean to—"

"Hit him?" Bria stepped between them. "Try to knock him out?" She shoved his chest again. "I can't believe you *did* that."

Simon cowered, looking at her with a wounded expression. "I'm sorry, Bri. It's just, you're here with him, and I got jealous, and he pushed me in the pool and—"

"And that's *not* an excuse for being a fucking—"

"Jerk," Tilly cut Bria off, stepping up beside Owen, in front of him a little. He wanted to chuckle at her protectiveness, but his head hurt too much. She flicked him a look over her shoulder, worry and rage warring in her eyes.

"I'm okay," he said for the third time. Or was it the fourth? Shit, he didn't know. Nor did he know if he *was* okay. It wasn't the first time he'd taken a punch. During his time working as a bouncer/stripper in his uni years, he'd learnt how to handle himself in a fight, but this *was* the first time he'd been blindsided by one. And the first time he'd almost been knocked out. The doc had told him to avoid doing anything too crazy while waiting for his results, and getting hit by a jealous ex probably fell firmly into that category. "I'm okay," he repeated, for his own sake more than Tilly's.

She frowned at him, just as Bria turned to do the same.

"You need to get to a doctor," Bria said, reaching a hand out toward him and then dropping it.

"Do you know one?" Tilly asked her, frown growing deeper as she stepped up and gently touched Owen's face.

Biting back a hiss, he pulled away. "I'm okay," he said. Again. "I just need to—" *get the hell out of here,* "—go get a Panadol or something."

"Panadol?" Worry flared in Bria's eyes.

"Paracetamol," Tilly clarified with a quick smile before turning her attention back on Owen. "I've got some in my bathroom, O. Let's go."

Behind them, Simon met his gaze, and Owen's gut clenched. Fuck, was that pity in the wanker's eyes as well?

He looked away, shaking his head. "No," he said, schooling the wince of pain before it could escape him. "I need—" *to get away from all the fucking pity,* "—to just go be calm and quiet for a while."

"O," Tilly growled.

Bria didn't say anything.

He shook his head again. "I'm going. I'll be okay."

The fifth *okay* since Simon punched him.

Around them, curious partygoers watched, zipping their stares between them all. Were they waiting for Owen to punch Simon back?

Owen let out a sigh. They'd have to deal with disappointment. He'd had enough. His head hurt, he'd clearly fucked up something that had the potential to be important, and the thought of engaging any further with Simon, giving the bastard any more of his time, made him angry.

What if someone had filmed this all on a smartphone and uploaded it to TikTok or Instagram or whatever the social media app of choice was at the moment? What if his students saw it? The last thing he needed was for them to see their teacher elevate a conflict even more. No one needed to see him acting like a macho bullshit caveman.

"I'm outta here," he muttered, rubbing the side of his head where Simon's knuckles had landed as he turned away. So it seemed he actually *would* make Tilly's curfew after all. God, he had a headache.

He heard Tilly call his name. He thought he heard Bria do the same. It might have been wishful thinking. Or maybe his brain was rattling around in his head so much he was hearing things.

Just get out of here.

He weaved through the crowd, although it seemed to melt away from his path. By the time he made it to the elevator lobby, he'd reached far enough away from the epicenter that no one gave a fuck who he was or why he was rubbing his jaw. He probably looked inebriated.

Hitting the button for Tilly's floor, he gave the rooftop party one more look. Still in the throng, Bria and Tilly—and probably Elisa and Zeta—were no doubt giving Simon hell again.

The bastard deserved hell.

For a second, a flash of copper-red caught Owen's eye in the mass of people. Bria? Coming after him?

The elevator door opened with a soft chime, and with a ragged breath, he stepped into the car and hit the close-door button.

Better to rip off that Bria-shaped Band-Aid quick smart. It had been fun, more than fun, it had been incredible and amazing and wonderful, but he wouldn't expect her to even think about taking what they'd discovered to the next level. Not knowing what he possibly faced. Not with the pity he'd seen in her eyes.

You don't think she should get a say in this? You're making assumptions, mate. What if—

He ground his teeth and shook his aching head. "No pity fucks or relationships for me," he muttered.

An unpleasant knot of guilt tightened in his gut, joined immediately by remorse and regret, but he ground his teeth harder, focusing on the sharp pain in his head instead of the pain in his heart.

"Band-Aid, Owen, Band-Aid."

"So the stubborn sod just took off." Tilly glared at the spot Owen had been standing and threw up her hands. "Great. Awesome. Fan-fucking-tasic. I'm going to kill him."

Bria liked Tilly instantly. It helped the pocket rocket dressed as a burlesque scientist had promised to kick Simon's ass—or *arse*, as Tilly had snarled—if he even looked at Owen again.

Of course, that didn't mean Bria wasn't furious with Owen for pulling a disappearing act, but his sister at least made the worry eating her up tolerable.

Biting her bottom lip, she shot her own sisters a look. Zeta and Elisa had appeared from behind the palm trees a few seconds after Owen had left, confusion twisting their identical eyebrows. "What did we miss?" Zeta had asked.

Tilly, God love her, had colorfully filled them in, jabbing

her finger at Simon and threatening him with bodily harm in a voice that hinted at it being not a threat but a promise. Bria watched the confusion on her sisters' faces morph into admiration as they observed Tilly. That admiration turned to something close to adulation when Simon stammered out an apology and scurried off.

Now, however, with Simon gone, Owen removing himself from the party, and Tilly angry with her brother, both Zeta and Elisa frowned at Bria again, the question in their eyes clear. What was she going to do next?

She didn't know.

She was pissed. At Owen for leaving, at Owen for keeping something as huge as possible brain cancer from the conversation, at Owen for making her believe love at first sight was actually possible, and at Owen for not hanging around so she could see he was okay.

Damn it, *was* he okay?

"I'm going after him," she declared.

She spun on her heel, stormed three steps away from Elisa, Zeta and Tilly, and then stormed the three steps back. "Where would he go?" she asked Tilly.

Frowning, Tilly studied her. "Sorry, I know the last few minutes have been a bit chaotic, but who are you?"

Bria opened her mouth. And closed it. Who was she to Owen?

Tilly narrowed her eyes and then smiled. "Ah, Scooby-Doo. You're Scooby-Doo, aren't you?"

"Yes." She had been. What felt like a lifetime ago.

"I interrupted you when you were making out with my brother." Tilly snorted. "He likes you."

"I like him," Bria said back. "A lot. I think."

"You know he's a shocker for leaving the loo seat up, right?"

"But he does pick up discarded bath towels from the floor."

Tilly snorted again, lips twitching. "I don't want to know

how you know that already, but, yes, he does. He's a bit of a neat freak." She paused, narrowing her eyes again as she looked at Bria. "So what are your intentions with O?"

Behind Tilly, Zeta covered her mouth with a hand—to muffle her laughter or to stop herself blurting out something, Bria wasn't sure. At Zeta's side, Elisa smirked.

"Originally?" Bria asked. "To fuck him senseless."

Tilly's eyebrows lifted. Slightly. Bria respected the hell out of her for that.

"But then," she went on, letting her mind flip through all the incredible minutes she'd shared with Owen since finding him at the party in his dead Steve Irwin costume, "as we spent time together, not just fucking, but talking and laughing, I realized I could genuinely see myself…"

She stopped. Would his sister think she sounded crazy if she said what was in her heart?

"Falling in love with him?" Tilly finished.

"Yes." Bria let out a ragged breath, nodding. "Very much yes."

"Yeah, he's a really nice, genuine guy." Tilly smiled, her love for her brother obvious. "Anyone would be lucky to be loved by him. To have him in their life." She paused for a beat, her eyes holding Bria's. "No matter for *how* long."

Bria didn't miss the subtle message. And she agreed with it one hundred percent. *Any* time spent with Owen was precious and wonderful, and she'd be damned if she was going to lose her chance. Besides, she was worried sick about him. If she didn't go after him now to find out if he was okay, she'd take out her frustration on Simon, and the last thing she needed was to end up in jail for the rest of the night after kneeing her ex in the balls again for being such a fuckwit.

"What's your apartment number?" she asked Tilly.

"165C." Tilly snagged her wrist. "C'mon. I'll take you to him."

"Hey?" Zeta called as Tilly began hurrying away. "Keep us in the loop."

Bria flashed a smile at her sisters and then let Tilly pull her through the crowd.

Waiting for the elevator doors to open, Tilly threw her a look. "Things you need to know about my brother," she suddenly said without preamble. "He yells at the TV when his favorite soccer team—the Newcastle Jets—are losing. And *also* when they're winning. He spreads way too much Vegemite on his toast, can quote whole scenes from *Star Wars*, snores, and is really bad at playing poker."

"What's Vegemite?"

Tilly's eyes widened and she laughed. "I'll pretend I didn't hear that. Oh, and you should know he was a stripper for a while during uni."

"He told me that. *And* showed off his dance moves."

Tilly pulled a face. "The sod *can* dance. Did he also tell you I'll unmake you on a microbiological level if you hurt him? I'm a scientist, in case the costume didn't give it away."

Bria laughed. "No, he didn't."

Tilly grinned. "I will. So don't. Okay?"

"I won't."

The elevator doors slid open, and they both hurried inside.

"Good," Tilly said, hitting the button for her floor, her gaze steady on Bria.

Silence stretched between them for a few seconds before Tilly let out a ragged breath. "Who's the guy that punched him? I should probably tell you I'm going to try to convince Owen to press charges."

Bria's stomach clenched. "My ex. And I understand that. And Owen is entitled to."

"Your ex?" Tilly's jaw bunched. "Hmm. Can I assume Owen protected your honor in some way during the party, and that's why your ex, what was his name, Simon, did what he did?"

"Yeah. I kneed Simon in the nuts earlier because he slept with my physiotherapist, and then Simon pushed me in the pool a little bit after that, and then Owen pushed Simon in the pool immediately after."

Tilly blinked. Frowned. And then burst out laughing. "I don't even know where to go with that."

"Your brother is incredible," Bria stated, "and as insane as it sounds, since I've met him, I've felt more alive and energized than I ever have. And I'm a sky-diving instructor."

"You're a what?" Tilly laughed again. "You really *are* crazy."

Bria grinned. "Life's about living to its fullest, right?"

"Yes," Tilly said. "It is." She studied Bria for a few seconds and then gave her a quick hug. "I think I'm going to like you."

A soft chime announced they'd arrived at Tilly's floor. The doors slid open, and Tilly released her. "As long as you don't hurt my brother," she clarified before hurrying out of the elevator.

Bria followed. Okay, if nothing else, whatever future she had with Owen, his sister was awesome, and she had no problems with spending time with her. Always a plus in a long-term relationship.

Long-term? Definitely still thinking that, 'eh? Even with the brain cancer pendulum?

"Yeah," she muttered, watching Tilly stop at a door a few feet away. "Even with that."

The door opened just as Bria came to a stop beside Tilly, and her heart slammed up into her throat as Owen filled the doorway.

"Owen," she breathed.

His hair stood awry, as if hands had constantly worried it, and something like exhaustion filled his face. Jet lag, like he'd said, or something else? A faint reddish mark marred the side of his jaw where Simon had hit him, sinking a tight bullet of fury at her ex into her chest.

He studied her, eyes impossible to read, and then gave Tilly a small smile. "Hey, sis. Why'd you leave the party?"

Tilly snorted. "Idiot."

"Seriously, I'm okay," he said with a warm smile and then returned his attention to Bria again. "I...had fun tonight. Thanks."

Her stomach clenched. Was that a goodbye? "Do we need to take you to a hospital?"

Jaw clenching, he shook his head. "Headache's almost gone."

Tilly cleared her throat, and flicked Bria a glance. "I'm just...going inside." She slipped through the open door and past Owen.

Gone.

Owen dropped his gaze, rubbing at the back of his neck.

Mouth dry, heart thumping—*why am I so fucking nervous?* —Bria let out a shaky laugh. "You scared me."

He lifted his eyes to hers, an unreadable tension now in their hazel depths. "Not my intention. Sorry."

She shook her head, reached out to take his hand, and then stopped and dropped hers. Everything about him, his expression, his body language, the way he couldn't hold eye-contact, seemed to scream *go away.* "How *are* you feeling?" she asked, aching to touch him. To run her fingers over the mark on the side of his head. To brush his hair back from his forehead and kiss him. "Really?"

"The pain's going. Panadol's taking care of it." His laugh was shaky. "My ego took a caning though. Been a long time since someone put me on the ground with a punch."

Her gut clenched at his unforced humility. Damn it, if Simon hadn't come along, there was a very high chance she'd be asking him to marry her by now.

Yep, you really really like him, don't you?

She really really did.

"You're going to press charges, right?" she asked. "Against Simon."

He let out another shaky breath, his attention sliding away for a second before he shook his head. "No. I just... I just want to forget it all happened. If I don't have that many days or months left, I don't want to spend them going after a wanker not worth my time or energy."

If I don't have many days or months left...

A cold band twisted around her heart at the words. She'd been furious at him for an irrational moment back up on the roof, when she'd first heard what he might have. Furious. How dare he come into her life, be so incredible and wonderful and make her believe in love at first sight and fantasy happy-ever-afters? And then the reality of what he was facing really hit her, and she realized how selfish she was being.

She wanted him in her life for a long time, she knew that, but he didn't even know if he *had* a long time left to live.

Now, looking at him battling demons she couldn't fathom, all she wanted was to give him all her strength and see him laugh.

Would he let her?

Giving him a small smile, she tilted her head in the direction of the elevator. "Wanna come back to my apartment? We can prepare for Elisa and Zeta's breakfast interrogation together?"

Another shaky laugh. The haunted torment in it twisted her gut.

He's going to say no. This is the end, Bria. He's ending it.

His eyes found hers again. "I think it's probably better if I don't."

A cold shiver rippled through her, but she didn't move. Didn't break eye-contact. "For who?"

"You."

"I don't have a say in this?"

He didn't say a word. He didn't have to. She could see it in his face. She didn't understand it, but he'd made the call.

She frowned. "You're throwing away the chance of something incredible. You know that, right?"

"I saw—" He stopped, looking away as he scrubbed a hand over his mouth and up the back of his neck.

"Saw what?"

He sighed and turned back to her. "You're amazing, Bria. The best thing that's ever come into my life. I'll never forget you."

"That's it? We're done?"

"It was only ever meant to be a hookup, remember?" he said with a small smile and took a step back. "Take care of yourself."

He closed the door between them.

She stood motionless, staring at it. Waiting for him to open it. To say he was kidding. To say he wasn't scared. To let her tell him she wasn't scared either.

The door didn't open.

In her gut, she knew it wouldn't.

It was only ever meant to be a hookup, remember? Her own voice whispered in her head. *He's right. Are you really insane enough to want to pursue a relationship with someone you've just met, someone who might have brain cancer?*

Throat thick, she turned from Tilly's door and headed for the elevator.

She *was*, in fact, that insane. Pursing a relationship with him, brain-cancer or not, was *exactly* what she wanted.

But it seemed the math teacher had cut her out of the equation.

She ground her teeth and hurried away, refusing to look back.

So much for him being good with numbers.

Clearly, he didn't know two was better than one.

CHAPTER EIGHT

"It's three a.m, O," Tilly mumbled.

Owen stopped pacing the floor of her living room and looked at her.

She lay stretched out on her stomach on the sofa, eyes closed, sexy-scientist make-up smeared over her cheek and the cushion she was using as a pillow. Gripped loosely in her hand, her phone pinged with an incoming message.

No doubt from Mick. Or their mum.

Huffing out a choppy sigh, Owen started pacing again. "Not my fault you're still having a conversation with the family," he grumbled. "You started it. I told you not to tell them what happened, but you had to go and fill Mum in, and of course, she then had to get Mick's medical opinion."

"Shut up," she rebuked into the cushion, voice muffled. "Be glad you have people who love you and care enough about you to be worried."

Guilt stabbed at him, and he let out another sigh.

She was right.

He *did* have people who loved him, who cared enough about him to be worried. Mick and his mum were going out of their minds back in Australia, and Tilly had lectured him since he'd closed the door on Bria about the situation.

Although, the situation Tilly lectured him about also included his "cowardly" treatment of Bria. She'd jabbed his chest with her index finger on each syllable when she'd said the word *cowardly*. His chest still ached.

His head... *It* had calmed down completely. If it weren't for all the drama from his family right now, there'd be no remaining evidence of Simon's attack.

Wrong. The fact you aren't with Bria right now...in her bed, in her...that's some big bloody evidence right there.

Guilt had another go at him, and he dropped onto the edge of the sofa, narrowly missing Tilly's side.

"Damn it," he muttered, rubbing at his face.

Tilly's phone pinged. Twice.

"Mum says you need to get on a plane and fly home right now," she muttered, lifting her head just enough to read the newest text message on the screen. "Mick says you probably should go to a hospital if your head still hurts."

"It doesn't."

She twisted on the sofa, fixing him with a level gaze. "No bullshit?"

"No bullshit. The only thing that hurts is my ego."

Rolling her eyes, she grunted and maneuvered herself into a sitting position beside him. "Your ego can suffer the pain."

"Thanks for the sibling support." He twisted his lips and let out a shaky breath, studying the floor between his feet. What was Bria doing now? Had she gone back to the party? Damn it, he missed her already. Which wasn't logical, given she'd hardly been in his life.

But when she had been... Fuck a duck, it had been the absolute best.

And you shoved her away. Now who's the wanker?

"Are you really just going to sit and mope around my place for the rest of the night?" Tilly asked, tossing her phone on the coffee table. Clearly, she was done with trying to calm his mother and brother. "I mean, morning?"

Guilt poked at him again. Different guilt. Maybe he should grab his own mobile from the charger and give it a go himself.

Chicken.

It seemed so. On every damn level.

He gave Tilly an askew frown. "Why do I feel like you're pissed at me?"

"I *am* pissed at you."

"Why?"

"Because you're being stubborn."

"About what? About not talking to Mum and Mick? I'm not sure I'm in the right headspace for a lecture from either of them."

You know that's not what she's talking about.

"Fuck, you're an idiot." She threw herself from the sofa and rounded on him, hands on hips, glare furious. "The way you shut down Scooby-Do was infantile and selfish and cowardly."

Owen's gut clenched. Rolled. Knotted. And then churned. He scrunched up his face and dropped it into his hands, shaking his head. "You don't get it, Til."

"No, you don't get it." She dropped back beside him on the sofa, giving him an ungentle nudge. "How many people get the chance to experience the instant connection you pair obviously have? You're the mathematician. You should know the numbers. How many people meet someone and know almost immediately that's the person they want to spend the rest of their life with?"

"Bria said that?"

Tilly's jaw clenched. "She did. She also said, and I quote 'as insane as it sounds, since I met him, I've felt more alive and energized than I ever have'."

Owen's gut went through the whole clenching-knotting-rolling routine again. "She said that?"

Tilly arched an eyebrow at him. "Who's the one who has hyperthymesia, brother?"

He rubbed at his face again. Tilly never forgot anything she personally experienced or heard. It had made for interesting ammunition when they were kids arguing. Clearly, it made for direct ammunition now.

"You like her, brother." She nudged him again. Gently this time. "You like her a lot. And who cares if you might not have many months left. In fact, isn't that more of a reason to stop being such a stubborn, selfish prick?"

He grunted, shook his head, and clawed his hands through his hair. "Everything in my gut tells me it's not fair to Bria to lump her with me. With what I might have, but..." He swallowed, throat thick.

"But?"

Ah shit, he really *was* an idiot.

He jolted to his feet. "I have to go talk to her."

Tilly slapped him on the arse. "That's the Owen Marcus Blackthorne I know."

He turned back to her. "Everything in my heart tells me I'm possibly fucking up a once-in-a-lifetime thing if I don't."

No matter how short that lifetime is.

Tilly grinned. "Your heart was always smarter than your gut, big bro." She threw a quick nod at her apartment door. "Now, go get her."

Pulse pounding, heart—clearly a wiser organ than his gut —thumping, he crossed to the door. "Don't wait up."

"*Oi!*" Tilly called behind him.

He turned just in time to snatch his mobile phone from the air as she tossed it to him.

She pinned him with a look. "Just in case you need to get in touch."

He didn't miss the undertone in her voice. She may have made him realize he was being an idiot when it came to Bria, but she was still worried about his head.

Shoving it in his back pocket, he let out a wobbly breath and smiled. "Love you, little sis."

She poked her tongue out at him.

Five minutes later, he stood in front of Bria's apartment door.

Stared at it.

Strained to hear if anyone was moving around or talking on the other side of it. Had Bria come home after he'd shut Tilly's door on her? Or *had* she gone back to the party? Had she gone back to find her sisters, to complain about the idiot Australian who refused to see a good thing even though it was staring him right in the face?

Or was she out having a great time with Zeta and Elisa, relieved she'd dodged a bullet?

Damn it, why hadn't he at least asked her for her phone number? He could've texted her, see if she was in there. What if he woke her up, and she told him to fuck off? What if—

Oh for fuck's sake, mate. Knock on the bloody door. One way or the other, you'll have your answers, and you won't have to live with regret.

Live. That was the critical word, wasn't it?

Or was it the optimal one?

"Stop wasting time," he muttered, squaring his shoulders. He glared at the door, knuckles poised, and closed his eyes.

It's now or never, Owen. What are you going to do?

"It's all insane," Bria muttered, shaking her head and turning back to where her sisters sat on Zeta's bed watching her pace. "I shouldn't feel like this so soon."

Elisa frowned, flicked Zeta a look, and then gave Bria a gentle smile. "Of course it's insane. Everything you do in your life is insane, Bri. You throw yourself into life one hundred and fifty percent. But that doesn't make it wrong."

"Obviously, the guy's a moron," Zeta declared, hugging one

of her pillows, resting her chin on it. "Only a moron would walk away from a life with you."

"A *cute* moron," Elisa offered.

"Hell yeah," Zeta agreed.

"You're not helping," Bria protested, scowling at them.

Identical grins flashed at her.

She threw up her hands and started pacing again, alternating between chewing on her lip and her thumb.

"Why is this irritating me so much?" she muttered.

"Because even though you've had years of knowing what you *didn't* want," Elisa said, her voice as gentle as her earlier smile, "you weren't really sure what you *did* want."

"What you *do* want," Zeta clarified.

"And what's that?" Bria asked, her pulse pounding harder than it should.

"Someone with a brain and a sense of humor," Zeta answered. "You *thought* you were meant to be with a brainless jock like Simon, because let's be honest here, Bri, that's all you've ever thought you were. You've never recognized your own worth, not really, so you've settled for those that didn't either."

"Like Simon," Elisa said.

"Ouch." Bria stuck out her bottom lip, even as her stomach clenched and a prickling heat crawled up over her scalp. "But fair."

Both Elisa and Zeta chuckled.

Bria rolled her eyes, stomped to the bed, and dropped onto it with a sigh.

"But here's the thing, Bri," Zeta went on, lobbing the pillow at her. "You're smart and funny and maybe, *finally*, you see that in yourself instead of just seeing the adrenaline-junkie sky-diver who is convinced she failed at the only thing she believes she's good at."

"Ouch." Bria tossed the pillow back at her. "Again."

Zeta raised an eyebrow. "But also fair. Again."

Bria threw herself backward onto the mattress. "Also fair. Again. Maybe."

"And *maybe*," Elisa said, wriggling over to Bria's side to brush a strand of hair from her face, "your cute Aussie math teacher has something to do with this sudden and long-overdue self-realization you're experiencing, and *maybe* that's why you're pissed. Because you're scared."

Bria stared at them both, her heart pounding in her throat. "Of what?"

"Of *him* not giving *you* the chance to live this new you?" Zeta asked. "The new you he's helped you find?"

Heart thumping faster, Bria moved her stare to the ceiling. "You know, for a zookeeper and a graphic artist, you're both very clever and savvy. Did both of you go to psychology classes without telling me?"

Zeta snorted. "Everything I know about people, I've learned through working with animals."

"And did you ever see the psychologist I went to for my anxiety back in high school?" Elisa asked with a wide smile. "He was so gorgeous, I practically hung on every word he uttered. He was like an addictive visual textbook."

Bria laughed. Zeta wacked her in the face with the pillow —softly—and then pushed her off the bed with her feet. "Go find the Australian, Bri," she instructed as Bria stood. "Tell him you're not letting him be scared alone. Tell him how you feel. Without any filters or hesitation."

"If nothing else," Elisa said, a mischievous light glinting in her eye, "it'll give us something to talk about the next time I have a panic attack in public. Hey, remember when Bri finally realized she actually liked nice guys with brains, and the nice guy with brains she really liked tried to run away from her?"

Bria rolled her eyes. "Ha ha."

Elisa grinned. "You love me."

"I do." Bria let out a wobbly breath, chest tight. "Both of you. More than you will ever know."

"Okay, now you're getting mushy." Zeta waved a hand in the direction of the bedroom door. "Go find Owen."

Elisa started to climb from the bed. "We'll come help you search, if you want? We can tell him to wake up to himself if he won't listen to reason."

Bria shook her head with a chuckle. "No. I've got this. I'll find him and make him see reason. He might be scared, and we might not have that long together, but if that's the case, every minute will be worth a life—"

Someone knocked on their apartment door.

Two soft, almost tentative knocks, but knocks all the same.

Zeta and Elisa both snapped their stares to Bria, identical excited expressions on their faces.

"It's him," Zeta whispered.

Bria's heart returned to her throat with a vengeance, something very close to fear slicing through her. What if it *wasn't* Owen? What if she got her hopes up, and it was someone else?

Who else would *it be?*

She swallowed, turning back her sisters. "Might be for one of you? Didn't either of you meet *anyone* at the party?"

Zeta snorted. "No. As if."

Elisa rolled her eyes. "Oh, for God's sake, Bri," she whispered, hurrying over to where she stood and giving her back a good shove. "Go answer the freaking door."

"Okay, okay," Bria whispered back, rolling her shoulders and tossing her hair over her shoulders. "I can do this."

"You jump out of planes for a living," Zeta muttered. "Of course you can do it."

With a quick scowl at her, and a quicker smile at Elisa, Bria hurried from Zeta's bedroom. "Jumping out of planes is easier," she tossed over her shoulder on way out.

Whoever was on the other side of the apartment door knocked again, softer this time.

She lengthened her strides, reached the door and stopped.

Pulling a deep breath, she closed her eyes, counted backwards from ten in Italian, and then opened her eyes.

"You can do this, Bria," she murmured and opened the door.

Owen stood on the other side of the threshold. His gaze locked on hers instantly. "G'day," he said, his voice cracking halfway through the greeting. He winced, cleared his throat, and let out a ragged breath, his smile almost shy. "G'day. Hi. Hello."

She regarded him, not saying a word.

His hair still hadn't seen a brush or a comb, and her fingers itched to run through the messy strands, not to control them or restrain them, but to just feel them sliding over her skin. He still wore the Steve Irwin costume—minus the stingray, of course—but the hiking boots were gone.

"You're wearing *thongs*," she said, smiling at his feet as she emphasized the Australian word for flip-flops.

"Hey, well done." He let out a low chuckle. "Also wearing *a* thong."

She snapped her stare up to his face, picturing his amazing ass in a black thong. "Really?"

With another chuckle, he ducked his head. "No. Sorry. Commando still. But it got your attention, right?"

She laughed. "It did. But you've had my attention from the second I saw you."

The forward confession fell out of her mouth, her heart, before she could stop it. So much for making him beg.

Ah, who was she kidding? She didn't want to waste any of their time together making him beg. Not unless it was making him beg in a filthy, sexy way.

Her stomach fluttered at the thought, and she bit her lip. Now was not the time for that.

Later, sure. But now...

"I'm sorry for knocking so early," he said, his gaze on hers again. "So late. So...whatever it is." A short little hiccup of a laugh burst from him, and he rubbed at the back of his neck. "Honestly, I actually have no bloody clue what time it is. My body thinks it nine p.m. I think. I'm stupidly sleep-deprived."

He let out another laugh, this one uncertain. "Of course, I didn't knock on your door at three a.m.—is it three a.m.? I think it's three a.m. I'm going with three a.m.—I didn't knock on your door at three a.m. to tell you I'm sleep-deprived. I knocked on your door at three a.m.—fuck a duck, Owen, stop saying three a.m." He turned away, burying his hands in his hair.

Bria held the doorknob, silent. *Well, that explains the crazy hair.*

"You knocked on my door…" she prodded, throat tight.

Sighing, he dropped his hands and looked back at her. "I knocked on your door to say sorry."

"Sorry?" Okay, so maybe she wasn't going to make it easy for him. Maybe she *was* going to make him beg. A little.

That hitchy little laugh fell from him again. "Yeah, I deserve this." He smiled. "Sorry for being a wanker. For shutting the door on you."

"For not letting me decide what I want to do with regards to us?"

He nodded. "Sorry for that as well."

She studied him, took in the worry in his eyes, the shadows beneath them. He did look tired, and what she wanted more than anything was to thread her fingers through his, led him to her bed, and curl up on it with him. Be the big spoon to his little one, if he was okay with that, and just hold him as he slept. If they missed Elisa and Zeta's breakfast interrogation, then they missed it. There'd be breakfast the next day, after all.

Will there? Or are you putting the cart before the horse?

"I just…" He stopped, clawed at his hair again, and shook his head. "I just… I've never believed in love at first sight, but there was almost immediately something about you, about *us*. And even as I was falling for you, there was a small voice in my head telling me I might be living on borrowed time, and I didn't want to mess up your life."

"And being with you will?"

Stop it. Hug him. Kiss him.

He pulled a face. "Might."

"It won't."

"Are you sure?"

She laughed. "No. But I'm not scared to try."

"Even if—"

"I don't care about the *even if*, Owen." She took a step closer to him, gently touching his chest, just over his heart. "I care about you. I want to *more* than care about you, if you're okay with that?"

His Adam's apple jerked up and down his throat. "I'm okay with that. I want it as well, and I'm okay with taking it slow and loose and easy, if that's the way it'll work for you, because any minute I get to spend with you is—"

She silenced him with a kiss.

She didn't want him to think about minutes. She just wanted him to think about her, making love to him, holding him, being with him...

He groaned into her mouth, his hands going to the small of her back and drawing her closer to his body.

She kissed him, gave him everything, promised him everything, and let out a shocked yelp when something near his ass started playing the beginning "Darth Vader's Theme" from *Star Wars*.

"Shit," he said against her lips, staggering back a step. "That's my—"

He shoved his hand into his back pocket, yanked out his phone, and stared at it.

Biting her lip, Bria watched him. His what?

His eyes darted over the screen. Back and forth. Back and forth. "Shit," he whispered. "Shit." He pressed a shaking hand to his mouth. "Shit," he mumbled into his palm.

"Umm…" She frowned, trying to see whatever was on the screen at the same time she tried to read everything on his face. "What…"

Dropping his hand, he lifted his stare from his phone and turned the screen to face her.

Negative.

Negative? She read it. And read it again. And looked up at him. "Negative?" she whispered.

His phone played the beginning of "Darth Vader's Theme" again, and another text popped up on the screen: ***Just thought you'd want to know while you're over in the States. Biopsy is benign. Will discuss treatment for meningioma when you return to Australia. Enjoy the rest of your trip.***

He looked at the new message and smiled. Beamed. Almost vibrated. "Negative," he said. "Benign."

Bria swallowed. "Is that from your…"

"Oncologist? Yeah."

She stared at him. "And your results…"

"Are benign." He wiped at his mouth again. "Negative for malignant cancer," he said a little louder.

"Negative," she echoed.

"Fucking negative." He murmured, thumb tapping over the screen of his phone. The swoosh sound of an outgoing text message filled the air and then he grinned at her. "And now Mum and Tilly and Mick know as well."

Her heart hammered in her ears. "That your results are negative?" She needed clarification. She needed to hear it aloud again. To be sure.

He laughed, elation flooding his face as he hauled her off her feet, spinning her around in the corridor. "Negative negative negative." He kissed her. Pulled back. Grinned wider. "Fucking negative."

"That's awesome, Owen," an excited voice called from behind them through the open door to Bria's apartment. Elisa? Zeta? They sounded so alike. "Congrats."

He laughed. "Thank you," he called before spinning Bria around once more and kissing her again.

She laughed against his lips. "Negative."

His phone burst into life in his hand but he ignored it, kissing her a third time, deeper and slower this time, and then, when her whole body began to thrum, he pulled away and gazed up into her eyes. "You are incredible."

She laughed, returning her feet to the floor. "So are you. Do you want to answer your phone?"

He flicked the screen a quick look, smiling, and shook his head, drawing her closer to his body. "Everyone else can wait for a sec."

She arched an eyebrow. "Can they?"

"They can. I've got to say this first."

"Say what?"

"I think I love you already, Bria De Luca. Is that all right?"

Heart racing, she tangled her fingers into his hair and drew his head down to hers. "That is *very* all right, Owen Blackthorne. I think I love you already as well." She nipped at his bottom lip and nudged her forehead to his. "Question; if I moved to Australia, do you think I could teach sky-diving there?"

Joy filled his face. "I am ninety-nine point nine percent certain you could."

She smiled. "I like those numbers."

"I'm very good with figures, remember."

"You're very good with everything," she murmured back, pressing her hips closer to his. "Now, ready to get livin' life together? Right this second?"

Chuckling, he brushed his lips to hers. "Hell yeah."

HOT AUSSIE NIGHT

THE DE LUCA SISTERS BOOK 2

DEDICATION

For my husband and my daughters. For believing in me when I'd lost all belief in myself.

And especially for Peanut. While you may be on your own journey with anxiety and depression, your inner strength is inspiring, and I am so proud to be your mum.

CHAPTER ONE

"Okay." Zeta rolled her neck and massaged her butt with the balls of her hands, indifferent to the people streaming by them on the gangway. Or more likely unaware, knowing Zeta. "I never want to set foot in a plane again."

Elisa shot a quick apologetic smile at the frazzled mom hauling three carry-ons and two crying toddlers trying to pass. The toddlers had started crying as the long-haul flight from LA to Sydney began its touchdown and hadn't stopped. Elisa understood their pain. She hated landings as well. Her ears always popped, and *she* knew why. Poor little kids had no clue.

"It's going to be hard for you to get home then," she said, scooping up Zeta's hobo bag from beside her sister's ankle. She slung it over her own shoulder—damn, what was *in* there?— and gave Zeta a pointed look. "It's a long swim from Australia to San Diego. Very long."

A tall man in an impeccable charcoal-gray suit hurried passed them, bumping into Elisa a little.

"Hey!" Zeta glared at him. "Watch it. You hit my sister."

He didn't slow down. Or acknowledge their existence.

"It's okay," Elisa mumbled, giving her shoulder a gentle rub. "We *are* standing in the way, after all."

"We're off to the side," Zeta pointed out, sticking her tongue out at the man's back. "Clearly he traveled first class. Who looks *that* good after a thirteen-hour flight?"

Elisa took a few seconds to admire the view—he definitely filled out his suit well, with his broad shoulders and tapered back and long legs that she bet were corded and strong—and shook her head. "C'mon, let's get moving. I want a shower more than breath right now."

"True." Zeta retrieved her bag from Elisa's shoulder, gave her a quick hug, and turned a narrow-eyed glare down the gangway. "Let's beat the douche in the suit through customs."

Elisa laughed.

A few seconds of power walking later, the man in the gray suit appeared in their sights, weaving through the other passengers heading for the custom gates.

"Do you think it's always this quiet here?' Elisa asked as Zeta picked up their pace. There weren't many people around at all. There was almost a calm sense to the area which messed with Elisa's mind. International airports were, in her experience, always crowded with stressed people. She was usually one of them.

"I think we were the first plane to land," Zeta said, determined glare drilling into the man's back. "It's only six in the morning here. I think. My watch went flat somewhere over the ocean. Quick, he's heading to the right."

Elisa noted the man *was* heading to the right, toward the Returning Australian Citizen checkpoint stations. "We can't go that way, Zet," she muttered, snagging her sister's elbow. "We're not Australian."

Zeta's eye narrowed. "Damn it."

Elisa laughed. Zeta had always been the competitive one. Bria, the eldest of them by a mere twelve minutes, was the adrenaline junkie. She was also the reason for the insane thirteen-hour flight to the other side of the world—and a different hemisphere, no less—ten days before Christmas.

Zeta spun to face her. "Quick, give me your best Australian accent."

Elisa dropped her jaw. "You're kidding?"

Zeta shook her head. "He's going to get there first. C'mon, you've been listening to Owen talk since October. Do an impression of him for me."

"I can't sound like an Aussie," Elisa protested. "Owen sounds like an Aussie because he *is* an Aussie."

Bria's fiancé had mentioned to them a few times he sounded more, what he called Ocker Aussie, because he grew up in a small rural town away from the multicultural big cities like Sydney. He'd even given Elisa and Zeta a few lessons in Australian slang.

"C'mon," Zeta pleaded, flicking the man in the suit—now much closer to the point-of-no-return for non-Australians than a few seconds ago. "He bumped into you without saying sorry. Just…"

"Push passed him and pretend I'm an Aussie?" Elisa cocked an eyebrow. "And then present the customs officer my *American* passport?"

Zeta blew out an exasperated sigh. "You're no fun."

"Exactly," Elisa agreed. "I'm the worrier of the family, remember?"

"Maybe we'll see him on the sidewalk and beat him to a cab?"

"He doesn't look the cab-catching kind." Elisa watched him stride with graceful confidence toward the Australian Citizen checkpoints. Tinsel and Christmas baubles hung from the various stations. For some reason, the decorations made her want to smile. She always liked Christmas, even if she constantly worried everyone would hate the presents she bought for them.

"More like a limo," she said.

"Do they have limos here?" Zeta wondered.

"No i— Oh crap." Elisa bolted, straight for the guy in the

suit, her stare locked on what he'd dropped without realizing. "Hey!" she called. "Hey! Guy in the gray suit. Hey!"

He didn't stop.

Rude.

"Hey," she called, cheeks burning as she noticed other people looking at her. She swooped up what he'd dropped—his passport—stumbling a little as gravity tried to control her jet-lagged muscles, and resumed her pursuit. "*Hey!*"

Still, he didn't stop. She burst into a faster run, bearing down on him as he reached the first available tinsel-adorned station. "Hey," she said again, trying to come to a halt as he stepped up to the counter and the waiting official.

Trying.

And failing. Spectacularly.

Her feet tangled beneath her, and she lost her balance, at the precise moment he turned around.

Wow, he's cute, she thought a heartbeat before she fell straight into him, her extended hand—the one gripping his dropped passport—punching straight into the middle of his chest.

"Oof," he grunted, stumbling back a step with the impact.

She yelped—damn it, that hurt her wrist—and suddenly he was sliding his firm hands around her waist and holding her still.

"What the—" he almost shouted, his frown both stern and confused.

"Your passport," she blurted, as he released her. "You dropped—"

Eyes the color of a cloudless summer sky locked on her as he reached up and plucked white earbuds from his ears. "What?"

"Your passport," Elisa finished on close to a whisper.

For a second, he stared at her, as if a second head had sprouted from between her eyes, and then his attention dropped to the passport she shoved up at him and dawning realization flashed over his face. "Shit, did I drop it?"

She nodded. Damn, she could gaze into his eyes all day. They were stunning. And he sounded so Australian.

Because he is, you idiot.

He took his passport, a smile stretching over his face. "Thanks. Saved me having a not so fun time trying to get back into the country."

"You're welcome." Wow, his smile was as gorgeous as his eyes. "I'm Elisa."

Now why the hell did she tell him that? She was so freaking shy she couldn't even tell her gynecologist her name was Elisa not Elise, and here she introducing herself to a complete stranger?

His gorgeous smile reached his gorgeous eyes. "G'day, Elisa. Welcome to Australia, I'm—"

"Holding up the bloody line," the customs officer behind the counter growled.

Heat flooded Elisa's cheeks. She jolted back a step, heart pounding. Oh no. She'd caused a problem. What if they didn't let her into Australia now? She'd miss Bria's and Owen's engagement party, and Zeta would have to find Bria and Owen in the arrivals terminal on her own, and what would their parents say? And think? And what would *Owen's* mom think? And oh no, she couldn't breathe, she couldn't breathe, she couldn't—

She turned and hurried away, her spine so stiff it ached, her face on fire.

"Thank you," the gorgeous Australian in the well-cut suit called after her. Was that confusion in his voice? Or laughter?

Her blood roared in her ears, and she quickened her pace. The air pressed down on her. Her vision blurred. Heart racing, she swallowed, flicking her stare from her moving feet to the space around her. God, where was Zeta? Where was her sister? What if Zeta had gone through customs, and now she was all alone and...and...and... Oh God, she couldn't breathe. She couldn't—

"I'm here, Lis." Warm arms wrapped around her, halting her frenzied walk, and Zeta hugged her tightly. "I'm here."

Elisa buried into Zeta's protective embrace, eyes squeezed tight, tears stinging at them.

"It's okay." Zeta smoothed a hand down over the back of Elisa's head. "It's okay. No one's angry with you. You did good."

Her stomach clenched. Damn it, what was wrong with her? It had been four months since her last anxiety attack, and she'd honestly thought she'd gotten her act together. Damn it.

Did good. You did good.

She forced her mind to cling onto Zeta's words. Played them over and over.

You did good.

Had she though? She'd made a custom official angry and probably embarrassed herself in front of the cute Australian and what happened if they pulled her aside and interrogated her about the Hershey Kisses in her bag? What if she'd forgotten to declare something on her entry card? Owen had told them before they left the US Australia was very strict about what it allowed to be brought into the country. What if the little watercolor painting she'd done for Bria of their child-hood dog on home-made paper was illegal here and she—

"Lis," Zeta whispered, smoothing her hand over her hair again. "You're going to be okay. You're amazing. You didn't do anything wrong. You didn't—"

"She okay?"

Elisa's frenzied heart smashed up into her constricted throat and she stiffened in Zeta's arms. That voice... So male and Australian...

"Hi," Zeta said, a wary happiness in her voice. "She's okay. Maybe. It's been a long flight."

"You just get in from the flight from LA?" the distinct Australian voice asked. "Yeah, me too. I never enjoy it. You sure she's okay? Anything I can do? It's Elisa, right?" Fingertips gently touched her shoulder—a barely there contact, but enough to let Elisa know the cute Australian in the gray suit was standing right next to her.

Oh boy.

Inching her way out of Zeta's arms, she gave him a wavery smile. "I'm okay."

Worry swam in those incredible eyes of his. His Adam's apple slid up and down the smooth brown column of his throat. "Sure?"

She nodded. Gave another smile. And a sniff. Worry moved to his frown. Great. No doubt he now thought she was broken or something.

Well, you kinda are. Sometimes.

He studied her, flicked a glance at Zeta, and then studied her again. If he was taken back by their identical likeness, he didn't show it. It was almost impossible to tell them apart on appearance alone—even their parents had difficulty sometimes. They were both five foot six, with strawberry-blond hair that hung around their shoulders in messy waves, freckles, and a subtly square jaw, thanks to their Sicilian father—but they were worlds apart in personality. For starters, Zeta would never be borderline breaking down with anxiety over a throw-away comment from a customs official. Anxiety and Zeta didn't gel.

Zeta was all snark and sarcasm. And occasionally, bite.

With another sniff, she gave herself a little mental shake and smiled at the hot Aussie in the suit. "I'm really okay. Thank you though, for checking. Nothing a shower, a bed, and some food won't fix."

"I can help with that," he said, his smile warm. Dio, he was so cute. "The food I mean. I can't help with the shower and the bed."

A tight sensation fluttered in Elisa's stomach, and she bit her bottom lip. Damn it, now she was thinking of what he would look like out of the gray suit and in a shower.

Oh baby…

"You could try," Zeta suggested with a sharkish grin.

"Zeta," Elisa groaned.

He chuckled, throwing Zeta another quick glance, and smiled at Elisa again. "If you're interested, I know a place that does an incredible breakfast."

Zeta slung her arm around Elisa's shoulder. "Sounds perfect."

"No it doesn't," Elisa said.

The gorgeous Australian stiffened. "Sorry." He took a step back. "I didn't mean…I wasn't trying to…" His Adam's apple jerked up and down in his throat.

Elisa blinked. Why was he suddenly—

Ah, crap. Of course. She must have sounded horrible. "I mean," she burst out, holding up her hand, "our sister is no doubt waiting on the other side of customs with her fiancé. They drove over two hours to pick us up." She fixed Zeta a pointed look, a tightness twisting in her stomach. Damn it, now she was going to freak out all over again for offending someone she didn't know. Why couldn't she just get a grip on her stupid anxiety?

"Dio, that's right." Zeta rolled her eyes, and shook her head. "I forgot. I'm brain dead from that long flight." She pulled an apologetic face. "We can't just abandon them for breakfast no matter how incredible it is."

The Australian chuckled. "It's all good. Next time, eh?"

Elisa's stomach clenched. Not from anxiety but something else. Excitement? Way too many years ago, any trust she had in people *not* her family had been utterly shattered by a simple act of betrayal that almost broke her. She didn't do social interactions. Not really. Bria's and Owen's engagement party here in Australia was going to be the biggest thing she attended since the Halloween rooftop party where they'd met.

So why was the ludicrous notion of having a fantasy breakfast with a complete stranger sending an unexpected tickle of a thrill through her?

"Next time," she said, letting her lips curl into a soft smile.

He smiled back, his gaze holding hers. "I'll hold you to that."

Another tight flutter bloomed in her stomach, and she flicked her tongue over her bottom lip. "Okay."

His eyes tracked the slight movement. The flutter in her stomach intensified. Was she…was she actually flirting? She didn't know *how* to flirt. Oh wow, was she flirt—

"Maybe you should give my sister your number," Zeta said.

Heat flooded Elisa's cheeks.

Ice-blue eyes held hers. "I think I'd like—"

AC/DC started singing about a highway to Hell from inside his suit jacket.

"Damn it," he muttered, shoving his hand into his jacket and taking a step back. "Sorry. Give me a sec…" He pulled out a smartphone, and swiped his thumb over its screen. "Sorry, I've got to take this," he said, raising his phone to his ear. "Hi Kara. Sorry, yes. I'm back. Still going through customs."

Kara.

Elisa swallowed. A cold itch crept over her. The flutter in her stomach twisted into a knot.

Kara.

Gripping at the strap of her carry-on bag, she shook her head. "We've have to go," she said to him, her smile wobbly. "It was nice meeting you."

He frowned, phone still pressed to his ear. "I won't be—"

Pivoting on her feet, she grabbed Zeta's arm and hurried toward the international arrivals custom stations. "Let's go."

"What's going on?" Zeta asked, stumbling into a scurry beside her. "Did I miss something?"

Elisa shook her head, increasing her stride. "Bria and Owen will be waiting for us."

"That's why we're suddenly running away from the cute Aussie who was about to give you his number?"

Grinding her teeth, Elisa walked faster, heading for the custom station farthest away from the returning Australian citizen stations.

"It was nice meeting you as well," a male voice with an Australian accent called behind them. Quite a way behind them.

Okay, so he wasn't chasing them. Good.

Really?

Zeta kept pace with her, her confused stare a prickling weight on the side of Elisa's face. "What's going on, Lis? Talk to me."

"I just..." She shook her head.

How did she explain without sounding like a freaking nutjob. The moment she'd heard the Australian say *Kara*, she'd thought of the way Bria's ex had cheated on her, and that made her feel sick in the stomach, and feeling sick in the stomach made her heart hammer and, what if she was responsible for someone feeling the way Bria had felt and how could anyone *want* her number, especially after she had an obvious breakdown over a customs official and he was probably only just being nice and who *was* Kara and...

Oh my God, stop. Stop it. Take a breath. Kara could be anyone and it doesn't matter anyway.

She knew that. And it wasn't even that. It was her stupid anxiety and her stupid fear of being betrayed and abandoned and mocked and—

"Hey." Zeta wrapped an arm around her shoulders, drawing them both to a halt. "Hey, Lis. It's okay. We're okay. *You're* okay."

Elisa looked into eyes identical to her own. Saw worry and compassion and understanding.

"I'm okay," she whispered. She would be. Zeta would make

sure of that. And so would Bria the second the three of them reunited.

"You're okay," Zeta repeated. "And hey! We're in Australia, finally, and I'm assuming the second we step outside the airport there's going to be kangaroos jumping all over the place and I know kangaroos everywhere will make everything better, even though you *did* just run away from a sexy Aussie in an exquisite suit wanting your number."

Elisa chuckled and threw her sister a grateful smile. "You're delusional."

Zeta grinned. "Yes." She curled her fingers around Elisa's arm and waved her hand at the row of Christmas decoration-adorned custom stations stretching out before them. "Now, which customs officer looks the grumpiest?"

"Why?"

Zeta's grin stretched wider. "I want to go through their counter so we can see who can make them laugh the most."

"Honestly, Kara," Angus Daniels tossed his overnight bag into the back seat of his sous-chef's Lexus, and then climbed into the front passenger seat, "your timing sucks."

Kara frowned at him as he closed the door. "So you didn't get to give the American your number. Boo hoo. You know how many women are lined up hoping to catch the eye of Australia's Most Eligible Bachelor?"

"Ah, sod off with that, will you?" He snorted, buckled in, and pointed at the busy traffic trying to navigate away from the international arrival pick-up zone. "Just drive."

"Yes, boss."

"I regret the day I ever answered the phone to that magazine writer. And I definitely should have said no to that stupid photoshoot."

Shoving the Lexus into a miniscule gap in the sludge of

traffic, Kara laughed. "C'mon. Admit it, you got off on the fame."

"I got off on the sudden uptick in patrons at the restaurant," he conceded. "But the fame... I'll leave that to Owen's cousin."

"Is the rock star going to be at the engagement party?" Kara blasted her horn at the car in front with the same gusto she ruled the kitchen of *Buckley's Chance*.

"No idea." Angus stopped himself from slamming on an invisible brake in front of him. Damn it, he'd forgotten how crazy Kara was behind the wheel. He would have thought two weeks driving on L.A. freeways should have prepared him, but nope. Was his life insurance up to date? "But Owen and Bria were talking about it being very low-key."

He'd been thrilled when his best mate from school told him he was getting hitched a month ago. Owen—the maths nerd—had been voted by their year to be the "most likely to die a virgin". Their year had voted Angus "most likely to start a harem". Interestingly enough, Owen had lost his virginity in the maths block at school on the second last day of senior year, and Angus had skipped the whole dating scene after school finished to concentrate on his chef's career. The decision had resulted in him being crowned *Australia's Good Food Guide's* Chef Hat Award-winner every year since he opened *Buckley's Chance*.

"Well," Kara said, slowing down a fraction to take a right turn. "Regardless, it's good to have you back in town."

He laughed, scanning the crowd of people on the footpath streaming out of the airport. What would he do if he saw the American from inside?

Jump out? Go talk to her?

"Yeah, yeah." Chest tight, he threw Kara a smirk. "You've been enjoying the power while I've been gone. Admit it."

"Of course I have." Kara swerved around a little purple hatch, blasted her horn, and shouted something in Portuguese as she shot past it. He'd missed his second-in-charge. Not so much her driving. "Bummed you're back," she said, flipping off a motorcycle rider in the lane next to her. "How did the meeting over there go?"

"Alright." The meeting to open a *Buckley's Chance* in Los Angeles had gone very well. The investors were ready to sign on the dotted line there and then.

Him though?

Angus wasn't sure why, but something was holding him back. Moving to Los Angeles sounded amazing six months ago when the ripple effect of that ridiculous magazine article was making his normal life hell. No, he didn't want to go on a singing show wearing some kind of costume to hide his identity. No, he was not interested in joining a group of twenty-somethings wearing almost nothing all wanting to hook up on an island for a television audience. And hell no, he did *not* want to be the bachelor ready to pick a wife from a bevy of eager women on an even more ridiculous show.

The producer for *that* show wouldn't leave him alone, calling him every damn week, coming into the restaurant for dinner every second day. She'd even started jogging the same route he did around Bronte Beach every dawn, insisting he at least take a look at the contract. And when she'd found out he'd flown to LA last week, she'd suggested flying out to conduct a meeting with him there.

Getting out of Australia had sounded perfect after *that* phone call.

But the fantasy of it and the actual *doing* it… Was he ready to leave his home country? To leave his half sister? His mates? His restaurant? Even for only a year or so while establishing the new restaurant?

And was Los Angeles *really* ready for his version of Australian cuisine? Not a single American he spoke to over there knew what 'Buckley's chance' meant. And don't get him started on the abomination they called a Bloomin' Onion.

"So," Kara's voice dragged him back to the car, "why *did* you ask for the American's phone number?"

He looked at her, just as she arched a pierced eyebrow at him.

"It's not like you need to hit on strange women you meet in the airport," she pointed out, returning her attention to the busy street. "If you want to find a woman you only have to give Nora a call. She's got a whole string of them lined up ready, remember."

He groaned at the producer's name.

Kara snorted. "I should warn you, she did come into the restaurant yesterday. Asking when you were coming back."

"Can she not take a hint?"

"I suspect when she looks at you, all she can see is record-breaking ratings. And from what I understand people in TV land aren't used to being told no." Kara flicked him a look. "But that doesn't answer my question. What's the deal with asking for the American woman's phone number?"

"She seemed...nice."

It was the truth. She had. In the short time they'd inter-acted, the woman who'd rescued his passport had seemed shy but friendly. And damn, she was gorgeous. But it had been something in her eyes that caught his attention more than her looks. He sensed a fragile strength to her, which he knew made no bloody sense. Something couldn't be fragile and strong at the same time, and yet something about the American made him think of those two contrasting states.

He didn't do relationships. It was easier not to. But some-thing about her had made him wonder...

"Nice?" Kara snorted. "You really using the word nice? I'm not sure that's actually a compliment these days."

Angus rolled his eyes. "Okay, something about *her* made something in *me* feel good."

She shot him a lewd look. "I bet."

"Get your mind out of the gutter, Santos."

She laughed.

"Something in my gut," he clarified, scanning the footpath again. "I just…wanted to talk to her a bit more."

"Your gut?"

"Don't knock my gut. My gut employed you when I had five other apprentice chefs with better experience and references to choose from."

"I applaud your gut then. Thank you, Angus's gut."

He chuckled.

She changed lanes, indicated, flipped off the person behind her, and frowned. "So what did happen? Why *didn't* you get her number?"

"You called," he pointed out. "And she seemed to…I don't know, freak out a little when I said your name."

"Why?"

Angus shrugged. "I don't know. Maybe she thought I was an unfaithful jerk? Maybe she thought I was taking a call from my girlfriend?"

"Girlfriend?" Kara burst out laughing. "Oh God, you are *so* not my type."

"I know."

"I mean, you're too tall for starters."

"Okay. True, I guess." At six foot five, he was too tall for a lot of people.

"And way too brooding."

"Brooding?"

"Too intense."

"Alright, alright. Stop piling on."

"Too much of a perfectionist. A control freak."

He raised his eyebrows. "You finished?"

"Oh, and you're my best friend's brother so the thought makes me throw up a little in my mouth."

"There is that."

Kara laughed again. "So…that's it, is it? Two ships passing in the night that could have been a big bang?"

"You're mixing your metaphors again," he pointed out. "But yeah, I guess so."

"Metaphors. Pfft." She shook her head and then gave him a smile. Not her normal don't-fuck-with-me smile he'd appreciated from the minute he'd first interviewed her for his restaurant five years ago, but a gentle one. "Sorry for my bad timing," she said. "I'll make it up to you. Work today even though I was meant to have it off."

"Yeah, nah." He chuckled. "It's all good."

Although it wasn't. As ridiculous as it sounded, the nagging feeling he'd missed something meaningful kept gnawing at his gut.

"You sure you're going to be awake enough to come in? Run the kitchen?" Kara shot him a quick look. "You look exhausted."

"Thanks." He pulled a hand through his thick dark hair, fighting back the yawn trying to claim him. "But Owen's future sisters-in-laws are arriving in Sydney sometime this morning, and I told him their first meal in Australia was on me at the restaurant. Plus, I promised I'd cook."

Kara whistled. "So the big boss is going to get his hands dirty? Wow."

Angus narrowed his eyes at her. "Shut up and drive, Santos."

"Yes, boss." She laughed, and flattened the accelerator.

He returned his attention to the footpath. Damn it, he *really* wished he'd gotten the American woman's phone number.

CHAPTER TWO

"Not a kangaroo to be seen." Zeta shook her head and let out a put-upon sigh as Owen, wearing a bright-red Santa hat with a fat white pompom hanging over his ear, deposited her suitcase into the back of his SUV. "Or a Hemsworth, for that matter."

Bria snagged Elisa's carry-on bag and tossed it to Owen. "We could possibly wrangle up a Hemsworth if you like. Owen's cousin knows them all quite well."

"Are you kidding?" Zeta blinked. "Don't mess with me, sis. You know I get nasty if you do."

"Maybe at the wedding," Bria mused, looking contemplative.

"Bria," Owen chuckled, repositioning the pompom. "Stop getting your sisters' hopes up."

Zeta narrowed her eyes at Bria. "You're going to pay for that."

Bria laughed. "I've missed you too, Zet."

Elisa stood back, taking in the interaction even as she tried not to stare into the cars pulling away from the pick-up zone. The chances of her seeing the cute Aussie in the suit were slim to none, but she still couldn't help but fantasize.

And what would you do if you did?

She let out a little snort. Throw herself at the car he was in? No, it was time to let him go. Bria might be able to fall in love at first sight and completely change everything in her life, but she wasn't Bria. Even if she *had* given him her number, even if he *had* called, and even if she *had* been able to pluck up the courage to meet with him again during the twenty-four hours they were in Sydney before heading to Owen's hometown, what then?

She wasn't staying in Australia for any longer than ten days, and she wasn't going to throw herself into any kind of long-distance relationship.

God, how would her anxiety handle *that* kind of stressful situation? She'd never sleep waiting for a text from the southern hemis—

"Lis!" A hand whacked her on the shoulder, and she blinked, jerking her stare from the passing cars.

Zeta stood in front of her, eyes narrowed.

"What?" Elisa asked, frowning. "What did I miss?"

Bria chuckled. "I asked if you and Zet wanted Owen to drive or if you're brave enough to experience my driving over here?"

"Oh God, no." Elisa shook her head. "Owen needs to drive. You were bad enough when you knew which side of the road to drive on. I guarantee you're worse over here."

"Ouch." Bria grinned. "But fair." She suddenly launched herself at Elisa, enveloping her in a bear hug. "Missed you, sis."

Elisa squeezed her back. "Missed you too."

Bria let her go, grin growing wider. "Now, to fill in time before dinner tonight, we thought we'd take you to the—"

"Hey!" Zeta burst out, grabbing at Elisa's arm. "Hey, Lis! There he is!" She pointed at a shiny black Lexus driving passed them, eyes wide. "There he is!"

"Who?" Bria asked, confusion filling her face.

"Who?" Owen swung around to frown at the traffic, pompom bouncing.

Elisa's heart jumped up into her throat and she looked at the expensive car as it went passed. Too late, it seemed. All she'd glimpsed was a possible shoulder covered in maybe gray material at the front passenger window.

"Quick!" Zeta shoved at Owen's chest and jabbed her finger at the Lexus. "Quick, follow that car!"

Bria burst out laughing. "What on earth are you talking about?"

"Follow that car, Owen," Zeta ordered again, almost vibrating. "We're on a mission to save Lis's love life."

"Oh my God, Zet." Elisa yanked her stare from the back of the Lexus—was its number plate really C00K 1?—and rolled her eyes at her sister. "We are *not* following a car."

"We're not?" Owen frowned. "Bugger."

Bria raised her eyebrows at him.

He shrugged, adjusting his pompom again. "Not gonna lie. I was game."

"Damn it," Zeta grumbled. "He's getting away."

"Okay," Bria said, fixing Zeta and then Elisa in a level stare. "I need an explanation. Now."

"Actually now we need to get moving ourselves, gorgeous," Owen said, giving Bria an apologetic look. "We're about five minutes away from needing to mortgage the house to pay for the short time we've been parked here. How 'bout we get the explanation over brunch? Or on the drive there? It's going to take us almost an hour to get to Angus's restaurant, after all." A scowl twisted his lips. "Bloody horrid Sydney traffic. I don't know how people can live in a big city like this."

Bria chuckled. "God, I love you, Owen Blackthorne."

He beamed. "Love you too, Bria De Luca. Now let's move."

"Who's Angus?" Zeta climbed into the back seat of Owen's SUV. "Is he cute?"

"Seriously, Zet?" Bria rolled her eyes before depositing herself in the front passenger seat.

"Hey," Zeta said as Elisa settled into the back seat beside her. "You got your hot Aussie—that's you, Owen—and Lis has her mystery hottie in the suit."

Elisa snorted.

"So it's only fair I get one as well," Zeta finished with a grin.

"Thanks for calling me hot," Owen said, starting the SUV's engine. "As for Angus..." He shrugged. "I guess he's alright. If you like that sort of thing."

"Then get us to brunch," Zeta instructed, tapping the back of Bria's seat. "Pronto."

Elisa laughed. "Remember, Zet. The next ten days are about Bri and Owen, not about you getting laid."

"Hey." Zeta gave her one of her sharkish smiles. "It *can* be both, you know."

"And on that note," Owen threw over his shoulder. The SUV pulled out into the traffic.

Elisa sat in the back, gripping her seatbelt. Not because Owen drove like a maniac, but because as far as she was concerned, they were on the wrong freaking side of the road. Dio, every turn was a hair-raising trip into near-miss collision.

"It takes a while to get used to it, sis" Bria said, dragging Elisa's stare from the streets ahead. "But Owen's a good driver. Promise."

"Look at the view out the side window instead, Lis," Zeta suggested. "It's what I'm doing."

Letting out a ragged breath, Elisa released her death grip on the seatbelt, forced her muscles to relax—as much as she could —and turned her attention to the world to her left. Shops, people, trees, cafes, more shops, more people, a cute dog, more shops... She frowned. Okay, so far, Sydney could be mistaken for any big city in the United—

"Oh wow," she whispered as Owen turned a corner and a

glittering swarth of blue water came into view. "Is that Sydney Harbor?"

"It is," Owen answered. "Angus owns a restaurant at Circular Quay West in The Rocks, which is a suburb right on the water. We thought we'd park at Darling Harbor and catch a water taxi to the restaurant. That way you both get a boat ride on Sydney Harbor and travel under the Sydney Harbor Bridge, which is kinda cool."

"That sounds awesome," Zeta said.

"The first time I was on a boat under the bridge, I…"

Whatever Bria said next faded away as Elisa sucked in a sharp breath. In the car next to them, in the front passenger seat of the Lexus waiting at the same red light they were, was her hot Aussie in the suit.

Oh wow.

Her throat tightened. She stared at what she could see of his profile through the open driver's window. The driver of the Lexus—a woman with spiky violet hair so vivid it was almost iridescent—was waving her hands around in what was clearly a very enthusiastic conversation about something. Was that Kara? Maybe. Beside her, Elisa's Aussie sat with a relaxed smile, his incredible blue eyes hidden by dark sunglasses as he no doubt listened to whatever maybe-Kara was saying.

"Hi," she whispered at him. Sure, he couldn't hear her. Sure, he had no idea she was watching him. "Remember me? I'm Elisa."

He laughed. At least, that's what it looked like he was doing, before the lights changed, and the Lexus took off from the intersection at a ridiculous speed.

"Tosser," Owen muttered from behind the wheel. "Where's a cop when you need one."

Elisa smiled, a wave of warmth rolling over her. Seeing her hot Aussie in the suit again, even only fleetingly, had for some reason made her feel better.

She released a shaky sigh, settled back in the seat, and closed her eyes. "Wake me when we get there," she murmured.

Zeta took her fingers in hers. "Will do."

She didn't sleep or dream; she just let her mind wander over memories and moments as the car moved through the Sydney traffic. Whenever it tried to linger on what her ex-business partner (and ex-collage best friend and ex-*partner* partner) had done to her—as it so often did—she turned her thoughts to the gorgeous Australian in the exquisite suit. Imagined him making eye-contact with her through the windows of their respective cars at the intersection. Pictured him getting out of the Lexus, striding around to Owen's car, and opening the back passenger door. Fantasized about him holding out his hand to her, his blue eyes on hers, his smile warm and relaxed and promising something wonderful, as he said—

"I *really* should have peed before we left the airport."

Forcing her eyes open, Elisa gave Zeta a bleary glare. "Thanks, sis. You just interrupted the hot Aussie in the suit saying something incredible to me."

Zeta raised her eyebrows. "I what?"

She let out a wry chuckle. "Nothing."

The car came to a stop and Owen pivoted in the driver's seat to smile at them. "And we're here. Ready?"

Elisa closed her eyes, her stomach knotting.

Would she ever be ready? Ready to live life without anxiety controlling her? Or was she destined to be crippled by it forever, escaping it only in deluded fantasies of being rescued by a nameless Australian?

"Adventure awaits." Bria's declaration floated through the shadows in Elisa's head. "Let's go."

Elisa opened her eyes. She didn't know the answers to any of those questions. All she could do was take each minute at a time.

"Hi," she whispered to herself. "I'm Elisa. And I'm trying to live life as best as I can."

And occasionally pretend I'm being swept off my feet by an Australian?

A soft chuckle escaped her. And it seemed, occasionally pretend that.

Cooking had always been an escape for Angus.

With a father who liked to express his dissatisfaction with life via his fists, and a mother who liked to express hers via as many empty bottles of vodka as she could, Angus had more than once saved his skin—and possibly his life—by keeping his parents' bellies full of food.

The first time he'd saved himself and his mother from another beating from his dad had been when he'd made scrambled eggs for dinner at the age of seven. His father had lost another job and had come home hellbent on taking out his frustration on the woman he'd promised to love and cherish and protect. The fact she'd been passed out drunk at two in the afternoon would have pushed him over the violent edge, had it not been for Angus—a terrified child older than his young years—realizing he had to do something.

At the sight of his father slamming the car door shut in the driveway and then kicking it repeatedly, Angus had bolted into the kitchen and started to make the only thing he knew how: scrambled eggs on toast. Heart pounding, eyes burning with unshed tears of familiar terror, he'd grabbed the ingredients and started cooking by a gut feel. By the time Barry Daniels stomped into the dilapidated house they lived in, face red with rage, fists already balled, the distinct aroma of freshly buttered toast and bacon-laced eggs filled the air.

Food hadn't always saved Angus from his old man, and it wasn't the only reason he'd cooked. Then or now. He cooked because he liked food—although he'd often gone without it as a child—enjoyed eating it, but more than that he liked the control and the chaos of cooking. Enjoyed losing himself in that conflicted state.

He'd cooked whenever he could growing up. And if there wasn't food at home to prepare, he'd head over to Owen's place and Mrs. Blackthorne would let him loose in her kitchen. Those times…with the laughter and love of the other family like a cloud around him…those were Angus's happiest times growing up.

When a mango chicken curry dish *hadn't* saved a fifteen-year-old Angus from his father's brutal, drunken wrath, it had been Owen who'd saved him. Owen—skinny, math-nerd Owen—who'd risked his life and knocked Barry out cold with Angus's cricket bat.

Angus lived with the Blackthornes for a month after that.

A drunk Barry had driven himself into a tree the day before Angus dared to move back home.

Two days after that, Angus discovered he had a younger half sister living in Sydney—thanks to a one-night stand his father had years ago while on a bender. Chelsea Parker had come to the funeral, nervous about meeting the brother she didn't know she had. Her mum had stayed in the car, no doubt living her own private torment over the man who'd fathered her daughter.

He'd cooked breakfast for Chelsea the morning of the funeral. It kept his own turbulent emotions at bay. They'd hardly spoken, but for the duration of the short meal, he'd felt a calming connection to her. A family member who didn't seem fucked up. It was nice. She'd hugged him and left to get ready for the funeral. His mother passed out from her liquid breakfast—vodka straight—in the bedroom, so he'd prepared all the food for the small wake. He'd poured his grief, his anger, his hope, into the appetizers and sandwiches and finger food.

He'd cooked dinner for Chelsea and her mum that night, discovering his newly found sister was everything his father wasn't, and her mum was everything his mum wasn't. They'd both made him smile. Made him ache for a life he'd never been given the chance to have. When they'd returned to Sydney the next day, he'd lost himself in kitchen again. The Blackthorne's kitchen. The only stable family he'd ever known.

He'd cooked dinner for Owen and his family every night until the pair of them finished high school and Owen moved to Newcastle for his teacher's degree and Angus moved to Sydney on a chef's apprenticeship.

Angus didn't doubt he'd be dead if it weren't for Owen. Today, he wanted to show his mate how much he appreciated that fact by wowing Angus's future in-laws with the most incredible meals he'd ever created.

Good food also helped make great first impressions, and he wanted Angus's fiancé—and her family—to like him. Probably lame, but the way it was, nonetheless.

He just had to get his mind back on focus.

Staring at the breathtaking sweeping views of the Sydney Opera House, the Sydney Harbor Bridge, and the iconic harbor itself from the dining floor of Buckley's Chance, he pulled a slow breath.

The kitchen was ready. His kitchen staff were ready.

Kara was ready. In fact, his sous chef was in the kitchen, ordering everyone around in her normal way, the best sous chef Angus had ever worked with or employed.

His wait staff were ready.

He…wasn't.

Damn it, why hadn't he ignored Kara's call for a few more seconds and got the American woman's number back in the airport? He was sure she'd introduced herself, but he couldn't remember. El…El…something. Ellie? Elsa? Argh. Why hadn't he got her number? Why hadn't he chased after her when she'd left?

Yeah, that's exactly what a woman wants; a strange man chasing after her. Idiot.

He pulled in a deep breath, drew an image of the woman

in his mind, and filed it away. A fleeting moment he would never forget. Ha, at least he finally understood that old James Blunt song now. They'd shared a moment—he and the American—and he'd have that moment to the end.

End of what? Your sanity? You interacted with this woman for a few minutes. Now get your shit together and get to—

"Boss?"

He turned away from his restaurant's famous view and gave Kara a sheepish grin. "I should be in the kitchen, right?"

"Depends on if you wanted to give it a going over before your friend and his table arrived."

He frowned. "Of course I do. I might be a little jet lagged, but I'm not going into the kitchen cold. God knows what you've done to it while I've been gone."

She pulled a face. "Got it running like a well-oiled machine, thank you very…ahh shit, Nora's back."

Angus stiffened as Kara scowled in the direction of the restaurant's main entry. Damn it, he didn't feel like dealing with the TV producer so soon after returning to Australia. He was tired, and when he was tired, he got angry quickly. When he got angry, the fear always whispering in his head that he was just like his father grew to a scream.

Letting out an exasperated sigh, he turned toward the entrance.

And froze.

"Fuck me," he murmured, his stare locked not on the beaming woman in a yellow power suit striding toward him, but on the woman walking into Buckley's Chance a few steps behind his best mate. "I don't believe it."

"What?" Kara muttered back. "You honestly thought Nora was going to back off? She told you she was making it her mission to get you on that show of—"

"No," he whispered, unable to take his eyes off the woman walking behind Owen. "It's the American."

"From the airport?" Disbelief laced Kara's voice. "You're kidding me?"

"I'm—" Angus's throat seized shut as the woman he'd thought he'd never see again looked at him.

Her eyebrows shot up, and then dipped into a frown. A wary frown. She stopped walking. Her identical twin stopped beside her, *her* frown puzzled as she said something to her.

Angus straightened a little as her twin shot him a stunned look, and then he straightened even more as another woman with copper-red hair who looked almost identical to the twins but not quite stopped on the other side of her, frowning at him as well.

"Daniels!" Owen's jovial shout sounded through the restaurant as Owen spied him. "We're here."

A shy smile curled his American's lips as she looked at Angus, and she gave him an equally shy wave.

Hell, he liked that smile.

Smiling himself, he stepped toward her.

Just as Nora Young, TV producer and professional annoyer, blocked his path, *her* smile growing sharkish. "Angus. Told you I wasn't going to accept no."

CHAPTER THREE

"Oh my God," Zeta whispered, her fingers curling around Elisa's wrist. "Your hot Aussie is Owen's *friend?*"

"What?" Confusion laced Bria's voice. "Who?"

Elisa stared at the man from the airport currently being spoken to by a woman in a yellow pantsuit. Except his attention kept flicking to her, and every time their eyes connected her stomach did a little flip-flop.

The woman in the yellow—was that Kara? Maybe?—either didn't notice she didn't have his full attention or didn't care. Elisa couldn't help but notice however, that every time he looked at the woman in yellow, he grimaced.

Bria jabbed Zeta in the ribs with her elbow. "Who's Owen's friend?"

"The hot Aussie in a suit," Zeta said. "The one from the airport. That's him."

"Hot Aussie in a suit?" Bria repeated. "Zet, are you making any sense right now?"

Elisa smiled at the Aussie from the airport. He was *indeed* very hot. If not for her sisters' conversation, she'd be half convinced he was a figment of her imagination.

"Hey, Owen." Laughter filled Zeta's voice. "Do you *know* the guy talking to the woman in yellow?"

"Angus?" Owen said. "Yeah, he's my mate from school."

Elisa shot her future brother-in-law a quick glance. "Your *what*?"

"My best friend. From school. He owns Buckley's Chance. He's one of the best chefs in Australia. Why?"

Zeta threw Elisa a grin. "Elisa shared a moment with him back in the airport."

Owen let out a soft whistle as Elisa's cheeks burned. "A moment, eh?"

"It wasn't anything," Elisa mumbled, throat growing tighter.

"He asked for her number," Zeta countered.

Owen's eyebrows shot up, and Bria's mouth fell open.

"Stop it," Elisa groaned, face burning hotter. Angus's gaze found hers once more over the woman in yellow's shoulder. A smile tugged at the corner of his lips and her stomach flip flopped again.

"So who's the woman in yellow?" Zeta asked.

Owen shrugged, turning his attention to Angus and the woman talking to him. "No idea. Let's go find out."

He threaded his fingers through Bria's, dropped a wink at Elisa, and hurried over.

Elisa didn't miss the relief falling over Angus's face as Owen and Bria drew closer.

"Mate," Owen almost drawled, slapping his palm to Angus in a firm handshake before they hugged each other.

The woman in yellow shuffled backward, lips twisting in obvious frustration. Beside Angus the woman with the spikey violet hair Elisa had seen driving the Lexus gave Elisa, Zeta and Bria a contemplative inspection.

"You're early, you bastard," Angus pointed out, laughing, as Owen let him go.

"Sorry," Owen said, not a hint of apology in his voice. He

slid his arm around Bria's waist and pulled her to him, even as he indicated for Elisa and Zeta to join them with a jerk of his head. "I've got three hungry Americans to feed, you know."

The woman in yellow let out a sigh. "Angus, if I can just have a moment of your—"

"Owen, this is Kara." Angus turned to the wild-haired woman, his smile relaxed even as he pointedly ignored the woman in yellow. "The scariest sous chef in the country."

Owen chuckled, shaking Kara's offered hand. "Ah, yes, I've heard about you."

"All good, I know," Kara answered with an accent Elisa couldn't quite identify.

The woman in yellow puffed out a louder, exasperated sigh. "And *I'm* Nora Young. TV producer." She stepped forward, almost into the middle of the casual circle. "And I *need* to talk to Angus for just a moment, so if I may—"

"How many times do I have to say it, Nora?" Angus said, frustration in *his* voice.

"Say what?" Owen asked.

Kara grunted. "She wants him to be the next man stud on that show." She slid her attention to Elisa, arching a pierced eyebrow. "The one where a single man supposedly picks a woman with a rose."

"What?" Elisa burst out. "*No!*"

Everyone snapped their stares to her.

*Every*one.

She froze.

Oh God. Oh God. Oh God. What...what...

"He can't... He can't do that," she stammered. Something invisible wrapped around her chest. Why the hell had she said that? What was she doing? This was not what she did. She didn't draw attention to herself, and she sure as hell didn't let her mouth run riot like this. Oh God, would the floor just hurry up and swallow her now? Please?

The woman in yellow—Nora Young—looked at her. "And *you* are?"

"Fiancée." The word erupted from Elisa.

His what? Her mind gibbered. *What are you doing?*

"His *what?*" Nora Young snapped.

Elisa swallowed. Why had she *said* that? Because she didn't like the idea of Angus giving a rose to some unknown woman? Because he looked irritated by Nora Young? Because her stupid brain had final switched all the way from anxious to insane?

"I'm sorry, Lis?" Bria asked. "His what?"

"His what?" Owen echoed, frowning at Angus.

Angus's eyes widened, his stare jumping around them all before locking on Elisa. His jaw bunched. His chest rose and fell with a deep breath.

Oh God, oh God, oh God. He's going to laugh at me and call me a liar, and I wish I was—

"My fiancée," he said, his voice smooth and controlled and relaxed as he stepped forward and took her hands in his. A world of enigmatic emotions shone in his eyes however, none of them relaxed and controlled.

Elisa blinked, her heart hammering in her ears. He was going along with this? Why was he going along with this?

"His fiancée!" Zeta clapped her hands. "Hell yeah!"

Kara clicked her fingers. "His fiancée. Ahh, of course she is." She shot Nora a borderline smug smile and then slapped Angus on the shoulder, hard enough for Elisa to feel the jolt through her hands. "I totally forgot you mentioned you got engaged, boss."

Nora narrowed her eyes on Elisa. "You're his fiancée?"

Elisa swallowed, meeting the other woman's drilling inspection. What did she do now? Confess? Laugh?

Run from the restaurant? Catch a plane back to the US, an Uber to her apartment, run into her bedroom and hide under the covers?

"Seriously?" Nora raked a slow look over her. "*You're* his fiancée?"

A finger of indignation ticking up Elisa's spine. Ignoring the knot twisting in her stomach, she met Nora's stare and flashed a wide smile. "Why *wouldn't* I be?"

Nora let out a soft grunt.

Elisa stretched her smile wider, extending her hand toward Nora. "Hi. I'm Elisa."

"*Elisa!*" Angus almost bellowed. "This is *Elisa*. Her name is *Elisa*. My fiancée's name is *Elisa*." He beamed at her, squeezing her fingers. "Hi, Elisa."

She bit back a soft chuckle. He'd never get a job as an actor. Clearly, Angus Daniels had completely forgotten he already knew her name.

"Elisa the fiancée," Nora said, as if tasting the words. Her lip curled. Obviously, they weren't that palatable to her. She leveled a direct look at Elisa. "I'm curious; why hasn't Angus mentioned a girlfriend before? In all the times I've talked to him about being on my show, he never once said he was in a relationship. Which would, of course, make him ineligible."

Elisa swallowed. Shit.

"We met while I was in the US," Angus said, inching a little closer to her. She could see the gratitude in his eyes. And the panic.

She smiled at him, and gently placed her palm over his heart. It was a thumping canon. Poor guy. Panic she understood. Panic was a creature she lived with most of her life. The best way to deal with it, in her experience, was distraction. "It was a whirlwind romance," she said, willing his panic away as she gave him a surreptitious wink.

Definitely in for a penny now. The desire to actually erase the small distance left between them and press her body to his swept through her.

His chest rose and fell under her hand, and he winked back.

"Whirlwind?" Nora repeated, her focus bouncing back and forth between him and Elisa.

"Whirlwind," Elisa confirmed. "I took one look at him and fell hard."

"Ditto." Angus smiled, his eyes warm and playful. "I asked for her number within minutes of first seeing her."

"Ain't that the truth," Zeta chuckled. "I was there. I saw it happen."

"I do not know what's going on," Bria muttered. She frowned at Owen. "Do you?"

Owen laughed. It dawned on Elisa he'd left his Santa hat in his car.

Bria gave her an askew smile. "Have you been keeping secrets from me, Lis?"

Elisa bit at the inside of her cheek. What did she say? They never lied to each other. Ever. It was an unspoken rule they had as triplets and they stuck to it.

Angus coughed. "Err...surprise." He gave Bria a sheepish smile. "Elisa, *Lis*, thought it would be best to tell you in person."

Elisa's throat thickened. No one but Bria and Zeta called her Lis. It was *their* name for her. She corrected anyone else who tried, and yet, it sounded good from Angus.

Dio, this is getting out of hand.

Owen burst out laughing again. "So you're about to become my brother-in-law? I know who's cooking Christmas dinner this year, then."

Angus snorted. "Me. I've eaten your food, mate. As a cook, you make a fantastic maths teacher."

"Oi," Owen protested with a mock frown.

"Fiancée," Nora said again. It was no doubt meant to be a question, but to Elisa's ears, it sounded like a skeptical denunciation.

"Fiancée," she echoed, straightening her shoulders and meeting Nora's gaze. The TV producer was beginning to irritate her. It took a long time for her to anger, but Nora was pushing her buttons. "I'm sorry, but do you have a problem with your hearing? Do you need me to speak up?"

Zeta laughed, and then muffled the sound with her palm.

Kara didn't bother trying to stop her own laugh. "I like her, boss. I approve of this engagement."

"Why thank you, Kara." Angus grinned, tugging Elisa closer to him. Her heartbeat doubled as he brushed his knuckle over her cheek, smiling down at her. His gaze held hers, and her heart beat faster still. "Me too," he murmured.

Elisa drew in a slow breath, her stomach fluttering in a wholly lovely way. Okay, she *had* to remember this was all a… a… Whatever it was. A sham? Subterfuge? She'd impulsively started it out of a deluded, dismayed reaction to Angus being with someone else, and surprisingly he'd gone along with it, no doubt eager to get the TV producer off his back, but it *was* all just a sham. Unfortunately, it was all too easy to lose herself in his blue eyes and his warm smile and santa merda, she was in trouble here.

"No sex on the restaurant floor though, okay?" Kara said.

Angus almost choked. Elisa's cheeks filled with heat.

"I'd watch," Bria declared with a grin. "Just so you know."

Owen burst out laughing. "I've seen Daniels's naked arse already. It's not pretty."

"Oi," Angus retorted, sliding his fingers down the outside of Elisa's arm and took her hand in his again. "It's a better-looking arse than yours, Blackthorne."

"Blackthorne?" Nora's attention snapped to Owen. "As in—"

"Not the famous ones," Owen cut her short.

Elisa bit at the inside of her cheek. It was very *much* the famous ones, but Owen never cashed in on his very famous cousins' famous name.

Nora narrowed her eyes at Owen, studying him.

"Sorry, but Owen's off the market." Bria slid her arm

around Owen's waist and yanked him to her side. "This sexy math teacher is taken."

Nora's lips twisted and she swung her attention back to Angus.

Elise ground her teeth. Per l'amor di Dio, could this woman be more annoying? And stubborn?

"So's Angus," she stated. "See?" She lurched up onto her tiptoes and planted a kiss on Angus's cheek.

He stiffened.

Oh no.

Her stomach dropped. Oh no, she'd taken the sham too far.

And of *course* she had. She was an idiot. This is what she got for trying to be brave and daring. Oh God, would the floor please, please, please just open up and swallow her? Why wouldn't the floor just—

Angus turned to face her. His eyes locked on hers, and then, with a slow smile, he murmured, "See?" and leant forward and brushed his lips over the left corner of hers.

It was the softest of soft kisses. Barely any contact at all. Lasting for barely a heartbeat.

And yet Elisa's entire body thrummed with an elemental, core-deep response unlike any she'd had before. She let out a hitching moan, the sound the sexiest noise she'd ever made, and closed her eyes.

Insane. This was insane. She'd never been so turned on, and so…so…centered. So grounded. So real and alive.

"See?" Zeta crowed at her side. "Fiancée."

Elisa pulled away from Angus.

His gaze found hers, a question in his eyes: *I hope that was okay?*

She could only answer with a smile: *It was perfect.*

He smiled back. "Fiancée."

"So it seems," Nora intoned.

Elisa grit her teeth at the suspicion in the producer's voice.

Angus drew Elisa to his side, smoothing his arm around her waist, and she had to bite the inside of her cheek to stop herself gasping in delighted surprise. His fiancée wouldn't gasp at the public display and body placement, even if it did feel so damn good to be snug against him. Solid and safe and calm. And normally she wouldn't even remotely feel two of those things. Being hugged by a guy she didn't really know, during a high-pressure situation, and here she was calm and feeling safe?

Could she convince him to spend the rest of his life with her?

Dio, I really am in trouble.

"Now if you'll excuse us, Nora," Angus said. "I'd like to spend some time with my friends and my fiancée's family."

"Of course." Nora waved a hand, as if brushing away a fly. "I don't want to be an annoyance."

Kara barked out a laugh.

Nora's eyes narrowed for a split-second, and then she flashed Angus a smile. "But while I'm here, I may as well have an early lunch. If I can't have you as my bachelor, I can at least have you as my chef. For a meal. Today. Right now."

Elisa wanted to scream. Nora clearly wasn't convinced.

Are you surprised?

Nora directed a sweeping gaze around the restaurant and then raised an eyebrow at Angus. "Can you point me to an available table? Or can I sit at your fiancée's?"

CHAPTER FOUR

Angus pulled in a slow breath as Nora settled herself into a chair at table three in the east quadrant of the dining floor. No freaking way was she going to be sitting at the same table as Elisa.

A part of his brain couldn't believe the TV producer's tenacity—or was it gall? The rest of his brain kept returning to the fact he still had his arm around Elisa's waist.

His *fiancée's* waist.

Why *had* she said she was his fiancée? A knee-jerk reaction to something? A slip of the tongue?

Going along with it hadn't been a knee-jerk reaction though. His first reaction when she'd said she was his fiancée had been confused shock, followed immediately by a powerful sense of relief. If he had a fiancée, Nora would have to finally move on from her stubborn, deluded quest for him to be the bachelor on her show.

Kara snorted. "So, she really *is* just going to sit over there and eat."

"Seems that way," Elisa's identical sister muttered, studying Nora.

As if aware she was being watched, Nora looked over and waved.

Elisa's sister waved back and then cast him a contemplative look. "Maybe you should poison her food?"

"Oh, I like you." Kara grinned at Elisa's sister. "What do I call you?"

"Zeta." Elisa's sister grinned back. "I'm the sane one of us triplets."

"Ha" Owen's fiancée, Bria, laughed. "Sane. That's funny."

"I'm so sorry," Elisa murmured, slipping out of his loose embrace. "I don't know why I... I can't really explain why I said..."

She trailed off, her gaze jumping everywhere except to him.

"It's all good." He gently snagged her hand before she could get too far away. For Nora's sake, of course. While the producer was here, they'd have to keep up the appearance of a newly engaged couple.

Sure. For Nora's sake. It has nothing to do with the fact you like holding Elisa's hand at all, does it. Or that when she smiles, you want to smile as well. Or that you want to control the situation? Jesus, brain, shut the fuck up.

"Don't apologize," he finished as her gaze finally rested on his.

"I still have no clue what's going on," Bria muttered, arching an eyebrow at Elisa. "But I'm enjoying whatever it is, so there's that."

"Yeah." Owen pinned Angus with a level look—what Angus thought of as his stern-teacher stare. "I'm equally in the dark. Care to explain, mate?"

Angus opened his mouth, closed it, and looked at Elisa. "Elisa saved me," he said, giving her a soft wink.

She bit her lip, the tiniest hint of playful mischief flickering in her beautiful blue eyes for a second, before she beamed up at Owen. "You of all people should be a believer in love at first sight, Owen."

"She's right." Zeta pointed at Owen, and then Bria. "Seriously, you two were fucking like rabbits fifteen minutes after you first met, and engaged four days later."

"Four days?" Angus looked at his best mate. "*Four* days?"

Owen shrugged. "Hey, why wait when you've found what you've always been looking for, right?"

"It probably would have been five minutes after they first did it, if he hadn't thought he had brain cancer," Zeta suggested, giving Owen a smirk.

Angus blinked. "Brain cancer?"

Owen snorted. "Old news. I'll tell you about it later. Now, I want to eat."

"Me too." Zeta nodded.

"And while we eat," Bria took Elisa's hand and gently tugged her from Angus's side, "Lis here is going to bring us up to speed. Isn't that right, Lis?"

Damn, he already missed the warmth of her body against his.

"That's right," Elisa murmured, cheeks blushing.

"The producer is watching you all," Kara muttered at Angus's shoulder. "Like a shark."

"You mean like a hawk?" he muttered back, trying to not glance at Nora at table three.

"A shark." Kara snorted. "Eyes nothing but cold blood-lust. She's just waiting for a hint of weakness in your happy engagement."

Angus ground his teeth. A hot finger of something tight and dark traced up his spine. Damn it.

He looked at Elisa. She met his eyes. The hot anger faded, and he pulled a slow breath. He liked looking at her. Liked the way it made him feel. If he kissed her again, what would she do? He took a small step toward her, faltered, stopped, swallowed.

She closed the tiny distance between them with a step, brushed her fingers over his chest and then her fingertips over his jaw, smiling up at him. "Go do what you have to do in the kitchen, sexy man," she said loudly. Louder than needed for her proximity.

He lifted his eyebrows. Sexy man?

She flashed a playful grimace at him, as if to say, *hey, go with it.*

"And come back to me when you're done," she finished just as loud, before raising up onto her tip toes and dropping a quick kiss on his cheek.

He had to physically stop himself from grabbing her arse, hauling her to him and making love to her mouth. Was it genuinely possible to *actually* fall in love at first sight? Was it?

You don't do relationships, remember, mate. Safer that way.

That was true. He wasn't going to fuck up another person like his father had. But still, spending time with Elisa wasn't a relationship.

Could be, though.

"Good plan," Kara declared. "The food isn't going to prepare itself."

Angus looked down into Elisa's eyes. *Thank you,* he said with his own.

"I'll be back out in a little while," he said as loud as she had, tucking a strand of her strawberry-blond hair behind her ear. That's what couples did, right? Any excuse to touch each other, to connect?

The only time his dad touched his mum was to hit her.

Then don't be like Dad.

He cleared his throat. "Don't miss me too much."

Jesus. As an actor, he made a brilliant chef.

Elisa laughed. The sound sent a ribbon of happiness unfurling through him. He leant forward and brushed a feather-light kiss on her forehead before he knew what he was doing.

Did you need *to do that?*

Did he? Was this all necessary? Was Nora still watching them?

"Do I have to go back there and cook my own breakfast?" Owen asked on a chuckle. "*Sexy man?*"

Angus threw him a grin. "You're just jealous because you don't have an awesome nickname."

"Hey." Bria held up a finger. "I call him stud muffin, thank you very much."

"You do not!" Owen laughed.

"*Blerk.*" Zeta made a face. "I'm about to lose my appetite."

Angus laughed again. Fake engagement or not, he liked this crazy family Owen had brought to him. And he liked Elisa the most.

He couldn't wait to introduce her to Chelsea.

Elisa's not your real fiancée, mate. Remember that.

Still, he could see his half sister liking Elisa immediately.

Jesus, you're in trouble. No relationships. Remember?

Elisa smiled up at him, a hint of shyness creeping into her face. "Will you come and join us after you've finished in the kitchen?"

This time there was no artificial volume to her voice. The question was for him, not Nora. Him.

It made him feel…good.

"Definitely," he replied, his answer for her and only her. "I honestly don't think I want to stay away from you for too long."

Whoa, mate. Tap the brakes. Don't scare her off.

Pink filled her cheeks again at his unplanned, impulsive, and thoroughly inappropriate confession and all shyness left her eyes. "I know what you mean. I feel the same."

He caught his breath. She held his gaze.

"Alright, alright." Owen gave his shoulder a playful shove. "Save up all the lovey-dovey for when I'm not waiting for food. Get your arse into the kitchen, Daniels. I'm hungry."

With one last look at Elise, Angus got his arse into the

kitchen. His staff were doing their thing in it, line chefs, commis chefs, kitchen hands—all dancers in a graceful performance that was the soul of the kitchen, preparing meals for those in the dining area who'd already ordered.

He stood for a moment, observing them. Their energy, their je ne sais quoi, thrummed through him and he let out a slow, calm breath.

Home. This was home. How could he go anywhere else?

"You going to just watch them, or you going to cook something?" Kara appeared at his side. "Or are you going to go back out to your fiancée and actually get started on the processes of making your new relationship a real one?"

A tight lump settled in his throat, and he pictured Elisa. He wasn't in the market for a relationship, not a real one at least. He was still trying to commit to a country to live in for a few years, let alone another soul to share a life with.

Share a life? Don't even think about it. You've seen how that goes. It only ends in pain.

And yet…

He flicked Kara a look. "Do you think Nora is convinced?"

"Hell no." Kara grunted. "I think you need to go out there and kiss Elisa until she has a screaming orgasm. Then Nora *might* be convinced."

"*Might?*" His body reacted to the notion of kissing Elisa. And reacted even more to the notion of making her climax. He arched his eyebrow at his sous chef, trying to ignore the hungry tightening of his groin. "And just out of interest, when was the last time *you* kissed your wife until she had a screaming orgasm?"

"This morning." She didn't blink. "And every morning."

Angus snorted. "And on that note, I'm going to go wash my hands." He shucked out of his suit jacket. Buckley's Chance's kitchen steward hurried over before he could call him, took the jacket, and hurried away.

His team knew him well. Had they missed him as much as

he'd missed them? What did they think of the possibility of him moving?

Kara grinned. "I've got your new fiancée's order, plus everyone else at her table. So hurry up so you can get started." She turned and snapped out a finger at his poissonnier. "Frank. Salmon. The best. Now."

Frank—one of the country's best fish-line chefs—flipped her off and hurried off to the fridge to select the morning's best salmon. Clearly someone in Elisa's party had ordered the smoked salmon mousse.

Elisa's party. Huh. Didn't take you long to think of them as Elisa's party instead of Owen's party.

It hadn't.

"What did Elisa order?" he asked, heading for the wash sink.

"The triple cheese omelet with a side of sautéed mushrooms. Speaking of which—" She jabbed her finger toward Buckley's Chance's saucier. "Luka, sauteed mushrooms to accompany a triple-cheese—"

"I got it," Angus cut her off.

"Still the control freak." She leant her hip against the wash sink's edge. "Cooking for the future missus, eh?"

He chuckled under his breath. Missus.

"I'm assuming you'll be buying her a ring from Tiffany's?"

Turning, he flicked warm sudsy water from his fingers at her, and then headed for the sauteing zone.

He'd designed Buckley's Chance's kitchen layout himself, preferring an open layout with dedicated stations so his team could move easily and not stumble over each other, particularly during the main dining periods. Each station was designed to his specifications; all fitted out with appliances and equipment he'd handpicked.

When it came to his kitchen, he liked—needed—control. He wasn't oblivious to what it meant: while he'd had no control

of the chaos of his father's violence and his mother's alco-
holism, he had control of the chaos of meal creation.

Control freak.

Arriving in the sauteing zone, he sought out his favorite
Henckels paring knife. The perfect knife for preparing mushrooms to be sautéed.

"Now, your engagement party?" Kara plucked the paring
knife from the block before he could, studying its edge as she
leant against the counter. "I'm torn between wanting to cater it
and wanting to just be there as a guest."

He held out his hand. "Knife."

She ignored the request. "And you'll no doubt be inviting
Nora to the wedding?"

"As if." Okay, he'd use the Wusthof instead.

"Given you're in *here* instead of being out *there* with your
fiancée," Kara placed his Henckels on the counter in front of
him, "I think the only way to convince Nora your engagement
is real is to invite her to the wedding."

He stopped reaching for his preferred knife. Turned his
frown to his sous chef. "You think…"

"I do." She nodded. "Get your ass back out there. Be seen
being the opposite of an available man. Be seen being taken. Be
seen being in love."

It made sense. Nora wasn't the type to admit defeat. But
how could he impress Elisa with his cooking if he wasn't
doing it?

Something tight curled around his chest. Impress her? Did
he want to impress her? Yes. Of course he bloody-well did.
From the second she'd handed him his passport, he'd wanted to
impress her. What was he going to do about it?

"Don't fuck up the mushrooms," he ordered, pointing at
Kara.

She snorted. "When have I *ever* fucked up the
mushrooms?"

Chest growing tighter, he turned and strode through his kitchen.

"Hey, boss?"

Kara's call stopped him at the door to the dining area. He frowned. "What?"

"What do *you* want to eat for this important meal?"

"My favorite," he threw back, before pushing on the swinging door and exiting the kitchen.

Eyes bored into him the second the door swung closed behind him, but he ignored their heavy weight. Nora didn't need to know he was aware she watched him.

He fixed his focus on the table where Elisa, her sisters, and Owen now sat. Elisa faced the window and its sweeping multi-million-dollar views of Sydney Harbor, her fingers threading through the long strands of her hair as if pulling if back into a ponytail.

What would it feel like, streaming through his own fingers? Cool? Silky smooth?

Owen's fiancée, Bria, leant forward and said something, a mischievous grin on her lips, and Elisa turned in her chair, her gaze finding his over her shoulder. She smiled. Raised her hand in the same tiny, almost shy wave she'd first given him on arriving at the restaurant. He smiled back. Time to be seen being in love. For some reason, he didn't think it was going to be hard.

He's coming over. He's coming over. What do I do? What do I do? Do I stand up? Do I kiss him? Oh God, I thought pretending to be his fiancée would be easier. Dio, what do I do? What do I—

Elisa tipped back her head, smiling up at Angus, as he stopped at the side of her seat.

"Hi," he said, his gaze holding hers.

"Hi," she croaked back. He'd removed his suit jacket, but it had not lessened the way he looked. Goddammit, he was gorgeous.

Sexy man. That's it, yes?

Yep, that was it.

Owen grunted out a laugh. "I can't help but notice a distinct lack of meals in your hands, Daniels."

Angus didn't stop looking at her. "I decided I wanted to be with my fiancée more than I wanted to be in the kitchen."

Elisa's heart thumped a little faster. A little harder. She had to remember this was all an act. A show for the TV producer watching them like a hawk.

"Awww," Zeta cooed. "That's adorable."

"I still don't understand what's going—oww, Zet?" Bria glared at Zeta across the table. "Why did you kick me?"

Angus chuckled.

"FYI," Zeta said, ignoring Bria, "we're being watched." Smile wide and cheesy, she flicked a glance toward the east.

Elisa's chest tightened. Nora. Of course.

"I was wondering," Angus murmured, holding out his hand as his eyes searched hers, "if you'd like to take a look at the private outside dining area?"

She jolted to her feet. "Yes, please."

He laughed. So did Owen. Heat filled her cheeks, and she ducked her head. Gentle fingers brushed hers and she looked up, straight into Angus's eyes. Without thought or hesitation, she threaded her fingers through his and stepped away from the table.

"We'll be back," she said loudly.

For Nora? For everyone at the table? She didn't know or care. She was holding Angus's hand. It felt…right.

Like an anchor.

A good one.

Ah Dio, she was never going to recover from this.

CHAPTER FIVE

"Wow." Elisa leant on the polished steel deck railing, gazing at the sweeping views before her. The water sparkled and glistened like a carpet of blue jewels, and the arcs of the Opera House gleamed pristine white in the morning sun. For a brief second, she couldn't believe she was actually here, looking at the famous building. A playful harbor breeze tousled her hair, a few strands tickling her lips and she let out a soft laugh, turning to face Angus. "That's an amazing view."

"I'm glad you like it." He beamed, and she couldn't help but smile. "Only amazing things for my fiancée."

"Is that so?" She bit her bottom lip, trying to restrain her grin. It was wrong to like hearing him say that so much.

"Absolutely." He nodded, the edges of his eyes crinkling. "What else would you like? Name it."

"*Name* it?" She snagged a strand of her hair once again blown across her face by the breeze and twisted it around her fingers. Was she flirting? Was that what she was doing?

Flirting with your fiancée.

"Name it," he confirmed, his gaze holding hers.

"Hmm…" Was he leaning a little closer to her? What would he do if she leant a little closer to him? "A cuddle?"

He drew in a swift breath.

"With a koala," she finished, unable to hide her grin.

He chuckled, and yes, he was definitely leaning closer to her. "And here I was thinking I was going to get lucky."

"Hmm, you never know," she said, not hiding her smile.

His eyes twinkled. "Are we flirting right now?"

"I think we are," she murmured. "But I'm not sure. I'm not good at flirting."

He drew a fraction closer still. Close enough his body heat kissed her. "I think you're *amazing* at flirting."

She swallowed, looking up at him. Craving…something… "I am?"

"You are." He dipped his head in a single nod. "With me."

"With you," she agreed.

Kiss him. He's right there. He's flirting with you. Kiss him!

He held her gaze, his body heat drawing her to him, even as *he* drew closer to her.

Dio, she wanted to kiss him. To be kissed by him. His lips were beautiful, slightly parted. Waiting for hers. All she needed to do was rise up on her tip toes and—

What if he recoils? What if he pulls away? What if you're reading it all wrong? What if he's all doing this just to throw off Nora? What if—

She stepped back. Almost a jerking stumble.

Angus blinked, jolting upright, his hand plunging into the front pockets of his suit pants as he took a step back and looked out over the harbor. "Sorry. Sorry."

A knot twisted in Elisa's chest. She licked her lips, turning away to grab at the rail. The steel cooled her palms, almost mocking the flushed heat prickling through her. "I like your restaurant."

"I can take you to hug a koala," he said at the exact same time.

They laughed. Also at the same time. The knot in her chest relaxed. A little.

Closing her eyes, she pulled in a slow breath. *I can feel the breeze, I can smell the salt water, I can hear the boats...* She needed to ground herself.

"Thank you," he said beside her, his voice low and warm and friendly.

She opened her eyes, giving him a quick glance. *I can see a gorgeous Aussie...* "For suddenly becoming engaged to you?"

His chuckle loosened the knot in his chest even more. "For saying you like my restaurant. But also for that."

She let out her own soft laugh. "Ah, I see. You're welcome."

"Why *did* you suddenly become my fiancée?"

The knot came back. She swallowed.

"Not that I'm complaining." He rested his elbows on the steel railing, his body loose and relaxed and too damn sexy. "It's just not the kind of thing that happens. To me."

Letting go of the railing, she let out a wobbly laugh, mimicking his pose. The harbor breeze played with her hair again. "You looked like a cornered animal."

He raised his eyebrows.

"I like animals," she said. "I wanted to help."

He studied her. She resisted falling into his gaze. Just.

"That's exactly how I felt," he finally said. "Cornered. Trapped. Thank you."

"You're welcome." She smiled. He was so easy to smile at. So easy to be with. "To be fair, I *was* in the middle of daydreaming what it would be like being with you—*dating* you, I mean—when what Nora was saying sank into my brain so my initial 'no' was more selfish than I'm making out."

Okay, she *hadn't* planned to confess *that*.

Because his is so easy to be with. So easy to be...to be open with.

He laughed. Her stomach fluttered at the tiny flash of dimples in his cheeks. "If it helps," he said, his gaze on hers, "I've pretty much thought of nothing else but you since the airport."

Oh Dio. What did she do with that?

Kiss him!

Silence stretched between them for a heartbeat. Elisa swallowed. If she went up on tiptoe and kissed him now, what would he do?

"Why *did* you take off so abruptly back at the airport?" he suddenly asked, his voice low and gentle.

"I…" The knot in her chest let her know it hadn't gone anywhere. She turned her stare to the Opera House again. *I can see the white arcs…* Did she tell him she freaked out when she heard another woman's name? That made her sound a little… unbalanced. Which she kind of was. Sometimes. "I struggle with anxiety," she said, keeping her stare on the famous building. The truth. The truth was always a good way to start a fake engagement. "It manifests sometimes at the worst moment."

"I make you anxious?"

Shaking her head, she looked up at him. "No. You make me feel…" She searched for the word. "Brave."

His nostrils flared. His gaze dropped to her lips for a second. She licked them.

"I really want to kiss you right now, Elisa?" His voice was husky. "Is that okay? Can I kiss you right now? This very second?"

"Call me Lis," she said. "And absolutely."

"Hi, Lis," he murmured, sliding his hands around her waist. "Thank you for being engaged to me."

A smile curled her lips, and she smoothed her palms up his chest, raising up onto tiptoe. "Any time."

He chuckled, the sound low and throaty and wonderful. "Until we get married?"

She laughed, just as he tugged her completely to his body and lowered his head to hers.

His lips moved over hers. Not confident or demanding. There was no arrogance to his kiss, nor expectation she surrender to him They brushed hers, hesitant, as if waiting for her response. Tasting with gentle nips, his hands ever so softly cupping her jaw, his fingertips laying lightly on her temples.

A delicious little shudder rocked through her, and she let out a hitching moan of approval, threading her fingers into the hair at his nape. Parting her lips to his.

I taste him…

His tongue touched hers with a tender sweep before he slowly pulled back. A low sigh left him, and he pressed his forehead to hers. "That was nice."

Her stomach fluttered at the husky quality to his low murmur. "It was."

With a soft chuckle, he straightened a little more, brushing his thumb along her bottom lip. "Can we do it again?"

She smiled, pulling his head back down to hers. "Only if you don't stop next time?"

His warm breath fanned her lips. "Deal."

Someone behind them cleared their throat. They both jumped, and Elisa yelped.

"Sorry to interrupt, boss," Kara said.

"What the—?" Angus ground out, swinging raised eyebrows to his sous chef. "We really need to have a word about your timing, Kara."

Kara flicked Elisa an apologetic smile and then turned her attention back to Angus, extending her phone toward him. "I think you should see this."

Angus took it from her, and Elisa realized how much she already missed his arms being around her. Was this what it had been like for Bria? Falling in love at first sight with Owen?

Dio, woman. Stop being so ridiculous. It's a kiss. A good one, a very good one, the best one you've ever had, but only a kiss.

"Jesus bloody Christ," Angus muttered.

The agitation in his voice made her frown. She bit her lip as he clawed a hand through his shaggy hair, his stare locked on Kara's phone.

"I have no justifiable reason," Kara said, "but my gut tells me Nora is behind this."

Elisa's frown deepened. Behind what? Would it be rude if she looked at Kara's phone as well? To see what they were talking about?

Angus lifted his head, scanning the distance of water on the other side of the railing. "You think she somehow contacted Chelsea?"

Elisa's stomach clenched. Who the hell was Chelsea?

Kara shrugged. "Maybe. It's a dick move, but I think she's capable."

"What's going on?" Elisa asked. Why was Angus so angry?

Anxiety bit into her. Had *she* caused this? Him being angry?

"Fuck," Angus growled, a muscle in his jaw knotting. "Now I've gotta…" He dragged his hands through his hair and let out a sigh.

"I…I should go inside," she mumbled. A fuzzy roar began in her ears. Her throat closed, a hot lump filling it. Her breath grew short. She swallowed. Her mouth was so dry.

"Damn it," Angus muttered, his voice distance. Like he was a mile away. "What am I going to tell Chelsea?"

She squeezed her eyes shut, taking another step backward. She didn't want… She didn't want to be here… She wanted…

Her stomach knotted. Her head began to swim.

She had to get out of here. She had to…to…to not be seen. She had to not be here. She had to be away.

Away. Where no one was. Where no one could see her and judge her and laugh at her and mock her and…and…

She hurried away, cheeks hot. Heavy pressure clamped down on her chest, her temples. Because of her, things had gone badly for Angus. She thought she was saving him, helping him out, but instead she'd made things—

"Hey?" A gentle hand curled around her fingers just as she moved into the dining area from the deck, halting her. "Lis?"

She turned, panic crushing her, and frowned up at Angus.

Were people looking at her? At them? Were they wondering what was going on? What she'd done?

"Hey," he said again, softer this time as he squeezed her fingers. "It's okay."

She flinched.

He sucked in a short breath. "Sorry, I didn't mean..." He stopped, dropping his gaze to where his fingers hooked hers. A battle she didn't understand warred in his face, and he dropped her hand. "Sorry, I didn't mean to grab you," he almost whispered, looking up at her as he took a step backward. "Or scare you."

"You didn't." God, why did she have to go and ruin everything. He was probably wishing he'd never met her. Probably wishing he'd caught an entirely different flight into Sydney this morning so they'd never have been in the same airport. "I'm sorry for causing all this problem."

He flicked Nora—watching them closely—a look and then dropped his stare to his hand once more.

Damn it, she wanted to thread her fingers through his again. She wanted to be hugged by him. She wanted to *kiss* him again.

Instead, she stayed motionless.

A smile, wry and wan, tugged at his lips. "You haven't caused any problem. Someone else—" another quick glance at Nora, "—has that honor."

Her own smile fought to surface. She wished she could stop worrying she was the cause of his anger. Pulling in a shaky breath, she gave Nora her own look. "True."

The TV producer watched them. Like a hawk. Elisa gave her a wide smile and friendly wave.

Angus chuckled. "God, I like you."

Heat filled her cheeks, and she ducked her head.

'I like you too'. Say it. Say 'I like you too'.

She lifted her eyes to his. "I—"

"I need to call my sister," he said at the same time, a distracted expression falling over his face. "She thinks I'm…" He trailed off, flicked Nora another frown, and cleared his throat. "Y'know. I'll be back. Promise." He turned and hurried away, disappearing through a pair of swinging doors on the other side of the restaurant.

Elisa bit at her bottom lip, studied the doors. Black-aproned waitstaff were striding in empty-handed and out with plates of food, so clearly those were the doors to the kitchen.

"Chelsea," a woman's voice said on her right, and she flinched.

"What?" She jerked around to find Kara at her side.

"Chelsea is Angus's sister." If Kara noticed she was a freaking nervous wreck, she didn't show it. "Just so you know. Not any kind of romantic partner or anything. Well, she's his *half* sister. *And* my best friend. She's going to be *very* upset that he didn't tell her he got engaged while in the US."

Sister? Dio, this was turning into a nightmare of Greek tragedy proportions. What was he going to tell his sister? That some crazy American had abruptly announced she was engaged to him?

She looked at Kara. Did she know? Suspect?

Tell her. At least then she will understand why Angus is so—

"Emily, is it?" Nora strode up to her, smile not meeting her eyes.

At her side, Kara began to hum the theme to *Jaws*.

"Elisa," Elisa corrected. Goddamn it, why hadn't she rejoined Bria and Zeta and Owen at the table when Angus hurried away?

"Elisa, yes." Nora ran a look over her. "I'd love to hear the story of how you and Angus met. It's the kind of thing a producer like me eats up. Was it romantic? Where did it happen? Can I see the ring?"

Elisa tucked her left hand under her right armpit.

Nora gave her another smile. It didn't reach her eyes. "Ah, that's right, you don't have one."

"*Yet.* She doesn't have one *yet.*" Kara draped her arm around Elisa's shoulder and bumped her hip with hers. "What's your point?"

Nora shook her head. "No point. I'm curious, is all."

"Good thing you're not a cat," Elisa said. She was getting tired. Not jet-lagged, just…tired.

Kara laughed.

Nora pursed her lips. "Do you want to know what I think?"

Elisa shook her head. "No." She turned and walked away, heading back to her table.

Screw Nora and her skepticism.

"Yep, it's official," Kara laughed, following. "I really do like you. You can marry the boss any day."

Elisa laughed.

"No, seriously." Kara nudged her gently with her shoulder. "Think about it."

And with that, Kara smiled, winked, and hurried toward the double doors Angus had disappeared through earlier.

Elisa swallowed. *Think about it.*

She was.

Which was mental.

CHAPTER SIX

So Chelsea was furious she'd learnt he *was* engaged from *TV Weekly* journalist who'd called her out of the blue to ask for her thoughts about his sudden betrothal to an American. She'd then been ridiculously excited *about* him getting engaged, even though he hadn't been the one to tell her. Hurt, but excited. She was then *very* bummed when he told her he *wasn't* engaged but trying to keep Nora off his back. And *then* she'd been really enthusiastic about the prospect of being a part of the ruse.

All in a whirlwind five minutes or so of telephone conversation.

His half sister was, in a word, awesome.

He'd promised her he'd call her if he needed anything. He also promised he'd introduce her to Elisa ASAP.

He tried not to admit to himself how much he liked *that* idea. It meant, if for no other reason, he had a—kind of— justifiable reason to keep Elisa in his life after Nora left the restaurant today.

That's what you're going with? How 'bout instead of more subterfuge maybe offer to really take her to the zoo to see a koala.

Or ask if she'd like to go to the art gallery or...or...climbing the Harbor Bridge or...

What was he thinking? He didn't do relationships. He refused to do relationships. But what about a fling? While Elisa was here in Australia? He did flings. Occasionally. When he had the time.

Is that what you want though? A fling?

"Boss, you better get your ass out there." Kara suddenly strode up to where he hovered at the sauté station. "Your fiancée is battling Nora alone."

A hot finger of anger drilled into his chest. He bit back a growl. "Seriously, if I ever hear the name Nora again..."

He stomped out of the kitchen.

Thankfully, Nora was back at her table, her meal being placed in front of her by Cassie, his head server. The producer looked over at him and waved.

He didn't wave back. Instead, he headed for Elisa's table, snagging a chair from an empty table on the way.

"I still see no food in your hands, Daniels," Owen protested with a laugh as Angus arrived.

Angus snorted. "You're a pain in the arse, Blackthorne."

Owen grinned.

"Can I join in?" Angus cast the table a smile before looking at Elisa. She smiled up at him and the anger in his chest evaporated. He really really liked her smile.

"Sure," she answered, shuffling her chair a little to the left to make room. Her sister, Zeta, did the same to the right, her grin full of mischief.

He positioned his chair between them, slightly angled toward Elisa, and sat. His knee brushed the side of her thigh and what felt like a soft electric jolt shot through him.

Her eyes met his, a question in them he truly wanted to answer.

He wanted to kiss her. He wanted to lose himself in her lips. He wanted to hear her laugh as he slowly undressed her, exploring each new inch of her exposed flesh with his lips and tongue and teeth.

He wanted to—

"Can I take you to the zoo after we eat," he said abruptly, cutting the thought short. If he didn't, things would...pop up that really shouldn't in the middle of the day in the middle of his restaurant.

Her little catch of breath made him catch his own.

An eternity hung between, a fraction of a second where everything he thought he wanted in his life somehow...pivoted.

"To hug a koala," he finished.

"I'd like that," she said, her smile as soft as her voice.

Yes.

"Oi," Owen said. "Can we come to the zoo as— Oow, Bri. Why'd you kick... Oh."

Angus didn't look at his best mate. Didn't want to look anywhere but at Elisa.

She laughed, no doubt aware of what had just happened on the other side of the table.

He bit the inside of his mouth to stop himself leaning forward and kissing her. His blood roared in his ears.

Elisa looked at him, her teeth catching her bottom lip.

"The omelet," Cassie's voice slid between them. He blinked, realizing how close to Elisa he'd been leaning, and sat straight in his chair, casting Cassie a smile as she placed Elisa's meal in front of her.

"Oh my God, that looks incredible," Elisa proclaimed.

He gave the dish a critical eye. Kara's hands were all over it. His sous chef had stepped up and done what he said he was going to do, and done it well.

"I'll make it for you myself next time," he said.

Elisa flashed him a grin, both mischievous and shy at once. "I'll hold you to that."

A hot, thick pressure pulsed through his body. He truly did

like the idea of being bound to Elisa, even for something as simple as a meal.

He liked the idea even more of making her breakfast in his own kitchen in his home, after they'd spent the night learning everything they could about each other.

Liked the idea a lot.

The rest of the table's meals arrived. He couldn't stop himself inspecting each one with what he hoped were surreptitious glances.

"Stop stressing, boss." Kara placed a large platter of freshly cut fruit in the middle of the table. "The kitchen crew did good."

Okay, clearly not surreptitious enough.

"Bloody oath," Owen approved around a mouthful of smoked salmon and scrambled eggs. "My compliments to the chef." He threw Angus an evil grin. "Not you, Daniels. All you did was hang out here making goo-goo eyes at your fiancée."

"Oi,' Angus protested with a chuckle.

Elisa bit her lip and smiled.

"Fiancée," Bria said. "That's still—" She looked at Elisa. "Does Mom and Dad—"

"Angus is taking me to the zoo after breakfast," Elisa declared, her voice louder than needed.

A prickling sensation crawled up the back of Angus's neck and he shot a quick glance over his shoulder. Yep, Nora was watching them from table three.

He turned back to Elisa, drawing a little closer to her. "You're amazing," he whispered.

Her smile stretched wider, and she picked up her knife and fork. "Happy to help."

And before he could move, she closed the small distance between their faces and brushed a quick kiss against his cheek.

His body erupted with warm delight, and he had to stop himself turning his head and capturing her lips with his. Instead, he let out a low, wobbly laugh. "Happy to *be* helped."

Her eyes held his. For a heartbeat. And then she settled back in her seat and dug into her omelet. They all ate. And while they all ate, they all talked. Five people, all enjoying each other's company. Angus hadn't felt so comfortable, so relaxed for…well, a long time. It'd been quite a while since he and Owen had hung out together—the bastard lived in Newcastle which was two hours' drive away, and Angus was a workaholic who rarely left the restaurant. Plus, there was the fact he'd spent the last two weeks in the US. But it wasn't just catching up with his best mate.

He enjoyed listening to Elisa and her sisters banter. He got a laugh out of watching Bria and Owen bounce off each other. He relished being included in all their conversations, whether it be about swimming with sharks off the coast of South Africa —Bria thought it a brilliant idea, Elisa thought it insane. Owen refused to give an opinion; about who was the best Batman—Owen was adamant it was Michael Keaton, Bria equally as adamant Christian Bale was the best, and Zeta lobbed Ben Affleck into the mix deliberately trying to cause a ruckus; or why Italians made the best pizza—on this one, he agreed with the De Luca sisters. The best pizza he'd ever eaten was in Rome.

And most of all, he loved sitting next to Elisa and just… existing with her. Listening to her talk—relaxed and at ease— with her family. Learning who she was.

He was right. Back at the airport something about her had told him she was kind and caring and quiet, and she was all those things. And yet, when she talked about design and art, she came to life. He drank in the enthusiastic energy radiating from her when she talked about her work as a graphic artist. He got lost in her excitement when she told him about her small but very busy graphic design business, and wanted to kiss her senseless when, after Bria mentioned Elisa had been chosen to design the new logo for the San Diego Zoo, she shyly ducked her head, cheeks growing pink.

He'd shared some amazing meals with some amazing people in his life—most chefs did—but nothing compared to this meal.

This moment.

These people.

Elisa.

Nothing compared to sitting next to Elisa, talking with her, being a part of her life, if only for this moment. A moment he never wanted to end.

He didn't believe in love at first sight. Wasn't sure he believed in love, full stop—not after living through his parents' marriage—but holy hell, right now, right at that moment…

A hand dropped onto his shoulder, and he almost let out a shout.

"She's gone, boss," Kara murmured in his ear, plucking his empty plate from in front of him.

Gone? He frowned at his sous chef. "Who?"

"Nora." She flicked a glance toward table three. "Left about fifteen minutes ago. On a side note, she didn't leave a tip."

He looked over at the table where the producer had been seated. Empty. Something heavy settled on his chest.

Nora was gone. That meant there was no reason for him and Elisa to pretend they were engaged anymore. That meant it was over. No. He wasn't ready for it to be over.

He swung back at Elisa. "Want to go to the zoo? Now?"

She blinked, startled. "Now? *Now* now?"

"Now." He jolted to his feet. "Right now. Let's go."

"All good over there, mate?" Owen asked.

"Lis?" Bria said. "Tutto okay?"

Elisa looked up at him, looked over at Nora's empty table, and looked at him again. What was she thinking? He couldn't tell. For all their gentle flirting and their…*intense* kiss out on the deck, what *he* wanted—them spending more time together —may not be what *she* wanted. He'd grabbed her wrist, after all. He'd startled her.

She caught her lip with her teeth. He swallowed. Held his breath. Waited.

A smile spread over her face, and she straightened to her feet, taking his hand in hers. "We're going to the zoo."

"What?" Bria blinked. "*Now?*"

"Can I come?" Zeta laughed. "Kidding. Kidding." She stabbed a finger at Angus. "Have her home by midnight."

Angus laughed.

Bria narrowed her eyes, first at Elisa and then Angus. "I really don't know what's going on, but if Lis is happy…" She flourished her hand toward the restaurant's entry.

"We're only in Sydney for twenty-four hours, mate," Owen said, pointing at Angus. "We've got two suites at the…at the…" He looked at Bria. "Where are we staying tonight?"

"At the CBD Mercure," she supplied. She arched an eyebrow. "We'll see you both there *before* midnight, yes?"

Elisa nodded. Angus did the same. "Before midnight."

"In that case," Bria waved, "Ciao."

Zeta grinned up at them both. "I want *all* the details later."

Something tight coiled in Angus's chest at the notion of there being *details*. Something tighter coiled in his groin at the thought of what those details could be.

The zoo. You're taking her to the zoo. To hug a koala. Stop thinking with your dick.

"We'll see you at the Mercure," Elisa said with a gentle laugh.

Angus tried not to beam and failed.

Fuck a duck, he really liked the fact she'd said *we'll*.

CHAPTER SEVEN

They didn't drive to the zoo. They caught a water taxi.

If anyone had told her before she left San Diego that she'd be traveling from one side of Sydney Harbor to the other with the hottest guy she'd ever met in a zippy little boat on her way to hug a koala, she would have told them adventures like that only existed in tourist marketing campaigns.

But that's what they were doing.

They'd walked out of his restaurant, Angus texting as they went, the fingers of his other hand loosely threaded with hers as they crossed the busy promenade, and climbed down into a waiting white motorboat.

The water taxi pilot smiled at them both, nodded when Angus said, "The zoo," and off they went.

Just like that.

Angus sat beside her now in the boat, his arm casually draped over the back of her seat, wind tussling his hair, his incredible eyes hidden behind dark sunglasses.

She'd stopped herself twice leaning into him. It was so enticing, his warmth so there. His grounded strength. All wrapped up in a killer suit. He was taking her to the zoo in a suit.

A soft chuckle vibrated through her, and he smiled. "Not what you were expecting to do today?"

"Not at all." She grinned. "But I'm having an insane amount of fun."

His lips curled more. "Me too."

She could feel his gaze on hers through his sunglasses. Normally she hated anyone looking at her. It always made her feel...exposed. Anxious. Right now, she felt...seen.

Dio, he was lovely.

So do what you want to do. Do it. Do it now.

She leant against him. His smile stretched wider still, and he moved his hand from somewhere near her shoulder to actually resting *on* her shoulder. It felt wonderful. *She* felt wonderful. Alive.

Safe.

"Have you been to Australia before?" he asked.

"This is my first time. We've been to Italy a few times. Mom and Dad's family are still there. But that's it for me. Bria's sky-dived in Spain once. And Zeta spent a summer in Hawaii on a student exchange program when she was sixteen."

"You don't like to travel?"

"No, I mean, yes. I do." She caught her lip with her teeth. "I just..." How did she explain how vulnerable she felt in places she didn't know without sounding pathetic?

"Like being at home?"

There was no judgement in his voice.

"Like being home," she confirmed.

"I get that." He tucked a strand of her hair behind her ear, stopping it from lashing in her eyes. "I'm the same. Home is safe. Known."

"Yes." She nodded. "Known is a good word."

"I'm sorry I grabbed you earlier," he said, his voice almost husky.

She blinked, looking up at him. An expression she couldn't quite decipher pulled at his features.

"I didn't mean to scare you." He turned his face toward the water, but the tension in his body told her it wasn't relaxing him like it was her.

"You didn't scare me," she said.

He let out a shaky sigh. "That's good. I'm glad. My..." He petered off, shook his head, and smiled at her. "I know the manager of the zoo. Catered her daughter's wedding a year ago. Might make cuddling that koala a little easier to organize."

I'm happy to cuddle you.

Once again, what she wanted to say stayed trapped inside her. Instead, she made an impressed sound. "I knew I got engaged to you for a reason."

His laughter slipped through her, like a wave of wonderful warmth. "Oh, I've got *all* the contacts," he chuckled. "If you want, I can introduce you to Henri Stefanovic."

She wasn't au fait with Australian celebrities. Hugh Jackman, Cate Blanchet, Chris Hemsworth, and Rebel Wilson. They were the only ones she was familiar with. Oh, and of course there was the Blackthornes. Still kind of surreal her future brother-in-law was a Blackthorne, although not one of the famous ones.

Was Henri Stefanovic an actor? A musician? She frowned, worried she wasn't as impressed as he might expect. "Who's Henri Stefanovic?"

"My butcher."

She stared at him and burst out laughing.

He grinned, smoothed his arm farther around her shoulder, tucking her into his side some more, and dipped his head to hers. She met him halfway. Her lips still curled in a smile, she kissed him.

It was the most natural, the most *normal* thing to do.

Kiss him. And be kissed by him.

Parting her lips, she touched her tongue to his, feathering her fingers over his jaw as she did so. He let out a low groan, the sound part surrender, part demand, and buried his other hand into the hair at the back of her head.

The action turned her insides to liquid. Her nerve-endings sparked and charged. Her nipples hardened. She deepened the kiss. Or maybe he did. She wasn't sure. Didn't care. The kiss was deeper and Dio, it was incredible and amazing.

His tongue slanted over hers, his fist in her hair relaxing a tiny bit before tightening again. Again, her body reacted, as if she'd suddenly been plunged into concentrated arousal. She moaned into his mouth, pressing her thighs together even as she wanted to part them, wanted to snag his hand—the one not fisted in her hair—and press it to their junction. If she straddled his hips right now, if she buried her own hands into *his* hair, would he—

He pulled away, a raw groan tearing from him as he released her hair. "I'm…I'm sorry."

"For what?" Hell, her heart was racing, her skin was on fire. Her sex…

"I didn't mean… Your hair… I…" He let out a shaky breath. "I shouldn't have been so aggressive."

Her hair? Was he worried about how he'd grabbed her hair? "You weren't. Not at all." Why would he think he was being too rough? Aggressive? "I… I liked it." Heat filled her cheeks and she smiled, ducking her head. "A lot."

His sharp intake of breath lifted her gaze to his, and for a moment a cold finger traced up her spine. She'd said the wrong thing. Oh god, she'd said the wrong—

Angus captured her lips with his. A gentle, but hungry kiss she responded to immediately.

She threaded her fingers into his hair and curled them into a soft fist, a low chuckling groan vibrating through her as he did the same.

He laughed into her mouth, and pulled away again. This time however, his hands stayed buried in her hair as he pressed his forehead to hers. "Have I mention how much I like you?"

She smiled. "Good thing we're engaged then, isn't it?"

He laughed again. Kissed her again. This time, he feathered his hand down the side of her face, along her jaw, the side of her throat… Her breasts grew heavy. Her nipples beaded. She wanted him to touch them, to drag his thumb over their harden points.

Show him.

She curled her fingers around one of his wrists and began to move his hand.

The boat juddered to a stop, the constant thrum of the motor replaced by the water taxi's skipper loudly saying, "Here we go."

Elisa jerked away from Angus. Just as Angus jerked away from her.

"Oh boy," he muttered, clawing a hand—the one she'd been about to put on her breast—through his hair.

"Dio," she whispered, staring at him.

She'd just been about to… In public…

Oh wow. Who *was* she and what had she done with Elisa?

Her heart pounded in her ears. A tight, hungry pulse throbbed in her very core.

No, this *was* her. She was still Elisa. It wasn't a *new* her, it was a different her. This was the 'her' she always wanted to be. Confident, brave. Honest. The Elisa she was, deep down where her anxiety couldn't reach.

She bit her lip. What happened now?

His eyes found hers. "If I asked if you'd like to take a raincheck on the zoo and come back to my place would—"

"Yes." The word fell from her in a gush.

He sucked in a quick breath. "You sure?"

Every fiber in her body thrummed with an urgency, a need she'd never experienced before. "Yes. Very much yes."

The edges of his eyes crinkled as a smile stretched his lips. "I am so glad you're my fiancée."

She laughed. Her insides did a little melted-puddle-of-desire quiver.

He jolted to his feet, steadying himself with a hand on the boat's canopy, and cleared his throat. "Umm…"

The water taxi's skipper paused in the act of setting out the dock lines and shot him a look over his shoulder. "Yeah?"

Angus gave him a sheepish smile. "Change of plans. We need to go back to the Quay. Sorry."

Elisa chewed her lip. Her stomach knotted. Would the guy get angry?

"All good." The skipper retracted the bow line. "Not my dollar."

Two minutes later, the boat was zipping back over the harbor toward Angus's restaurant.

A surreal sensation bubbled in the pit of Elisa's stomach, a nervous eagerness. Was she about to have a one-night stand? A one-day stand? Or was this the beginning of something… more? The butterflies in her stomach fluttered in a frenzied dance at the thought.

She flicked Angus a glance and found him looking at her.

"I'm nervous," she admitted.

Removing his sunglasses, he let out a soft chuckle. "Me too."

"Really?"

He nodded. "What if I don't live up to your expectations? Will you break off our engagement?"

She laughed, and nudged his shoulder with hers. "Break off our engagement? Before you introduce me to Henri Stefanovic?" She shook her head. "Never."

"In that case…" he lowered his head to hers, his breath a delicate tickle on her lips as he feathered his fingertips along her jaw. "You will *never* get to meet Henri. Are you okay with a vegan life from this point onward?"

She laughed again, a heartbeat before he kissed her. As before, the moment his lips touched hers, every fiber in her body sizzled and thrummed with an elemental need. His kisses, his touch, awoke her in ways no other touch or kiss had. A low moan vibrated at the back of her throat, and she tangled her hand in his hair, parting her lips and seeking out his tongue.

He gave it to her. And she gave herself fully to the moment.

All that existed was this kiss. She knew, on a distant level, they were zipping across the water on a boat and all the skipper needed to do was turn his head to see them, but it didn't matter. It should. The thought of being judged, being watched would normally make her chest squeeze tight and her head swim and her stomach knot.

But it didn't.

It didn't matter at all.

She kissed Angus, right there in the boat, for the world to see. She moaned, uncaring who could hear her, when he deepened the kiss, his hand gently cupping her jaw before sliding down to brush over her breast.

She arched her spine, pressing closer to him, aching for him to not just brush her breast, but to cup it, squeeze it.

He pulled away, breath ragged, and stared into her eyes.

"How far away is your home?" she asked.

"Too fucking far away," he answered.

Her core throbbed at the husky hunger in his voice.

CHAPTER EIGHT

He had no fucking car.

Of course, he hadn't thought of that on the water taxi when he'd suggested they skip the zoo and head to his place instead. All he'd been thinking about is how much he wanted to lay Elisa out on his bed, slowly peel her clothes from her body and taste every inch of her skin he exposed.

Now, all but a minute away from docking at the jetty, it dawned on him he had no way of driving to his place.

His home was a twenty-minute drive away—in *good* traffic. Uber it?

The water taxi docked. Elisa's fingers—threaded through his—squeezed a little firmer. He gave her a look. She smiled up at him, and every molecule in his body burned. He needed to be alone with her. He didn't want to be sitting in some stranger's car making small chat. He wanted it to be only him and her. He wanted to chat with her. No one else. He wanted to hear her voice, her laugh. He wanted to kiss her at every red light. At every stop sign. He couldn't do that in a stranger's car. Not when he didn't have any control—

"Done," the skipper declared, killing the boat's engine.

"You actually getting off this time, or are we heading back to the zoo?"

Elisa's fingers closed around his tighter. Her eyes met his.

"We getting off?" he asked, keeping his voice low, calm. "The boat?"

A small smile curled her lips. "Yes."

The husky quality to *her* voice made his dick pulse.

"We're getting off," he confirmed to the skipper, rising to his feet. Elisa followed, and before he knew what he was doing, he lowered his head to hers and brushed a kiss over her smile.

"Yay." The skipper intoned with sardonic joy. "We're getting off." The boat listed to the side a little, and Angus stumbled into her.

She steadied him, her palms on his chest beneath his suit jacket, her fingers brushing his nipples. "I got you."

He gazed into her eyes. "You have no fucking idea."

They disembarked from the water taxi. The skipper smirked at them both, giving Angus a chuckle as he paid for both trips. "Thanks, mate."

Angus dipped his head. "Cheers."

The exchange finished, the skipper tapped his forehead and climbed back into his boat.

Angus's stare fell on Buckley's Chance, his restaurant looming up on the other side of the busy promenade barely a few yards away. He could see the lunch-time diners inside, see his staff busy at work.

Maybe he could go in there and tell everyone to sod off, patrons and staff alike, and make love to Elisa on the—

Elisa threaded her fingers through his and she gave a tiny grin. "Just in case the TV producer is still watching."

He gave her a gentle tug and, without releasing her hand, lowered his head to hers and kissed her. Soft. The kind of kiss that promised a hunger not allowed in public. "Just in case Nora's still around."

She chuckled. Bit her bottom lip. Swung her shoulders side

to side. "Better do it again," she whispered, her grin stretching wider. "Just in case."

He did. But this time, he didn't give a rat's arse they were in public. Didn't give a flying fuck they were on the busy sidewalk of Australia's busiest quay. He hauled her to his body, his hands raking down her back to squeeze her arse. To bring her hips to his.

He plundered her mouth, his blood running hot as her tongue slid over his. He groaned, almost desperate, and forced himself to pull away.

"Dio…" she breathed, swaying a little on her feet as she gazed up at him.

"Dio?" His heart raced. "That's good, right? I didn't…"

She stepped back into his body, pressing her hips to his again as she slid her fingertips up the side of his neck and into the back of his hair. "Very good."

He sucked in a shaky breath. "If I don't get you somewhere private soon, I'm going to—" He ground his teeth. *Fuck you here on the sidewalk* probably wasn't the best thing to say. He didn't want to scare her.

You're scaring yourself, mate. You need to tap the fucking brakes. At least take a breath.

"We're going to your place, right?" She frowned. "That's the plan."

"That's the plan." He gave her a sheepish grimace. "But here's the thing. I forgot I don't have a car. Not here. Kara picked me up from the airport."

And I don't want to share a single minute of being with you with an Uber driver.

Again, probably not a good thing to say aloud. Not without sounding like a jealous, possessive nut job.

"Hey, boss."

He jumped at the sound of Kara's voice. So did Elisa. Turning, he found his sous chef standing behind him.

"Here." She tossed something at him, and he snatched it out of the air without thinking.

Keys. Car keys.

Kara grinned. "The Lexus is yours for the day."

"How…" Elisa began, before stopping, drawing a little closer to his side. She ducked her head, and his heart squeezed at how shy she suddenly looked. He smoothed his arm around her back and drew her closer, wanting to let her know it was okay. Kara was bombastic and an extrovert, but she had the heart of an angel. Just a loud one without a filter.

Kara chuckled. "I saw you both get off the water taxi and as I was wondering if everything was okay, I saw you both… publicly cementing the engagement, shall we call it?"

"Dio…" Elisa's face grew redder, a shy smile curling her lips.

"So then I thought, get a room you two," Kara went on. "And *then* I though how the hell *can* the boss get a room, given he hates Ubers and I picked him up from the airport." She grinned again. "So here I am. Giving you the means to get a room. Aren't I fucking awesome?"

Elisa laughed. "Definitely."

Angus snorted. "And so very humble."

Kara bowed at the waist, waving her arm behind her in a flourish, before straightening. "Absolutely. Now I'm going back to work. Someone has to run the restaurant."

"Oi." He protested, although his heart wasn't in it. All he wanted now was to take Elisa back to his place. To discover everything about her. What made her tick. What made her laugh. What gave her pleasure…

Me. I'll *give her pleasure.*

Heart thumping, he slid her a look.

"Well?" She smiled up at him. "What are we waiting for?"

It took five minutes to reach Kara's Lexus, twenty-six minutes to arrive at his place on Bronte Beach, forty-two seconds to park in front of his garage, and thirty seconds for him and Elisa to climb out of the SUV and walk to his front door.

Or thereabouts.

The whole time, they talked. About everything. About nothing. He'd never felt more connected to someone. It was almost terrifying. And at the same time wonderful. Now, standing at his front door, with Elisa beside him, he was fucking close to trembling. Trembling. Like a teenage boy finally getting to first base. He flicked her a quick glance, his heart racing.

She smiled, that part shy part playful smile he was already completely addicted to. "I like your Christmas wreath," she said, lightly touching the wreath made of gum leaves, wattle and banksia hanging on his front door he'd hung before flying out for LA.

"It's very Christmasy." He pulled his keys from his pocket.

Hurry the fuck, mate.

"Very." She traced her bottom lip with her tongue.

He fumbled with his keys. Missed the lock. Dropped them.

"Sorry," he muttered, bending down to scoop them up.

"It's okay," she murmured when he straightened, her eyes twinkling with that same shy playfulness.

Hell, he wanted to kiss her.

He tried the keyhole again.

Missed. Missed.

In.

"Thank fuck," he ground out under his breath. "Finally."

She laughed.

Pulse pounding in his ears, he looked at her. "Ready?"

For an answer, she pressed her body to his, rose up onto tiptoes, and kissed him. His body went from nervous anticipation to full-blown impatient lust. Kissing her back, his left hand fisting in her shirt at the small of her back, he shoved open his door. They tumbled through it. Laughing even as their mouths and tongues continued to mate, even as their hands worked desperately to remove their clothes.

She started with his suit jacket. He helped her, shucking it off as he fumbled with the tiny buttons of her dress. His feet tangled in his jacket, and he stumbled sideways, just as Elisa snagged his tie. He coughed. Grabbed at the front of her dress. She gasped.

"Shit," he rasped, taking a step back, holding up his hands. "I'm good. We're good. It's all good."

"I almost choked you," she protested.

He laughed, yanking his tie off himself. "I almost tore your dress."

She looked down at the disheveled front of her dress. He did the same. The top button of the V neckline was open, revealing a taunting hint of her incredible cleavage.

His cock throbbed. He sucked in a breath. She lifted her hand, touching the second button with her fingertips. He drew in another breath, this one shaky.

"Don't move," she said softly, calmly, a heartbeat before she popped the second button.

Fuck me…

The raw thought growled through Angus's head as more of the swell of her breasts became visible.

She undid the third button.

He groaned. Shifted his feet. He wanted to rip the rest of her dress open.

"Don't move," she repeated, a playful steel in her instruction.

He tore his stare up to her face, his mouth dry. His cock throbbed harder, so thick it strained against his pants with painful pressure.

She released the fourth button.

The soft fabric of her dress parted completely. He wanted to look at what she'd served to him. Wanted to cup them, squeeze them, taste them. Instead, he held her gaze. Let *her* take control. Didn't move. Just like she told him.

He was a control freak. He knew that. But with Elisa...he didn't want to be. She'd already confided she struggled with anxiety. More than anything, he wanted this moment to be safe and wonderful and everything she wanted it to be.

So, for the first time since escaping the brutal unpredictability of life with his father, he relinquished power.

Stood motionless. Watching her watch him.

Her hands moved again. Another button.

His body tightened. His blood raced.

Something flickered in her eyes, something that made his breath catch, something intimate and intense and...and *trusting*, and then she slowly inched her dress off her shoulders.

The soft fabric slipped down her body.

He followed its path with his eyes, unable not to, noting the delicate mint-green lacy bra and matching undies she wore. He sucked in a shaky breath. Ground his teeth. Forced the base male urge wanting to control him down.

Lifting his stare to her eyes again, he showed her she was in control. Promised her this would be on her terms without a word.

Slowly, with a quick bite of her bottom lip, she stepped out of the puddle of dress at her feet, and walked toward him.

"Hi," she whispered when she stopped directly in front of him. Her smile—part shy, part mischief—curled her lips. Her body's heat seeped into his own.

"Hi," he said back.

"I think I'd like to take your clothes off," she said.

A low chuckle rumbled deep in his chest. "I think *I'd* like you to take my clothes off."

She laughed.

And began.

CHAPTER NINE

Dio, this is crazy.

The thought whispered through Elisa's mind as she gently slid his unbuttoned shirt from his shoulders.

His stomach hitched as he sucked in a short breath, drawing her attention to his abs. A six-pack. Subtle but sublime. In fact, *subtle but sublime* perfectly described what she slowly uncovered.

Underneath the exquisitely cut suit and shirt was a body that spoke of exercise and life. He was fit. Healthy. But not untouchable.

Not at all.

Crazy, but wonderful. And right.

Lifting her eyes back to his face, she trailed her fingertips over his pecs, a little thrill shooting through her at the soft tickle of his chest hair. Her ex—once her college best friend, then her business partner, then her partner in more than just business—had waxed his chest. Touching Angus's chest, touching the soft but course hair there... A hot, damp tension throbbed in her core, and she pressed her thighs together. Who knew she had a chest hair kink?

Holding his gaze, she trailed her fingers down his abs to the waistband of his suit pants. A shaky breath fell from him, and his stomach muscles contracted.

"Ticklish?" she asked, loving the way his body responded to her touch.

"Yes," he replied on a husky chuckle. "And horny."

She unbuckled his belt, popped his pants button, and moved her fingers to the tiny toggle of his fly without breaking eye-contact. When had she ever held someone's gaze for so long?

"So fucking horny," he groaned, his eyelids fluttering almost closed.

"I know the feeling," she whispered, before slowly lowering his zipper.

His pants opened and—mouth dry—she dropped her gaze, taking in what she'd uncovered.

A thick, rigid bar curved upward behind the snug black material of his boxer briefs. A *large* thick, rigid bar.

Oh ragazzo…

For a few seconds, she couldn't move. The reality of the moment, of the direction the day had taken, overwhelmed her. How had this happened? She'd rescued a gorgeous guy's passport from an airport floor five minutes after touching down in the country, and now she was in his home, a heartbeat away from undressing him entirely and having her first ever… What? Fling? One-day stand?

A shiver rippled through her, and she returned her focus to Angus's face.

I feel his heat. I hear his breath. I smell his cologne. I see him…

"Kiss me," she ordered. "Now."

He feathered his fingers along her jaw, cupped her face in both hands and did just that. A soft sensation told her his pants had pooled at his ankles. A harder sensation told her his boxer-brief-trapped erection pressed to her stomach.

Both sensations made her heart quicken and her skin flush. Her nipples pinched into aching tips.

She reached up, even as his lips explored hers, and gently wrapped her fingers around his wrists and moved his hands to her breasts.

A hoarse groan rumbled deep in his chest, and he kneaded the heavy swell of each one through the lace of her bra, his thumbs teasing her puckered nipples with soft strokes.

She moaned in return, raking her nails along his arms and up over his shoulders, arching her back to push her breasts deeper into his hands.

It wasn't enough. The lace…it stopped her experiencing his skin completely on hers.

With another moan, she pulled her lips from the hungry kiss and stepped backward.

He stared at her, nostrils flaring, chest rising and falling with ragged breaths. "Did I—" he began.

She reached behind her back and unfastened her bra, letting it fall to the floor.

"Ahh." He breathed out a chuckle, his stare falling to her fully exposed breasts. "I see."

She'd never exposed herself like this to anyone. It had been lights-out, under the blankets with Scott for their whole sexual relationship. It was easier that way. If she was hidden, her fear he was disappointed with her body and her responses wouldn't gnaw at her too much.

But with Angus…

She *wanted* him to *see* her. Completely.

It was freeing.

It was wonderful.

It was…*empowering*.

She brushed her fingers over her nipples, watching his face. "Touch them. Suck them. Please?"

He stepped out of the crumple of suit pants at his feet, destroyed the distance between them and cupped her right breast, dragging his thumb over its distended nipple before bending down to capture it with his mouth.

Heat. Wet heat. Wet suction.

Her head swam, pleasure rushing through her. She whimpered, fisting her hand in his hair, swaying on her feet and he feasted on her right breast.

Drowning in the raw pleasure, she closed her eyes. "Oh...God..."

He moved his mouth to her left nipple, and she whimpered again, the exquisite pull on her flesh almost too much to bear. "I like that so much," she rasped.

Cupping her right breast with gentle possession, he worshipped her left breast with his mouth and tongue, coaxing noises from her she'd never made before. Sparks of liquid need sank into her belly. The junction of her thighs grew damp and warm. She swayed again, keeping herself anchored by her grip on his hair. "Santa cazzo," she groaned.

He lifted his head from her breast, charting a path of nibbling kisses up to her temple. "I have no bloody clue what you're saying, but I fucking love the way it sounds."

Letting out a throaty laugh, she pulled away from him a little. "It roughly translates as holy fuck."

His nostrils flared. "In that case..."

He returned his mouth to her left breast, this time giving her nipple a tiny bite with his teeth before sucking deeply again.

"Holy *fuck*," she burst out, laughing even as pleasure erupted through her at the rough sensation.

He pulled away again, mischief and hunger in his eyes as he suddenly scooped her up into his arms. "You okay with us taking this to the bedroom?"

Stomach fluttering with impatient delight, she raised her eyebrows. "Depends."

A knot bunched in his jaw, and he became still. "On what?"

"Does your bedroom have the same kind of view?" She indicated toward the sweeping view of beach and ocean beyond the floor to ceiling window of his living room. It was stunning; if they hadn't been so busy making out, she would have found it breathtaking.

Instead, it was Angus that had taken her breath away.

A beautifully decorated artificial Christmas tree stood off to the side of the window, a shiny cooking spatula adorning its top where her family placed a star.

God, she liked this man so much.

He chuckled. "I don't know whether to be happy you approve of my home's location…or insulted you think you may have ability to focus on the view when we're—"

She silenced him by kissing him, laughing against his mouth before tearing her lips from his. "Take me to your bedroom, Angus."

He took her to his bedroom.

"View," he pointed out, carrying her passed the massive bed in the middle of the room to its window.

"View," she confirmed, taking in the equally breathtaking view of the beach and ocean through the expansive window for a second before brushing her fingertips along his jaw, turning his face to hers. "Seen. Amazing. Breathtaking. Now…" She tangled her fingers in the hair at his nape and drew his head to hers.

She loved kissing him.

Loved the way her body awoke when his lips touched hers. Loved the way her blood raced when his tongue touched hers.

Loved the way every doubt and fear and worry she had evaporated.

Could he kiss her forever? If she asked nicely?

With a shaky groan, he lifted his head from hers. "I want to throw you on the bed now and utterly worship your body. That okay?"

A hot beat throbbed in her core. "That's very much okay."

His nostrils flared and, with two steps, he crossed to the side of his bed and dropped her onto it.

Laughing, she adjusted herself on it, smiling up at him as he shook out his shoulders, rolled his neck and cracked his fingers.

She laughed again, and let out a delighted squeal as he snared her ankles and inched her legs apart. "Now, if it's okay with you," he said, pressing one knee to the mattress in the middle of the space he'd made, "I'm going to kiss my way up the inside of your thighs until I get to your…y'know."

Raising her eyebrows, she held his stare. "My y'know?"

He ducked his head, rubbed at the back of his head, and gave her a hungry smile that turned her insides to liquid lust. "Your y'know."

Before she could respond, he smoothed his hands up the inside of her spread legs, his fingers almost brushing the lace of her panties' crotch, and dipped his head to trail his lips and tongue in a line high along her right inner thigh.

A choppy breath escaped her, and she closed her eyes, pressing her head into the soft mattress. Her hands flittered over his hair, her stomach, her breasts, back to his hair.

He nibbled at the sensitive skin where her leg disappeared behind her panties, his tongue flicking wicked little stabs before nipping gently with his teeth.

She spread her legs more, already aching from the need to feel his tongue on her sex. In her sex. "Please…" she moaned.

His fingers moved closer to her wet heat, skimming so close to her folds—hidden behind her panties—a ripple of rapture rushed through her.

"Please…" she repeated. Her clit throbbed. Her very center clenched and contracted. She'd never wanted to be touched, licked, there as much as she did, waiting for Angus to do so.

His hot breath fanned the skin of her left thigh, high, higher, and then…

His tongue swiped the seam of her sex through the lace of her crotch.

"Oh yes!" she groaned, toes curling.

He did it again, harder this time. A shiver claimed her. Her nipples pinched so tight they almost hurt. She cupped her own breasts, kneading them, even as she bit her lip.

"Tell me to take your undies off, Lis," he murmured against the skin of her upper left thigh. "If you don't, I might not be able to stop myself tearing them off you."

"Take my undies off," she instructed on a raspy breath. "And eat me—"

He yanked her panties down over her hips and off her legs with a savage urgency, throwing them aside.

She gasped, the sound turning to a throaty whimper as he hooked his forearms under her thighs and buried his face between her legs.

His tongue—Dio, his incredible, talented tongue—took her to the edge. Over and over. He teased her clit, sucked on it. Licked at her folds, sucking on them as well. He parted them, his tongue entering her wetness with strokes both deep and insistent.

She fisted her hands in his hair, the duvet beneath her, his hair again, her own hair, his hair once more.

She cried out his name, implored him never to stop, told him over and over how fucking good it felt.

Three times she balanced on the precipice. Three times he brought her there with his mouth, only to refuse to let her fall over the edge into sweet release. She reveled in the exquisite torture. His complete mastery of her pleasure pushed it to an intensity she'd never experienced before. She thrummed. Burned. Craved all of it. More of it.

Head swimming, she arched on the bed, planting the sole of her feet on his shoulders. "An...Angus," she panted. "Pl-please...please..."

He lifted his head, eyes smoldering. Until that point, she didn't believe it possible to be more turned on, but the way he looked at her with open, unadulterated desire... Her nipples pinched hard, and a shiver rippled through her. "Please what, Lis?"

She licked her lips, her breath shallow. "Please...make...*let* me come."

His nostril flared. He drew in a deep, slow breath, as if steadying himself, as if something about her request had shaken him. And slowly returned his mouth to her sex.

His tongue found her clit. Licked it. Flicked it. Over and over. And as it did, he gently slipped a finger passed her fold and into her very wetness. Two fingers. Two talented fingers that stroked the sweetest spot within her walls. Her climax exploded through her. She cried out, bucking her hips upward against his worshipping mouth. He lapped at her release, his fingers stroking her higher and higher, until another bone-melting shudder wracked through her, and she cried out again.

Wave after wave of exquisite tension crashed over her. Concentrated pleasure enveloped her. She rode each wave, just as she road Angus's mouth and fingers.

Until, exhausted and spent, she slumped flat onto the bed, limp and sated. "Dio..." she whispered, eyes closed. Or maybe she croaked it. She'd never made so many guttural, carnal noises in her life. "That was incredible."

"That was the entrée." He rained a line of kisses up from her sex, over her belly, her ribs, to the peak of her right breast. "Or as you would call it in the US, the *appetizer*."

He captured her nipple with the seal of his lips, giving it a gentle suck, even as he slipped his fingers from inside her, moving them to her clit.

"Il aperitivo," she breathed, her body instantly responding to his mouth on her breast.

She let herself drown in the pulling sensation. Let herself surrender to the tight, hot pleasure. Stretched out beneath him on the bed, sliding her heels up and down the back of his thighs, one hand tangled in his hair, the other raking at the back of his shoulder.

And once again, the building pleasure inside her grew. With every suckle on her nipple, her sex squeezed tight, impatient for a cock that wasn't there. When he lifted his head, moving his lips from her breast up over the column of her throat, along her jaw, it was all she could do not to flip him onto his back and impale herself on his erection.

"God, I fucking want you," he groaned against her temple, his fingers still teasing her clit. "It's like I've finally found the only food that can nourish me." He nipped her earlobe. "And I just want to gorge myself."

She moaned out a low chuckle, sliding her heel up the back of one of his legs to push it against his butt. She understood exactly what he meant; *she* wanted him inside her more than breath.

Then tell him.

Rolling her hips up to his, she tugged his head from the side of her neck by a fistful of hair.

Eyes burning with open desire and hunger, he frowned. "Did I…was that too much?"

"Do you have a condom?" she asked for an answer, pushing her hips harder to his.

A choppy breath burst from him and, before she could say another word, he scrambled off the bed. "Don't move." He hurried into the en suite bathroom. "Don't move."

"I'm moving," she called back with a grin. "I'm waving my arms in the air like I just don't…"

The jest died on her lips as he strode back into the bedroom.

In the brief moment he'd been in the bathroom, he'd removed his boxer briefs and now stood at the side of the bed as naked as she was.

"Oh boy…" She pushed herself up on her elbows to look

at him.

He was...was...

"Dio, you're perfect."

And huge.

He ducked his head, rubbed at the back of his neck, and shot her a smile. Shy. Not smug or proud. Shy. "Thanks."

God save her, she could fall in love with this man without any problems at all.

He held up a little square packet the color of the ocean. "Would you like me to put it on, or would you?"

She'd never been asked that before. In all her sexual interactions, not once had she'd been given the option. All her sexual partners—of which she'd had a total of three—just did it. Without asking for her involvement. For a split-second, a finger of cold worry snaked up her spine. What if she tried to put it on and got it wrong? What if Angus was disgusted by her lack of finesse, her obvious inexperience, and told her to get out of his bed and—

"I'd like to put it on." She smiled up at him. Screw the worry. Whatever this was between them, her worry and anxiety didn't have a place at the table. Not right now.

He bunched his fist and let out a little *yes* under his breath. And ducked his head again. "Sorry. I just...really was hoping you'd say that."

Heat spreading through her in a delicious wave, she held up her hand.

"Ribbed," he said, giving her the packet. "For your pleasure. So the box tells me."

She smiled, opening it. "And what kind of graphic artist would I be to argue with the box?"

With a shaky laugh, he positioned himself on his knees before her on the bed.

Heart pounding, hands trembling, she looked up at him. "This may not be the right time to say this, but I have to. I don't know what it is about you, but you make me feel safe."

His chest rose as he sucked in a deep breath. "It's the perfect time to say it," he murmured, cupping her jaw in his palm before brushing his lips over hers. "And I'm glad."

He straightened, and—hands trembling even more—she slowly rolled the condom down over his very impressive length.

CHAPTER TEN

S teady. Steady. Just...count to ten.

He held his breath and began counting off, watching Elisa's fingers work the condom down to the root of his dick. Fuck, if he wasn't careful, he'd fucking come already. Her hands being there... Her breath tickling the lower plane of his stomach...

Five...six...seven...

"Finito," she murmured, lifting her gaze to him.

"I know that one," he said, his voice a wobbly rasp. Holy hell, he was so hard, so horny, he could hardly breathe. It was almost borderline painful. "Finished, yes?"

She nodded, even as a playful smile curled her lips. "Yes. The condom is on. But *we're* not even close to finished."

She rose up from the bed, kneeling in front of him, one of her hands encircling his sheathed dick, the other trailing up his chest.

He swallowed, straining for more.

Eight...nine...

Her tongue touched his nipple and he hissed, his cock jerking in her grip.

"Like that?" she asked.

"Do it again," he said.

Nine and one quarter...nine and a half...

She did it again.

Fuck...nine and three quarters...

He couldn't stop the groan tearing from him. A groan that turned to a guttural growl when she sealed her lips around his nipple and sucked.

Jesus fucking Christ, he was going to erupt.

Think of something else. Think of something—

She moved to his other nipple and sucked it, pumping his dick in perfect rhythm with her mouth's suction.

A bone-deep heat began to consume him. His balls throbbed. The soles of his feet began to tingle.

Steps to frying the perfect egg. One. Make sure the egg is room temperature.

Elisa's fingers slid down his cock again, dancing over his balls. Cupping them. Gently kneading them. Her tongue flicked at his nipple. Her teeth nipped at it.

Fuck. Fuck fuck fuck.

Heat cold pressed virgin olive oil in a stainless steel pan over a medium heat.

She slid her mouth from his chest, up to the side of his throat. Her fingers moved from his scrotum, inching closer to his—

"*Crack the egg!*" he burst out.

She pulled away, confused laughter dancing in her eyes. "Is that some kind of Australian sex term?"

He shook his head, placing his palms lightly to her jaw. "The way you make me feel... Your hand on my cock, my balls... Your teeth on my nipples... Fuck, Lis, I'm trying to stop myself from fucking exploding right now. Going through the process of frying an egg in my head."

She stared at him. And then laughed. "Oh my God, you're amazing."

"So are you," he rasped.

"Be inside me?" She feathered his nipples with soft finger-tips, her other hand closing around his dick once more. "Now? I don't care if you explode straight away. I just want you inside—"

He crushed her mouth with his, pressing her back to the bed. Covering her body with his.

She wrapped her thighs around his hips, her hands in his hair once again. His cock nudged her folds, the thin film of latex not even close to dulling the exquisite reality of her pussy kissing his cock.

He pictured the frying egg in the pan. Pictured his spatula...

Lifting his head, he stared down into her face. "Fuck frying an egg," he muttered.

She laughed, and then cried out as he sank his length deep into her heat. He froze. Held his breath. Held her stare. Lost himself to the feel of being surrounded by her tightness. Surrendered to its sublime perfection.

"Oh yes..." she sighed, eyelids fluttered closed. "Oh yes..."

He moved. Rocked his hips backward. Slowly. Forward. Just as slow. Back again. Faster.

Pleasure sheared through him. Consumed him.

He reached back and hooked his hand under one of her thighs, holding her leg higher. Rolled his hips faster, sinking deeper and deeper into her with each thrust.

"Yes..." she moaned, her nails raking at the backs of his shoulders. "Don't stop. Don't stop."

He slammed harder into her. Harder. Faster. Deeper still. She arched beneath him, driving her hips to his, rocking with his movement in perfect harmony.

"Don't stop," she ordered, her walls squeezing around his length. "Keep...keep..."

He dropped his head, buried his face into the side of her neck, and sucked on her skin.

"*Yes!*" she cried out, her sex constricting.

Her orgasm detonated his own. He clung to her leg with one hand, his other punching the duvet beside her head. Rhythm deserted him. His thrusts turned frenzied. Frantic. He came over and over, emptying himself into the condom, reveling in the way her body squeezed him, enveloped him. Responded to him.

Loved the way she fit with him. Moved with him.

Until finally, there was nothing left.

He came to a stop, his heart wild, his head still buried into the side of her neck, his cock still buried in her sex.

"That's one way to fry an egg," she panted, her leg sliding from his hand, her fingers slipping from his shoulders.

His laugh wobbly, he lifted his head and smiled down at her. "Every time I fry an egg now, I'm going to think of this moment and get a hard on."

"Fried eggs for breakfast then?" She raised her eyebrows, a devilish grin on her face.

His chest tightened at the notion of waking up with her in his bed tomorrow morning. He didn't want her *not* be here come sunup. He wanted her to stay with him, in his home, in his bed, and not go back to the Mercure where Owen and her sisters were staying. He sure as *hell* didn't want her to leave Sydney and go to Newcastle tomorrow.

Maybe he could convince Owen to move his engagement party here, to his house? Sure, most of Owen's guests didn't live here. Sure, his brother and mum lived up north in Newcastle as well, but surely Owen would get that Angus didn't want to miss out on a second of being with Elisa? His best mate understood all about love at first sight after—

Love at first sight?

His stomach clenched. It wasn't a thing. Not for someone like him. He had to stop thinking like that. Love led to relationships and relationships were a minefield of hurt.

Sex. This was sex. Amazing, incredible, soul-shattering, life-changing sex.

Just sex.

There's nothing just *about this, and you know it.*

"Fucking fried eggs for every meal, I say," he growled, before capturing her mouth with a kiss. He lifted his head a little. "To hell with the cholesterol."

"To hell with it," she murmured, combing her fingers through his hair and tugging his head back down to hers.

This kiss lasted long, hot moments. He had to force himself to pull away. To withdraw from her tightness. "I'll be back," he whispered.

He disposed of the used condom, grabbed a bottle of Sanpellegrino from the fridge, two glasses from the bar, and headed back to his bedroom.

His heart thumped up into his throat at the sight of her sitting, naked, on the edge of his bed, looking out the window.

She was gorgeous. Funny, sweet, stunning.

Would it be so bad, waking up every morning with her in your bed? In your life?

He cleared his throat. "I brought water. And glasses."

She turned. "Is it okay if I take a shower? I haven't had one since leaving San Diego."

He nodded. "Absolutely. Through that door—" He pointed toward the en suite. "There's clean towels on the shelf. Help yourself to the shampoo."

A smile—shy? After what they'd just shared?—played with her lips. "Thanks. You're welcome to join me." She bit her lip, her cheeks growing a soft pink. "If you like."

He liked very much.

Angus didn't do long showers. Ever. You couldn't grow up in rural Australia—a place ninety-nine percent of the time in drought—without having it ingrained in your psyche showers didn't last longer than four minutes.

When the warm water started to turn cool, Angus realized how long they'd been in the shower for. He didn't give a fuck. He'd spent the shower doing everything he could to Elisa to make her come over and over.

He'd started by sucking on her nipples, teasing her clit with his fingers as she washed her hair. He'd sank two fingers into her heat as she rinsed the shampoo off, scissoring them inside her until she shuddered and collapsed against him under the water. He'd then lowered himself to his knees and shampooed the trim nest of her pubic hair, teasing her clit again as he rinsed the suds away with the jet massage function of the shower head.

She'd cried out in surprised shock as another orgasm shook through her. And before she could recover, he replaced the jetting water on her pussy with his mouth, languidly eating her out as the water streamed over them. Exploring her folds, her tangy sweetness, her very center with his tongue. She'd raked her nails over his scalp when she came that time, and his name had torn from her in a raw way that made his dick so fucking hard it was a wonder he still had blood left in his brain.

Licking his way up from her pussy to her nipples, he teased them with quick flicks of his tongue and then kissed her once more.

The water's cooling temperature judged him, but he really didn't care. All that mattered was giving Elisa pleasure, and taking his own pleasure in doing so.

He should have brought a fucking condom into the bathroom.

The water cut off and he tore his lips from hers, looking down at her.

"Did you want to get—"

Before he could say *out*, she sank to her knees, took his erection in her hand, and lowered her mouth down over its length.

It didn't take long for him to explode.

He threw back his head, trying not to fist the heavy strands of her wet hair too much as a tsunami of concentrated pleasure smashed over him.

His knees wobbled. A rough, shaky laugh fell from him. Followed by a shakier, "Holy fuck, that was good."

She released his spent cock, the soft pop reverberating around the shower walls, and slowly straightened to her feet. "I am so glad you dropped your passport," she said, before stepping from the shower.

He supported himself with one hand against the tiles, watching her wrap her wet body in a dry towel and exit the bathroom. His chest tightened and he closed his eyes, clawing his other hand through his wet hair. Everything had changed. Everything. No way could he let her go. Not to the motel. Not to Newcastle. Not back to the US. He couldn't. He'd fallen for her. On every possible level. Completely. Utterly. Irreversibly.

He wanted her to stay tonight. He wanted her to stay for Christmas. He wanted her to stay forever. Opening his eyes, he stared blankly at the open bathroom door.

Fuck, what the hell did he do now?

CHAPTER ELEVEN

Sitting on the padded bench seat positioned next to the bedroom's floor-to-ceiling window, Elisa looked at the emoji she'd just typed into her phone, licked at her dry lips, and then hit Send.

"Here we go," she whispered as the text shot off to her sisters.

She'd lost track of how long she and Angus had spent in his bed, his shower, his bed again. After their last epic bout of amazing sex, they'd chatted a little about getting something to eat. "I'm pretty good at cooking," Angus had said with a grin—but somehow, neither of them had actually made it out of his bed.

It wasn't until Elisa had woken and noticed the dusk sky outside that she realized they'd both fallen asleep. She'd carefully extracted herself from his arms, resisted the insanely compelling urge to kiss him awake—and not necessarily on the mouth—and tiptoed out of his room. She'd located her crumpled dress on the floor in the living room, her discarded handbag a little closer to the entry way.

She'd slipped her dress on, sans underwear, dug her phone from her bag and, making sure her phone was on mute, headed back to the bedroom. The view from Angus's living room was just as stunning as the view from his bedroom, but the problem with the living room was he wasn't in it.

Being with him, whether he was asleep or awake, was...soothing.

She'd curled on the bench seat next to his bedroom window, woke up her phone, and read all the texts from her sisters she'd missed.

Basically a list of curious face emojis from Zeta, and a koala with a question mark from Bria, and finally one from Bria received only ten minutes ago that simply said **Safety Check Time.**

When one of them texted **Safety Check Time**, the sisters receiving the text would answer with an emoji specific to each sister that let the others know they were okay.

The emoji she'd sent—the artist palette—was her secret code everything was, in fact, okay.

Within a few seconds of sending the artist palette, her phone vibrated with an incoming message.

Zeta: About time you sent us the safe emoji! It's 8pm!!! I'm going to guess you're no longer at the zoo? Where are you? In bed? In Angus's bed? Tell me you're in Angus's bed. Was it good? Tell me it was good. It was good, wasn't it. Reeeeeally good.

A warm pressure wrapped around Elisa's chest, and she smiled. Very Zeta: kiss and tell was her motto. No, kiss and shout loudly was more like it. She hovered her thumb over her phone's screen, her stomach fluttering.

Life-changing. she typed. **I think**

She stopped. What did she think? That she was already in love? Impossible.

Not really. Aren't we here in Australia because Bria fell in love almost straight away?

But Bria was Bria. Bria was fearless. Brave. *She* wasn't Bria. She was—

Her phone vibrated with a new message. This one from Bria herself.

Bria: We need more than the emoji, Lis. You don't have to tell us all the details – yet – but at least tell us you're enjoying yourself. And that we'll see you at the motel tonight.

Elisa deleted **I think** and **Life-changing.** Swallowing, she glanced over her shoulder. At the sight of Angus, sprawled naked on his bed, sound asleep and snoring softly, that wonderful warm pressure wrapped around her again.

I'm very much enjoying myself. she typed. **And you might see me at the motel. Or you might not.**

Adding a winking emoji, she hit Send, switched her phone to Do Not Disturb, and placed it facedown on the bench beside her. Bria's and Zeta's heads were going to explode.

She turned back to the view beyond the window. Angus had told her at some point through the day the glass had a privacy film on it. You could see out, but no one could see in. She liked the idea. Liked that she would watch the world without the world watching her.

What would Angus think if she asked him to make love to her right here on the bench? Her hands pressed to the glass, supporting her as he took her from behind…

"Dio, he's made me insatiable," she muttered, shaking her head.

"If you're talking about me," a low, husky rumble came from the bed, "I'm making no apologies."

Her stomach burst into butterflies. Horny, excited butterflies. She turned to him, tucking her knees under her chin, and gave him a grin. "I was. And you have."

He studied her, lying on his side, head rested in one hand. "I like waking up with you in my bedroom." A slow smile spread his lips. "Even better would be waking up with you in my bed."

The implication behind the declaration whipped the

butterflies into a frenzy. She looked at him. Straightened from the bench and slipped her dress from her shoulders. His swift intake of breath sent wicked licks of delight through her.

She lifted an eyebrow, feathered her fingertips over her nipples—already rock hard and aching for his attention—and turned her back to him, placing her palms on the window and pushing her butt back toward him a little. She cast him a look over her shoulder. And burst out laughing as he scrambled off the bed, arms and legs thrashing with the tangle of sheet.

He crossed the tiny distance between them in a heartbeat. Pressed his body to hers, his erection nestling between the cheeks of her backside, his stomach to the small of her back. He kissed the base of her neck, smoothing his hands over her ribcage to cup and squeeze her breasts. She moaned her appreciation, wriggling her butt closer to his hard length.

"Here?" he murmured against her skin, his fingers plucking at her nipples. "Like this?"

"Yes," she whispered. "Here. Like this."

He palmed her breasts, his mouth exploring the back of her neck.

For long, languid moments, he worshipped her breasts with his hands, and the back and sides of her neck with his mouth. Her core turned to liquid need. She kept her hands pressed to the glass, trembling with hungry desire.

When he slowly began working his lips down along her spine, she knew exactly where he was heading.

When his lips and tongue touched her damp folds…

He made her come with his mouth. She stood, legs spread, palms on the window, staring blankly at the view beyond, pleasure fogging her vision, her mind, as he brought her to an almost savage orgasm.

She slumped forward, pressing her forehead to the glass as his lips and tongue left her sex. Took long slow breaths.

Bria and Zeta were just going to have to accept she wouldn't be joining them at the Mercure tonight. She wasn't walking away from this. Not at the moment. Maybe tomorrow? Maybe after she and Angus exhausted themselves, gorged themselves on each other —as he'd put earlier—maybe then she'd be ready to walk away.

Maybe not even then.

The soft whisper—hers but not the *her* she was used to— made her heart thump harder.

What was she thinking?

If Bria can…

Pushing from the window, she bit her lip, the knot still twisting in her stomach, and turned around.

Angus entered the bedroom from the en suite, naked, hard, and erect, a condom packet in his hand.

She met him at the base of the bed, plucked the condom packet from his fingers, and—holding his gaze—pushed him onto his back onto the bed.

He didn't resist. Allowed her to take control. Completely.

She climbed onto him, straddling his thighs.

They didn't speak.

She opened the packet and sheathed him in the slick latex. He drew in a choppy breath as she did so, his jaw bunching as he watched her.

Tossing her hair over her shoulder, she raised up onto her knees, aligned her sex to the jutting tip of his cock, and slowly, slowly impaled herself on his thick, hard length.

All the way.

"All the way," she murmured, losing herself in the pleasure on his face.

"All the way," he echoed, his hands coming to her hips.

She controlled their movements. Rolling her hips, riding his length. She splayed her hands on his chest, still holding his gaze. She wanted to see his eyes when he came. When they came together.

His fingers dug into her flesh, the pressure adding to her

own rising pleasure. He stretched her, to an almost painful limit, and that too increased her pleasure.

She rode him, her breasts swinging gently with her movement, his fingers gripping her hips tighter. He drove up into her, his thrusts in perfect sync with her rhythm, each stroke pushing her closer and closer to another bone-melting release.

"You are perfect," he moaned, eyes half shuttered, breath ragged. "Fucking perfect."

The declaration pushed her over the edge. Or maybe it was his powerful strokes, stimulating her clit, filling her. She came, the quake starting deep in her core, radiating out. Consuming her. Possessing her.

She cried out, her muscles contracting, squeezing him.

"Fuck." The exclamation tore from him, and his thrust grew wild, his seed filling the condom.

They rode out their climaxes together, Elisa slumping with spent exhaustion on Angus's chest for a few moments before letting out a soft squeal as he rolled her onto her back. He looked down at her, his shaggy hair hanging around his face, his eyes shadowed in the deepening dusk.

"Elisa…" he whispered, her name barely a breath.

She waited, her heart pounding into her throat.

Stay with me. Say it. Say, stay with me. Forever.

He lowered his head, kissed her, a gentle brush of his lips on hers, and then withdrew from her body, climbed off the bed, and disappeared into the bathroom.

She closed her eyes and let out her own breath.

"Stay."

His deep voice snapped her eyes open, and she pushed herself up onto her elbows.

He stood in the en suite's doorway, one shoulder leaning against the doorframe, the light spilling from the bathroom turning him in a silhouette.

"Stay," he repeated. "With me. Tonight."

She swallowed.

"Please?"

A smile pulled her lips as a wave of warm joy rolled through her. "I thought you'd never ask."

———✦———

Buttoning up the loose cotton shirt Angus had given her just before leaving the bedroom to go make them some supper—right after they'd made love, again—Elisa walked into the living room. "My god, that smells good."

He'd also given her a clean pair of his boxer briefs and she'd put them on after having another, quicker, shower. She found the empty bulge in the front of the crotch particularly funny and found herself patting it more than once since pulling them up over her hips, grinning every time. She'd never worn men's underwear before. Who knew they were not only comfortable, but also comical?

The second the delicious aroma of whatever he was cooking slipped into her nose, she forgot all the fun of his briefs. Her mouth instantly flooded with saliva, her stomach growling.

Not surprising. She hadn't eaten anything since the omelet she'd had at his restaurant how many hours ago?

"Chilli prawn larb lettuce cups," he answered from the kitchen, flicking her a quick look over his shoulder as he expertly handled a large wok on the burner. "Finger-food with a little bit of a kick. One of my signature dishes."

"It smells divine." She made her way through the open living room toward the kitchen, combing her fingers through her hair. She hadn't paid any attention to the kitchen on first arriving, but wow. It was clearly a chef's kitchen. Stainless steel, expansive granite countertops, with preparation space to spare.

She was jealous.

"Divine?" He chuckled. At some point while she'd been showering, he'd pulled on a pair of faded-blue jeans and an equally faded-chambray shirt, which he hadn't bothered tucking in. "Well, I guess I *am* a…" He shot her another quick look. "Wait for it… *God* in the kitchen."

"Good grief," she mocked groaned.

He laughed. "God in the bedroom, then?"

She stopped at the large granite island counter and leant her elbows on it. "I'll need more intensive practical study before reaching a conclusive answer for that one."

He laughed again and turned back to what he was preparing. She loved chilli.

"Prawns." She admired the ease with which he moved. "That's shrimp, yes?"

"Yes. And no. But close enough." He plucked some kind of spice from a small container and sprinkled it into the wok. "Hand me the lime, will you?"

She scanned the counter, spying a fat lime sitting on a wooden cutting board, sliced in half.

"Shrimp have plate-like gills and are mostly found in salt water," he went on, his shoulders moving with fluid grace as he quickly moved the wok back and forth on the burner. "Prawns have branching gills, more claws on their legs and are usually found in fresh water. And they're bigger. And they're sweeter and meatier—in my opinion. Plus, there's the whole Aussie thing with prawns. Next time I cook us prawns, I'll throw them on the barbie for you."

Next time I cook us. Picking up the lime, she smiled, rounding the counter to give it to him. She liked the idea of him cooking for them both again. Often. Every day.

"Here you go." She stopped at his side.

He kissed her. A searing kiss that made her toes curl. "Thank you."

"Anything else I can help with?" Anything else she could do to earn another kiss like that?

"There's a bottle of Pinot Gris in the fridge. The glasses are on the table. Feel free to pour us both a glass if you like?"

She turned to the dining table, noticing it was already set. Two plates, two long-stemmed glasses, a candle—already lit.

"I could get use to this kind of life," she murmured.

"Me too."

She turned back, finding him plating up what looked—and smelled—like the most delicious meal ever.

He lifted his gaze to hers. "Have you ever thought of moving to Australia?"

CHAPTER TWELVE

Her breath caught in her throat.

He cleared *his* throat, and returned his attention to arranging their meals on large, white plates.

"I'll get the wine," she said, her voice husky.

He nodded, his expression enigmatic.

Standing in front of the open refrigerator, she let the chilled air cool her flushed cheeks.

Maybe I should just strip naked and offer myself to him again right this second? When we're having sex, I don't have to think about how much I actually want to have more of...of...this.

She grabbed the bottle of white wine, pressed its icy side to her cheek, and turned to the dining area.

Angus stood at the table, watching her.

Heart thumping fast, she joined him, pouring them both a glass.

He took his, that enigmatic gaze never leaving her.

She caught her lip. Not nervous, just...anticipating... something. But what?

Or wanting something? Something impossible?

"I like this label," she blurted out, drilling her attention onto the wine bottle's simple white and gray label. "The design,

I mean. The graphic design. I've never had the wine before, but I like the label."

God, she was babbling like a fool.

"It's a small winery in the Hunter Valley," Angus said. "Owen's cousin owns it."

"The rock star?" Elisa lifted her glass to her lips, realized she hadn't eaten anything for a long time and abruptly lowered it. Dio, why was she suddenly so nervous? It was ridiculous. "Or the cellist?"

"The rock star." He pulled out the chair beside her hip. "Ready to eat? Before we do something crazy like drink on an empty stomach?"

A wobbly laugh fell from her. "I was just thinking that." She lowered herself into the chair. She couldn't remember the last time someone not a waiter had held a chair for her.

Her stomach rumbled and she pressed her palms to it. She was hungry. *And* nervous. Hungry she understood. Nervous? Not at all.

Yes, you do. Because you think what's happening between you both could be more and you think he *does as well and you're too scared to make the first move and* too scared of what might happen if you do, let alone if you don't.

"What makes a signature dish?" she asked as he moved to his seat on the other side of the table. *Stop stressing out. Enjoy the moment.*

"Well, all the food magazines and blogs and food critics will tell you it's a recipe unique to a chef or restaurant. In a blind test, a well-informed gastronome can identify the chef from taste alone. But to me..." He rested his fingers on the stem of his glass, pivoting it slowly on the spot. "It has a soul."

She frowned.

"Okay, that sounds wanky, I'll give you." He chuckled. "Cooking has always been a...an escape for me."

Something about the way he'd said the word *escape* made Elisa think that wasn't the word he was originally going to use.

"But this meal…" He looked down at his own plate. "This one I made at a particular time in my life when I needed an anchor. I spent almost half a day in Owen's parents' kitchen experimenting with flavors, textures." A stillness fell over him.

Owen's parent's kitchen? Not his own parents? Now she thought about it, she had no clue about his family apart from the fact he had a half sister he adored.

And an anchor? A person only needed an anchor when their life was chaos. She'd needed an anchor in her life once. Her sisters and mom and dad had been hers. Owen and his family had been Angus's. Why not his own family?

She nibbled on the inside of her lip. He was still a closed book. A closed book she felt comfortable with, but a closed book all the same. One she wanted to open.

He lifted his head, his smile once again relaxed. "Owen was the very first person to try it. He loved it. Ate all of it. Didn't share a single bite with anyone. And that's how we all discovered he was allergic to shellfish."

Elisa's eyebrows shot up. "Oh boy."

Mischief twinkled in his eyes. "Oh boy, indeed. His face blew up like a balloon. An itchy, red balloon. It was hilarious."

"Hilarious?"

"Well, Owen and I thought it was hilarious. Mind you, we *were* only fifteen at the time. Idiotic teenage boys. The doctors and nurses in the emergency department didn't think it was hilarious. Nor did his mum and dad. His brother and sister…*they* thought it was funny. His sister made us all T-shirts for Christmas that year with Owen's bloated face printed on the front. I've still got mine. Was contemplating wearing it to the engagement party."

She blinked. "I thought I understood Australian humor by now, but…" She shook her head, chuckling. "So this is your signature dish? The most popular at your restaurant?"

He turned his wineglass again, his smile wide even as a

pensive stillness fell over him again. "I've never put it on the menu rotation at Buckley's Chance. It's too...personal."

She swallowed, the weight of his declaration making her heart thump faster. It was an important dish to him, very important by the sounds of it. Too important to share with the general public, but he'd made it for her.

"In that case," she picked up her knife and fork, and began dissecting one of the plump shrimp nestled in the crisp lettuce leaf amongst the chopped peanuts, green beans, mint and coriander, and red onions. God, it smelt good, "thank you. For making it for me."

He dipped his head in a single nod. "Bon apetit."

Holding his gaze, she took her first bite.

Oh. My. God!

"Dio," she groaned, hand covering her full mouth. "This is *amazing*."

It was. She'd never eaten anything so good. Ever.

He shrugged, turning his wineglass again. "It's all right."

Swallowing, she shot her eyebrows up.

He laughed. "Okay, it's bloody delicious."

"That's an understatement." She ate more. Closed her eyes. Groaned. Succumbed to the ambrosial moment. "So good."

"I should let you know, watching you enjoy my food is making me horny."

Laughing, she opened her eyes and licked her lips. "Is this foreplay? Is that what this is?"

His nostrils flared. "Something like that."

The intensity in his eyes, the huskiness in his voice sent a tight, warm pulse through her core.

Something like that indeed.

He cleared his throat, and picked up his own knife and fork. "So, graphic design. How did that come about?"

A little butterfly tested her wings in her stomach. She loved talking about graphic design. How she became a graphic designer however… "It started in high school. I studied art but I wasn't really into the traditional stuff."

Angus raised a curious eyebrow, drawing a laugh from her. "Paint and pencils and charcoal. That kind of art. Mom and Dad bought me a Wacom when I was sixteen—they're both academics, so they've always encouraged anything Bria, Zeta and I were interested in."

"Wacom?"

"A drawing tablet that uses a stylus."

"They existed before iPads?"

She laughed again. "They existed before iPads. The second I got it I was lost. It was amazing. The artworks I created with that tablet…" She smiled. "Teenage me was very impressed with myself back then."

Angus caught her gaze, smiling. "Adult Angus is very impressed with you now."

The butterfly in her stomach fluttered again, though this time with happiness, and she lowered her gaze to her plate, piercing more food with her fork. "I discovered with my Wacom that I wasn't into drawing people or landscapes," she continued, letting the memories of school flood her mind. "I liked design. I was good at design. I *am* good at design. Very good."

Being so open about her talent wasn't normal, but with Angus she felt okay doing so. It was nice.

"I got accepted into The School of Art and Design at SDSU after high school, and won a partial scholarship, in part due to a fictitious print campaign I created selling Italy as the perfect tourist destination…using its least attractive elements."

"That's one way of doing it." Angus laughed, sitting back in his chair. "Did you start *De Lucreative Designs* straight after uni, or did you work for someone else for a while?"

He'd remembered the name of her design studio. Her heart clenched. She'd mentioned it only once back in his restaurant, and yet, he'd remembered. It was wonderful.

If only the answer to his question was wonderful as well.

An ache settled in her chest. A familiar one. The one that had made itself at home from the second she'd discovered what Scott had done.

"Yes. And no." She let her lips curl in a small smile. This was going to hurt. It always did when she thought about it, but *talking* about it?

Then stop. Don't talk about it.

"I had a rival in art school," she said instead. "Scott O'Dea. He was insanely talented."

Angus rotated his wineglass around in a 360 on the spot, watching her. "Should I be jealous? I want to be jealous. Can I be jealous?"

She let out a wry chuckle, even as her chest tightened. *I can hear the beach. I can taste my meal. I can smell the candle. I can touch the table. I can see Angus…* "He had this annoying habit of coming up behind me in class and watching what I was doing over my shoulder. I hate being watched. I'd freeze up every time he did it, and he knew it."

Still do.

Angus turned his wineglass again. And again. He hadn't taken a single sip of its contents since she'd poured it. Not once. Just…played with the stem. "Ah, maybe not jealous. He sounds like a bit of a wanker."

She bit back her wry grunt. She knew that word, thanks to Owen and his Australian vocabulary lessons. *Wanker* was entirely accurate.

"One day, I snapped," she said, studying her plate. "Told him to stop it. Told him to stick his nose in someone else's artwork. He apologized. Profusely. And before I knew it, we were somehow friends."

She still couldn't remember when the line between rival and friends got blurred, but somewhere before the first year of art school finished, she and Scott were always together. Partnered projects? Elisa and Scott. Group projects? They were always in a group together. He was adamant about it.

She should have seen the red flags, but she hadn't. She'd trusted him.

Angus shifted on his seat. "Just friends?"

She bit the inside of her lip, a tightness crawling over her scalp. What was she doing? Starting so far back? She could have just told Angus she started her own studio after working with someone and left it at that. Why was she talking about Scott?

Maybe she should change the subject? Whenever the topic of Scott came up—thankfully less and less these days—Elisa would change the subject. Thinking about Scott was a sure-fire way of stirring up her anxiety; like poking a wasp nest with a stick and being surprised when you got stung.

Or if she didn't change the subject, she'd press fast-forward on the whole ugly, sordid affair and skip straight to the *And I decided to open my studio* part.

So why wasn't she now?

Because she wanted Angus to know. So he would understand…her.

No one learns anything from a closed book.

"Friends." Her voice dropped an octave.

Angus shifted in his seat again.

She moved her dinner around on her plate. She should be eating it. It was too good to let get cold. "He was very open about his admiration for my work," she said, trying to force herself to sound relaxed. She collected some of her meal onto her fork and put it in her mouth. Chewed. Swallowed. Damn Scott for ruining this. Damn him.

Is he ruining it, or are you?

"Back then I was always doubting it," she clarified. "Always insecure. But he kept praising me. All the time. By the end of our first year, we were inseparable. Even when working on our separate designs we worked together, bouncing feedback off each other, and sharing ideas." Sharing ideas. Ha. It had taken her way too long to realise the *sharing* hadn't gone both ways. Way too long. "When graduation time came around, Scott and I were talking about starting a graphic design studio together. We were *more* than just friends by then, and it seemed to make sense to do so."

What an idiot she'd been.

"More than just friends." Angus let out a low laugh. "See, *now* I'm jealous again."

She looked at him. As crazy as it was, she felt like he was trying to diffuse her tension. Or was she just hoping that was the case?

"Trust me, there's no need to be jealous."

He dipped his head in a single nod, not a hint of judgement on his face. "Okay. I won't be."

She smiled.

He smiled back. "And you did? Start a business together?"

Let's make it a partnership, Scott's whispered words snaked through her head now. Uttered when they'd first had sex. When he'd first entered her. *In bed and in business.*

She shuddered at the memory. The world seemed to be darkening a little, losing its color. And Dio, her hands were shaking. Her stomach rolled. Was it anxiety? Or self-disgust?

I can hear the beach. I can feel the table. I can see Angus...

"We did," she said. "Before I think either of us were ready, we did." She hovered the prongs of her fork over her meal. It was so delicious, so special, and she was ruining it all. Which was so typical of her. Didn't she just ruin everything? Isn't that what she did? Ruin moments and make people agitated and wish she wasn't—

"Lis?"

She lifted her head at Angus's gentle voice. He studied her, worry in his eyes. "It's okay. You don't have to."

"I'm okay."

"Sure?"

She nodded. She wasn't, but she also was. She had to be. "Six months after we opened *O'Dea/De Luca Studio*, we were so busy we were turning new clients away. It was crazy. I was working twenty-four seven, and I loved it. But then our new client numbers began to fall." Sweat formed on her brow. Her upper lip. The room seemed to go a little fuzzy.

I see Angus. I hear the waves outside. I smell my meal...

"And as weeks went past, we began to lose *existing* clients. Jobs that were already booked were cancelled. I was heartbroken, and Scott was abnormally distant. He was rarely in the studio, and I assumed he was out trying to land new clients. I was scared but I didn't want to make him more upset. So I worked harder with the clients we had. Desperate to keep them. To make *him* happy. And then he stopped coming into the studio completely. And he stopped returning my messages."

Her heart thudded.

Stop talking. Stop. You're ruining the moment. Angus doesn't want to hear any of this. Just shut up. Shut up.

She swallowed. Licked her lips. Stared at her plate. "It turned out *we* hadn't lost our clients. I had." She let out a shaky breath, anxious nausea twisting her insides until they knotted in her chest. "He still had clients. *Our* clients. All our clients. He'd stolen them. Claimed all the credit for my work and took them." Her eyes tingled and she squeezed them shut, swallowing the hard lump in her throat. She was going to be sick, and that was wrong. It would offend Angus so much. After the meal he'd made for her... "He told them I wasn't able to handle the pressure, mentally, and took them to the new studio he'd set up without me knowing. *His* studio. He'd been lying to me for months."

"Fucking prick," Angus's low whisper made her blink. Or was it the stupid hot tears prickling the backs of her eyes?

Every emotion she'd felt at that moment rushed back into her heart in an instant. The waves of anger and pain and confusion almost too much to bear, still every bit as unexpected and raw as the first time.

Scott had betrayed her. She'd confronted him. He'd abused her. Said she was mentally unbalanced, too emotionally fragile for him to deal with. That her anxiety suffocated him. Strangled him. Blamed her for the fall in their sales. Said her insecurity only held him back.

She'd cried for days. Her mental state couldn't handle it. She'd never felt so alone, so abandoned. So empty. Even with Bria and Zeta to comfort her, even with her parents ready to unleash legal hell on him, she'd felt…discarded.

"It took me a long time to find my confidence again," she said, her voice somehow devoid of the anger and grief she'd kept locked away since Scott had destroyed her. "But tentative steps with small clients led to bigger jobs. And more clients. And all on my own, I created *De Lucreative Designs*. And now it's one of the most in-demand graphic design studios in Downtown San Diego. And occasionally, I land a client who's come from Scott's studio, dissatisfied with the work being done there. And when those clients come my way, I have a little party for one in my soul. Which is probably very petty, but that's the way it is."

She nodded, staring at her plate. Staring at her meal. The most amazing meal she'd ever had. And she'd blurted out all her shit instead of eating it.

"And I figured you should probably know that about me," she finished, with a self-deprecating shrug.

"He's a fucking prick."

She lifted her head and locked stares with Angus, her heart clenching when he offered her kind smile.

"A massive fucking prick."

She straightened her shoulders and shook her head, letting out a choppy little laugh.

God, she really had ruined supper. "So *that's* how I started my own business." She gave him a sheepish grin, aching to turn back the clock to stop herself blurting this out. She'd wanted him to understand who she was. No doubt, all she'd done was scare him away. "Bet you wish you hadn't asked, right?"

He stood and rounded the table, crouching down beside her chair. "I wish I could take all the pain he gave you away," he murmured, brushing his knuckle along her cheek. "But all I can do right now is make you feel loved." He cupped her jaw and leant forward, his lips tender and gentle on hers.

She smiled, his words, his soft kiss sweeping a warm calm through her. Taking away the knot in his stomach and the dark whispers in her mind.

He pulled back, tucking a strand of her hair behind her ear, his smile playful. "And well-fed," he finished with a wink.

She laughed.

Loved. That was exactly how he made her feel. Loved. And while it wasn't possible to fall in love so quickly, Angus made her feel like it was. And as impossible as it was, she loved him for it.

She'd cross whatever looming bridge that unexpected emotion caused later.

For now, she was happy to feel loved.

And, Dio, she was more than happy for him to make her feel well-fed.

CHAPTER THIRTEEN

They finished eating, their conversation relaxed and light. A deep, dark anger seethed inside Angus the whole time. He had to keep unclenching his fist. The betrayal Elisa had experienced... If he ever met her ex...

No. Stop. That was Dad's way. Not yours.

Still...

"Dessert?" he asked. "I make a mean bowl of ice cream."

Elisa's eyebrows raised. "You make ice cream?"

"Well, by *make* I mean I'm very good at taking the lid of the tub I have in the freezer and scooping it into a bowl."

She laughed.

He grinned. "I suck at desserts. I'd offer to call Heather, my pâtissier, and have her come make us one of her famous deconstructed passionfruit pavlovas, but she's rostered on tonight and well, I don't want to share you with anyone, if that's okay?"

Her cheeks blushed with a delicious faint pink tinge. "I don't want to share you with anyone either."

Fuck, he was totally in love with this woman.

He rotated his wineglass. If she'd noticed he hadn't drunk any of the pinot gris in it, she hadn't commented. In fact, she'd only had a few sips of her own.

He didn't drink alcohol. Ever. But he enjoyed the way wine moved in a glass. The beauty of the glass itself. The delicate scent of a good wine on the air, accompanying good food.

Good company.

His father had drunk whiskey. His mother, vodka. Neither ever drank wine of any sort.

"Ice cream then?" he asked.

She nodded.

He straightened from the table, collected their dirty dishes and cutlery, and walked into the kitchen. He didn't need to look to know she followed him.

Depositing the plates, knives, and forks into the sink, he gave her a smile. "Can I get you something else to drink? Water? Juice?"

She shook her head, leaning her elbows on the counter, watching him.

"You have a question?" He snagged a glass from the cupboard and poured himself a water from the tap. "I can see it in your face."

"I thought all chefs were control freak bastards."

He chuckled. "Oh, I *am* a control freak. In the kitchen. At the restaurant."

"But not a bastard."

"Not a bastard. I hope." He let out a soft snort. "My father was a bastard. A bastard with fast fists and swift kicks."

Her soft intake of breath made his own stick in his throat. "I'm sorry," she whispered.

He shook his head, rinsing the plates. "Don't be. Nothing to do with you. I remind myself when I'm in the kitchen the people working with me love food—preparing it, cooking it— as much as I do. Plus, I had a good family life."

A confused frown pulled at her forehead.

He turned off the tap. "It just wasn't mine. The love in Owen's family was amazing. There's a lotta heart in that family.

In all of them. Owen's heart is bigger than Mars, I think. Your sister has definitely got herself a keeper there."

Elisa studied him. Didn't say a word.

Something tight coiled in his stomach. "You don't think so?"

"Oh no, she's *definitely* got a keeper. Owen is amazing." She smiled. "I was just thinking your heart is bigger than you think."

"Maybe." He let a low chuckle fall from him. For a split-second he'd been prepared to defend Owen, but it was clear Elisa was a fan of his best mate. "I've got a *few* big things, as it turns out."

She groaned around a grin, rolling her eyes. "Your prowess in the kitchen and the bedroom isn't surpassed by your word play prowess."

Gasping with mock indignation, he leant his elbows on the counter opposite her and pinned her with a steady stare. "You mean I'd never be Australia's next poet laureate? Or make it as a TV star? What kind of fiancée are you?"

"The honest kind." Her lips curled, and she leant closer to him. "The kind who would never *ever* let you go on a TV show like that."

"I knew I asked you to marry me for a reason."

It was her turn to gasp, eyes twinkling. "Mi scusi? *I* asked *you*, thank you very much."

"A mutual asking?"

She laughed. "A mutual asking."

"We'll go buy the engagement ring after breakfast tomorrow." He was joking. He really was. And yet the thought of slipping a massive chunk of a diamond on her finger…

"If it's at breakfast time, I'm assuming we're going to Tiffany's?"

"Of course."

"As it should be," she said with melodramatic sternness. "But be warned, I'm going to be very picky."

"Wouldn't want you any other way."

They grinned at each other. It was ridiculous how much he never wanted this to end. Could she feel it? Could she see it in his eyes? Could she see his heart, thumping like a cannon in his throat? Could she hear it?

"You wouldn't?" she asked.

"I want you *every* way, Lis. *All* the time."

She pushed herself from the counter and rounded to where he stood. He turned to face her. Met her gaze. Breathed her in.

Felt her warmth.

Without a word, she rose up onto tiptoe and kissed him.

He smoothed his hands around her waist, pressing them to the small of her back, holding her closer to his lower body.

His blood licked through his veins: hot and fast. His heart thumped harder.

He gave himself to the kiss, to her. Let his lips and tongue tell her everything he couldn't say aloud: not to her, nor to himself. He didn't do relationships, and she hardly knew him. But he never wanted her to go.

Finally, he pulled away. "Stay the night," he said. "Or maybe longer. Just…stay. With me."

She stared up at him, her eyes impossible to read. "Okay."

As simple as that. One word, and everything changed.

He scooped her up in his arms. She let him. Moved with him. As if aware of his every thought. "Ice cream can wait," he declared, his voice a husky growl.

He carried her to the long sofa in the living room and lowered her onto it. Gently removed his clothes from her body. Kissed every inch of her skin he revealed. Her shallow breaths, her swift intakes, her soft whimpers as he did so drove him wild with need and lust, but he didn't rush.

He explored her entire body with his fingers, his lips. He spent long languid moments worshipping her breasts, her throat, the soft skin high on her inner thighs. He nibbled the back of her knees, the inside of her wrists. He charted a path with his lips from her belly button to her nipples, to her temple, to her mouth.

She moaned and writhed on the sofa, sometimes fisting her hands in his hair, sometimes cupping her own breasts, sometimes directing his mouth to where she wanted it the most.

He made her come twice with his fingers and once with his mouth.

And when she begged him to enter her on a shaky, breathless whisper, he rose to his feet to get a condom, so hard it hurt.

"I'll be back," he murmured against her forehead. "Just getting a—"

She caught his fingers with hers and he lifted his head to find her gaze locked on his. "You...you don't have to."

A prickling heat swept over him. His breath caught. He searched her eyes, his body thrumming. "Are you sure?"

"I trust you," she answered. Not whispered. A declaration.

"I trust you," he said, before brushing his lips over hers.

She helped him undress.

And then, holding her gaze, he pressed her back down onto the sofa again, nestling between her thighs, and entered her.

Lost himself to her.

Completely.

Her heat enveloped him, moved over his skin. He stroked into her, the unadulterated, pure sensations of their bodies sliding together heightening a moment already beyond perfect.

"Dio," she moaned, suddenly locking her legs around his hips. "I'm...close. Don't...don't stop..."

He didn't. Adjusting his weight, he thrust deeper and deeper and deeper into her. And when her breath began to hitch, when pleasure etched her face, he reached between their bodies, his fingers finding her clit.

She came. And he came with her.

Spent, their bodies still joined, he looked down at her,

brushing her hair from her temples with shaky fingertips. "I think I'm in love with you."

She grew still.

Shit. Shit shit. What...why had he said that? Why—

Tangling her fingers in his hair, she pulled his head down to hers. "Penso di amarti anch'io," she whispered against his lips.

Breath stuck in his throat, heart hammering, he swallowed. "Penso...?"

The corners of her eyes crinkled with a smile. "I think I love you too."

He let out a wobbly laugh, kissed her, and rested his forehead on hers. "I am so fucking glad I asked you to marry me."

She laughed, her tight heat still gripping his length. He kissed her again. Thoroughly. Deeply. He surrendered to everything she awoke in him. Everything he never thought he wanted or could have. And when he finished kissing her, he carried her to his bed and made love to her again. And after that, finally, got the ice cream. One container, two spoons.

"I love the way you've served this." Playful mischief danced in her eyes as—sitting up in his bed, naked and clearly uncaring—she scooped a spoonful from the tub. "Very...rustic?"

He stuck his own ice-cream laden spoon into his mouth, grinning. "It's an artform."

She closed her lips around her spoon, letting out an appreciative moan. "There's nothing quite like vanilla—"

From living room, Silverchair's 'Tomorrow' started playing faintly.

Angus flung a look at the bedside clock. "Shit. It's one a.m." He clawed a hand through his hair. "That's Owen. I should have called him by now."

He'd promised Owen to have Elisa to the motel by midnight, and even though *he* knew damn well she was spending the night, Owen didn't. All Owen knew was Angus had whisked his future sister-in-law away and hadn't returned her. Or had the courtesy to let Owen—and Elisa's sisters— know why. Owen was going to kill him.

He scrambled from the bed. "Yeah, I'm in deep shit now."

Dismay fell over Elisa's face. "It's one a.m.? Dio! Bria and Zeta are going to *kill* me."

Angus chuckled. "We're both busted. I'll take Owen's call. You get in contact with your sisters. Before they call the police and we start an international incident."

She grinned. "On it."

He hurried out of the room, Silverchair still singing from the living room. God, where was his phone? In his jacket's inside pocket? Where was his jacket? Everything was a blur since touching down in Sydney.

His whole world had been turned upside down.

He'd landed wondering if he had it in him to move to the US for a few years, if he wanted to leave his restaurant here for a new one over there, and now he was legitimately planning on taking Elisa to Tiffany's in the morning and—

He spied his crumpled jacket on the floor, damn near sprinted over to it—jogging buck-naked was not comfortable. At least his balls weren't enjoying themselves—and snatched it up. Dug his phone out, connected the call and slammed it to his ear. "I'm here, mate," he almost shouted.

"Where the hell is Elisa?" Owen growled.

"With me." Angus's gut clenched. Yeah, his best mate wasn't happy. "Safe. We've been…" He petered off. How the hell did he tell Owen what they'd spent the last…what? fifteen hours doing?

"The fact you can't finish that sentence kinda pisses me off a little, mate," Owen stated.

"It's not what you think." He raked his hand through his hair again, his blank stare jumping around the floor at his feet. "It's…"

Once again, he trailed off.

Behind him, Elisa's voice wafted softly from the bedroom. She no doubt was talking to her sisters. How was she faring? Better than him, he hoped.

"It's what?" There wasn't a hint of Owen's normal, relaxed good humor in his voice. "You've got thirty-six seconds to answer, Daniels, before I get in the car and drive to your place. Thirty-five. You know me and numbers, mate. I'm not mucking about."

Angus swallowed. *It's what?*, Owen had asked. Could he answer his best mate? Honestly?

What *was* this thing between him and Elisa? What was this thing he felt for her, deep in his…his…his soul? Honestly, what *was* it?

Love.

He was certain it was love.

It sure as hell was more than just sex. He'd walk through fire to make Elisa happy. The thought of not seeing her smile, hearing her laugh, holding her, talking to her, existing with her every day pressed a damn-near suffocating weight on his chest. So yeah, he was pretty fucking certain love was exactly what it was.

Thinking it though, was one thing. Saying it aloud to someone else?

"Thirty-one…" Owen said flatly.

"Love," Angus declared. "It's love. I've fallen in love with her. She's incredible. I want to wrap her up and protect her from the world and care for her and—"

"She's not one of your sister's rescue dogs, Angus," Owen cut him off. "She's a person. And she's gone through some shit. And I know *you* have also gone through some shit, mate. More than anyone else in your life, I know what you've gone through. *And* I know you've come out the other side of that shit with some baggage. You've told me more than once you don't do relationships. No-strings fucking; that's what you do. That's what you've told me. And I'm okay with that, but not when it comes to Elisa. She's fragile. Amazing, and sweet and gentle, but fragile. And as much as I love you, mate, as much as I love my own brother, I'm not going to—"

"Owen," Angus said, eyes closed. Hell, how was he even breathing with the size of the lump in his throat? "Stop. Listen. Please?"

Owen fell silent.

Angus swallowed at the lump again.

"I…" He licked his dry lips. Jesus, he wished he had a glass of water right now. "I know it makes no sense, but I love her. If it's *not* love, it's this…" he waved his hand around in front of his chest, curled his fingers on the air, as if trying to grip the impossible, "…this big…big *thing* that makes every breath worthwhile. This *massive* thing that makes everything alive. Makes it all make sense. I can't *not* see her in my life. When I think of tomorrow, the next day, the next month, fuck, the next decade, I see her there. With me. Being loved by me."

Owen didn't say a thing.

"And I get it," Angus went on, staring at the floor. If he gripped his phone any harder his knuckles would pop. "It's not possible, but it *is*. And you of all people shouldn't be telling me it isn't. That I'm not. I *am*. So you can just accept I'm legit, that I love her and—"

"Angus," Owen said.

"Just trust me. Trust me that I feel what I feel, and trust me that I will treat her the way she is meant to be treated and never—"

"Angus," Owen cut over him, a chuckle in his voice. "Will you shut the fuck up for a second."

Angus stopped. Swallowed.

"*I* get it," Owen said. "I do. I get it. Falling in love when you least expect it…it throws everything into chaos. I know that first hand. But you? Your whole life you've actively *fought* against falling in love, so I bet right now that control-freak mind of yours is completely in a spin." He paused. "I hear everything you're saying, and I get it. I'm *not* saying you can't have anything to do with Elisa. And I'm not saying you don't feel how you feel. I don't have the right to do that. Or the inclination."

A heavy pressure wrapped around Angus's chest. "So what are you saying?"

"I'm saying if you hurt her, if you make her cry, or abandon her, I won't protect you from her sisters. In fact, I'll drive them to your place straight away, and screw the speed limit."

Angus sucked in a slow breath. "So you believe me?"

"I do. But a word of warning, mate," Owen said, his tone serious. "I know your baggage. And I won't hold back on calling you on it if I think I need to. Understand?"

"Wouldn't have it any other way, Blackthorne."

"Good. Don't forget."

"I won't." Smiling, Angus lifted his gaze from the floor. And froze.

Elisa stood, watching him, only a few feet away, her expression unreadable.

He stared at her.

"I'm pretty certain Bria and Zeta have been handing Elisa a new one while we've been talking," Owen said. "So I'm going to let you go. But right now, imagine I'm making the *I'm watching you* fingers back and forth, got it?"

"Got it," Angus replied. Or maybe he didn't. All he could do was look at Elisa. Nothing existed but her.

His blood roared in his ears. His heart hammered. He lowered the phone, and swallowed. "That was Owen."

She nodded.

"How much did you hear?"

She bit her bottom lip. Licked it. Hugged her elbow. "From where you said, *I can't not see her in my life.*"

His gut knotted. "From there, eh?"

She nodded.

He swallowed again. "And?"

She crossed the space between them, and threaded her fingers into his hair. "And I can't *not* see you in my life either. Tomorrow, the next day, the next month, fuck, the next decade."

And with that, she pulled his head down to hers and kissed him.

CHAPTER FOURTEEN

The bedroom smelt delicious.

Bacon, eggs, bacon, fresh toast, and bacon.

Elisa's stomach rumbled and opening her eyes, she smiled, stretching out in the tumble of sheets.

The morning sun streamed through the window, bathing her in warm light. Outside, the sound of the breaking waves joined the soft sound of seagulls and even softer sounds of people enjoying the beach.

Elisa stretched some more and smiled wider. She could truly get used to waking up like this.

Waking up like this means living in Australia. It means Christmas in Summer. It means no country-wide July 4th celebrations. It means starting all over with your work: new business, new clients, new everything.

The thought should have turned her stomach to a churning maelstrom of anxiety. It didn't.

Bria was already living in Australia. She loved it here. The only things she said she missed about no longer living in San Diego was not living with Elisa and Zeta, and not being able to see their mom and dad whenever she wanted.

If Elisa lived in Australia with Angus... What about Zeta?

How could Elisa move away from Zeta? They were the twins of the triplets. Zeta was almost a part of her. How could she not be where Zeta was?

What if Angus moves to San Diego?

She scrunched up her face and pressed her palms to her face, chuckling into her hands. She really needed to slow her head down. Take some breaths. Live in the moment, not… whatever lay beyond Angus's front door. Now, now the only thing that mattered was breakfast.

And making love to Angus again after breakfast.

But first, breakfast.

Her stomach rumbled again, agreeing wholeheartedly with the plan.

Breakfast. Eggs. Bacon. Bacon.

Hmmm…bacon.

She climbed out of bed, slipped her arms into the shirt Angus had given her last night, and headed into the en suite. She cleaned her teeth with the toothbrush he'd given her somewhere around two in the morning, brushed her hair with her fingers, rubbed the sleep from her eyes, and made her way to the kitchen.

Like yesterday when she'd left his bedroom, the delicious aroma pulled her along. Quickened her pace. Her mouth filled with saliva and her stomach growled again.

At the sight of him working in the kitchen, shirtless, black boxer briefs covering his gorgeous ass, and what looked like a garland of bright-red tinsel wrapped around his head, her pulse quickened.

Yes, she could *definitely* get used to waking up to this.

She made her way over to him, slid her hands around his waist, and kissed the spot between his shoulder blades. "I am starving."

He chuckled, twisted a little, and gave her a smile. "Admit it, you're only my fiancée for my amazing cooking."

Going up on tiptoe, she stole a quick kiss from his lips. "You've found out my secret."

He chuckled again. "I'm not complaining. Table is set. Ready for the best fried eggs and bacon you'll ever have?"

"Ready."

Making her way to the table, a wave of happy warmth rolled over her. The table was indeed set. And wow, talk about impressive. There was a stack of freshly made toast, what looked like a glass pitcher of fresh OJ, a fruit platter that looked like it came from a tropical island resort's website, a bowl of what she guessed was some kind of yogurt, two steaming mugs of coffee...oh Dio, coffee, yes, she needed a coffee...and their plates.

She froze, her heart slamming up into her throat as she stared at the plate set at the chair she'd sat at last night. "Is that a key?"

"It is." His voice was steady, low. "It's symbolic really, because Kara has my spare, but...well... I thought it could be an early Christmas present. From me. To you."

She feathered her fingers over the key on the plate.

Oh boy. Oh boy, this is happening. Is this happening? This is happening.

"So I know geography isn't on our side," Angus's voice caressed her senses and she tried to lift her head, tried to look at him, but all she could do was look at the key, "but we can work it out, right?"

The metal was cool under her fingertips.

"I know the original plan was for you and your sister to head to Newcastle with Owen and Bria today. And you were both staying in Australia until after Owen and Bria's engagement party, but I was wondering...hoping...you'd stay here instead. With me. And we can both head up to Newcastle the day of the party and then...maybe...you'd stay and have Christmas with me here."

She swallowed, stare locked on the key. Christmas with

Angus sounded perfect. And not just Christmas with Angus, but every day with Angus. All the days. From this day onward.

Her mom and dad were going to have a meltdown, of course. Two daughters lost to Australians on the other side of the world, but they'd be okay. Eventually. Especially if Angus *did* open a restaurant in LA. She could travel back with him, see them then. And Zeta. And Zeta would definitely visit her and Bria here. So would her parents; their frequent-flyer miles would sky-rocket.

She smiled, a soft warmth spreading through her.

"And you are one-*hundred* percent allowed to tell me to pump the breaks," he said, a huskiness to his voice. "One-hundred percent. If I do go ahead with a restaurant in the LA, I will date the hell out of you whenever I'm there." He made a weird noise. "Okay, that sounds weird. What I mean is…crap, I'm not good with words. I'm better with food. I just…I just… really want us to be a thing. A real thing. Not just a…"

He trailed off as she looked up at him.

He stood on the other side of the table, a platter piled high with bacon and eggs and grilled tomatoes and haloumi and mushrooms in his hands, a string of red tinsel hanging over his eye, and oh god, she was never leaving this guy. Ever.

He gave her a smile; shy and nervous and hopeful all at once. "Ready?"

"Ready," she said, her heart…actually, her heart wasn't wild or racing. She felt calm. Wonderfully calm. "I've never been more ready."

A grin replaced his smile and he placed the platter on the table. "In that case, dig—"

The doorbell rang.

Angus cocked an eyebrow at her. "What's the bet that's Owen?"

"I'm not sharing this, if it is." She dropped into her seat with a defiant smirk. "Especially if Zeta and Bria are with him. Those two inhale food."

Chuckling, he rounded the table, and dropped a kiss on her upturned face. "Be right back. Don't wait for me."

"I wasn't going to," she declared, impishly, as he hurried toward his bedroom.

He reemerged a few seconds later, faded jeans now hiding his gorgeous ass and legs. "Actually," he said, head for the front door, "*do* wait. Watching you eat makes me horny, remember?"

She snagged a plump strawberry from the fruit platter and slipped its pointed bottom past her lips slowly.

He groaned. "Well, that's not playing fair."

She gave her eyebrows what she hoped was a sexy wriggle.

Laughing, he turned to the door and opened it.

"Now, I *know* this is highly unethical," an unseen female said from the other side. A *familiar* female voice. "But I wanted to give you one last chance."

Elisa's breath caught. She stared at Angus, unable to see who was on the other side but knowing who it was all the same.

Even if she hadn't recognized the TV producer's voice, the way Angus stood stiff, the way his knuckles whitened as he gripped the doorknob, the way the very air around him turned heavy, told her who it was.

Nora.

Elisa jolted to her feet. Her chest tightened. Dio, what was this woman's problem?

"Before you say anything," Nora went on, an edge to her voice. "Hear me out."

Elisa hurried around the dining table, heading for Angus. What did she have to do to make the producer leave him alone? Actually marry him?

Sounds like a plan.

"You've overstepped the line, Nora." Angus's low growl sent a chill up Elisa's spine as she approached them. "You need to leave."

"No, no," Nora said, stepping forward a little. Enough for

Elisa to see her now. She didn't look contrite or apologetic or even respectful; she looked haughty, as if there was no reason why she shouldn't be there. "I know you've been a tad reluctant in our previous negotiations, but I firmly believe the contract I've been authorized to offer you will change your mind. We're talking twelve-months free advertising for Buckley's Chance on all the network's channels, social media accounts and—"

"Hi," Elisa said, coming to a halt a few feet behind Angus.

Nora's stare snapped to her. For a split-second confusion and surprise flickered over her face, replaced finally with a frown. "What are *you* doing here?" She flicked a glance over Elisa's attire—Angus's loose button-up shirt and nothing else—and frowned deeper. "No, seriously, *why* are you here?"

"Nora," Angus's voice sounded strained. "Enough."

Nora squinted, as if something unpalatable suddenly filled her mouth. "I mean, I know you're not his fiancée. I know you didn't even know each other before touching down in Sydney."

Elisa's stomach dropped. A cold chill crawled over her scalp. "How do you know—"

She stopped. Swallowed. Shit. Shit, shit, she shouldn't have said that. Shit.

"Nora," Angus warned again, an icy anger in his voice. "Give it a rest."

"I have a contact at Qantas, you see." Nora waved her hand with a disdainful flick of her wrists. "They told me you didn't board together, sit together or disembark together. You didn't even buy your tickets at the same time. Although it's of no real concern, I guess. I *am* surprised to see you here, to be sure, but no one, viewers or contestants alike, ever expects the bachelor to be an innocent virgin so it honestly doesn't matter if—"

"*Enough,*" Angus shouted. "*Jesus fucking Christ, enough.*"

Elisa squealed, shock stealing the sound from her throat before she could stop it. He jerked around, his fist in his hair, and she stumbled back a step, heart racing. He stared at her, a tormented shadow filling his eyes. She swallowed. Took another step back. Bit her lip. If she didn't, she'd yell at Nora herself. What was the woman's deal? Did her job depend on this? Or was she just that obstinate? Or was Angus the first person to ever say no to her?

She opened her mouth. Closed it. An enigmatic stillness fell over his face and, pulling the makeshift tinsel garland from his head, he turned back to the TV producer, his shoulders bunching. "I've had a gutful of this, Nora. Please get off my property. Now."

Nora raised her finger, mouth opening, and he closed the door.

"Wow," Elisa whispered, hugging her elbows. "Wow. That was...something."

He slumped against the door, face in his hands, motionless.

A prickling tension scraped up Elisa's spine. "Angus?"

He didn't move. Except for his fingers that clawed at his hairline. Slowly. As if trying to gouge his skin. As if trying to cause pain.

"Angus?"

Was he okay?

"This isn't going to work," he muttered.

The prickling sensation spread over her skin. Her stomach clenched. "What isn't?"

He shook his head, his head still in his hands. "This isn't going to work," he repeated, lower this time.

Elisa frowned. He sounded...broken. "What isn't going to work?" she asked again.

A ragged breath left him, and he lifted his head, his eyes finding hers for a heartbeat before he straightened from the door, stare locking blankly over her shoulder. "I was fooling myself. I can't... I won't do this." For a fleeting second, he looked at her again, his expression empty, his eyes hollow. "I'll take you to the Mercure now. Your dress is hanging up on the back of my bedroom door. We can leave as soon as you're ready."

She blinked. "What?"

Without a word, he strode back into the dining room, discarded the length of tinsel on the table, and started collecting up their untouched food.

"What?" she said again, following him. Maybe she was still asleep? Maybe this was a stupid dream, and she was currently sound asleep, tucked into Angus's body?

He picked up the platter of fried eggs, bacon, and haloumi from the table, his focus locked on it. His hands trembled.

She narrowed her eyes and gripped the back of the chair she'd been sitting in only a few moments ago. "Angus, I don't understand. What happened? What's going on?"

He turned and carried the platter to the kitchen and placed it on the counter. Every muscle in his back and shoulders seemed at breaking point. For a heartbeat he didn't move, his head hung, his hands planted on the counter beside what was meant to be their breakfast.

The prickling tension making its way over her skin slithered up over her scalp. She stared at his back. "Please explain what's going on?"

"I can't do this to you, Lis," he muttered, head still low. "I won't."

"Do what?"

He turned, and she stepped back, the tortured pain in his face stealing her breath.

"I saw you flinch. When I lost my temper with Nora. I heard you squeal."

"Yes. But it wasn't—"

"I'm a control freak with a temper, Elisa. I don't do relationships. It's better that way. I let myself think I could with you, but…" Eyes haunted, he swiped his hand over his face.

"Better for who, Angus?" she whispered.

His jaw knotted. "Better for you."

She shook her head. No. This wasn't happening. It wasn't. "Don't," she objected.

"I saw you flinch," he said. "Saw your fear. I heard it. You were scared because of me, because of my temper. I can't do that to you again." He scrubbed at his mouth with his hand, as if he hated it.

God, he didn't just look broken; he looked destroyed.

"It's not like that, Angus," she said, taking a step toward him. "I was startled and—"

"I'll take you back to the hotel." He turned back to the counter, not looking at her. "I'm sorry. This isn't what I wanted, but…I can't…I won't…"

She stared at his back. Her heart pounded in her chest like a trapped bull.

Bria had told her last night—well, at one a.m. this morning while she'd been giving Elisa advice about love-at-first sight—that Angus apparently had some baggage.

Elisa had dismissed it. Everyone had baggage. Dio, hers was so freaking heavy she could barely breathe carrying it around. But watching the man she'd spent the last twenty-four hours with, the amazing, funny, confident, relaxed, warm, calm, sexy, self-effacing man she'd fallen in love with, being torn apart from the inside… God, what had his father done to him?

She pulled a slow breath, forcing her heart to slow. Forcing the prickling heat crawling over her to the back of her mind. Now was not the time to let anxiety gnaw at her.

I can hear the seagulls. I can feel the summer warmth. I can smell the bacon. I can see…

"Angus," she said, taking another step toward him. "I'm not going anywhere."

His shoulders bunched. His fingers on the counter curled. A little. "It's for the better, Elisa." Her throat thickened at the raw grief in his voice. "I swore my whole life I wasn't going to be my father. I swore I wasn't going to do to anyone what my father did to me. To…"

The hoarse words faded, and his head dropped again.

Biting her lip, she studied his back. How much had his

father hurt him? Or maybe it *wasn't* just Angus his father had hurt?

"You're scared you'll hit me one day," she said softly. "Like your dad hit your mom?"

His fingers curled fully into fists on the counter. And then uncurled, splaying flat on the granite. An almost imperceptible shudder rocked through him. "Yes."

Her heart tore at the wretched emptiness in the word. "You won't."

"You flinched. When I lost my temper with Nora. You stepped backward, away from me. And the second that happened… It broke me." He turned, his eyes red. "You are the most amazing, incredible, amazing person I've ever met, with the most gentle soul, and the thought of scaring you, of hurting you… I can't let that happen. I won't let that happen. Not to you. I love you too much."

The softest of smile pulled at her lips. "You said amazing twice."

He frowned.

She shook her head, letting her smile grow wider as she walked toward him. "Angus, I wasn't scared of you. I was furious with Nora. I wanted to scream at her. And I was damn close to doing just that. If I hadn't forced myself to take a step back, to take a breath…"

His Adam's apple jerked up and down his throat.

She stopped, barely a foot away from where he stood. "I have suffered with anxiety as long back as I can remember. I take daily medication to help my brain produce serotonin. I panic often that I'm letting anyone I care for down and that I'm pathetic and woeful and no one wants to be with me *because* I'm me. In crowds, I want to fall through the floor. In situations I've never been in before I want to crawl into a hole. I don't do strangers. I don't do impulsiveness."

He studied her. Seemed to search her eyes for something.

She took the final step until she rested her fingers on his

chest. "And yet, here I am with you, a stranger. Here I am, ready to spend the rest of my life with you, after only twenty-four hours. I'm standing here, not wanting to fall through your floor, not thinking you hate me, not even thinking you might be sick of me. I feel calm with you. From the beginning. I'm here with you because from the moment I saw you at the airport, I knew..." She pressed her right hand to her chest, over her heart, "right here, you were what I wanted, needed. I want to be impulsive with you for the rest of our lives. I want to make you horny every day eating your cooking. I want to travel with you, stay at home with you, I want to live my life with you. I wouldn't do that if I was scared of you."

His nostrils flared. His chest rose and fell with a choppy breath.

She tilted her head, letting her lips curl into a gentle smile. "My therapist told me once that people who suffer from anxiety have a sentry's brain. Do you know what that means?"

He shook his head, his eyes holding hers.

"It means, my brain is kind of hardwired to worry about everything. Back in the day, when our lives where constantly threatened by wild predators or rival tribes, a sentry would be alert for any threat at all. Any tiny hint of danger. Today, when as a species we're *not* needing to worry about being eaten by sabretooth tigers or giant pythons or killer caveman, a sentry's mind has nothing really to worry about...and so it seeks things out; and thus we have anxiety." She closed the tiny space left between them. "But not once, in all the time I've been with you, have I worried about you and what you think of me. All I've felt is safe. And wanted. And loved."

His chest rose and fell again.

"So, no, I'm not going to let you take me to the hotel." She feathered her fingers up his chest, to his jaw. "Because the only thing that scares me is not living my life with you." She gave him a serious frown. "Do you hear me?"

"I do," he murmured.

She lifted an eyebrow. "And?"

He lowered his head to hers and kissed her.

Slid his hands around her waist, hauled her hips to his, and kissed her.

And kissed her.

And when he finally stopped kissing her, he nudged his forehead to hers and let out a wobbly breath. "Do you think Bria and Owen would be mad if we got married before them?"

She laughed, tangling her fingers in his hair. "Maybe. But they'll get over it."

EPILOGUE

Christmas Day

"Ta-dah!" Angus strode into the living room, arms akimbo, grin wide. "I'm ready."

Looking up from buttering her toast at the kitchen counter, Elisa snorted out a chuckle. "Owen says if you wear that shirt to lunch today, he's going to throw you in the pool."

Angus crossed to where she stood, smoothing his hands over the front of his T-shirt and the image of mid-shellfish-reaction-Owen printed on it. "He can try." He stopped at her side, lowering his head to brush his lips over hers. "Happy Christmas, gorgeous one."

"Gorgeous one? I like that." She rose up on tiptoe and kissed him back. "Merry Christmas, handsome one."

He laughed, stole a piece of her toast, and took a playful bite. "Still no Vegemite, I see?"

"Don't even," she warned, pointing at him. "You try to make me eat that stuff and I'll help Owen throw you in the pool."

Two weeks since she landed in Australia, two weeks since she first met Angus, first pretended to be his fiancée, first fell in love with him, and every day was still the best day of her life.

Every day she fell in love with him more.

Her mom and dad were still refusing to believe she wasn't coming back to the US—but she knew they were happy for her. They'd told her so at Bria's and Owen's engagement party a few days ago. Her mom was especially impressed with Angus. As it turns out, her mom had known she was going to marry her dad the very first time he'd cooked her dinner a week into their courtship (as her mom called it). Elisa—and Bria and Zeta—had been amazed to discover that little nugget of information about their parents at the party. A wonderful sense of happiness had swept through Elisa; falling in love almost at first sight was, it seemed, a family tradition.

Still didn't stop her parents refusing to believe her and Angus weren't going to make their future in the US. Of course, she and Angus hadn't decided. For now, they were just living each day together, and each day was the best day.

"What if," Angus said, opening the fridge, "I make my famous Vegemite and chocolate truffles to take to Christmas lunch today?"

"Vegemite and chocolate?" She gaped at his back. "Please tell me you're kid…"

She trailed off as he turned around to face her. Stared at him. Stared at what he'd taken from the fridge. What he now held in his left hand.

A small blue box, the color of a robin's egg. The famous Tiffany and Co. blue. *Pantone 1837*, her graphic-artist's brain whispered, even as her heart slammed into her throat. Not at the color of the box, but the distinct size and shape.

Angus looked at her, and—with the fridge door still open behind him—slowly lowered himself to one knee.

Dio…

"I'm not kidding," he said, gazing up at her, "about my famous Vegemite and chocolate truffles. *Or* about this."

He opened the small box.

Inside, nestled on a black velvet pillow, sat a simple, elegant, and ridiculously stunning square-cut diamond solitaire.

Swallowing, she stared at it. Lifted her stare to him.

"Will you really *really* become my fiancée, Elisa De Luca?" A smile played with the corners of his mouth. "*Will* you marry me?"

"Yes," she whispered. "Yes, yes, yes."

He stood, closed the distance between them and removed the ring from the box, ready to slip it onto her finger.

She pulled her hand away a little, curling her fingers loosely. "On one condition," she said, trying not to grin.

A soft frown dipped his eyebrows. "Which is?"

She grinned. "We don't invite Nora Young to the wedding."

He laughed. "Deal."

ANGUS'S CHILLI PRAWN LARB LETTUCE CUPS

INGREDIENTS
- 1 1/2 cups (300g) long-grain rice
- 1/3 cup (110g) chilli jam
- 1 tbs sambal oelek (Indonesian chilli paste)
- 1/4 cup (60ml) olive oil
- 1/3 cup (100g) green curry paste
- 1 tbs fish sauce
- 1kg large green prawns, peeled, deveined, chopped
- 150g snake or thin green beans, thinly sliced on the diagonal
- 1 red onion, thinly sliced
- Juice of 1 lime, plus wedges to serve
- Cos lettuce leaves,
- Roasted peanuts, to serve
- Mint leaves, to serve
- Coriander leaves, to serve

METHOD
1. Cook the rice according to packet instructions. Drain and set aside.

2. Combine the chilli jam, sambal and 1 tbs oil in a bowl. Set aside.

3. Heat remaining 2 tbs oil in a wok or frypan over medium-high heat. Add curry paste and cook, stirring, for 2-3 minutes until fragrant. Add fish sauce, prawns, beans and onion, and cook, stirring, for a further 3-4 minutes until prawns are opaque. Stir through the lime juice and remove from heat.

4. To serve, spoon rice into the lettuce cups and top with prawn larb, chilli jam dressing, peanuts and herbs. Serve with lime wedges to squeeze over.

You can find this recipe (as well as many more) at Delicious.com.au

AUSSIE ACTUALLY

THE BOUNDARIES BOOK 3

DEDICATION

For the amazing Newcastle Romance Writers group. Especially Michelle Douglas and Kaz Delany, who took me to lunch and gave me back my self-belief.

And Rhian Cahill, who made me take a breath.

CHAPTER ONE

S tudying her reflection in the full-length mirror, Zeta scowled at her older sister. "I'm still angry at you there's no tulle."

"Tulle was never an option, Z." Bria crossed the spacious room and stood behind Zeta, meeting her gaze in the mirror as she did up the long zipper of the dress Zeta wore.

Zeta smoothed her palms over the emerald-green satin slip dress now hugging her body. She grinned at Bria. "Boring."

"My wedding, my choice," Bria said with her own grin, adjusting how her boobs sat in the exquisitely beaded bodice of the ivory chiffon and satin sleeveless dress she wore. "When *you* get married, you can have as much tulle as you like, and I will happily wear it."

"Ha, jokes on you." Zeta smirked. "I'm never getting married."

"Sure you're not." Bria tapped her on the nose. "I believe you. But when you *do*, I'll wear as much tulle as you want."

"Hold her to that, Z," Elisa said, joining them in front of the mirror. She too adjusted her breasts in the dress she wore, the style and color identical to Zeta's. Almost. "My boobs are getting so big." She turned, running her hands over the gentle swell of her stomach pushing against the satin. "Twins. I can't believe I'm having twins."

"I can't believe you *also* denied me tulle at *your* wedding, Lis." Zeta bent over, drawing her head close to Elisa's baby bump. "Your mom is a party pooper, little ones. And so is your Aunty B."

"Hey, hey, hey." Elisa covered her belly with her palms, mock indignation in her voice. "Stop telling them I'm no fun."

Laughing, Zeta straightened and smoothed her bridesmaid dress down again. Despite her jest, it truly was stunning, and she looked stunning in it.

It was a huge difference from her normal attire. The wardrobe of a zookeeper tended to be dominated by khaki chinos, khaki shirts, khaki boots, and jeans. Lots of jeans. Usually faded. And smelling of, in her case, cheetahs. No matter how many times she washed them, the clothes she worked in always smelled like the cheetahs at the San Diego Safari Park. And because she worked almost all the time, almost all her clothes were clothes she worked in.

But not this dress.

This dress…

"This dress truly *is* bellissima, Bri," she said, turning to give Bria's cheek a soft kiss. "Even without any tulle. I feel amazing in it."

Bria stopped fiddling with the small white roses pinned in her hair at her right temple and looked at her. "You are amazing, Zeta. And I've missed you so much."

A hot lump filled Zeta's throat. "No, no. No talking sad stuff. Not on your wedding day."

Sad stuff. Like the fact both Bria and Elisa now lived in Australia with their respective partners, Owen and Angus, and had done for a few months now. Not sad for her sisters, but sad for Zeta. She missed them.

More than she could comprehend.

They were triplets, after all.

The fact she hadn't seen either of them until midnight last night made it doubly important not to get sad now. Three months was a long time between hugs.

Thank God, she and Elisa were identical in every physical way. It made sizing and fitting her bridesmaid dress hassle-free despite her not being in Australia. Well, identical in every physical way until Elisa's pregnancy had started to show, that was.

"You could always get a job at Taronga Zoo," Elisa said, sliding her arm around Zeta's waist, her smile warm in the mirror as she looked at Zeta. "The one on Sydney Harbor."

Zeta rested her cheek on Elisa's shoulder and smiled back. "I can't leave my boys. I love them too much."

Her boys were Kagiso and Mandla, born to the park's dominant female cheetah, Noxolo, only six weeks ago. With cheetah numbers critical in the wild, the cubs were a precious gift for the park *and* the world, although the world didn't know it yet. Their birth was still a secret, given they were still in the dangerous period. Their little sister, Thadie, had died at only a week old, breaking the hearts of everyone at the park, especially the close-knit cheetah keepers. Kagiso and Mandla were strong and healthy and entirely full of feisty spirit though. Zeta had a good feeling.

But still, a nervous good feeling. Only Bria's wedding here in Australia could tear her away from being at work since their birth. As it was, she'd given Dani—the other cheetah keeper—strict instructions to send her regular updates on their progress. Very regular.

Four times a day regular.

Except for today.

Today was a phone-free day.

Besides, everyone she wanted to be with, to talk to, was already here—Bria and Elisa, their mom and dad, Owen and Angus.

But then three days after the wedding, you head back to San Diego, and leave Bria and Elisa, and Owen and Angus here.

She would. And not only that, her mom and dad were making the most of being in Australia and had decided to have a second honeymoon in the country. They were hiring a car and doing a six-week self-drive tour to as many places and sights and locations here as they could.

She'd be alone back in San Diego.

Maybe she should just move into the cheetah enclosure's staff annex?

No sad stuff, remember. This is a huge day for Bri. Stop being selfish.

Good point.

"Hey!" she burst out, looking at Bria and Elisa in the mirror, eyes wide. Serious. Stern.

"What?" Bria asked.

"What?" Elisa echoed.

She stuck her tongue out at them.

They all laughed. Sisters to the end, no matter where any of them lived. Or how far apart.

A soft knock sounded on the door and Tilly, Owen's sister, popped her head into the room. "It's showtime." A smile spread across her face, and she let out a happy sigh. "You all look gorgeous, by the way."

"Absolutely we do," Zeta agreed. "Even with a decided lack of tulle."

Tilly laughed.

Zeta found Bria's gaze in the mirror, and she lifted an eyebrow. "Ready?"

Bria closed her eyes, drew in a deep, slow breath, and then nodded. "Hell yeah," she said, looking at Zeta and Elisa in the mirror. "Let's go get hitched."

"I'm already hitched," Elisa pointed out with a laugh. "And am now up the duff."

Zeta blinked. "Up the *what?*"

Elisa laughed, running her palms over her belly. "Up the duff. Pregnant."

Zeta rolled her eyes. "This is what happens when you marry an Australian. You start speaking gibberish."

Tilly cleared her throat. "Not that I'm not enjoying this sisterly moment, ladies—" she gave Bria a grin, "but Mick has Owen almost convinced you're going to realise you're actually *marrying* him today and decide that's a *really* bad idea, and take off back to the States so…"

Bria burst out laughing. "Of course he is."

Zeta ground her teeth. Mick. Owen's brother.

She'd only met him once at Bria's and Owen's engagement party a few months ago, but once was once enough. ER Doctor. Opinionated. Far too impressed with himself. Way too good-looking for his own, well, good. And unfortunately, her partner in the bridal party.

The only irritation of the day.

But still, for Bria, she'd grin and bear the annoying, arrogant pain in the ass.

For Bria.

Even if he *had* called her—

"Scusi, Matilda," a male voice uttered behind Tilly, and a towering man with steel grey hair, ice-blue eyes, and a glorious moustache appeared in the doorframe, his smile wide. "Mie belle ragazze, tutti stanno aspettando."

"We're coming, Papà," Bria said, turning from the mirror. She held out her arms. "Do you like?"

Their father entered, dropping his customary kiss on the tops of all their heads, before mimicking Bria's pose. The dark-grey tux he wore looked perfect, especially with the pants rolled up to just below his knees. "I like very much, mia figlia. You are more than beautiful." He crooked his elbow. "Now let's go, before your future husband thinks you're not coming. His brother has him convinced you're running off with some mysterious skydiver you met last week."

Bria laughed, hooking her finger over his biceps. "I'm going to kill Mick."

Zeta rolled her eyes. Mick. What a pain in the ass. Perhaps she'd accidently kick him in the shins during the bridal waltz?

She'd thought about wiping that smug grin off his face more than once since meeting him. In fact, he'd popped into her mind often, ruining her day, making her grumpy. Making her wish she could see him again so she could prove to him just how insignificant and inconsequential he was.

Tilly snorted. "Everyone wants to kill Mick at some point. It's his superpower. That and the fact he's so damn loveable when he wants to be." She wrapped her knuckles on the doorframe. "Ready?"

Bria nodded. "Ready."

"Shit," Zeta burst out. Pain in the ass Mick had almost made her forget what was about to happen. "Wait."

Everyone stopped and looked at her.

She pulled a face at them and toed off the sneakers she'd pulled on way back at seven a.m. to go to the resort's hairdressers. "Sorry. Wrong shoes."

Hurrying to the bag of supplies and other wedding paraphernalia she'd dumped on the bed on arriving at the beachside resort, she dug around in it and yanked out what she needed.

Gold rubber flip-flops, complete with gold glitter on the straps. "Got 'em. Sorry."

Grinning, she dropped them to the floor and shoved her feet into them. You had to love Bria. Getting married on a beach really made for far comfortable footwear.

"I'm gonna kill you, Mick," Owen muttered under his breath, tugging at his tie.

"Your fault, big brother." Mick tried to keep his grin under control. The celebrant was scowling at them both, the gentle coastal breeze flapping the old guy's combover about in a way that made Mick want to laugh. Behind him, the pristine beach and surf connected to the remote luxury resort where Owen and Bria were getting married stretched on forever. "You'll think twice about beating me in poker again."

"But bright pink?" Owen shot a look at his feet, currently buried almost to the ankles in the beach's cool, white sand. "Really? Bright pink? On my wedding day?"

Mick snorted out a chuckle. "You thought I was going to play fair?"

Owen looked down at his hidden toenails, now painted the most shocking shade of neon pink. "I thought I was going to lose. You had that look on your face that says *I am so fucking good.*"

"Hey." Mick mock pouted. "I *don't* have a look that says—"

"Yes, you do, brother." Owen threw a quick sideways glance at him. "You very much have that look. But still, how is it *I* won the poker game and yet I ended up with *my* toenails painted bright pink?"

Mick shrugged. "Retaliation. It's a word. Look it up. Besides, that's what you get for dozing off this morning after Angus made us breakfast."

"Hey, don't drag me into this," Angus protested with a low chuckle from Mick's other side, adjusting the cuffs of his suit's jacket. "*I* didn't paint his toenails. You did."

The celebrant scowled at them all again, before shooting the sand at Owen's feet a curious look.

Owen let out a ragged sigh. "Neon pink."

The celebrant raised his eyebrows. "An interesting look, to be sure."

Angus chuckled again. Mick grinned.

Finding Owen asleep that morning on the deck Mick had booked at the luxury resort for the wedding day and night, hands crossed on his chest, bare feet up on the railing, had been too good an opportunity to pass up. The sod had beaten him at poker at the bachelor party, after all. He'd bolted to the closest cabin—a good sixty meters away—where a family with at least three young teenage daughters were holidaying. He'd knocked on the door, turned on the charm, and asked if he could borrow the brightest nail polish they had.

After a few dubious frowns, he'd explained the situation. His brother was getting married today on the beach. He was the best man. Owen had beaten him in poker a week ago. Revenge was due.

The mum, God love her, had laughed and told him he was a brave man and a woeful brother, but she hadn't stopped her youngest daughter handing over the neon-pink polish.

"Remember," the mum had called as he'd started running back along the path to his own far-more secluded cabin. "Revenge can go both ways."

It was true of course. Owen *would* get him back for this, but that hadn't stopped him painting Owen's toenails. Nor had it stopped him hiding Owen's dress shoes. The ones he would put on after the beach ceremony.

"Just let it be known," Angus muttered, tugging at his collar as if he'd never worn a suit before, "that I'm innocent in all of this."

Owen snorted. "For once."

Angus grinned. "Oh, and when the time comes for the reception, I have no clue where your shoes are, Owen."

"Traitor," Mick gasped around a laugh.

"My shoes?" Owen looked confused. And then horrified. "Fuck a duck, Mick. What the hell have you done with my…"

He trailed off, his stare locked on something, or some*one*, over his shoulder, a heartbeat before Chloe Blackthorne—world-famous cellist and Owen and Mick's second cousin—started playing something Mick didn't recognize but was probably romantic and soppy.

"Oh boy," Owen whispered, his AWOL shoes seemingly forgotten, his face going just as soppy as the music. "Oh boy."

"Here we go," Angus intoned, twisting a little to look behind them.

"So she didn't do a runner, after all?" Mick grinned, giving Owen's shoulder a gentle squeeze. "Guess she truly *does* love you, mate." He tossed a look over his shoulder to check out the bride.

And forgot how to breathe.

Holy fuck, she looked gorgeous.

Not the bride, although Bria *did* look incredible.

Not Elisa either, who glowed with pregnant beauty.

Zeta.

Zeta looked gorgeous.

Zeta, his counterpart in today's events. The chief bridesmaid to his best man.

Zeta, the annoying, no-filter, manic-energy American who'd rubbed him the wrong way the very second he met her at Owen and Bria's engagement party last year. Zeta, who'd insisted he was an arrogant, inconsiderate "ass" because he made a joke about Owen's previous brain-cancer scare. Zeta, who'd taken up space in his head, rent bloody free ever since.

Zeta.

"Wow," Owen murmured at his side.

Mick tore his stare from Zeta—had to, otherwise she'd notice and who the hell knows *what* she'd think—and shot his brother a glance.

Owen was gazing at Bria, and any doubts Mick harbored that Owen was rushing into things were obliterated. Pure, one-hundred percent love radiated from Owen as his bride approached them across the beach.

"Wow," Owen murmured again.

A warm beat of happiness throbbed through Mick for his brother, and he looked back at the bridal procession making their slow way across the sand towards them.

Elisa came first, her eyes only for Angus, her smile shy and proud and promising Angus things Mick didn't want to know about. At the back of the procession, Bria walked on her father's arm, all sorts of promises on her face as well as she looked at Owen. Promises, Mick was pretty certain, that shouldn't be made while walking next to her dad.

And in the middle...

Of its own accord, his stare moved to Zeta.

The last time he'd seen her, the first and *only* time he'd seen her, her golden-auburn hair had been pulled back in a ponytail so tight his own head had ached. Now, it tumbled around her face in a mess of soft waves that made his fingers itch with an unsettling desire to touch it. Last time, her direct blue eyes had been framed by fair lashes. Now they were framed by dark sooty makeup that sent a hot lick of something filthy straight to his groin. At Owen and Bria's engagement party, she'd been wearing faded denim jeans and an oversized jersey for some sports team from San Diego.

Now, the bridesmaid's dress highlighted all the curves and dips and planes of her body, and fuck a duck, she had no damn right looking so fucking gorgeous.

He swallowed. Tried to drag his stare away. Tried to turn back to the beach. The celebrant. Hell, the clouds in the sky.

But he couldn't. He couldn't stop looking at her.

And he couldn't stop his body *reacting* to her.

Damn it.

This was a serious fucking problem.

Because the last time they'd met, she'd accused *him* of being an arrogant, insensitive jerk, and he'd accused *her* of being an ignorant American.

Following Elisa, Zeta drew closer to where he, Owen, and Angus stood under the wedding arbor made from ghost-gum eucalyptus, wattle flowers, gum leaves, and draped in a long, flowy length of white gauzy fabric.

Closer.

Her unreadable gaze seemed to pin him to the spot. Indecipherable. What was she thinking? Was she even thinking about *him*?

Of course, she wouldn't be. Why would she? She hated him. Had made it very clear the last time they'd met. Whereas, he *hadn't* been able to stop thinking about her. About how annoying and snarky and...and...American she was.

His mouth turned to a desert. His heart beat faster. Harder. His groin tightened. Grew heavy.

Shit, what was going on with him? This was mental. She was annoying, not...not...

"You're in big trouble, Mick," Elisa whispered, giving him a cheeky smile as she arrived at the end of the sandy stretch of beach acting as the aisle.

His already pounding heart hammered faster. He swallowed.

Wait. What? "What?" he whispered.

Elisa let out a soft laugh and then, with a very seductive wink at Angus, she veered off to the left, taking up her place on the bride's side of things.

"God, I love her so much," Angus muttered at his side, the tone of his voice making it very clear exactly what he was planning to do with Elisa when they were next alone.

Mick swallowed again. His skin began to prickle. His pulse quickened. Not because of Angus's obvious lust and adoration for his wife, but because Zeta was now barely a foot away from him, about to follow Elisa to the left.

She was looking at him.

And for whatever fucking reason, all he wanted to do was grab her arse with both hands, haul her to his body, and kiss her.

Really fucking kiss her.

Senseless.

Fuck, what the hell is going on?

CHAPTER TWO

Zeta tried not to fidget during the ceremony. She focused on wriggling her toes in the cool sand. She focused on the smooth stalks of the bouquet of ivory-white roses in her hands. She focused on... Oh, who was she kidding? She was almost entirely focused on Michael Blackthorne.

"Mick to my mates," he'd said to her and Elisa the night they'd first met at Bria and Owen's engagement party. "But don't get me confused with *Nick* Blackthorne. All that bastard can do is sing songs and play a guitar."

Zeta's mouth had fallen open at the insult towards one of the world's greatest rock stars. She'd made a shocked noise and shot Bria and Owen a worried look, but Owen had just snorted, clapped Mick on the shoulder, and said it was a good thing their cousin wasn't there to hear him say that.

Mick had laughed. "What's he going to do? Sing me to death?"

"Can *you* sing?" Zeta had shot back. "Or is this some kind of inferiority complex hiding in bravado?"

"Oh God." He'd rolled his eyes. "A groupie?"

"No," she'd protested. "Just respectful of people's talent."

His eyes had held hers for a fleeting second, an expression she couldn't quite decipher on his face, and then he'd excused himself and crossed to someone else at the party.

She'd found her gaze moving to him often throughout that night. For some reason, she'd always seemed to know where he was—and somehow, he'd caught her looking every time.

It had irritated her.

He'd irritated her. Every time their stares collided, a smile had curled his lips.

Jerk.

She'd tried to stay clear of him for the rest of the night, but at one point, they'd ended up standing next to each other at the bar. She'd done her best to pretend he wasn't there, but he'd started singing Nick Blackthorne's "Gotta Run". Not loud enough to draw anyone else's attention, of course, but loud enough for her to hear.

She'd snapped around to face him. "You're not funny. And you're a bad singer."

Grinning, he'd leant his elbow on the bar and looked at her. "I *am* funny. And trust me, singing's not my talent."

She'd cocked an eyebrow at him. "Clearly."

He'd arched one in return. "Could still beat Nick at a karaoke contest though."

She'd snorted. "You're delusional. God help your patients."

He'd narrowed his eyes. "Are you always this snarky?"

"Are you always this arrogant?" she'd shot back. "I mean, I know he's your cousin, and you Australians are weird with the whole insulting each other thing, but Nick Blackthorne isn't *just* a singer. My God, he's one of the biggest philanthropists for animal rights causes around the world. Did you know a hundred percent of profits from his last album—*The Best of Blackthorn*—was donated to the World Wildlife Fund?"

He'd chuckled an irritating know-it-all laugh. "So you *are* a groupie."

"I'm *not* a groupie," she'd snapped. "His music is not my

taste at all. Too angsty and melodramatic and—" she'd searched for a word to shut down his insistence she was a groupie, "—contrived."

Mick had pulled away from the bar a little, and turned to the tall, lean man with shaggy salt-and-pepper hair standing on the other side of him. "Contrived. There's one I bet you haven't heard before, cousin."

Nick Blackthorne—*the* Nick Blackthorne—had laughed. "Nope. Haven't heard that one before." He smiled at Zeta, a gleam in his eye, and lifted the glass in his hand. "To being contrived."

The floor had engulfed Zeta. Or at least, she'd wanted it to.

She'd stared at the famous rock star for a heartbeat, blustered out an apology, thrown Mick a glare, and almost bolted from the bar back to where Elisa and Angus were talking to someone she didn't know on the opposite side of the party. The bastard had walked her *right* into that with premeditative ease.

And that had been it for her and Mick.

Except for the times she'd found herself looking for him, practicing in her head the absolute roasting she would give him if they came face-to-face again.

They hadn't.

Not for the rest of the engagement party.

Their stares had clashed more than once, but he'd stayed away from her, and she'd stayed away from him.

Far away.

Which was good, because he was an arrogant—

"Zeta," someone whispered at her. "Earth to Zeta?"

She blinked, her attention focusing back on the beach and the wedding, on the here and now.

Bria was looking at her. No, *everyone* was looking at her. Elisa, the celebrant, Owen, Angus, Mick…

Her cheeks grew hot.

"What?" She frowned, yanking her stare away from Mick and back to Bria.

Bria flicked a glance downward.

Zeta did the same, more heat filling her cheeks as Bria gently shook the large bouquet of ivory roses and gum leaves in her hand.

Dio, they'd reached the do-you-have-the-rings part of the wedding.

She'd zoned out for most of the ceremony.

Goddamn Mick Blackthorne. This was all his fault.

Really?

Snatching at Bria's gorgeous bouquet, she mumbled she was sorry and shuffled back a step, eyes downcast, but not before catching the look on Mick's face.

Judgey jerk.

The celebrant cleared his throat. "As I said before, *now* for the vows and the rings."

A soft chuckle went through the guests, and Bria laughed.

"Hey, gave me a few more seconds to remember mine," Owen declared.

Bria laughed again. "God, I love you."

"I bloody well hope so," he said. "Given what we're about to do."

Everyone laughed again.

A deep rumbling chuckle caught on Zeta's sanity and, face still aflame, she looked up through her lashes.

Mick was laughing along with everyone, and when his gaze found hers, he lifted his eyebrows at her.

She poked her tongue out at him.

God, what was she? Eight?

You're going to ruin Bria's wedding.

The thought sheered through her, and she sucked in a breath. Okay, enough. Mick was a pain in the ass, but she wasn't going to let him get under her skin. Not today. She was going to be a responsible, sophisticated adult.

Straightening her spine, she shook out her shoulders and tilted her chin. *Bite me*, she mouthed.

He arched another eyebrow, lips twitching.

"Owen?" the celebrant said, jerking Zeta's attention from Mick. *Again.* "Your vows?"

Zeta fixed her stare on Bria and Owen. She wasn't going to acknowledge Mick for the rest of the ceremony.

That'd teach his ego.

Owen pulled in a deep, choppy breath and took Bria's hands. "Here we go."

Mick chuckled. "Here we go indeed."

Zeta ground her teeth. God, what did she have to do to stop him getting under her skin?

Kiss him. Grab him by the ears and kiss him. Hard.

She blinked. Kiss him?

What?

No seriously, *what?*

His brother was saying something. Mick was probably meant to be listening, given it was almost at the point in the ceremony where he was to give Owen the wedding rings, but he kept trying to not look at Zeta.

Unfortunately, since she'd silently told him to bite her, all he could think about was, for some weird, unsettling reason, doing *just* that. Biting her. Image after unnerving image filled his head of him nibbling on her smooth, creamy skin. Nipping at the curve of her exposed shoulder, the side of her neck, her hip, her inner wrist, her inner thigh…

Fuck.

He squeezed his eyes shut, heart a thumping jackhammer against his breastbone.

Fuck. Just because she looked incredible in her bridesmaid dress, that didn't give his body permission to suddenly behave like it belonged to a horny teenager. He needed to stop this. She wasn't even a blip on his radar.

Yeah, like you haven't *thought of her more than once since—*

"Mick," Owen's low growl scraped through the thought. "Mick, the rings."

Mick sucked in a breath. Shit.

He gave Owen an apologetic grimace and shoved his hand into his jacket's inside pocket, searching for the matching gold bands tucked in there.

The invisible prickling weight crawling all over him told him very clearly that he was being watched.

He snagged the rings, yanked his hand free, and gave Owen another grimace. "Sorry." He passed the rings to Owen, or tried to. Both slipped from his fingers and fell to the soft sand at his feet.

Shit. Again.

A collective gasp went through the guests. Everyone gaped at him for a beat.

Except Zeta.

She stood watching the waves kiss the beach, the ocean breeze playing with her strawberry-blonde hair. Completely indifferent to what was going on.

Why did that bug him so much?

He bent down and snatched both rings back up.

"Good thing you're not a surgeon," Angus muttered with a laugh.

"Shit," he muttered in return, blowing grains of sand from the bands. He shot Owen another apologetic look and —carefully—delivered the rings to Owen's palm. "Sorry, brother."

"All good." Owen chuckled and then frowned at him. "You okay?"

"I'm awesome," he declared, swiping the sand from his fingers on the seat of his suit pants.

Owen snorted. Angus did the same.

Zeta's light-blue eyes flicked his way, and his heart thumped a little faster.

"And I'm going to be late for my next ceremony," the celebrant stated softly, leaning forward with a pointed expression.

Bria laughed, plucked the smaller of the two bands from Owen's palm, and slipped it on her left ring finger. "There. Done. Now, my turn."

She began her vows, and Owen's attention locked onto her. Mick's slid to Zeta. He tried to stop it, but it just…did.

What did her skin smell like right now? Was she wearing perfume? Would her hair tickle his cheek if he pressed his lips to the subtle curve where her neck became her shoulder?

Stop it.

Yeah, stop it. What was going on with his brain? Maybe he needed to get a CAT scan? Maybe he was having a stroke? No, not possible. He wasn't smelling burnt toast. And he was only in his thirties and healthy and fit and—

A raucous cheer jerked Mick back to the here and now. Bria and Owen were kissing. Seriously kissing. Serious-public-display-of-affection kissing.

He caught himself before he could check Zeta's reaction. Instead, he clapped a hand on Owen's shoulder. "Alright, alright, big brother," he admonished loudly, grin wide. "Save it for later."

Owen and Bria pulled apart, both tossing him a smirk. "Spoil sport," Bria laughed.

And just like that, his gaze locked with Zeta's again.

She studied him, bottom lip bit by her white, even teeth, a frown pulling at her forehead. She was always frowning at him. Why didn't she like him? Everyone liked him.

Why are you worried?

He didn't know. But it irked him. He was awesome. She *should* like him.

Holy shit, Mick. Check your ego at the door, mate.

Still… Maybe he could *make* her like—

"Mick?" Angus nudged him with an elbow. "You're needed."

He blinked.

"Signing time," Angus muttered, indicating toward the small table to the side of the arbor draped in a white cloth and adorned with white roses and gum leaves. Bria was lowering herself into the seat as the celebrant pointed something out on the table in front of her. Owen was standing behind her, and beside him was Zeta.

Watching him.

Before he knew what he was doing, he smiled. For the briefest of seconds, the softest of smiles curled her lips, and everything in Mick's world imploded.

Oh shit.

He had the hots for Zeta De Luca.

CHAPTER THREE

Zeta had never eaten a meal like the one served at the wedding reception.

"Angus," she said, leaning forward over her plate full of crisp pork belly, corn puree, and almond croquet to look down the table at the chef. "This is incredible."

Angus dipped his head. "Of course it is."

She laughed, settling back into her seat to continue the first course of the wedding feast—all prepared by the staff of Angus's restaurant. Her gaze found Mick's, and for a heartbeat, they just stared at each other. Then he smiled, and a liquid shard of something intense and terrifying shot through her. Lust.

"I'm getting a drink," she muttered, jolting to her feet.

If anyone at the table responded, she didn't hear. She was already hurrying away across the empty dance floor—the one she was meant to be on in Mick's arms soon.

What was going on with her?

The bar was devoid of guests when she got there. Phew, thank fucking God for that. She needed a drink to clear her head. "A gin and tonic, please." The barkeeper, a very cute guy she would normally flirt with, nodded and turned away to start her order.

"No, wait," she almost shouted. The barkeeper turned back. "Ice water."

Drinking probably wasn't a good idea. Not before she had to dance with Mick. He was no doubt going to be the best dancer in the world, or at least think he was, and she needed to make sure she could hold her own.

The barkeeper nodded again. "Sure." He turned away again.

"No!" She burst out.

He turned back.

"Gin and tonic." She bit her lip. "And lime."

He lifted an eyebrow. "You sure?"

"Yes. No. Oh shit." She grabbed the counter. What was going on with her?

"Would you like me to suggest something?" Mick said, his voice low and full of a warm laugh as he stepped up to the bar beside her.

"Vodka," she blurted out at the barkeeper. "Straight."

The barkeeper flicked a look at Mick and then back at her. "Vodka?"

"Two ice waters," Mick said. "With a wedge of lime in each."

She spun to him. "Who said I want water?"

"Who said the second glass is for you?" he asked, his smile playful.

Her heart quickened, and the pit of her stomach tightened. *Oh God.*

"Two ice waters." The barkeeper placed two glasses on the counter in front of Mick.

"Thanks, mate," Mick said, picking up both.

His jaw was so square. His nose so...so...hawkish. Damn it, why was he so good-looking?

He turned back to her, that playful smile still dancing on

his lips, and held out one of the glasses to her. Zeta swallowed, opened her mouth, closed it.

"Thanks," she muttered, taking the glass and capturing the straw with her lips.

His stare dropped to her mouth.

She sucked. Ice water flowed down her throat.

Mick chuckled. "Thirsty?"

She ignored him and drained the glass without stopping. Well, she tried to ignore him.

He leant on the bar with one elbow, his smile tormenting her. It did things to her she didn't want to examine. It hadn't before. Whenever he'd smiled at her before, she'd wanted to hit him in the face with a pillow.

Did you really? Or have you been telling yourself that?

Putting the empty glass on the counter, she licked her bottom lip.

His gaze dropped to her mouth again, and his nostrils flared.

Her pulse quickened. Of course, with his ego, he probably thought she'd licked her lips on purpose to draw his attention to her mouth.

And you didn't?

No. She hadn't.

Had she?

"The food is incredible, isn't it?" Mick raised his own glass toward his mouth. "Angus did it again."

"The guy can cook." She watched his lips close around his straw. A pulse somewhere low in her body throbbed a bit faster. "Or in this case, tell people how to cook."

Mick chuckled, lowering his glass. "True. Although every time he told me how to cook when we teenagers, what I made didn't taste as good."

She raised her eyebrows in mock surprise. "The *Mick* Blackthorne isn't perfect at something?"

A devilish glint shone in his eyes. "It was when we were teenagers."

She snorted.

"I'm an amazing cook now." He drew his head a little closer, lips twitching. "Better than Angus."

Zeta laughed. "Of course you are." Damn it, why was she enjoying this interaction?

Mick chuckled again, straightening. "Okay, maybe not *better* than Angus." He pulled a melodramatic face. "Let's go with *almost* better than Angus."

She rolled her eyes, her own lips curling. "Almost better."

"But—" he held up a finger, "—I'd still wage my signature breakfast dish against his."

"And what's your signature breakfast dish?" Why did she want to know?

If he says he'll cook it for you tomorrow morning, what will you say?

Her stomach knotted. What would she say? Groan at the lame pick-up attempt, scowl at his assumption that she'd even contemplate having breakfast with him, let alone the inuendo behind the whole *I'll cook you breakfast* line, or say—

"Vegemite on white bread toast," he said.

She burst out laughing. Again. Damn him. He had no right to make her laugh like this. "That's your signature dish?"

"Hey, don't scoff. There's a skill to mastering the perfect Vegemite-to-butter ratio. Plus, the bread has to be just the right level of toasted. Not too brown, but not a wussy, pale tan either."

"The perfect Vegemite-to-butter ratio is all butter, no Vegemite," she stated. Her blood licked hot with a little thrill of excitement, anticipating his response.

He gasped. "No. You're not one of *those* Americans, are you? The kind that doesn't like Vegemite?"

"Yes." She tapped his chest. Once. "I am."

A violent sigh burst from him, and his shoulders slumped.

"And here I was thinking we might have finally found a way to be friends."

"Us?" She twisted her lips to stop her smile. "Friends? No way."

No, no, no. Stop being charmed by him. Stop it.

"In that case." He raised his glass. "To breakfasts."

She raised her empty one. "To breakfasts."

He took a sip from his. She tried not to watch his lips close around his straw again. Tried and failed.

"So what's *your* signature breakfast dish?" he asked, his smile relaxed.

"A breakfast burrito from Super Bronco Authentic Mexican Diner. Curb-side pick-up." She waited for the judgement to fill his eyes.

"Oh, I know the place," he said instead. "Amazing food. Tilly took me there the last time I visited her."

"Hey, your sister took *me* there as well. It's how I found the place."

Something flicked over his face. "You hang out with Tilly often?"

"Not that much. Although she's the closest thing I have to a sister now Elisa and Bria live here in Australia. I'm usually at work, and she's usually in the lab, but when we do..." The memory of her and Tilly's most recent night out made her chuckle. It had been a wild night of dancing, followed by a hangover that even a breakfast burrito wouldn't fix.

Mick snorted around a grin. "Don't believe anything she says about me."

"Hate to bruise your ego, but she's never said a word about you."

He huffed. "Well, I'll have to have a word with her about that."

"Should I point out you just told me not to believe anything she says about you?"

"Good point. From now on, only believe anything you hear about me from me."

She narrowed her eyes. "So I'm to believe you're a better singer than Nick Blackthorne, and a better chef than Angus?"

He laughed. "Okay, only believe anything you hear about me from me starting now."

"What are you like at dancing?"

Why did she ask him that?

"The worst."

Narrowing her eyes, she studied him. "I have no idea whether to believe you or not right now."

He drew a little closer. Enough to make her heart skip a stupid beat. "It's all part of my plan to keep you guessing about me. Keep you thinking about me."

Her chest tightened. The deep timbre of his voice, the blueness of his eyes, the way his words made her nipples grow hard... "I hate to burst your bubble, Mick, but I don't think about you at all."

Something glinted in his eyes, and his head dipped closer to hers. "Hmm, why don't I believe—"

The distinct *ting ting ting* of a spoon tapping against a crystal glass filled the air and silenced the room. Heart pounding, Zeta stepped away.

Oh God. Oh God, what...what...

"Alright everyone," the wedding's MC—a man wearing a purple velvet suit, black shirt, and Kermit-green tie—called, tapping a spoon to the glass in his hand again. "We need your butts in your seats and your attention on the dance floor, because it's time for Owen to make a fool of himself with the beautiful woman I'm still convinced he paid a ridiculous amount of money to marry him."

"Oi!" Owen protested, rising from his seat and holding out his hand to Bria. "Enough of that, Lawso."

"It wasn't a ridiculous amount," Bria said, taking Owen's

hand and getting to her feet. "Maybe a stupid amount of money is more accurate."

Mick chuckled beside Zeta, and before she could stop herself, she flicked him a smile.

Their eyes connected. Held.

Her breath caught.

His jaw bunched.

And then *the* Nick Blackthorne started singing "Tonight", and Zeta tore her focus back to her sister and her new brother-in-law as they moved together on the dance floor. If she didn't force herself to watch the bridal waltz begin, she'd do something really stupid like tangle her hand into Mick's hair, draw his head down to hers, and kiss him.

For fuck's sake, mate, think of something gross.

Mick formed an image in his mind of the infected puncture leg wound he'd treated two days ago in the emergency department.

It didn't help.

Nothing could change the fact they were but a few song lyrics away from the rest of the bridal party joining Owen and Bria on the floor. A few more moments before he and Zeta would be chest to chest, his hand on the small of her back as they moved together and Nick sang the most romantic fucking song ever written.

Zeta stood beside him, her stare locked on Owen and Bria. Was she cursing the fact they had to dance together? Or was she thinking about the moment they'd shared just before the bridal dance started?

They *had* shared a moment. He was sure of it. For a heavy, tight moment, their eyes had connected. Held. And he'd had to fight like fucking hell not to reach up and brush his fingertips along the line of her jaw and lower his head to—

"And now the rest of the bridal party will do their thing," Lawson proclaimed, and for a split second Mick wanted to kill the IT security expert he'd known since they were all teenagers.

Lawson Mauboy stood microphone in hand and pointed at Mick. "C'mon, doc. You're not getting out of it this time."

On the dance floor, Owen laughed. Angus, walking towards the dance floor holding Elisa's hand, did the same.

"This time?" Zeta echoed.

He flicked her a look. "You don't want to know."

Her lips twitched. "Oh, I do. I very much do."

He snagged her hand in his. "Too bad. It's dancing time."

He pulled her onto the dance floor, spun her around, and smoothed his hand to the small of her back as they joined Owen and Bria, and Angus and Elisa dancing.

Infected puncture wound, Mick. Infected puncture wound.

No, no good. All he could think about was how his palm rested just above the curve of her butt, how amazing she smelled—coconut and vanilla and…and…jasmine?—and how close their bodies were.

"Are you okay?"

He blinked at Zeta's low whisper, jerking his stare from the empty air above her head down to her upturned face. A frown pulled at her eyebrows, but not the contemptuous one she normally directed his way. Confusion swam in her eyes. God, how had he never noticed how pretty her eyes were before?

'Cause you're an idiot?

"Yeah." He frowned back. "Why?"

"You're as stiff as a tree trunk."

He sucked in a sharp breath. Did he have a— No, no he didn't. Well, not exactly, although it was bordering on one.

"Loosen up, doc," she whispered. "I'm not that horrible to dance with."

He bit back a groan. She wasn't. That was part of the problem. The curves of her body seemed to align with his perfectly. Clearing his throat, he tried to create a little more space between their hips without her noticing. Just in case. Her frown indicated he'd failed.

"What?" he grumbled.

Her lips twitched. "Honestly, I was a little worried you'd show me up out here, but—"

He dipped her. Effortlessly and gracefully. Before she could finish.

A shocked laugh burst from her as he yanked her upright again. Her palm splayed against his chest, and her hips pressed to his. His breath caught in his throat as their gazes locked. Shit, he hadn't thought that through.

For a second, for barely a heartbeat, they were utterly motionless, as if frozen, and then he sent her twirling away from him, as far as their arms would allow. A part of his brain registered people were cheering and laughing. Another part recognized it was more than just the bridal party on the dance floor now. The rest of his brain was locked on the fact that all he wanted to do was kiss Zeta De Luca.

That one split second of stillness with their bodies pressed together, her palm over his heart, his on the small of her back, had rocked him to his fucking core.

There'd been a…a…*want* in her eyes. And a question.

A question and a want that echoed his own.

He looked at her now. Saw her lips part. Saw that question again even as her eyebrows dipped into a confused frown.

He flicked his wrist, and she twirled back to him.

She didn't have to, but she did.

Her fingers slid up his chest to rest on his shoulder, and her thighs almost brushed his as they moved together to the music. Nick was no longer singing "Tonight". Now his world-famous rock star cousin was singing "Bleed", a song the world knew he'd written for his wife after they'd rekindled their relationship after fifteen years of separation. It was a song about being unable to deny what was between them any longer.

Swallowing, Mick looked down at Zeta. Her stare was locked on the space above his shoulder. Adamantly.

Stubbornly.

A soft chuckle fell from him before he could stop it.

She scowled. "What?"

He grinned. "I can tell you're trying not to look at me."

Something flickered in her eyes, but her gaze stayed locked on the same spot above his shoulder. "Why would I *want* to look at you?"

He chuckled again but didn't answer. What he did do was use the hand on the small of her back to draw her a little closer to his body.

She didn't resist.

Fuck, he liked that. A lot.

They continued to move together. He knew someone was still singing. Was it Nick? Or maybe it was Josh, Nick's son and a rock god in his own right. It was just background noise to Mick. Both the rock stars would find it hilarious their cousin had reduced their multi-platinum voices to mere white noise, but that's the way it was.

Right now, the world was a fuzzy cloud with only one thing in focus—Zeta.

Say something. Anything.

"So you *can* dance?" she murmured, a gentle rebuke in her voice.

"Dancing lessons until I was seventeen," he confessed.

Her stare slid to his then.

"For footy."

A frown replaced her shock. "For what?"

"Sorry," he said, smoothing his hand a little farther up her spine and then back down to the small of her back again. She moved closer to him, and her hips were pressed to his now, not just brushing up against him as the danced. Did she know that she'd done that? "Football. I mean, rugby union." He snorted out a laugh. "Almost every sport involving a ball and feet is called footy here."

She rolled her eyes, smiling as she shook her head. "Of course. Why not?"

Her smile turned impish, and something purely carnal and male in him reacted to the expression. What would it be like to see that same expression playing with her lips when they were both naked together and—

"So you learned to dance to play a sport requiring no dance moves at all," she clarified, humor dancing in her voice.

"Best way to keep from being crushed on the field," he said, trying to keep his body under control. Maybe he should dip her again, just to get some space between them.

"I see," she said. "So you really *do* know how to move."

His heart thumped faster, and he risked everything by drawing his head a little closer to hers. "You better believe it, baby," he whispered.

"Oh, I do," she whispered back.

His gaze dropped to her lips, and they parted. A little. Just enough to tease him. To flood him with a maddening need to brush his own over them. To discover if hers were as soft as they looked, as sweet.

He dragged his stare back up to her eyes, his heart a fucking canon in his ears. "Zeta…"

Why do I want to kiss you so much right now?

"Mick." His name fell from her in a breath.

A distant part of his mind realized they'd stopped dancing. They stood motionless, his hand pressed to the small of her back, her hand almost buried in his hair at the back of his neck, her hips pressed to his, their heads close. Close.

They didn't like each other, and yet this moment felt more…more *right* than any other he'd ever experienced.

Holding her stare, he drew his head closer still to hers. She combed her fingers deeper into his hair, pressing her body—

hips, belly, thighs—to his. Her heat seeped into him. Seared him. Stirred him.

Consumed him.

"I know it's crazy," he murmured, drowning in the exquisite blue of her eyes, "but I really want to—"

A monumental cheer shattered the air. People clapped, *wooted*, and stamped their feet. Zeta jerked back from him, out of his arms.

He staggered back a step himself, swinging a confused look around the dance floor. What the...

Ahh.

It seemed Owen had dipped Bria and was now snogging her quite thoroughly in the middle of the polished parquet flooring.

CHAPTER FOUR

"Onya, Blackthorne," the MC called from the side of the dance floor.

Zeta shot the speaker—Lawson something-or-other—a quick glance before looking back at her sister and her new husband.

Mick had dipped her a few moments ago on the dance floor, but he sure hadn't kissed her like that when he'd done it.

And you'd wanted him to?

Hell no.

The tight flutter between her thighs suggested that was an outright lie.

Fark.

"Get a room," someone else shouted on a laugh.

For some reason, she flicked a glance at Mick.

He stood a few feet away, stiff and hardly moving, watching the married couple. His Adam's apple jerked up and down his throat. She snapped her stare back to Bria and Owen just as Owen zipped her sister upright again with dramatic gusto.

More cheering and clapping from the guests.

Bria beamed at everyone and then at her husband. "God, I

love you," she told him before snaking her arms around his neck and kissing him again.

And again, Zeta found herself looking at Mick.

She'd been a breath away from doing the same thing to him before the cheering interrupted them. A heartbeat away from tugging his head down to hers and kissing him. Just to show him she knew how to kiss as well as he knew how to dance. Just to throw him off-kilter.

That is so not the reason.

There was more fluttering between her thighs. It was a wholly excited, horny sensation that confused the hell out of her. It wasn't possible she was sexually attracted to Mick Blackthorne. Not possible at all.

And yet, if you'd had one more moment on the dance floor...

Scrunching up her face, she pivoted on her heel and stormed off the parquet floor. Her untouched champagne waited for her at the bridal table. She snatched it up, down it in one swallow, and then wiped her lips with the back of her hand.

Classy, Zeta. Real classy.

"Oh, shut up," she muttered.

She grabbed Elisa's glass and downed it as well and then burst out coughing. Water. Sparkling water.

Of course. Elisa was pregnant. She wouldn't be—

"You okay?" Mick's voice came from behind her.

She froze.

"If I made you uncomfortable back there on the floor," he went on, not a hint of his normal arrogant confidence in the words, "I'm sorry. I just... There's something about you that just... I don't understand what's going on, but I can't stop thinking about you and how much I want to—"

She spun around, buried her hands in his hair, and kissed him.

Really kissed him. A kiss to rival Owen's dip-kiss with Bria.

Bad idea. This is a bad idea. A bad i—

He kissed her back. Really kissed her back.

His hands grabbed her hips and hauled her to him. She moaned, a liquid need blooming into hungry, horny life between her thighs, and she fisted her hands in his hair and rolled her hips to his.

Their tongues touched, battled. He nipped her bottom lip with his teeth. She fisted his hair harder. He groaned, squeezing her ass. An explosion of pleasure rocked through her at the far-from-subtle touch. Something hungry and wet tightened in her core. Dio, she wanted to fuck this man so—

Jerking out of his embrace, she stared at him, heart racing. Her whole body thrummed. Her blood roared in her ears.

She wanted to fuck him. She wanted to be fucked *by* him. And that right there was a problematic situation. An unexpected, problematic situation.

Did she act on it?

Mick studied her, wordless. His breath sounded as ragged as hers.

"I don't like you," she said, the words close to a whisper. "But I want to—"

"Alright you lot," Lawson's voice boomed through the cacophony of guests enjoying themselves, the MC's mic amplifying the relaxed laughter in his voice. "It's time for La Tarantella. Everyone get their butts onto the dance floor."

Throat thick, Zeta met Mick's gaze for a second, and then she hurried away. No way was she going to be standing next to him for this Italian tradition. The last thing she wanted was to hold the arrogant son of a bitch's hand as all the guests danced a circle around Bria and Owen. Not after what she almost confessed.

The tarantella was a fun moment, a way to wish the happy couple good luck in their future together, but the only future Zeta had in her head was the strictly never-going-to-happen future of her and Mick screwing each other's brains out. Holding his hand was just asking for trouble.

She weaved through the guests all making their way for the dance floor. She'd grab Elisa's hand and…and…

Dio. She had two hands. Fuck. What if Mick took the other before she could stop him?

Spying Lawson returning the mic to its stand, she made a beeline for the MC. She'd only interacted with him a couple of times since Bria and Owen announced their wedding, but an almost-stranger was better than Mick.

"Ciao." She snagged his wrist just as he was about to move away from the mic stand and beamed at him. "Come with me."

She didn't slow down as she scanned the guests already starting to form the linked-hands circle around the dance floor's perimeter. Where was Elisa?

"Where we going?" Lawson chuckled, putting up no resistance. "Am I getting lucky? Or am I in trouble?"

Ah, there was Elisa. *And* Angus. Making lovey-dovey faces at each other as they stepped onto the dance floor together.

"This way," she threw over her shoulder at Lawson, hurrying across the floor toward them.

"You in trouble, Mauboy?" someone called, laughing.

"No idea," Lawson laughed back. "Wish me luck."

"Lis." She quickened her pace—and by default, Lawson's—until she was but a foot away from Elisa. "Give me your hand."

Elisa did without question. Relief rushed through Zeta, and she let out a wobbly sigh as she settled into the circle with Elisa on her left, Lawson on her right.

Wait, relief? Are you sure that's what you're feeling?

"This is how we're tarantellaing," she muttered, throwing Elisa a wide smile. "'Kay?"

Angus raised his eyebrows at her and then slid a look to Lawson. "Shouldn't you be on the mic explaining what La Tarantella is for the guests who don't know?"

"Ah shit." Lawson snorted out a wry laugh. "Yeah, I should be."

Zeta swung her stare to him. No. No, no.

He disengaged his wrist from her grip, grin apologetic. "Sorry, Zeta. Next dance?"

She opened her mouth and snapped it shut as he partly turned and slapped his hand on the shoulder of the person beside him in the forming dance circle.

"Mick'll look after you," he said, giving her a smile.

Mick's lips twitched.

Bastard!

"Don't do anything I wouldn't do," Lawson warned, eyes twinkling with mirth, and before she knew what he was doing he'd somehow managed to place her hand into Mick's.

Delicious jolts of sensations shot up her arm, into her breasts, down into the pit of her stomach, and she had to stop herself letting out a low, hitching whimper.

"That leaves us pretty much wide open to do anything and everything," Mick shot back, giving Lawson a smirk.

"True." Lawson grinned again. "Gotta go be awesome. I'll catch up with you crazy kids later."

And with that, the towering, broad-shouldered MC hurried back to the mic stand.

Mick studied her. Silent. For a wild heartbeat. He leaned a little towards her. "I'm not going to bite."

She leant a little toward him in return and, holding his stare, snapped her teeth together.

He laughed, and the junction of her thighs grew warm. Tingley.

God help her.

A distant part of her was aware Elisa held her other hand. If her sister was watching her and Mick, Elisa would no doubt be forming all sorts of erroneous conclusions. Conclusions like her and Mick were flirting, or that they had chemistry, or that maybe there might be a reason for Zeta to move to Australia after all.

Like that was ever going to happen.

She wasn't going to abandon her life, her team, her cheetahs back in San Diego. It didn't matter how hot Mick was, or how sexually attracted to him she was, or how much she wanted to peel his clothes from his body and ride him like a bronco, and— Oh *God*, what was she *thinking*? Ride him like a bronco?

She jerked away from him, snapping her stare to the center of the dance floor where Bria and Owen stood, fingers entwined, making goo-goo eyes at each other while their guests finished making the tarantella ring around them.

On her right, Mick let out a low chuckle.

Bastard. He probably assumed she was flustered because of *him*. No, she was just worried about Kagiso and Mandla. Maybe she should go call Dani after La Tarantella and find out how they were doing. Yeah, that's what she'd do. She'd find somewhere quiet after the raucous dance, maybe out on the beach where Bria and Owen had gotten married, and touch base with the other cheetah carer and her team back in San Diego.

Anything to get away from your unexpected feelings for Mick, eh?

"Stai zitto!" she muttered through her teeth. *Shut up!*

"Didn't say a word," Mick replied.

She shot him a look. "Since when you do speak Italian?"

He shrugged. "Thought it might be come in handy."

His gaze held hers for a second, and then he looked away, an expression she couldn't decipher on his face. Was he embarrassed? Like he'd been caught out? Or was he smug? Like of *course* he spoke her second language. Why wouldn't he?

Zeta's heart hammered in her throat, and her head spun. He hadn't spoken Italian the first time they'd met. She knew that for a fact. She'd uttered something under her breath during that first meeting, something about arrogant bastard Australians thinking they were so funny, and he'd replied with, "What was that? I don't speak Klingon."

But now he spoke Italian. Why? And why did it make her feel...something? Something almost scary, almost wonderful? She bit her lip.

"Okay everyone!" Lawson's voice rose over the noise of the wedding guests—and her thudding heart. "Ready to dance to the happy couple's future? Clockwise first, then counterclockwise. Aaaand....go!"

He collided into her.

Everyone went clockwise, the way they were meant to move.

He went counterclockwise.

Because he couldn't stop thinking about Zeta and the question and confusion in her eyes. And the way she'd kissed him. And the way *he'd* kissed her back. *And* the way he wanted her on a level he truly didn't want to analyze because it was a level beyond just physical, carnal lust, and fuck a fucking duck, he went the wrong way when the music started and slammed into her.

She stumbled. He instinctually went to stop her from falling, and in doing so, grabbed her boob. She lurched back from him, colliding into Elisa, who stumbled backward into Angus, who let out a surprised, "What the fuck?". Suddenly, their side of the tarantella disintegrated into a mess of people going clockwise, counterclockwise, forward, backward, sideways and — Jesus, he had to get his shit together.

"Onya, Mick," Owen laughed from the middle of the chaos as Bria laughed.

"And that was Michael Blackthorne messing everything up, boys and girls," Lawson cheerfully announced over the microphone. "Give him a round of applause."

And of course, everyone started laughing and giving him a hard time. Except Zeta. She studied him with that same confused question in her eyes that had started the whole thing.

He stepped forward a little, bowed with a flourish, and then grinned at Owen and Bria. "Sorry about that. Brilliant doctor I may be, I clearly don't know my left from my right."

Owen snorted, his own grin wide. "My brother, everyone. Always trying to be the center of attention."

Mick bowed again.

Someone tossed a bread roll at him. Most likely Lawson. Food had been the cyber security expert's projectile of choice back in their high school days.

He scoop up the bread roll, bounced it off his biceps, and snagged it mid-air. "Let's dance!"

Everyone in the room laughed, and he turned back to his spot in the circle, his smile directed at Zeta.

Who wasn't there.

He blinked and flicked a glance at Elisa. Frowned. Yep, definitely Elisa, not Zeta. The pregnant belly gave it away, as did Angus nuzzling a laughing kiss on her temple.

So where the hell was Zeta?

Go find her.

He pivoted on the spot.

"Any time now, brother," Owen protested with a chuckle behind him. "No rush."

"Get your arse back in the circle, Mick," Lawson instructed over the mic, jerking a thumb at him.

No sign of Zeta. No sign at—

Mick sucked in a sharp breath.

There she was. She was hurrying through the room's massive sliding glass doors leading out to the resort and beach and night beyond. She stopped and shot a look over her shoulder back into the reception and then she was gone into the night beyond.

"Mick!" Owen shouted with a laugh. "Get back in the circle and stop hogging all the attention."

Mick hurried back into the circle and took Elisa's offered hand. "Where's Zeta gone?"

"She got a phone call from her work," Elisa answered, a slight frown on her face. "Something about one of the cheetah cubs."

"Cheetah cubs?"

Before Elisa could respond, Lawson restarted the tarantella, and this time, Mick went the right way.

Just.

The raucous dance—all the guests ringing the happy couple clockwise and then counter-clockwise, cheering their marriage and their future together—kept his mind off Zeta.

Also just.

Well, not really. He kept looking over his shoulder every time his part of the circle neared the doors leading out of the venue and to the beach.

No sign of Zeta.

Which, given it was her sister they were doing the tarantella for, was worrying. He knew how close the triplets were, and none of them would miss something like this unless something was wrong.

He shot Elisa a glance.

Yeah, that was definitely a concerned lip chew right there. She was still dancing, but her expression told him she was also worried about Zeta's absence.

Are you sure? Or are you just looking for an excuse to go find Zeta?

A boisterous *hooray* almost split the air, and suddenly his hands were free, and everyone was clapping.

He blinked. The tarantella was done? Finished?

In the middle of the dance floor, Owen and Bria marked the moment with a kiss far more passionate than was accepted in polite circles. There was more cheering, more clapping. It was the perfect cover to take off and find Zeta. Make certain she was okay. And not abducted by a serial killer or fighting a deadly rip in the dark surf.

He bit back a grunt at his own melodramatic and obviously woeful reasoning and took off. Heading straight out the doors and into the dark night. Looking for Zeta. Just in case she was in trouble.

Yeah, right. You want to kiss her again.

He did.

That and so much more.

Bloody annoying American.

CHAPTER FIVE

S lipping her phone back into the small pocket of her dress —God love Bria forever for demanding pockets in her bridesmaid dresses—Zeta scowled at the waves crashing on the sand under the moonlight.

Tendrils of thick clouds creeped across the white ball, mirroring the turbulence of her thoughts.

Mandla, the littlest cheetah kitten, wasn't feeding as often as he should. And Noxolo, his mom, had occasionally started to reject him.

Her team back at the wildlife park couldn't work out why.

She'd gone through everything she could think of with them as she'd walked away from the reception, questioning everything from the cheetahs' food supply, the enclosure's temperature, to the deodorant her team was currently using. It was only when cool sand slipped around her toes that she realized she'd followed the meandering path through the lush resort gardens that led to the beach.

An almost ten-minute conversation with no conclusion.

Staring at the cloud-encroached moon, she balled her fists. Dio, she felt useless. And disconnected.

Hot tears prickled at the back of her eyes, and she blinked

them back. She pictured the two adorable kittens. Remembered how Noxolo had nuzzled the little form of her stillborn female kitten. Perhaps Noxolo was in trauma? Perhaps if Zeta went back home now and was there for the mother cheetah, Mandla would start to get the attention he needed and would start to thrive?

Surely Bria wouldn't mind if she flew back to the States earlier than intended? Like tonight?

"Well, at least I know you weren't abducted."

Heart slamming into her throat, she spun around.

Mick walked toward her across the sand, the pale moonlight barely revealing the lopsided smile on his lips. "By aliens, I mean. When you didn't come back, I was worried you'd been…" he paused, a frown replacing his smile. "Hey, everything okay? You look—"

She burst into tears. She didn't mean to. But she did. Stupid hot fat tears.

"Hey?" Mick's arms suddenly smoothed around her. "Hey, hey, hey?"

She buried her face into his shirt, her fingers gripping his jacket lapels. Poor Mandla. Being cut off from his family, feeling alone and lonely and…and…abandoned.

"Shhh," Mick whispered against the top of her head, his breath warm. "Shhh, what's up? How can I fix it?"

She shook. Shuddered with more stupid hot fat tears. Poor, poor little guy. She should be there for both the kittens, to help them. Why had she left them? Being left hurt so much. Family wasn't meant to do that. More tears squeezed from her eyes, and she pressed her face harder into his chest.

"Shhh," Mick whispered, holding her. Just holding her. His chin rested on the top of her head while his hands smoothed small circles over her back. "Shhh, it'll be okay. Don't cry, beautiful one. It's okay. It'll be okay."

She pulled away a little, still holding his lapels, and looked up at him, studying his face in the soft moonlight. Of all the people to find her in this moment, to be the one to see her so weak and vulnerable, of course it had to be him. He'd never let her live this down.

A tender chuckle, so soft it barely feathered over her senses, fell from him.

"What?" she mumbled, her heart aching. "Why are you laughing?"

He lifted one hand and lightly brushed his thumb over her cheek just below her right eye, his lips curling in a gentle smile. Worry swam in his gaze. "Clearly not waterproof mascara."

She gave an entirely unladylike sniff but didn't look away. He was there, so warm, so strong, so solid and holding her so gently. He didn't look at her like she was annoying. He looked at her like he genuinely cared. And her heart hurt so much. She was losing everything she held dear—her sisters—and now, one of her kittens wasn't thriving, and Dio, he was so warm, and his smile was so gentle, and his gaze so concerned.

He brushed his knuckle over her cheek again, softer this time. "Are you okay, beautiful one? Can I help? In any way at—"

She pulled him down to her height by his lapels and captured his mouth with hers again. He kissed her back. No hesitation. No question. His hands smoothed over her shoulders, down to the curve of her butt to pull her closer to him. To fit her to his body.

She moaned and tangled her fingers in his hair, pushing her hips to his. It felt right to be held like this by him, to be distracted and comforted like this by him. It was what she needed right at this moment.

And every moment?

She growled into his mouth, silencing the annoying thought, and rolled her hips again. He growled in return, his hands cupping her ass cheeks. His tongue slid over hers, and she met his hunger in return. Dio, he was an incredible kisser. He knew exactly what to do with his tongue, his teeth, his hands. A tremble swept through her, and the junction of her thighs grew damp. Her breasts ached, wanting his hands on them. Her nipples puckered, wanting his mouth.

If he flattened her to the sand right now, if he shoved his hand under the hem of her dress and found her wet sex, she wouldn't stop him.

She wanted him to do that. She wanted—

She yanked away and took a step back. Her breath fell from her in ragged bursts, and she studied him in the dark, the faint moonlight highlighting the lines and planes of his face. Goddamn it, why did he have to be so good-looking even in the freaking dark?

"You kissed me," he said. A roughened huskiness scratched through the words. He was as shaken as she was. Good.

Licking her bottom lip, she gave him a jerky nod. "I did."

"Again," he said.

"Again." Could her pulse be any faster? Maybe she was having a stroke? Maybe that's why she kept on kissing him?

That's not why, and you know it.

He tilted his head to the side a little. "Is this something you're going to do now? Randomly kiss me?"

"Maybe." Her heart pummeled hard. "Maybe not. I don't know. I—"

He closed the space between them, cupped her face in his steady hands, and kissed her.

Slowly.

Kissed her until her knees began to tremble and her toes curled in the cool sand.

Kissed her like he wanted to thoroughly understand everything about her.

Or like he already did.

He seemed to know exactly what she wanted his lips and tongue to do, where she wanted them to be. He explored her mouth, her throat, back to her lips again. A shiver rippled through her, bursting delicious little blooms of desire deep in her core. Dio, it felt good.

She whimpered a soft sound of surrender. She'd been kissed many times—she'd been the biggest earner of the homecoming fair's kissing booth back in her senior year, not to mention her various exes and flings—but she'd never, ever been kissed like this. Mick's kiss sent a flood of pleasure and hunger through her. Mick's kiss seemed to awaken a carnal ache in her. Mick Blackthorne, of all people.

And she didn't want him to stop.

In fact...

She tugged his shirt free of his pants, slid her hands under the loose material, and feathered them over his abs.

God damn, they felt incredible under her fingers, all sculpted and hard and warm and smooth.

Liquid need pooled between her legs.

He groaned into the side of her neck as she skimmed her fingertips up over his tight nipples.

"Holy fuck, Zeta," he ground out, his lips scoring a path up to her temple while his hands kneaded her butt. "What are you doing to me?"

He rolled his hips to hers, and fresh blooms of desire spread through her body at the impressive bulge pressing into her lower belly.

"Questa," she whispered back, pinching one nipple lightly as she rolled her hips back. She wanted that impressive bulge in her hand, her mouth, her sex. Pulling away a little, she captured his stare and freed her hands from under his shirt. "This."

She lowered his fly.

His jaw bunched.

Way off in the distance, a low grumble boomed across the dark sky. Or maybe it was the thudding of her heart? She wanted him on a purely carnal, sexual level.

Did he want her?

Still holding his gaze, she popped the button on his fly.

His jaw bunched again, his chest swelling as he sucked in a breath. "Zeta, are you serious about this?"

As an answer, she trailed her fingertips up the length of his engorged erection, now jutting free of his pants but still trapped by what felt like cotton briefs of some sort. His eyes fluttered closed, and his whole body shuddered with a low groan.

"I don't understand how I feel about you, Mick," she confessed, her throat tight, her voice almost a rasp. "But right now, at this moment, all I want from you is this." She flattened her palm to his erection, inched her fingers into his open fly and gave his balls—as impressive as his erection—a gentle caress. "Please?"

His nostrils flared. He opened his eyes and looked down at her, wrapping warm, strong fingers slowly around her wrist. He held her hand motionless and lowered his head to hers, his breath a warm fan on her lips. "Zeta, if this is some kind of weird retaliation for what I did with Nick back when we first met, I—"

She closed the minute space between their mouths with a silencing kiss. She didn't want to think about that. She didn't want to think about her sick cheetah cub. She didn't want to think about her sisters no longer living with her in the US. She wanted all that confusion and uncertainty and emptiness to be gone. Care of Mick's lips and hands and arms and abs and cock.

For whatever reason, Mick's kisses and touch eased the ache doing its best to undo her. If she was going to be undone, she was going to be undone by sheer no-strings, no-expectations, no-future fucking.

With Mick.

Right here. On the beach.

He growled into the kiss, driving his thick erection harder

into her palm. His other hand cupped the back of her head, fingers tangling in her hair.

His tongue lashed over hers, his hold on her wrist guiding her hand on his cock; up and down, up and down.

Dio, he was fucking huge!

Her sex contracted at the thought of it moving inside her.

He groaned, tearing his mouth from hers and staring down into her eyes once again. His breath burst from him, choppy and rapid. "You have no fucking clue how much I want you right—"

The night detonated in brilliant-white light followed immediately by a crack of thunder so loud Zeta squealed. Mick pulled her to him, his eyes wide as he looked up into the darkening night sky. "Jesus, where did *that*—"

It started raining. Zeta turned her face up into the fine droplets, a chuckle falling from her. "Sex on the beach in the rain? How romance novel can we be?"

He snorted out a chuckle. "You read romance novels?"

A cold finger danced up Zeta's spine. She narrowed her eyes at him, taking a step back out of his arms. "What's wrong with reading romance novels? What? You think they're stupid? Of course you do. I forgot. You think *everything's* stupid except for you." Her stomach clenched. "God, what was I thinking? You might be a kissing god, but you're still an arrogant jerk."

Mick's eyebrows shot up. "I *was* going to say my sister reads romance novels as well. And *then* I was going to ask if you've checked out her massive collection, but seeing as *you've* already judged me guilty of being an arrogant jerk, how about I say this instead. You are the most judgmental, mercurial—" he held out his hands in front of him as if trying to strangle the air, his gaze jumping all over the place, "—*frustrating* woman I've ever—"

The night bleached white a second before thunder cracked the world. Deafening. Bone-rattling.

Zeta yelped, ducking and slamming her hands to her ears.

The heavens really opened then, pelting torrential rain down on them.

"Let's go, let's go," Mick shouted, holding his hand out to her, the other trying to shield his eyes from the attacking raindrops.

She went to take his hand. Lightening blinded her. Thunder deafened her. She squealed again, hands rammed to her ears once more, staggering backward, sideways. Wet sand oozed between her toes. Grains of it stung her bare ankles and thighs, flung up by the rain striking around her feet.

"It's okay." Mick's fingers brushed at her elbows as the rain tried to drown out his shout. "I'm here."

She squinted up at him. Blinked over and over as water pelted her face. "This storm's timing sucks!"

He laughed. At least, she thought he did. She could barely see him through the downpour, and all she could hear was the storm and the waves—now angry and pounding the wet sand.

His fingers found hers.

Just as the world shattered in a blinding white, deafening crack again.

Dio! She flinched, almost falling on her ass.

Mick snagged her hand. "We gotta go," he shouted, his hair plastered to his head. Water streamed off his nose, his chin. She nodded, tightening her grip on his hand.

He began running for the sandy path that led through the dense bushes and trees and palms back to the wedding reception venue. Zeta ran behind him. Then beside him. The rain grew heavier, and by the time they'd reached the tree line and the path, it was so heavy it was almost impossible to see anything.

"Is this a normal storm?" she yelled.

"We turned it on just to impress you Yanks," Mick yelled back.

At least, she *thought* that's what he yelled. Now they were in the bushy area, the rain sounded like a furious roar, as if a hurricane was about to park its ass on top of them.

"Yanks?" She grunted under her breath. "I'll show you."

She released her grip on his hand and bolted ahead.

A distant part of her mind wondered where the low lights that had illuminated her way *to* the beach had gone. Were they here but turned off? Or was she on a different path without lights? Another distant part of her mind acknowledged Mick was yelling something behind her.

Yeah, yeah, whatever. She'd beat him back to the reception. And then, as they drip-dried under cover, she'd apologize for the romance-book misunderstanding. Maybe. Unless he really had used the term *yanks*.

"Zeta?" Something swiped at her wrist. Mick's fingers? "Zeta, the—"

Her foot plunged into water. A lot of water. Past her ankle. Halfway up her calf.

"What the—" She recoiled, pinwheeling her arms to the side as her momentum tried to send her face-first into... What?

Mick's fingers snagged hers again, stopping her tumble, and he stopped at her side. "The creek."

She squinted up through the rain at his shadowy shape. Where the hell had all the light gone? "The what? You mean the tiny trickle of water I skipped over walking to the beach?"

"That one."

"You're kidding?"

She peered into the darkness, trying to make out how much water surged past them through what had been a calm, gentle trickle of water flowing over a rocky indent in the path barely fifteen minutes ago.

"Storm water run-off creeks," Mick shouted. "Never trust them."

She shook her head. "How do we get back to—"

He scooped her up in his arms. Just like that.

One second her feet were on the wet ground, the next they were dangling in the air as he hoisted her up into his arms.

"What the?" she yelped.

"Hold on," he yelled, taking a couple of steps back.

"Wait, wait, *wait!*" she squeaked, squeezing her eyes shut.

And then he ran forward and jumped.

CHAPTER SIX

His foot landed in water, and his heel slid forward. Fast. Gravity grabbed his body, hard, and he fell. Backward. He landed on his arse. In the creek. Still holding Zeta in his arms, like some kind of uncoordinated, good-intentioned but utterly idiotic romance-novel-hero wannabe. His tailbone protested the abrupt and brutal landing. So did the rest of his bones and muscles.

"I've done this poorly," he muttered, the rapid creek barreling into them, over them.

Writhing out of his arms and onto her feet, Zeta snorted. "You think?"

She grabbed under his armpit and helped him up, letting out a low grunt as the rushing water tried to knock her off-balance.

They looked at each other, the rain pelting down.

Say something, idiot!

"I ruined your dress," he said. "And your hair."

And yet, God help him, she still looked so fucking sexy he could barely breathe. Her hair clung around her cheeks and throat and shoulders in a wet, tangled mass of wavy strands. Her dress stuck to her body like a green muddy second skin, highlighting curves and dips and plains, the junction of firm thighs and swell of full breasts and cold nipples and... Fuck a fucking duck, he was getting a hard-on.

He cleared his throat.

She studied him, rain streaming down her face. "*I* ruined the moment. Back on the beach."

He let out a low chuckle. "Well, there is that."

She grinned, ducked her head, and brushed wet hair from her face. "I guess we should head back to the recep—"

The night lit up a split second before thunder cracked. Zeta clapped her hands to her ears and hunched her shoulders.

He destroyed the small space between them and wrapped her in his arms, fighting to stay balanced as the rising creek slammed into his legs. "It's okay."

"I'm not good with storms," she mumbled, almost—almost —turning into his chest. God, he wanted her to. He wanted to know she felt safe in his arms, that he was a safe place for her.

Wait, what? What this thing is between you both is purely sexual, right? Not emotional. Just carnal. Right?

She pulled away a little, her smile wobbly. "We should get back."

He nodded. "Okay."

Just sex, Mick. That's all it's going to be. That's all it could be. Just sex.

Nevertheless, he took her hand in a gentle grip, a warm happiness spreading through him as she threaded her fingers through his.

No, no. You don't like her. She doesn't like you. It was just going to be fucking. Remember that.

But the only thing he wanted to remember was how incredible kissing her was. How amazing holding her to his body was.

"C'mon," he murmured, sloshing his way out of the flooding creek.

Fresh lightning and thunder rocked the sky overhead, and

Zeta's fingers squeezed his. Then the first tiny ball of hail struck and hit him on the head. Followed by another. And another.

"Are you fucking kidding me?" he shouted, throwing his arm up over Zeta's head as hail rained down.

"Come to Australia, they said," Zeta yelled. "It'll be wonderful, they— *Ouch!*" She winced, wrapping her arms around her head.

"We gotta get inside," he yelled, shucking off his suit jacket and throwing it over her head. "My cabin's closer."

"Your *what?*" she yelled back. At least, he thought that's she yelled. The roar of hail and rain smashing down into the trees filled the air.

"My— ah, shit, just trust me, okay?" He snagged one of her wrists and started running along the path again. His cabin, the one he'd booked for the next two nights, was situated amongst the lush gardens of the resort off the path leading to the beach. He'd passed the private path when he'd come looking for Zeta. No doubt she had as well, although she probably hadn't noticed it. If you didn't know it was there, you would miss it, hidden as it was by palms and ferns and all types of trees and bushes and flowery plants. He'd gotten lost trying to find it when he'd first arrived.

The resort described it as "private and exclusive luxury". He distinctly remembered thinking when he'd booked it, that if he had to put up with Zeta De Luca for the event, he was going to treat himself to some "private and exclusive luxury" when he needed to get away from her.

Ha. And now here he was taking her to it.

Irony had a weird sense of humor.

The hail pelted down harder. So did the rain. A war of extreme weather.

He increased his speed, holding her wrist, no her *hand*. Her fingers were linked with his again. "This way," he threw over his shoulder, swerving off the main path onto what he hoped to hell was the path to his cabin. It was so fucking dark.

Zeta swore behind him, both in English and Italian.

Something large and blocky and dark loomed right in front of them, and he almost slammed into the front door of his cabin.

"What?" Zeta stumbled to a halt beside him, his jacket a sodden shield on her head.

He dug his hand into his hip pocket, ignoring his phone—most likely dead now with how saturated and full of water his pocket was—and pulled out the cabin's key.

A good, old-fashion key.

He'd snorted at its quaintness when he'd checked in. He thanked fuck now the resort had embraced its rustic theme, given there wasn't a single light to be seen anywhere, and the chances were the whole resort had lost power.

How were Owen and Bria and everyone in the reception faring?

He'd find out later. After the storm died down.

All that mattered now was getting Zeta out of Mother Nature's wrath and getting them both out of their wet clothes.

"Is this your cabin?" Zeta shouted at his ear.

Stabbing the key into the lock, he flicked her a look. "Yep."

"Then open the freaking door!"

He opened the freaking door, and they damn near fell inside.

He slammed the door closed behind them, shutting out the insanity of the storm, but not the noise.

The cabin—in typical Australian architectural fashion—had a corrugated iron roof. Rain and hail smashed against it in a deafening tattoo.

But at least they were inside, out of immediate risk of injury, even if they were in complete darkness.

"Shit!" Zeta exclaimed a second before Mick heard a dull thud. "Ouch."

"You okay?" He waved his hands around waist height. "What did you trip over?"

"Shoes." Zeta's disgruntled voice came from the floor in front of him. "I think I tripped over your shoes. Or maybe a body. Have you murdered anyone recently?"

Cautiously shuffling his feet across the floor in her direction, he chuckled. "Not since before the wedding."

"I'm not even sure how to respond to that," she said, her voice floating to him from the blackness.

He grinned, still waving his hands in front of him. "Just be grateful I like you."

Ah shit. Had he said that? Aloud?

A beat of hail-peppered silence followed, before Zeta said, "*Do* you like me?"

Shit. Shit.

He stopped shuffling in the dark and straightened, drawing a steadying breath. *Did* he? A tight band wrapped around his chest as the unexpected answer filled his heart. "As it turns out, I think I do."

"Annoyingly," Zeta's voice—low and soft and directly in front of him—quickened his pulse, "I think I like you too."

Warm fingers brushed against his face, clumsily at first as she found his cheeks, his jaw, and then she kissed him.

Deprived of light, of seeing anything but blackness, Mick's other senses took over. The sliding warmth of her parted lips moving over his, the gentle invitation of her tongue, the feathering caress of her fingers down the sides of his neck...

His body reacted, charged and aware and ready. He slid his hands around her back, finding the tiny toggle of her dress's zipper with steady fingers, lowering it, lowering it, lowering it.

She hummed into their kiss and shimmied against his body. Her dress didn't fall. The damp fabric clung to her skin with a persistence he both admired and despised. He wanted her naked. In his arms. Against his body.

Deepening the kiss, he found the open back of her dress and peeled it downward, only surrendering his occupation of her mouth with his own so he could step back and completely remove the sodden item of clothing.

Tossing the wet, heavy dress aside, he wished to fucking God he could see her. His eyes were starting to adjust to the darkness, but not enough to allow him to take in what he'd revealed. Instead, he relied on his hands, skimming his palms up over the shape of her waist, her ribs. His thumbs brushed the underswell of her breasts, and he couldn't stop his shaky breath. The soft warmth of her skin against his made his blood run hot. Hotter. He was already on fire with lust and need.

She let out a hitching breath. "Mick…" she whispered.

"If you want me to stop…" he said, his voice a rasping croak. *God, please don't want me to stop.*

Firm fingers closed around his wrists, and she placed his hands completely on her breasts. "What do you think?" she asked.

The heavy perfection of her breasts warmed his hands. Her taut nipples pressed into the center of his palms. His head swam with a rush of raw desire. No bra.

"I think I want to do this," he said in reply, bending until his mouth found one of those pebbled nipples in the dark.

She let out a choppy groan, burying her hands in his hair as he sucked gently on her breast.

He lingered, getting lost in the way her nipple pressed to his tongue, how it moved in his mouth with each drawing suction he made, how she moaned and fisted her hands tighter in his hair and demanded he suck harder. Harder.

He did, skimming his hands up and down her legs, her waist, her arse as he did so. Every time his palms ran over the bare cheeks of her backside, his cock pulsed. What colour was her G-string? Green like her dress? Black? No G-string at all?

Find out.

He released her nipple with a pop and lowered himself to his knees, slipping his hands down the curve of her waist to her hips as he explored the flat plane of her stomach. His lips found the shallow dip of her navel as his fingers encountered...nothing.

No lace or cotton on her hips.

He moved his lips down below her navel, nibbling on her smooth, warm skin. Her smooth, warm skin.

The curve of her smooth, warm pussy.

His cock jerked.

"Oh God, Mick," she groaned, fingers still in his hair. "Yes..."

Pulling away a little, he looked up at her, a distant part of his pleasure-fogged brain realizing that while rain still drummed the cabin's roof, the hail had stopped. The rest of his brain, however... "You're not wearing underpants."

The redundant statement fell from him on a husky breath. His cock jerked again, so fucking hard it hurt.

"Never do," she replied, her fingers combing his damp hair back from his temples. "Got a problem with that?"

"Fuck no," he growled before finding her labia with his thumbs, gently parting the soft folds of flesh, and stroking his tongue along the tiny bud of her clitoris.

She made a noise that almost made him blow his load. It was a raw groan of unabashed lust, surrender, and greed, and then he got lost in the taste of her. He licked at her clit, flicked it over and over with the tip of his tongue. She fisted her hands in his hair and drove her hips forward, grinding her sex to his mouth.

"Sì, sì," Zeta gasped, holding his head harder to the junction of her thighs. "Non fermati. Don't stop. Don't stop."

He didn't. No way in hell was he going to stop until she came, until she screamed his name.

He parted her labia lips a little more with his thumbs and sucked her clit, teasing it with his tongue as he did so.

She shuddered, her thighs shook, and she let out that same carnal noise. Blood rushed into his cock, engorging it completely. He couldn't wait to bury it deep inside her, to have her inner muscles grip him, slide up and down it… But not until he made her come with his mouth first. He wanted to make her erupt, to give her so much pleasure her knees collapsed.

He laved her slit with hungry swipes of his tongue, cupping and kneading the sublime curves of her arse cheeks before slipping the tip of his tongue as deep into her wetness as he could.

"Sí, Mick," she groaned, rolling her hips into his mouth. "Non fermati, non fermati."

Stopping was the last thing he was going to do. He lapped her up, tasted her, gave himself over completely to the salted sweetness of her pleasure.

"Oh, Mick." Her nails scraped against his scalp. Her moan caressed his senses. "Oh God, Mick… Mick… Oh God, Mick…" She fisted her hands tight in his hair, slamming her hips forward. A shudder rocked her. Her belly hitched. "*Mick!*"

He growled into her climax, squeezing her arse, tonguing her clit over and over.

She bucked again and again, and then, as he slowed his licking strokes down, she released her grip on his hair and staggered back a step.

"Oh wow," she rasped.

He looked up, barely able to see her in the darkness, and smiled. His whole body ached with a need beyond carnal, beyond elemental. "Just so you know, I'm taking *oh wow* as a compliment."

She laughed, the sound throaty.

Slowly rising to his feet, he pulled in a steadying breath. He knew what *he* wanted to happen now, but he was one hundred percent leaving it in Zeta's court. Rain still poured down outside, loud and persistent. If he moved, touched her in the dark when she couldn't see him, and she wasn't ready for him…

Her shaky breath teased him. Fuck, he wished he could see

her. He imagined her face flushed with sated pleasure, her lips parted, her breasts rising and falling, her hair a damp, tangled mess falling around her bare shoulders.

His cock pulsed, demanding attention.

"Mick?" Zeta's whisper flayed his control.

"Zeta?" he rasped back. He could sense her move in the darkness. Stepping closer to him.

His cock pulsed again. Impatient. Eager.

"Bedroom or sofa?"

He swallowed. His heart slammed up into his throat.

"To be honest," he said, shaking his head. "I don't think I can last until the bed—"

His right hip pocket started vibrating. He stopped, shoving his hand into the damp cavity. How the hell was his phone still working with all the water he'd been in and been drenched with?

He pulled it out of his pocket and winced at the sudden assault of bright light from its screen.

Owen's face grinned up at him.

He flicked a look up at Zeta, his heart skipping a beat as the light from his phone spilled faintly over her naked form.

She stood barely a foot away, her arms loosely folded across her chest. The muted light kissed the exquisite curves and lines of her body, teased him with the promise of what the lack of light denied him.

He swallowed. He should answer Owen's call. His brother was probably wondering where the hell he was? Was probably wondering where the hell Zeta was as well. He *should* answer the call...

Zeta closed the distance between them. The light from his phone was a faint sheen on her face, her throat, her breasts, her nipples...

His cock throbbed. His phone vibrated in his hand with Owen's incoming call.

Her shadowed gaze holding his, Zeta plucked his phone

from his hand, swiped her thumb across the screen, and raised it to her ear. "We're busy, Owen."

Mick's lips curled into a smile. Ah fuck, she was incredible.

A tinny voice burst from the phone—Owen, responding in some way to Zeta's statement. Was he asking if they were okay? Was he shocked she'd answered Mick's phone?

She tilted her chin, the darkness almost hiding the devilish glint in her eyes. "I'm sure Mick will tell you later. Bye."

Without waiting, she pulled her phone from her ear, ended the call, and held it out to Mick. "Well?"

He took his phone from her, tossed it in the direction he *hoped* was the sofa, curled his arm around her waist, and drew her to his body. "I am going to fuck you senseless," he stated. "If that's okay with you?"

She rose up onto tiptoe, her warm, naked body driving him insane with lust, and buried her hands in his hair. "Promises, promise—"

He crushed her mouth with his.

CHAPTER SEVEN

They somehow found the sofa.

It took a lot of fumbling around in the dark, but they made it. Rain continued to fall, and thunder continued to rumble way off in the distance. There didn't seem to be any more lightning, and there was no illumination, no matter how brief.

They kissed each other non-stop, stumbling and laughing and colliding their way through the unfamiliar room to the sofa. The backs of her knees bumped into it first, and she fell onto her ass on the cool leather. She released her grip on Mick's damp shirt just in time to stop pulling him down on top of her. He laughed, kneeling between her spread legs to find her lips again.

His hands cupped her cheeks, her jaw, and then travelled down to her breasts. She sought out his clothes in the darkness, wanting him naked. She may not be able to see his body, but she wanted to feel it, every inch. Refusing to tear her lips from his, she shoved his shirt—still open from their beach tryst— over his shoulders and dragged her nails down his chest and pinched his nipples.

He growled into her mouth, pinching her nipples in return before sliding a hand between her legs and fingering her clit.

She groaned her approval and reached for his pants. His cock jutted free of the open zipper, the button the only thing keeping his pants up. He must have done it up before they bolted from the beach. Well, she'd take care of that problem right—

He pulled away, breaking their kiss. "Let me," he said on a shaky breath.

She sensed him rising to his feet before her. The soft sound of material and belt buckle hitting the floor sent her heart racing. Her pussy contracted, impatient.

Warm fingers feathered against her cheek, her shoulder. She lifted her hands in the dark and found her prize. His erection filled her grip, thick and solid and warm and hard.

"Dio," she whispered, running her thumb over its tip. A small bead of moisture wet her skin, and her pussy contracted again.

"Oh fuck, Zeta," he groaned. "I—"

Whatever he was going to say dissolved into a raw growl as she took his length in her mouth.

His hands clawed into her hair, and he thrust his hips forward, pushing his cock deeper into her mouth. She hummed with hungry delight, grabbing at his ass cheeks. Tight and muscular and smooth, and God, she couldn't wait to see them in the light.

She sucked harder on his length, moving the tight seal of her lips up and down as she did so.

"Fuck..." he groaned again, his fingers fierce in her hair. "That's good. You're good. So good."

She pulled off him with a pop. "Say that again."

His throaty chuckle fell down on her in the darkness. "You're good."

Grinning, she pumped his cock with slow strokes of her

hand. "Of course I am. Took you long enough to realize though."

His hand fisted her hair, tilting her head back before his lips brushed hers. "A mistake I'm sure you will never let me live down," he murmured.

"Never," she confessed before cupping his balls with her other hand and giving them a gentle tug. "Now straighten up so I can show you just how good I am."

He laughed and did as she asked.

She took him in her mouth again. Brought him close to the edge more than once. She loved that he told her, warned her just how close he was. She hated it when men just blasted into her mouth without warning. Mick did the opposite, telling her just how incredible it was, that he was close, so close, so fucking close. Every time he did, she'd tease him by easing off a little. Every time she did, he'd groan out a guttural laugh and promise retribution.

His words turned her on as much as the carnal noises he made, the thrusts of his hips, the pulsing spasms of his cock in her mouth.

She kneaded his sac with her palm, aligned her middle finger to the sensitive area behind it, just before his anus, and pressed.

"Oh fuck!" he ground out, slamming his hips forward.

She laved her tongue against the underside of his length, took him deeper, and then let out a little gasp as he jerked back a step and his cock popped free of her mouth.

"I..." His breath tore from him, turning the word to a choppy exhalation. "I don't want...in your mouth...the first time..."

Ahh. She smiled, wishing she could see his face. Goddamn storm. "Do you have a condom?"

"I do," he rasped. "In my toiletry bag."

"Go get it, Michael Blackthorne," she ordered.

He let out a wobbly chuckle. "Yes, ma'am."

He hurried away, and it was only when she found herself admiring the broad strength of his shoulders and the narrow leanness of his hips that she realized her eyesight had adapted to the lack of light.

Enough to watch him collide, shins first, with the living area's ottoman.

"Fuck," he mumbled, recovering and continuing to what she assumed was the bedroom.

She straightened off the sofa and followed him.

"Where the fuck are you?" she heard him mutter under his breath from deeper in the dark room.

"Me?" she called on a laugh from the door.

"My toiletry bag," he called back. "I can't— Ah-ha! Got it!" The sound of items clattering onto a surface filled the darkness. Zeta smiled, picturing Mick upending his toiletry bag onto the bed. "Where..." More clinking and rustling. "Are...you, you... little...fuck— Yes!"

And just like that, the power came back on.

The distinct sound of electrical appliances activating buzzed through the room. 00:00 flashed on the room's bedside clock, announcing it had returned to life with bright-green happiness.

"Hey! Did the..." Mick's outline moved to the left, and the room filled with a soft warm glow as light from the bathroom spilled through the open door.

Zeta stood motionless at the end of the bed, finally able to see him naked.

She swallowed.

Dio, he was a fine specimen of the human male. Toned muscles, the most exquisite lats she'd ever seen, sculpted pecs, corded thighs... She bit her bottom lip, admiring his erection for a second before raising her attention to his face.

Her breath caught.

He studied her, hunger and desire and something she wasn't prepared to analyze—yet—burning in his eyes. His nostrils flared as her stare found his, and his jaw bunched. "You are the most gorgeous, sexiest woman I've ever met," he declared, slowly walking toward her.

She tilted her chin. "Of course I am." Why was her heart racing so much?

He stopped a mere foot in front of her. "Of course you are," he echoed on a murmur. One side of his mouth curled, and he lifted his hand to beside his face, presenting her the condom. "Ribbed. For your pleasure."

She closed the distance between them and plucked the small square packet from his fingers. "As it should be."

His nostrils flared again, and she was hauled off her feet and thrown on the bed. She landed on her back, in the middle of the soft mattress, laughing.

Her laugh melted into a moan as he shoved her legs wide, crawled onto his knees between her ankles, and took possession of her sex with his mouth. He brought her to the precipice with his tongue, only stopping when she begged him to.

Settling back on his heels, he gazed down at her, his lips and chin glistening with her juices. Dio, she could come just looking at him.

"I want you inside me," she stated, dancing her fingers over one of her nipples as she parted her thighs a little farther. She wriggled the condom packet at him. "Chop-chop."

He laughed, snatched the condom from her fingers, and with a skill and speed that took her breath away, covered his cock—long, erect, and demanding attention—in bright-purple latex.

"Love the color choice," she said, trying not to giggle.

He grinned, first at his condom-covered erection and then at her. "To be honest, I had no clue it was a colored one."

The confession set off a little squiggle of delight in her. Mick Blackthorne confessing to not knowing something? It was as if he was letting his guard down. What else would he reveal? What else would she discover about him? She couldn't wait to get to know him more.

*Couldn't wait? No, no. There is no more, Zeta. This is a one-and-done situation. It's just sex. Just a crazy, got-an-itch-to-scratch one-night stand. Not even a one-night stand. A one-*moment *stand. Not the beginning of a relation—*

Mick planted his hands on either side of her ribs and slid himself up along her body. "Hello," he murmured, the tip of his erection kissing her folds. A slow, warm smile stretched his lips as he gazed down at her. "My name's Dr Blackthorne. How can I help you today?"

She stared up at him and snaked her arms up around his neck. "Make me come, Dr Blackthorne," she ordered. "Fuck me hard and fast and make me explode."

He frowned. "Hard I can do. But fast? Isn't that the opposite of what I'm meant to be doing?"

She laughed, and he sank into her with one long, slow, powerful thrust.

He filled her. Stretched her. Embedded himself completely in her.

Pleasure washed through her.

He moved inside her with perfect rhythm. She moved with him, her hips rolling with his, their bodies fitting together in all the right places.

She gazed up at him, held his stare as they moved as one. One moment. That's all this was. Just one moment. But damn, what a moment.

He skimmed one hand down along the length of her side, over her hip, her butt, the back of her thigh, coaxing her leg up. She bent it, the slight change granting him even deeper penetration.

His breath fell from him in a ragged groan, his hand anchoring on the back of her thigh, his cock sinking deeper, deeper with each powerful thrust.

She arched beneath him, surrendering to the concentrated

pleasure consuming her. She clawed at the back of his neck, his shoulders. One moment, but she wanted to leave her mark on him forever.

Why?

Because…because he was hers? Because she didn't want it to just be one moment?

"Fuck, Zeta," he groaned, his eyes finding hers again, his breath a shaky pant. "This… I've never…" He thrust into her, bringing her knee up closer, higher. "This…"

She arched again, driving her hips higher. He didn't need to finish what he was saying. This was incredible. Amazing. Different.

Significant.

She felt it, not just in her body, not just in her core, but in her soul.

"This…" he ground out again, shaking his head, his eyes closed.

"This," she whispered back, a delicious, tight heat beginning to bloom deep in her core. She arched. Curled her toes. Wrapped her legs around his hips, locking him to her body. She didn't want him anywhere else but where he was. "This…"

His rhythm began to quicken. Grow erratic. His thrust grew wild.

Her heart quickened. Her breath turned shallow. Hitching. The tight heat in her core began to unfurl, to spread, to flow.

"Oh God, Mick," she whimpered, tightening her legs around his hips, drawing him into her.

He buried his face into the side of her neck and grabbed her ass, his strokes growing faster, harder. Harder.

"Mick," she groaned. "Mick."

His teeth found the curve of her shoulder. His cock slid back and forth over her clit. His length stretched her. His width filled her.

He slammed deeper into her, over and over, and with a

keening cry, her orgasm detonated, her entire body thrumming with release.

She came, and with a ground-out cry, he came with her.

"Oh God, Mick." She clawed at his back, his shoulders. "I can feel you... I can feel you..."

He lifted his head and stared down into her eyes. His were ablaze with a pleasure she understood. It was the same pleasure consuming her.

They moved together, holding each other's stare, and at some point, his hand found hers, and their fingers threaded together on the bed. Their hearts hammered as one, and he buried his face into the side of her neck again and let out a wobbly groan as his hips grew still.

Eyes closing, she smiled and let her legs fall from around his hips. "Well then..."

He chuckled, and his warm breath fanned against her skin.

For a few seconds, they didn't move, their fingers still as interlocked as their bodies. His heart pounded against her breast.

Finally, he lifted his head and gazed down at her. "Well then."

She smiled and reached up with her free hand to feather her fingers over his cheek. "I *want* to tell you that was incredible and amazing, but I *also* don't want to feed that ego of yours."

A low laugh fell from him. She loved the way she could feel it move through his body.

"My poor starved ego," he murmured. "If it helps, *I* want to tell you that was the best sex I've ever had."

She grinned, wriggling a little beneath him, enjoying the fact he was still embedded deep inside her. "In that case, that was incredible and amazing."

His expression grew melodramatically smug. "Of course it was. I don't do anything any other way."

Laughing, she shoved at his chest.

"Wait, wait." He laughed in return. "Don't want to leave…" Twisting a little on her, he looked down between them to where their bodies joined. After a quick readjustment of hands and weight, he withdrew from her and climbed off the bed.

A sense of no longer being complete washed through her for a heartbeat, and she bit her bottom lip, watching him hurry into the bathroom. Stretching out on the bed, she stared at the ceiling and listened to him deal with the used condom and go through the post-sex wash.

It was insane how much she missed his weight of his body on hers—*in* hers. Would it be rude of her to ask him not to go back to the wedding reception? To ask him if they could stay here, in his cabin, for the rest of the night?

What about Bria? And Elisa? What about Mandla? How will he survive if you don't go home ASAP?

Go home. Yes, she needed to stop being silly and selfish, and get back to San Diego as soon as possible.

A tight knot twisted in her chest. The cheetah kittens needed her, but if she left, she'd likely not see Mick for a long time.

And? That shouldn't be a problem, right? This was only an itch scratched. A one-wedding stand.

The mattress dipped a little, and she repositioned herself on the bed. Rolling onto her side to rest her head in her hand, she studied Mick where he sat on the end of the bed.

Smoothing his palm along the back of her calf, he looked at her, his expression unreadable.

"You want to say something," she noted.

Ask me to stay the night. Ask me to stay the weekend.

A slight frown pulled at his eyebrows, and he let out a soft snort. "Remind me never to play poker with you."

She laughed. "Oh, I suck at poker."

"I'm brilliant at poker," he said. "But you seem to have a knack for reading me."

Her stomach clenched. Why did she like knowing that? Why did she like he'd confessed it to her?

Because you really do like him. And you like being with him.

"What do you want to say?" she asked, ignoring the lump in her throat and the knot in her stomach.

His hand grew still, his fingers loosely cupping the back of her calf. "Why were you upset when I found you on the beach? I know it's none of my business, but if there's anything I can do to help…"

The question took her by surprise. Or maybe it was her reaction to it…that sense of wanting to tell him. Wanting him to share in her worry for moment, the absolute conviction he'd make her feel better somehow if she did.

Oh no. She swallowed, and a prickling heat crawled over her scalp. *Don't fall for him, Zeta. Don't fall in love with him. Don't.*

"Mandla, one of my newly born cheetah kittens, isn't doing well," she said. "He's not thriving. And Noxolo, his mom, seems to be rejecting him for some reason. I think I need to go home ASA—"

Someone thudded on the cabin's door.

Loud. Insistent.

"Oi," a muffled male voice shouted outside. "Mick? Mick, you in there?"

Zeta flinched. Mick frowned, shoving himself from the bed. "What the…" He scanned the room, snagged up a pair of colorful boardshorts slung over the chair in the corner, and yanked them on. "Who the hell…"

He stormed from the room, muttering.

A small smile pulling at her lips, Zeta scrambled off the bed and hurried into the bathroom. She'd do a little post-sex care herself and—

"Zeta?" Mick's shout sounded from the front door. "We gotta go."

He hurried back into the bedroom, and her breath caught at the icy calm expression on his face.

"What's wrong?" she asked, snatching a towel from the rack and wrapping it tightly around her body.

He opened the cupboard, searching for something in there. "Elisa had a tumble," he said without looking at her. "Just before the blackout ended. She needs medical attention."

CHAPTER EIGHT

Z eta stared at him. Eyes wide.

She bolted from the bathroom, heading for the door.

He snagged her wrist just as she ran by him, stopping her.

"What—" She glared at him, trying to yank her wrist free. "Mick, let go. I've got to get to Lis."

"Zeta, you're only wearing a towel." He kept his voice calm. Gentle. He'd been here before, with family members of sick or injured patients. Many times. Freaking out didn't help anyone. He handed her the pair of running shorts he'd brought with him, and one of his T-shirts. "Put these on."

Worry swam in her eyes. She didn't move for a second, and then she nodded and snatched the clothes from his hand.

He turned back to the open cupboard and removed a black leather bag. His doc-on-the-go bag, Owen called it. He mainly took it with him whenever there was a family event, just in case something happened to their mum, or if Owen or Tilly, or even himself, did something stupid—which was entirely possible when they all got together. Their family gatherings were prone to be rowdy. He hadn't ever needed to use it, but bringing it with him whenever he went anywhere had become a bit of a habit. A ritual.

Thank fuck he had.

The rundown Lawson had given him at the cabin's door a few moments ago was concerning.

Elisa, it seemed, had fallen onto the edge of a table during the blackout and was now experiencing both pain and a bit of vaginal bleeding. Lawson, the most laidback guy Mick knew, had been like a charged wire in their brief interaction at the door. According to Lawson, Elisa was calm but scared. Angus, according to Lawson, was coping—barely.

Mick had sent Lawson back with instructions for both Elisa and Angus, as well as a couple for Owen and Bria. "I'm coming," he'd told Lawson. "Tell Elisa and Angus it's going to be okay."

He gave the contents of his black bag a quick but thorough inspection and then turned to Zeta. In the few seconds she'd spent getting dressed, she'd managed to calm down.

Somewhat.

"Hurry," she ground out before running from the room.

He followed.

The path back to the reception area was a chaotic aftermath. The storm had left a sodden mess of puddles, fallen palm leaves, tree branches, and wet sand. Rain still peppered down, not as heavily or wild as before, but it was still there stinging his face and eyes.

They ran, wordless. Barefoot.

After this, he'd need to check both their soles for puncture wounds.

Bursting from the path through the bush, Mick's heart slammed up into his throat at the sight of a slew of guests waving frantically at them on the grass outside the reception venue.

Panic and worry hung on the air, palpable even from this distance.

A choked sob sounded from Zeta, and she threw herself into a sprint.

He followed her and caught up. She tossed him a look of sheer terror as he passed her, but he had to put that to the side. The focus was Elisa.

"Here! Over here!" Lawson met him at the entry. The guests outside parted like a wave. The security expert hurried into the reception, striding through the tables and heading for the bridal table. Mick followed with Zeta.

A distant part of Mick remembered he'd been here, in this room, at this table, only a little while ago. An hour? Is that how long he and Zeta had been gone? It felt like a whole new life had started in that time.

If he'd been here instead of getting his fucking rocks off—

No, that wasn't logical. And wasn't helpful.

He saw Elisa lying on the floor behind the bridal table, her head propped up on someone's jacket—Angus's probably—her knees were bent. Angus knelt beside her, holding her hand and brushing her hair from her face. Worry ate up his face, but he smiled at her. She kept shaking her head. It looked like she was saying sorry over and over. Hovering beside Angus stood her parents. Her father was hugging her mother, rocking her back and forth. Next to them, Mick, Owen and Tilly's mum wrung her hands together as Tilly hugged her. Bria sat beside Angus, her wedding dress a cloud of ivory chiffon and satin around her. Owen stood behind her, hair a mess, his hand holding hers.

Owen looked up as Mick approached, relief replaced with confusion when he saw him. He was probably expecting Mick to be dressed in more than boardshorts.

"Lis!" Zeta bolted passed him and threw herself onto the floor next to her sister.

Elisa and Angus looked at her. Both their eyebrows shot up.

A weak laugh fell from Elisa, and she shook her head again. "What are you *wearing*?"

"A few items from the Michael Blackthorne Summer

Collection," Mick said, dropping to his knees beside Elisa's hip. He placed his bag on the floor next to him and gave her a gentle smile. "I always knew you were an attention seeker."

She chuckled and winced.

"Stop being a bastard and help her," Zeta snarled.

"Zee." Elisa scowled at Zeta, shaking her head. "Shush."

"I see you're wearing only *one* item from the Michael Blackthorne Summer Collection, brother?" Owen deadpanned.

Mick gave Owen a relaxed grin. "They're actually *yours*, mate. You left them at my place last summer and I keep forgetting to give them back to you." He turned his attention back to Elisa. She looked at him, a question swimming in her eyes. "Okay, Lis. Talk to me. Tell me what happened."

"I fell over." She pulled a face, part embarrassment, part frustration. "Lost my center of balance, tripped on my own feet, and my stomach hit the corner of the table. I then fell to the floor."

"She was trying to get a glass of water in the dark," Angus offered, his voice grumpy. "Wouldn't wait for me to get it for her."

"I was thirsty," Elisa protested. "And I'm not an invalid."

"She shouldn't have been on her feet in the dark," her mother said.

"She should've stayed sitting," her father muttered.

"She should have listened to me when I said I was going to get it," Angus joined in.

"Okay." Mick looked up at everyone hanging over Elisa. "I need you all to shut up and let Elisa speak. And if you can't do that, I need you to bugger off. I know you're all worried, but right now, I need to talk to Elisa. No one else. And all Elisa needs is calm. And an ambulance." He arched an eyebrow at Angus. "Has anyone called one?"

"I have," Lawson said from behind Mick. "It's on its way."

Mick threw him a glance. "Thanks, mate. Can you get everyone to give us some space here? Help Mr. and Mrs. De

Luca, and Mum to find a seat nearby." He gave the worried older couple and his mother a kind but pointed smile. "That last thing Elisa needs is one of you having a stroke from worry."

Alfonso De Luca opened his mouth and shut it. "Sí. Sí. That makes sense."

"I'm okay, Daddy," Elisa said, directing a wan smile up at her parents. "Mick's an amazing doctor."

"Even if his bedside manner is somewhat dubious," Angus grumbled.

Mick grinned. "I wasn't first in my class for my bedside manner."

"No, you were last," Owen snorted.

Elisa laughed. That was a good sign.

"But I was first in my class for everything else," he assured her, opening his black bag. "Now, I'm going to touch your abdomen and then do a little listening. Is that okay?"

She nodded. Tears shined in her eyes.

"Alright everyone," Lawson's voice rose above the murmur of concerned guests. "Not that there's nothing to see here, but I need you all to take some serious steps back. Don't make me put my angry pants on. They're bright green with pink polka-dots, and they are stomach-turning."

A low chuckle rippled through the other guests.

Elisa let out a wobbly laugh.

Angus snorted. "I've seen those pants. He's not wrong."

"For fuck's sake, stop talking and help her," Zeta ground out.

Mick turned to her. Her eyes were wide, terror burning in them. His chest tightened. She was trying to cope with her own stress about her cheetah kittens back in San Diego. Add this to the situation, and she was likely on the brink. He hated the idea of her feeling so helpless, so panicked.

"Zeta?" he said softly. "Zeta, look at me."

She jerked her stare to his face. "What? What?"

"Can you find my stethoscope in my bag, please?"

Movements jerky and abrupt, she nodded and looked in his bag. He knew exactly where it was in there and didn't need Zeta to locate it for him, but Zeta needed something to do. Something to help with.

He turned back to Elisa. "Ready?"

She squeezed Angus's hand and nodded.

Chest tight, breath slow and calm, Mick took off his close-friend hat and put his emergency-department-doctor hat on.

———————

"First thing first, the heartbeats are good. Steady," he said, keeping his voice soft as he removed his stethoscope from Elisa's stomach.

Relief burst from Elisa—and Angus and Zeta and Bria—in audible breaths. No matter how stern Lawson was, he couldn't get Zeta or Bria to leave their sister's side. Fair enough. He wouldn't leave Owen's or Tilly's side either in a similar situation.

He placed his palm gently on the swell of her stomach and gave her a smile. "That's a good sign."

She smiled back. "It is."

"Now, there is a risk of trauma," he went on. "But I need to know where the pain is before I can ascertain that."

Elisa bit her lip, frowning as she nodded. "Trauma?"

"It's a horrible word, so don't get hung up on it." He smoothed his hand softly over her stomach. "Where is the pain now?"

Her frown deepened, and she tentatively touched low on her right side, near her hip. "Here."

"Cramping?" He moved his fingers to where she'd indicated and explored the area with a light pressure. "Like contractions? Do you feel like you want to poo?"

Her eyebrows shot up, and a nervous giggle fell from her.

"Evacuate your bowels, I mean." He grinned. "Sorry, I'll keep my doctor language going."

She laughed and looked up at Angus, who brushed his fingers across her forehead again. Mick wanted to point out to Angus there was no more hair on her face to sweep away, but he knew the repeated move had nothing to do with Elisa's hair and everything to do with Angus keeping himself calm.

"No," she said, looking at Mick again. "No pain like that."

"Okay, this is good. Really good. It means the chance of the fall instigating labor is low. We definitely don't want you going into labor yet."

"No, we don't," she said, at the exact same time Zeta and Bria said the exact same thing.

The sisters looked at each other, and then all three smiled.

Mick's chest tightened. Not just because of the way the triplets existed for and with each other, but because it was the first time Zeta had visibly relaxed since they'd arrived at Elisa's side. As soon as this was finished, he was going to pull her into his arms and hug her, hold her and let her know everything was wonderful and that he was there for her.

All the time.

Forever.

Forever?

His throat thickened. He flicked Zeta a quick look. Their eyes connected for a split second, and he jerked his stare back to Elisa.

He patted her hip gently and then pulled a face. "Now I'm going to need to know something that's probably way more personal than we ever thought this relationship was going to get. Okay?"

"Oh God, help us," Angus muttered, shaking his head.

Mick threw him a grin. "Remember this the next time I ask for a table at Buckley's Chance."

"There's going to be a permanent table for you at Buckley's

Chance after this," Elisa declared, touching his arm. "The best table in the restaurant is yours. Always."

"Hey, hey, hey!" Mock dismay filled Angus's protest, even as a grin stretched his lips. "Steady on now. He's not that awesome."

Mick laughed, returning his focus to Elisa. "We'll just ignore him for a while. How's that sound?"

She smiled. Worry, however, still swam in her eyes. Not as intense as when he'd first arrived, but it was there, which was only natural. She was a few months pregnant with twins and on her back on the floor of a wedding venue after a fall. If she wasn't worried, he'd be... Well, worried.

"Okay," he said again, resting his palm lightly on the apex of her stomach. "Now the personal part. I need to know how much blood you've lost. I need to know if it's light spotting, or clots, or a steady flow."

She stiffened.

"It's okay, Lis," Zeta murmured, squeezing her hand. "We're here."

"Can *I* tell you?" Angus asked, frowning at him. "Do *you* need to look?"

Mick let out a steadying breath. "I'm going to let Elisa decide. It's up to her completely. You, one of her sisters, me. It doesn't matter at this very moment in time as long as it's accurate."

Elisa chewed on her lip again, looked up at Angus, and then at Bria and Zeta.

"I've got this," Zeta stated, nodding her head.

The calm confidence in her voice sent a wave of something he didn't want to analyze through him. Falling in love with Zeta De Luca wasn't on his agenda tonight. But then tending to his honorary sister-in-law's medical emergency wasn't on his agenda either and yet, here he was.

His chest tightened. He'd deal with this unexpected

emotional turn later. After he made sure Elisa was going to be okay.

Zeta crawled on her knees to Elisa's feet. "Sorry, sorella," she whispered, giving Elisa a grimace. "Say goodbye to your dignity."

Elisa laughed.

"Everyone turn their back," Owen instructed on a raised voice from somewhere behind Mick.

Feet shuffled. Voices mumbled. A detached part of Mick's brain registered he couldn't hear rain any more, and then Zeta grinned at Elisa.

"Hey, Lis?"

Elisa looked at her.

Zeta blew a raspberry, and Elisa burst out laughing just as Zeta ducked her head, looking for what he needed to know.

And, before he had any chance to stop himself, Mick fell head over heels in love with her.

One hundred percent irrevocably in love with her.

Fuck a fucking duck.

CHAPTER NINE

Zeta stood on the edge of the gravel driveway, hugging her elbows. The red and blue flashing lights of the ambulance lit up the night, growing fainter as it drove away from the reception venue, taking Elisa and Angus to the local hospital. Behind the ambulance, in a big matte-black pickup, Lawson Mauboy drove her mom and dad. Lawson was taking them to the hospital and was going to wait with them while Elisa and Angus were in the ER.

That made Zeta feel a little better. Her mom had been insistent she stay at the reception with Bria. "We'll let you know how your sister is as soon as we know anything," she'd said, tucking Zeta's hair away behind her ears in the same way she used to when Zeta was a little girl and upset or hurt or angry.

Zeta let out a choppy sigh and looked up at the night sky. Stars twinkled above, no longer shrouded by storm clouds. Not the stars she was used to, but stars all the same.

"Well, this is not how I imagined my wedding going," Bria said at her side, a wry laugh dancing on her words.

Zeta shot her sister a look, trying to ignore the churning knot in her stomach. "No? You didn't imagine a crazy wild storm, a blackout, a medical emergency, and Lis being rushed to the ER? Dio, *I* did."

Bria laughed, shook her head, and squeezed Zeta in a tight hug.

"I'm in on this," Owen's voice sounded beside them, and warm, strong arms wrapped around their hug.

Bria laughed, and Zeta smiled, burrowing into her sister's embrace, wondering if other arms were going to join in?

They didn't. Whatever Mick was doing, it wasn't joining the group hug.

She pulled away, looking for him. He'd chatted with the paramedics before the ambulance drove away, his expression serious but calm.

Elisa was going to be okay. Her twins were going to be okay. Mick had declared that was the case, and she believed him. It seemed the paramedics did as well. And so did Angus and Elisa.

The trip to the ER—or ED, as they called it here in Australia—was a precautionary thing. Mick and the paramedics—or ambos, seriously, did Australians have slang names for everything?—agreed it was the best course of action. Elisa's bleeding was only mild spotting, and her pain had completely gone, but Mick suggested some scans would put everyone's mind to rest, especially Elisa's and Angus's.

"Coming back in?" Bria asked on Zeta's left now, making her jump.

She glanced at her sister, her heart thumping faster than it should. "I should go get changed. My dress is still in Mick's cabin." She looked down at herself, scowling at Mick's T-shirt and shorts. Or maybe she smiled at them? As stupid as it was, she liked wearing them. Liked that they smelt of Mick. It made her feel good. Safe. Warm.

A hot lump filled her throat, and she jerked her head up, staring out at the darkness surrounding the reception venue.

Oh God. Oh God, was she…was she in love with Michael Blackthorne? Was she?

"Mick's inside, at the bar, dressed only in his boardshorts," Owen stated, tugging Bria to his side. "I mean *my* boardshorts." He let out a melodramatic shudder. "I am never wearing those boardies again. Yech."

An image of Mick in nothing but the brightly colored boardshorts he'd pulled on back in his cabin filled Zeta's head. "At the bar?"

She could picture him standing there shirtless, shoeless, hair a damp, tousled mess tumbling around his eyes, those incredible shoulders and lats of his moving as he lifted whatever he was drinking to his lips. Lips that only a short while ago she'd kissed. Lips that only a short while ago had been all over her body…

Swallowing, she frowned. It was too easy to imagine him leaning up against the bar like that. Too easy to picture him, full stop. Too easy to remember how amazing being with him had been.

Too easy to imagine herself with him again.

Over and over.

"I thought he'd be out here?" she murmured, looking around the grassy, lush area of the reception venue's main entrance. "Making sure the ambulance got away without any problems?"

Owen let out a soft grunt. "He mumbled something about needing a drink. Apparently, he needs to clear his head over something." He pressed his lips to Bria's temple and smiled at his new wife. "Wanna come in and dance with me? Or eat ice cream with me?"

"Or both?" Bria suggested.

"Both is it." Owen kissed her and then smiled at Zeta. "Coming in?"

"In a moment," she answered. Her heart pounded too fast in her chest. Going inside meant she'd see Mick. And she wanted to see him now. Way too much. And that terrified her somewhat. "I'm going to look at the stars for a while."

Bria nudged her shoulder with hers. "It takes a while to get used to how different they are. But you do. And then you love them as much as the stars back home."

Zeta studied her, remaining silent.

Bria's lips curled in a soft smile. "Just in case you were wondering what it's like to look at that sky every night."

Zeta looked up at the stars.

Bria cupped the side of her head with a gentle hand and kissed her cheek. "Miss you, sorella," she whispered. "The miles between us makes my heart hurt."

And then Bria and Owen went back inside, returning to their marriage celebration and leaving Zeta alone to think about everything.

Everything. *And* Mick Blackthorne.

She hugged her elbows, the softness of Mick's T-shirt a taunting caress against her arms and breasts.

The tiny pinpoints in the sky twinkled back at her. Offered no answers.

She missed Bria and Elisa. Every day, her soul seemed to ache with a gnawing emptiness.

Being here with them, laughing with them, hanging out with them, existing with them… It had filled that emptiness. But the emptiness had still been there waiting, a nibbling hollowness reminding her that as soon as she got on the plane to fly home, she'd be away from them again.

At some point tonight, that niggling, nibbling sense of separation had faded. Completely. At some point, she hadn't thought about a life without her sisters.

But at what point?

When had that hollowness disappeared?

When Mick found you on the beach. When he took you in his arms and promised it was all going to be okay. That he was going to make everything okay.

"Dio," she whispered, scrunching her eyes shut and shaking her head. "I really have fallen in love with the son of a bitch."

And now the son of a bitch was inside at the bar. Trying *to clear his head about something*, Owen had said. Probably regretting every second they'd spent together.

Her stomach rolled.

She ground her teeth, glaring up at the different stars.

Well, screw that. She wasn't going to let him just brush off what they'd shared. He might be an arrogant jerk, but she was a stubborn Yank, and she wasn't going to let him just…just *ghost* her.

Besides, her bridesmaid dress and her phone were still in his cabin. She had to get those back. He could just take her to his cabin, listen to her lay out what was going to happen going forward with their relationship, if that was the word for whatever they were about to begin. And it *was* a beginning.

Maybe he could come to the US sometimes, and maybe she could come back to Australia often? And—

She stiffened. Blinked.

Was she really thinking this?

This was insanity. Only a few hours ago, she was in tears about Mandla and thinking she should rush home, and now here she was seriously thinking about some kind of future with a guy who, only a few days ago, she thought was the most annoying, irritating, arrogant bastardo. A guy whose feelings for her she was completely clueless about.

"Dio, I'm screwed," she groaned, rubbing her hands over her face.

A cool breeze flowed around her, bringing with it the sweet smell of rain and moist earth and eucalyptus. Like the stars, it was so different to back home.

Dropping her hands, she looked up at those stars again.

First things first, she needed to go find Mick. She needed her phone, and it was in his cabin, still in the pocket of her bridesmaid's dress.

She needed to find out how Elisa was doing. Then she needed to check in with her team about Mandla. Then she'd turn her full attention to the problem that was Mick Blackthorne.

Hopefully, her subconscious would have a solution by then.

"Are you going to drink that?"

Mick looked up from the scotch sitting on the counter in front of him and frowned at his brother.

Owen arched an eyebrow. "You've been staring at it for the entire time we've been standing here. It's twenty-six-year-old single-malt Glenfiddich. If you're not going to drink it, I will."

Mick snorted and slid the whisky over. "Go for it."

Laughing, Owen shook his head and slid it back in front of Mick. "How 'bout you tell me what's going on in that big brain of yours first? Clearly, it's got something to do with Zeta. It doesn't take a genius to connect the dots. You both disappear during the reception. You both turn up after the blackout wearing different clothes. She turns up wearing something of yours. Spill. I've got a twenty-buck bet with Bria, and she won't pay up until I get confirmation."

Mick snorted. "What's the bet?"

Owen smirked. "That you bonked like rabbits. Bri reckons you did it on the beach, I say you did it under a tree."

"And here I was thinking you were worried about your little brother." He looked at his scotch, turned the glass a few degrees to the left. To the right. The left again. "And you're both wrong."

Owen rested his elbows on the counter, studying him. "Is it serious?"

Mick scowled. "I don't know."

"Bullshit."

Mick turned his scowl to Owen.

"Look, Mick, we both know Tilly is the smartest out of the three of us, but out of you and me?" He waved a finger back and forth between them. "When it comes to really knowing what's going on, you run rings around me. Always have. I'm just a numbers guy. But I've watched you fool around with the idea of romance for years, and I've watched you and Zeta circle each other since you first met. And I gotta say, not one single girl or woman you ever sank any serious time into made you come alive like she does. You're too bloody smart for your own good, Mick. Your ego knows that. And Zeta calls you on it. There's a part of you that knows that's a good thing. So I'm going to ask again if it's serious?"

Mick stared at his brother. Swallowed. Let out a choppy breath. "It is."

A smile split Owen's face.

"On *my* end," Mick clarified. "I don't know what she feels."

Owen looked at him like he'd grown an extra head. "Then tell her how you feel, idiot. Ask her how *she* feels."

Mick's gut clenched. "Pretty certain she'll laugh in my face."

Owen snorted. "Pretty certain you have no idea what she'll do until you do it." He reached across and took back Mick's drink. "You don't deserve this."

"Oi!" Mick protested on a laugh. A laugh. Here he was contemplating his very future, and Owen was making him laugh over a scotch. Life was weird. Surreal.

"What doesn't he deserve?" a male voice chuckled on their right as Nick Blackthorne joined them at the bar.

Owen threw their famous cousin a smirk. "Young Michael here won't tell a girl he likes her."

Nick's eyebrows shot up, and then he tossed back his head, laughing.

"You two can just sod off," Mick muttered, throwing both his brother and his cousin a glare.

The rock star shook his head, still chuckling. "Mate, take it from an idiot who took way too long to tell a girl he liked her... Tell her. Now!"

Owen grabbed Mick's shoulder and gave it a squeeze. "Do it."

"Do it," Nick Blackthorne echoed, as he reached down the bar and picked up the glass of scotch from in front of Mick. He held the glass aloft. "Do it."

"Hey," Owen protested, as the rock star downed the liquid in one go. "That's my scotch!"

"That *was* my scotch," Mick pointed out.

Nick grinned. "It was delicious. Good choice, cousin."

With a shake of his head, Mick turned back to the bar and stared at the racks of bottles and glasses on the other side. Behind them, the wedding reception partied on. He could feel Owen and Nick studying him.

What should he do? This whole feeling for Zeta had blind-sided him so much. He *always* knew what to do. *Always* had the answer. *Always*.

But now...

What if Zeta *did* laugh in his face when he told her how he felt?

What if she says she feels the same?

He thought of not getting to see her anymore. He thought of her flying back to the U.S. to care for her cheetahs and not seeing her for who knew how long.

A heavy weight pressed on his chest, and his breath quickened. Grew shallow.

Holy shit, what was this? A panic attack? Seriously?

Was he seriously freaking the fuck out at the thought of not getting to see Zeta De Luca?

Fuck. Fuck, fuck, fuck.

"Hey?" A hand squeezed his shoulder and gave it a shake. "Hey, Mick? You okay?"

He sucked in a sharp breath, held it for a few heartbeats, turned to Owen, and let it out.

His brother stared at him, frowning. Nick did the same.

"You look like you were about to pass out, cousin," the rock star said.

"I'm okay." He let out a wobbly breath. "I just...need to get my head around things."

Owen squeezed his shoulder again. "What you need to do, brother, is go put a shirt on."

Mick laughed.

Owen slapped him on the back, grinning. "You know what you have to do, Mick. You always do."

"And on that note," Nick Blackthorne pushed himself away from the bar, "I'm going to go find my wife, kiss her stupid, and ask her to dance with me." He pointed at Mick. "Stop fucking about, cousin, and do it. Tell her how you feel. Show her."

Stop fucking about...

"Hey, Nick," Mick called as the rock star started to walk away.

Nick turned back. "Yeah?"

Stop fucking about. Tell her how you feel. Show her.

Mick straightened, pulling in another breath. "Can I ask a favor?"

"Where's Mick?" Zeta stopped her stomping stride and fixed Bria—currently snuggled up against Owen's side at the bridal table—with a stern look.

"Mick?" Bria pulled a confused face and looked at her new husband. "Do we know anyone called Mick?"

Owen chuckled, kissed her temple, and grinned at Zeta. "I got sick of him parading around without a shirt on and told him to go find one. Ab-envy is real between brothers, I'm afraid."

Zeta's pulse kicked up a notch. "So he's…"

"He went back to his cabin, Zee," Bria clarified. "A few minutes ago. Why?"

Zeta turned on her heel and hurried through the reception. She weaved through the guests moving together on the dance floor to a Nick Blackthorne classic.

She saw the rock star himself dancing with his wife, and then she was outside, striding across the damp grass, heading for Mick's cabin.

The path lights glowed once more, reflecting on leaves and bushes still wet from the storm. Her feet squelched on the path, mushy grass and sand oozing up between her toes. Mick's shorts and T-shirt flapped around her legs and torso in the cool breeze.

As soon as she got to his cabin, she was going to demand he take them off her, stretch her out on his bed, have wild, crazy monkey sex with her, and then they were going to have a conversation about whatever the hell their relationship and future was.

How dare he freaking take off and hide in his cabin after everything that had happened? How dare he not come and talk to her?

When she came to the creek they'd both fallen into during the storm, she realized she'd missed the turnoff for his cabin. She threw out a few choice curses—in both English and Italian —and headed back the way she came, fists clenched, jaw the same.

Goddamn it, he was an infuriating man. Even his choice of accommodation was infuriating. She was going to give him a piece of her mind when she found him.

The path almost eluded her again., but a few stomping steps later, she arrived at the rustic cabin tucked away amongst palms, trees, and bushes.

"Huh," she mumbled, frowning at it. "So this is what it looks like?"

A warm glow filled the window beside the door. Someone was inside.

Mick. Mick is inside.

Fists still clenched, heart racing, she stomped up to the entrance, raised her hand, and froze when the door swung open.

Mick stood on the other side of the threshold.

His stare locked with hers.

She swallowed. "Listen, you arrogant bastard. You can't just take off and not talk about what we—"

He reached out, cupped the back of her head with his hand, and crushed her lips with his.

She fell into him, into the kiss.

He staggered back into his cabin, taking her with him. Their lips and tongues and teeth battled, and for a moment the world seemed to spin.

She pulled away just as he slammed the door shut behind her.

Breath bursting from her in choppy pants, she glared at him. "Listen," she started again.

"I'm listening," he rasped.

She glared more at him. He still only wore his running shorts. "Didn't Owen tell you to put a shirt on?"

What was she doing? She wasn't here to critique what he did or didn't wear. *Oh God, Zeta, focus.*

"He did."

She waved her hands at him. "Well?"

"I've been busy."

"Doing what?"

Dio, what was she doing?

An unreadable expression fell over his face. "Making phone calls."

"About what?" *Zeta, stop it! It's not important. Focus!*

A tiny smile tugged at the corner of his lips. Lips she'd only just been kissing. "About taking time off work."

"Well, you should have been putting on a— Wait." She frowned. Narrowed her eyes at him. "What? Why?"

"I made some phone calls about taking some time off work," he said. He snagged her fingers lightly in his and walked backward into the cabin, taking her with him, until he reached the back of the sofa. He perched his butt on it and pulled her to him until she was nestled between his spread thighs. "Turns out, I have quite a lot of paid vacation leave, given I haven't taken a day off work since I started at the hospital."

"I don't..." She frowned again and shook her head. "Where are you going?"

"To San Diego."

Her heart slammed into her throat. "When?"

"Tomorrow?" He flicked his watch a quick glance. "Well, I guess, technically today, given it's just gone midnight."

Zeta opened her mouth. Closed it.

"I figured," he said, smoothing his palms over her hips, "you need to go back to San Diego and check up on your cheetahs ASAP, so I asked Nick for a favor."

"A favor?" She shook her head. Was it possible to be so confused you pulled a muscle frowning? "I don't understand."

Mick's smile stretched a little wider. "I asked if we could borrow his private jet to fly you back to San Diego so you can get to your cheetahs, and he said sure. It's at our disposal as soon as we get to Sydney."

She stared at him. A tingling sensation began to sweep over her. Her heart hammered fast in her chest, her throat, her ears.

"We can stay there as long as you need. I've got plenty of leave. I'll take care of you while you take care of your cheetahs. I'm actually a really good cook. And I give amazing massages."

She continued to stare at him. Gape at him, really.

He stared back. His Adam's apple jerked up and down the smooth tanned column of his throat. "If that's okay? If it's not,

I'll just get you back home safely, and then…then… I'll come back to Sydney. Maybe we could FaceTime a few days a week? If…that would be okay? I don't…" He let out a shaky breath and shook his head. "Either works, as long as I get to see you, talk to you. If that's… If that's o—"

Cupping his face in her palms, she shut him up with a slow, deep kiss. He slid his hands from her hips to her ass and pulled her closer into the V of his spread legs. She liked it there. A lot.

Tearing her lips from his, she leant back a little, and shook her head. "I hate you, Mick Blackthorne. You know that?"

He let out a low chuckle. She couldn't tell if it was wry or smug. Either would be very Mick.

"That's a shame," he said, smiling at her. "Because I love you. Seriously. I have no fucking clue how it happened, but it did. I love you. Completely and utterly."

A grin stretched her lips. She couldn't stop it. Didn't want to. "Oh, okay then. I love you too."

He grew still. "You're not messing with me, are you? I mean, I've been a bit of a jerk, so…seriously?"

"Seriously." She kissed him again, just to prove how serious she was. His body reacted. Her body reacted. There were a lot of reactions. She liked that a lot as well.

She ended the kiss with a quick nibble on his bottom lip and pulled away a little again. "And yeah," she said, snaking her arms around his neck. "It took me by surprise as well. But that's why I came here to find you. To tell you that you're stuck with me now. Capicse?"

He nodded. Kissed her. Grinned. "Capicse."

She preened.

"So you're okay with me living with you in the US while you take care of your cheetahs?"

"I'm okay with you living with me," she said. "Full stop."

It was his turn to preen.

She laughed, and he kissed her again, a quick, playful kiss

that made her heart quicken. It was so natural to be kissed by him. So right.

"Now," he said, squeezing her butt, "let me put on a shirt, and we can get back to the reception and tell everyone we're heading off to San—"

She shook her head, fisting her hands in his hair. "Hell no. The reception's done for us. We're staying here, getting naked and having wild and crazy monkey sex until sunup."

"Wild monkey sex, eh?" He arched an eyebrow, even as his cock—now a hard pole pressing against her lower belly—spasmed. "So no wedding cake then?"

She went up on tiptoe and pressed her lips to his. "No wedding cake."

He chuckled against her lips, grabbed her ass, and pulled her harder to his groin. "I'm not hungry for cake anyways."

EPILOGUE

*S*ix months later

Mick looked up from the pink-wrapped bundle cooing and gurgling and wriggling in his arms. "Babies are so squirmy."

Lowering herself onto the sofa beside him, Zeta gently repositioned the blue-wrapped bundle of amazingness in *her* arms. Two-week-old Isaac and Lily were the most perfect niece and nephew a person could have. She smiled at Isaac—cooing softly like his twin sister, but without the wriggling—and then lifted her smile to Mick. "Squirmy? That's the official medical term, is it, Dr Blackthorne?"

Grinning, he nodded. "Definitely." He readjusted Lily in his arms and his butt on the sofa. "I take it Elisa is asleep?"

Zeta let out a soft chuckle. "Both her *and* Angus fell asleep before I even walked out of the room."

Mick snorted. "So much for Angus's *I'm just going to sit here with Lis in case she wakes up and wants something.* His snoring will probably wake her."

"I don't think anything is going to wake Lis for a while." She pulled a face at Isaac, who gazed up at her with dark blue eyes that were wide and solemn. "Being a parent is hard," she told him on a lilting whisper.

Mick laughed, the sound as soft as her whisper. "Being an uncle is easy." He looked down at Lily, who was now gazing up at him with the same solemn concentration as her brother, and gently booped her nose. "I could do this all day."

A wave of warmth rolled through Zeta, and she let out a happy sigh. They'd both arrived back in Sydney yesterday, ready to be the best aunt and uncle for the babies, and to give the exhausted new parents as much help as they could. Elisa and Angus were coping well, according to Bria and Owen. They were just very, very tired.

The moment the safari park's resident vet confirmed that Mandla was doing well and thriving, she'd booked their flight to Sydney.

Staying away from her sisters had been hard.

Staying away from her new niece and nephew had been damn near torture.

She didn't like it. Not at all.

A thick lump filled her throat, and she lifted her focus from Isaac to Mick and watched him pull faces at Lily.

He was amazing. He'd been living with her in San Diego for six months and had been accepted into an emergency medicine fellowship working in the university hospital network as an ER doctor. Although no matter how many times she corrected him, he still said ED instead of ER. She was beginning to suspect he was doing it on purpose as part of his winning Australian charm.

Six months. But that couldn't last. For starters, his work visa would run out soon. Secondly...

The lump in her throat flowed down into her chest, turning into a warm pressure. "Mick?"

He looked up from Lily with a goofy smile on his face. "Zee?"

She pulled in a steady breath. "I got a job offer yesterday."

Lily squirmed in his arms a little, and he gave her a gentle jiggle, patting her butt in a steady rhythm as he did so. Instinctual. Everything about Mick was instinctual. And wonderful and caring. She loved that about him. So much.

"From who?" he asked. "The San Francisco Zoo still trying to convince you to go work there? I'm happy to move to San Francisco, if that's what you want. The public hospitals there are crying out for good doctors, and if I apply for a new work visa soon, I'll—"

She shook her head, and the warm pressure around her chest spread to her whole body. "Not the San Francisco Zoo."

He frowned. "Who then?"

Here we go…

Nerves fluttered in her stomach. No, not nerves, excitement.

"It turns out," she said, trying to keep her grin from splitting her face, "Taronga Zoo is establishing a brand-new cheetah enclosure and are looking for a full-time zoologist specializing in cheetah care."

He blinked. Stared at her. Blinked again. In his arms, Lily let out a happy little gurgle. "Taronga Zoo?" An emotion danced on his words. One that made Zeta's heart soar. "As in Sydney Harbour Taronga Zoo? As in Sydney *Australia* Taronga Zoo?"

Unable to hold back her grin anymore, she nodded. "As in Sydney *Australia* Taronga Zoo. I'm wondering if you're okay with us living here. In Sydney? For good?"

"Living in Sydney together forever?" He pulled a mock frown. "Hmm, let me think about it."

She laughed. "God, you're an asshole."

He grinned. "True. But I'm *your* arsehole."

"You are. Forever. Now, show me just how clever you are and kiss me while holding a baby."

He showed her.

He was, as it turned out, remarkably clever.

MORE ROMANCE FROM LEXXIE COUPER...

The Always Series

Unconditional
Unforgettable
Undeniable

The Outback Skies Series

Bound to You
Breathless for You
Burn for You
Bare for You
Better with You

The Heart of Fame Series

Love's Rhythm
Muscle for Hire
Guarded Desires
Steady Beat

Lead Me On
Blame it on the Bass
Getting Played
Blackthorne

See the full book list...

ABOUT LEXXIE COUPER

Lexxie Couper started writing when she was six and hasn't stopped since. She's not a deviant, but she does have a deviant's imagination and a desire to entertain readers with her words. Add the two together and you get erotic romances that can make you laugh, cry, shake with fear or tremble with desire. Sometimes all at once.

When she's not submerged in the worlds she creates, Lexxie's life revolves around her family, a husband who thinks she's insane, an indoor cat who likes to stalk shadows, and her daughters, who both utterly captured her heart and changed her life forever.

Lexxie lives by two simple rules – measure your success not by how much money you have, but by how often you laugh, and always try everything at least once. As a consequence, she's laughed her way through many an eyebrow raising adventure.

You can find details of her writing at
www.LexxieCouper.com

ABOUT LEXXIE COUPER

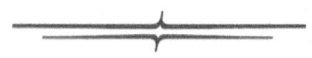

Lexxie Couper started writing when she was six and hasn't stopped since. She's not a deviant, but she does have a deviant's imagination and a desire to entertain readers with her words. Add the two together and you get erotic romances that can make you laugh, cry, shake with fear or tremble with desire. Sometimes all at once.

When she's not submerged in the worlds she creates, Lexxie's life revolves around her family, a husband who thinks she's insane, an indoor cat who likes to stalk shadows, and her daughters, who both utterly captured her heart and changed her life forever.

Lexxie lives by two simple rules – measure your success not by how much money you have, but by how often you laugh, and always try everything at least once. As a consequence, she's laughed her way through many an eyebrow raising adventure. You can find details of her writing at
www.LexxieCouper.com

www.ingramcontent.com/pod-product-compliance
Lightning Source LLC
Chambersburg PA
CBHW020252120726
47904CB00001B/168

* 9 7 8 0 6 4 5 3 8 1 9 5 5 *